"WHO ARE YOU—AND WHAT ARE YOU DOING ON MY SHIP, MISTER?"

Kirk kept his voice even, but his hands were clenched tight at his side.

A starbase security trooper in full armor blocked the airlock door. The trooper lowered his phaser rifle and saluted. "Lieutenant Abrand, sir. Commodore Wolfe requests your immediate presence on the bridge."

"Commodore Wolfe? On my bridge?" Kirk looked over the trooper's shoulder. There were more of them in the lock—all armed. "Where the devil is Spock? What's the meaning of this?" If Kirk's eyes had been phasers, the lieutenant would have been a dissipating blue mist.

"Commander Spock is in interrogation, sir. Commodore Wolfe will explain."

"You can be damn sure about that," Kirk said, pushing past the startled trooper and through the airlock.

Look for STAR TREK Fiction from Pocket Books

Star Trek: The Original Series

Final Frontier
Strangers from the Sky
Enterprise
Star Trek IV: The Voyage Home
Star Trek V: The Final Frontier
Spock's World
#1 *Star Trek: The Motion Picture*
#2 *The Entropy Effect*
#3 *The Klingon Gambit*
#4 *The Covenant of the Crown*
#5 *The Prometheus Design*
#6 *The Abode of Life*
#7 *Star Trek II: The Wrath of Khan*
#8 *Black Fire*
#9 *Triangle*
#10 *Web of the Romulans*
#11 *Yesterday's Son*
#12 *Mutiny on the Enterprise*
#13 *The Wounded Sky*
#14 *The Trellisane Confrontation*
#15 *Corona*
#16 *The Final Reflection*
#17 *Star Trek III: The Search for Spock*
#18 *My Enemy, My Ally*
#19 *The Tears of the Singers*
#20 *The Vulcan Academy Murders*
#21 *Uhura's Song*
#22 *Shadow Lord*
#23 *Ishmael*
#24 *Killing Time*
#25 *Dwellers in the Crucible*
#26 *Pawns and Symbols*
#27 *Mindshadow*
#28 *Crisis on Centaurus*
#29 *Dreadnought!*
#30 *Demons*
#31 *Battlestations!*
#32 *Chain of Attack*
#33 *Deep Domain*
#34 *Dreams of the Raven*
#35 *The Romulan Way*
#36 *How Much for Just the Planet?*
#37 *Bloodthirst*
#38 *The IDIC Epidemic*
#39 *Time for Yesterday*
#40 *Timetrap*
#41 *The Three-Minute Universe*
#42 *Memory Prime*
#43 *The Final Nexus*
#44 *Vulcan's Glory*
#45 *Double, Double*
#46 *The Cry of the Onlies*

Star Trek: The Next Generation

Encounter at Farpoint
#1 *Ghost Ship*
#2 *The Peacekeepers*
#3 *The Children of Hamlin*
#4 *Survivors*
#5 *Strike Zone.*
#6 *Power Hungry*
#7 *Masks*
#8 *The Captains' Honor*

STAR TREK®

MEMORY PRIME

GAR AND JUDITH
REEVES-STEVENS

POCKET BOOKS
New York London Toronto Sydney Tokyo Singapore

An *Original* Publication of POCKET BOOKS

POCKET BOOKS, a division of Simon & Schuster Inc.
1230 Avenue of the Americas, New York, NY 10020

ISBN: 0-671-74359-7

First Pocket Books printing October 1988

10 9 8 7 6 5 4 3

Printed in the U.S.A.

For Robin Kingsburgh,
who has chosen the final frontier.

Chapter One

THEY WERE ALL ALIENS on that planet. From the worlds of the Federation, the empires, and the nonaligned systems, each was a visitor on a planet where indigenous life had vanished in the slow expansion of its sun more than five hundred centuries before.

The scientists from a dozen races had come and gone since then. Andorians had sifted through the heat-stressed sands in search of clues to understanding and controlling their own prenova sun. Vulcans had beamed down a network of automated planetary sensors and warped out of system in less than one standard day. Terrans had conducted a six-month colony assessment study, with negative results. Even a Klingon heavy-assault scientific survey vessel had passed by, scanned for dilithium, and departed.

Through all these incursions, the planet spun on, unclaimed, unwanted, littered with the debris of sprawling survey camps and unbridled exploration. In the end, it was not even given a name and became little more than a footnote on navigation charts, identified only as TNC F3459-9-SF-50, its T'Lin's New Catalog number. It was an abandoned world, a dead world, and for some beings in that part of the galaxy, that meant it was perfect.

* * *

This time, his name would be Starn, and he would wear the blue tunic and burgundy guild cloak of a dealer in kevas and trillium. Legitimate traders were not unknown on TNC 50. The disguise would serve him well.

As he walked through the narrow streets of Town, Starn cataloged everything he saw, comparing it to the scanmap his ship had produced while in orbit, already planning his escape routes. The slender needles of Andorian prayer towers stretched up past the squat bubbles of Tellarite communal baths, casting dark shadows through billows of fine sand that swirled like vermilion fog. A group of Orion pirates appeared, wearing filters against the sand. There were no authorities on TNC 50 for pirates, or terrorists, or any type of criminal to fear. There was only one law here. Fortunately, Starn knew it.

The Orions slowed their pace, coolly assessing the resistance that a lone trader such as Starn might provide. Starn pulled on his cloak, stirring it as if the wind had caught it for an instant. The Orions picked up their pace, each touching a green finger to his temple in respect as they passed by. The sudden glimpse of the black-ribbed handle of Starn's Iopene Cutter had shown them that, like most beings on TNC 50, Starn was not what he seemed.

Starn continued unmolested. Most of the other oxygen breathers he passed also wore filters. A few, like Starn, did not. For those whose lungs had evolved in an atmosphere scorched by the relentless heat of 40 Eridani, this barren world was almost like coming home.

As Starn approached the center of Town, he felt a tingle and slight resistance as if he had stepped through a wall of unmoving wind. It was the transporter shield, projected and maintained by the merchants of Town. A strong enough transporter beam could force its way through, Starn knew, but the transmission time would be on the order of minutes, long enough to make an easy target of anyone trying a quick escape after an act of vengeance. Everyone who came to TNC 50 had enemies and Town could only continue to exist as long as it offered safe haven.

As the swollen red primary set, Starn approached his rendezvous site: a tavern pieced together from scavenged survey structures. A sign swung above its entrance, clattering in the rising wind. It told Starn who the proprietors of the tavern were. Other races might secretly whisper the name of the tavern, but only a Klingon would be insulting enough to display it in public.

The sign carried a two-dimensional image of a monstrously fat Vulcan clutching two Orion slave women to his folds of flesh. The Vulcan's face was distorted in a terrible grimace. Beneath the image, set in the angular *pIqaD* of Klinzhai, glowed the tavern's name: *vulqangan Hagh.* Starn pulled his cloak around him, an innocuous gesture that served to position the handle of his weapon for instant access, then stepped into the tavern to keep his appointment.

The central serving area was smoke-filled and dimly lit. For a moment, Starn was surprised to see a fire pit set in a far wall, blazing away. An open fire on a desert planet without plant life could only mean that that part of the tavern had come from either a Terran or a Tellarite structure. Starn studied the fire for a moment and failed to detect an appropriate amount of heat radiating from it. It was a holoprojection.

Terran, he decided. Tellarites would have shipped in plant material especially for burning. Starn knew the fire was there for a purpose, most probably to hide sensors. His host must already know that Starn had arrived.

Starn stepped up to an empty space at the serving counter. A multilegged creature made an elaborate show of sniffing the air, then moved several stools away. Starn ignored it.

The server behind the counter was, as Starn had deduced, a Klingon, and an old one at that. He limped on an improperly matched leg graft and wore a veteran's ruby honorstone in the empty socket of his left eye. Starn was troubled. A Klingon with an honorstone would be revered on Klinzhai, given line and land. A veteran with such a medal would never submit to being a menial tavern server, which meant the tavern server had *stolen* the honorstone. The concept of a Klingon without honor was as unsettling as the laughing Vulcan depicted on the tavern's sign. Starn decided that the stories of Town's depravity did not do it justice.

After ignoring him for several trips back and forth, the server finally stopped in front of Starn. "*NuqneH, vulqangan?*" the Klingon growled.

Starn considered for a moment that in this setting the standard Klingon greeting actually made sense. "*bIQ,*" he snarled in reply.

The Klingon paused as if puzzled by Starn's perfect accent, then filled the trader's order for water by spitting on the counter in front of him.

Other beings nearby, who had listened to the exchange, froze. Had Starn also been Klingon, a glorious blood feud would have started that might have lasted generations. But Starn was not Klingon, though his knowledge of the empire's customs was comprehensive.

The server waited tensely for Starn to respond to the insult, his single eye burning with expectation. Starn slowly slid his hand beneath his cloak, and just as slowly withdrew a carefully folded white cloth. Keeping his eyes locked on the Klingon, Starn delicately dabbed the cloth into the spittle on the counter and began to raise the cloth to his forehead.

The server began to tremble. Starn moved the cloth closer to his forehead. Two Klingon mercenaries standing farther down the counter began to snicker. The cloth was centimeters from Starn's forehead when the server finally realized that the mad creature was not going to stop.

"*Ghobe!*" the server spat, and snatched the cloth from Starn's fingers. Starn sat motionless as the server used the cloth to wipe up the counter and then stormed away, his rage almost comical in its intensity. The mercenaries broke out in gales of harsh laughter. One of them motioned to a server, who guided an antigrav tray of food and drink through the tables. A few moments later, the server stopped the tray by Starn and passed him a sealed bubble of stasis water.

"With the compliments of the officers, trader," the server said.

Starn looked down the bar at the Klingon mercenaries. They smiled at him and made clumsy attempts at saluting him with third and fourth fingers splayed. Starn nodded in acknowledgment, to more laughter, then broke the seal on the bubble and waited for its field to collapse. Around him, the business of the tavern returned to normal.

Whatever else Starn was, he was a connoisseur. From its bouquet, he identified the water as coming from a desert world, high in complex oxides. With his first sip, he ruled out TNC 50 as its origin. The water had once been part of a photosynthesis-based ecosystem and this planet was lifeless. A second sip was all he needed. The water was from Vulcan. The mercenaries had sought to honor him. Starn placed the bubble on the counter and would not touch it again.

A pale blue hand reached out to the counter beside Starn. The movement was cautious and he turned slowly. An Andorian girl looked at him nervously. She was young, clothed in a tattered and obviously contraband Starfleet jumpsuit that matched her skin color, and she suffered from an atrophied antenna. Even the smallest and poorest of her people's families would have sacrificed everything to treat that twisted hearing stalk. The girl was something no Andorian should ever have been forced to be: alone.

Starn greeted her in flawless Federation Standard, again no accent to suggest it was not his first tongue.

The girl looked nervously from side to side. "Wass it a present brought you here, trader?" she asked in a sibilant whisper.

Starn nodded yes. He couldn't detect anyone nearby trying to eavesdrop, but noticed that the girl stood so that as he turned to speak with her, he looked straight across the serving area into the sensors hidden behind the fire. He didn't try to block them.

"And where was that present from?" the Andorian asked, shuffling and looking over her shoulder. Her withered antenna twitched and she winced in pain.

"Iopene," Starn answered. Another dead world whose now-extinct indigenous life had proven to be too competent in building lethal weapons. Even the empire banned Iopene relics from all but the noblest houses. The cutter that Starn carried had been the "present" that had convinced him to take the invitation to come to TNC 50 seriously.

"Thiss way," the girl said, and headed for the back of the tavern. Starn followed. Behind him, he could hear the mercenaries begin to laugh again.

The girl slipped quickly through a series of dark corridors. Starn kept up with her, ducking his head beneath the low Tellarite ceilings. They passed an entrance to a smaller serving area where Starn could hear Orion dancing music pulse in time to the cries from an unseen audience. He detected the scent of drugs outlawed on a hundred worlds, heard screams of pain and pleasure above the hum of cranial inducers, and committed to memory every twist and turn, every dark stairwell, for the long run back.

At last the girl stopped by an unmarked door. She gripped a gleaming gold handle on the doorframe and trembled as the embedded sensors read her palm prints and analyzed her sweat. The door clicked, then slipped open. The girl entered and motioned for Starn to follow.

A young Klingon waited behind a simple desk. A single glowpatch lit the room from directly above him and his eyes were deeply shadowed beneath his prominent crest. The Andorian scuttled to a corner. The Klingon rose gracefully and waved toward a chair across from his desk.

"Good of you to come, Trader Starn," the Klingon said in Standard. "I am Karth."

Starn took the offered chair, comfortably proportioned and padded for humanoids, and studied his host. Even for a Klingon, the being was large. The taut fabric of his tunic stretched across an impressively muscled physique. Starn compared the tunic with hundreds of military designs he had memorized in order to place his host within the Klingon hierarchy. With something close to amazement, he finally realized that what Karth wore was that rarest of Klingon garb—a civilian outfit.

"Do you want something?" Karth gestured to a serving unit on the wall. "Perhaps . . . water?" The Klingon smiled, respectfully keeping his teeth unbared.

"Sensors in the fire pit?" the trader asked.

"Of course. The crime rate in Town is one of the lowest in the Federation."

"And in the empire?"

"Trader Starn," Karth began seriously, "all beings know there is no crime in the empire." Then he smiled again. "Though if you had touched that server's spittle to your head and become betrothed to him before all those witnesses, that would have qualified him for criminal proceedings. A very clever way out of a potentially disastrous situation. *Kai* the trader."

"*Kai* the Karth who gives such generous presents."

The Klingon settled back in his chair. The chair was massive, but Starn's sensitive ears heard it creak.

"As there is no crime in the empire," the Klingon said, "there are no presents, either. The Iopene Cutter is a down payment."

"Understood. What service do you require?"

Karth shook his head. "This is a foul language. So many ways around the point. Nothing direct. What service do you think, trader?"

"*ChotneS,*" Starn replied instantly.

Karth glanced over at the Andorian girl. "We shall stay with this *tera'ngan* chirping. She speaks *Hol* much better than Standard." The girl stared blankly. Karth shifted his gaze back to Starn. "I want no heads of state removed, no leaders killed. This will be a simple act of murder, trader, not assassination."

"Whatever you wish to call it, the service is the same." Starn shrugged. "Who is to be the victim?"

"Don't you want to know the price?"

"After I know the victim."

Karth shook his head again, hands moving slowly to the edge of the desk. "You accept the contract now. You accept the price now. There will be no negotiation once the victim is revealed."

Starn considered his options. It was probable he could walk away from this now. But the opportunity for expansion that this meeting offered might not come again. However, if he did commit to the contract, in the end he would still be able to make a final decision concerning who would be the more difficult victim: the one who was now unrevealed, or a certain Klingon civilian.

"Very well," Starn agreed. Karth moved his hands back to the center of the desk. "But since I cannot know the cost or effort involved in this service, I must call on Klingon honor to seal our bargain. State your price." Starn was puzzled when he could detect no physiological response to his subtle insult. For a non-Klingon to bargain on Klingon honor implied either that the non-Klingon was an equal of a Klingon or that Klingon honor was suitable for animals. At the very least, Karth should have demanded a test of blood, if not death, but Starn could not hear any quickening of Karth's breathing rate or see any change in his skin color.

"Two hundred Iopene Cutters with feedback shields."

Two hundred! Starn concentrated on not disrupting his own breathing rate. Whole planets could be taken with a handful of cutters whose beams could tunnel through any force shield by turning the shield's own energy against itself in perfect counterphase.

"I was not aware that there were that many in existence," Starn said flatly. *Two hundred!*

"Do you doubt my word?" Now Starn picked up an immediate flush in Karth's face and a rapid escalation in breathing rate.

"I simply stated a fact. For such a price I will accept your contract. Again I ask, who is the victim?"

Karth motioned for Starn to approach the desk. He

touched a keypad and images formed on the desk's surface. Starn watched intently.

At first he was stunned. Then impressed. The concept was brilliant. By this one single action Starfleet could be reduced to an uncoordinated swarm of helpless ships and starbases. The entire Federation could be brought to its knees. So many past wrongs would be repaid. Starn knew he would have accepted this contract without fee.

He leaned over the desk, studying the words and pictures, memorizing the diagrams and timetables. Already a plan was forming. It could be done. He was just about to step back from the table when he noticed Karth's hand on the keypad.

"Bring up the initial timetable again?" Starn asked.

Karth tapped out a three-key sequence. Starn watched the Klingon's exact hand movements carefully, then stepped back.

"I will be proud to carry out this service," Starn stated. "But I do have a question."

"I expect you to have many."

"Federation officials will not rest until they discover who is behind this action."

"That is not a precise question."

"What do you wish the officials to find out?"

"That is not a clear question."

"Should I leave evidence implicating the empire in this crime?"

Karth leaned back and snorted. He gestured to his dark face. "Who has set this crime in motion, trader? What do you think?"

Starn took his opening. "I think it is intriguing that I am being hired to commit this crime by a mechanical device attempting to pass itself off as a Klingon."

Karth's hands disappeared beneath the desk with unnatural speed. Starn twisted sideways and reached beneath his cloak. Karth jumped back from the desk, aiming a disruptor at Starn. The cutter's particle beam sliced through the air with a thunderous crackle, disassociating dust and smoke molecules. But Karth *dodged!* The beam erupted on his shoulder instead of his chest.

Starn stumbled back against his chair. The cutter whined as it cycled up to discharge again but it would take too many seconds. Karth's shoulder dripped with thick blue coolant. Wires and transtators glowed and sparked in the mechanical ruin. The Klingon robot leveled its disruptor and fired. Starn braced himself for disruption. The Andorian girl was engulfed in a sputtering orange corona and collapsed onto the floor. The robot placed the disruptor on the desk.

Starn looked over to the Andorian. Her body had not disintegrated. She was still breathing. A Klingon disruptor set for *stun?* What kind of madness was this?

"Neural disruption only," the robot said. "She won't remember anything of the last twelve hours. She didn't know." It pointed to its shoulder.

The cutter beeped its ready signal in Starn's hand.

"You won't need that," the robot said, pushing small silver tendrils back into its shoulder. The arm beneath fluttered erratically, then jerked once and hung limply.

Starn replaced the cutter beneath his cloak. "You didn't kill her?" he asked.

"Low crime rate in Town. She'd be missed. There'd be questions. The important thing is that there be no witnesses." A flesh-colored foam sprayed from the robot's good hand to cover the open circuitry of its blasted shoulder. "Not now, and not when you carry out your contract."

Starn watched with fascination as the robot began to repair itself. He suddenly doubted that the Klingons had anything at all to do with this.

"That sounds quite . . . logical," Starn said and, thinking of the image that hung above the tavern door, he began to laugh.

Chapter Two

SPOCK DID NOT NEED LOGIC to know that another attempt was going to be made. The only question was, who was behind it: the captain or the doctor? He finally decided that the instigator would be the one who entered the *Enterprise*'s recreation lounge last. Satisfied, Spock returned to his meal. His theory was disproved when the lounge door puffed open and Kirk and McCoy entered together. Spock realized then that they were both in on it. Whatever this one was going to be, it was going to be big.

"Mr. Spock, mind if I join you?" Kirk was already seated by the time Spock could swallow and begin his reply. McCoy sat beside the captain, not even bothering to ask Spock's permission. The table for eight was now filled. As were the two tables closest to it. The fact that the two chairs across from Spock had been left empty, even as other crew members decided to sit as close to him as possible, indicated that everyone else knew that Kirk and McCoy were expected. It had also been Spock's first clue that he was, as McCoy would put it, being set up.

"Well, Captain?" Spock decided to play white and take the advantage of the opening move.

"Well what, Spock?" Kirk's wide-eyed innocence confirmed his guilt.

"I merely assume that you have come to tell me something and I wonder what it is."

Kirk pursed his lips. "Tell you something?" He looked over to McCoy. "Bones? Did you have anything to say to Spock?"

McCoy smiled brightly, his expression calculatingly cheerful. "Not a thing, Jim."

The captain and the doctor smiled at Spock. Spock constructed a decision tree. He could excuse himself and return to his station, though he concluded that would be interpreted as a resignation from whatever game was being played. Or he could regroup his position.

He took another forkful of salad.

"Good salad, Spock?" Kirk asked.

Spock chewed carefully and nodded warily, assessing the captain's counteropening gambit. He prepared himself for the next attack. But the captain turned back to McCoy instead.

"So, Bones, who do you think is going to take the top spot for the Nobel and Z.Magnees Prize in medicine?"

So that was it, Spock realized. Something to do with the prizes. But what? He had not been nominated, and his work would likely remain too specialized to ever qualify. Sarek, his father, had been awarded the Peace Prize more than twenty years ago but, logically, that had nothing at all to do with Spock. So what were they hinting at?

"Well now, Jim, I think that Lenda Weiss has made a remarkable contribution to our understanding of resonance fields. Half my portable scanners are based on her work. I really don't see how she has any competition."

"Not even from Forella?" Kirk suggested. "I hear his work with shaped stasis fields will make the protoplaser obsolete in just a few years."

"I'll believe that when I see it," McCoy said definitively. "Dr. Weiss is the front runner. No doubt about it."

"I believe you'll find the work of Stlur and T'Vann merits the attention of the prize committee as well," Spock offered. He suspected he shouldn't get involved but logically he could see no other choice. The captain and the doctor were grievously misinformed. "They have opened up the whole new field of transporter-based surgery. Surgeons might never—"

"Stlur and T'Vann?" Kirk interrupted. "A Vulcan team?"

"Department heads at the Academy of Science," Spock added.

"So you follow the prizes, do you, Spock?"

"Doctor, the winners of the Nobel and Z.Magnees Prizes represent the forward thrust of Federation science and culture. From their work today it is possible to deduce the shape of tomorrow. They represent the finest minds of all the worlds of the Federation. Who would not follow them?"

Kirk and McCoy exchanged glances. Spock observed them and felt as he did when he stepped into one of the captain's intuitive mates in three-dimensional chess, but he still couldn't determine what Kirk and McCoy were trying to accomplish.

"I suppose you keep up with all the latest news about the prizes then?" Kirk asked.

For a chilling moment, Spock was afraid he was about to be informed that Dr. McCoy had been named a nominee, but quickly discounted the notion. The prize committee had some standards, after all. There were Vulcans on it.

"I follow the news as much as I am able, Captain," Spock replied.

"And you know about the ceremonies coming up?"

"I have read about them in the updates."

"Ah, good then. You know all about it. C'mon, Bones." Kirk started to stand. McCoy followed.

Is that all? Spock thought. Where was the logic in creating an elaborate setup such as this just to determine if he had been keeping up with the news about the prize ceremonies? Had he missed something?

"Excuse me—know all about what?" he asked, knowing the odds were overwhelming that he shouldn't.

"The prize ceremonies," Kirk said.

"The scientists who will be there," McCoy added.

"Where it's being held."

"How they're all getting there."

"You *do* know, don't you, Spock?"

Spock prepared himself for the worst. "I'm afraid I must say I obviously do not know. Please be so good as to inform me." Kirk and McCoy exchanged glances one more time.

"Why certainly, Spock," Kirk began, then paused for a moment. Everyone in the lounge looked at Spock expectantly.

"The *Enterprise* has been assigned to carry a delegation of sixty prize-nominated scientists to the ceremonies on Memory Prime."

Checkmate, Spock thought. Again. "That is indeed splendid news," he managed to say evenly.

Kirk turned to McCoy. "Well?"

"He blinked, Jim. I'm sure of it."

"How about a smile? A little one?"

"Maybe. But the blink was definite. I think he's excited. Think of it, an excited Vulcan! And we were there."

Spock stood up from the table. "Captain, may I ask what arrangements have been made to accommodate the delegation on board?"

"You may ask, but I can't answer. The person in charge hasn't told me what's been planned yet."

"I see. And who is the person in charge?"

"You are." Kirk checked with McCoy. "Another blink?"

"I might have to write this up."

Kirk looked back to Spock. "If that's all right with you, that is?"

"I shall be honored, Captain."

Kirk smiled. This time it was genuine. "I know, Spock. We all know."

"If you'll excuse me, gentlemen, I find I have considerable new work to attend to."

"Of course, Mr. Spock. Carry on."

Spock nodded, took his tray to the recycler, and headed for the lounge door. As he stepped out into the corridor, he could hear McCoy complaining.

"I was sure we were going to get a smile out of him this time. I'll admit two blinks are a good start but—" The doctor's voice was lost in the puff of the lounge door.

Spock walked through the ship's corridors at a measured pace, contemplating his feelings. Despite what most of his crewmates believed, Vulcans *did* have emotions. It was just that they chose not to express them. Though Spock supposed that Dr. McCoy would be surprised to discover how close he had come to seeing Spock smile back in the lounge.

In fact, if Kirk and McCoy had not made it so obvious that they were setting him up, Spock thought he might well have been startled and pleased enough at the news of the prize nominees to have actually smiled in public. Then again, Spock thought, perhaps that's why the captain had made it so obvious, so his friend would be forewarned and spared committing an unseemly act.

The captain has such an illogical way of being logical, Spock thought. He knew he would think about that for a long time, though he doubted he would ever totally understand. And as in most of his personal dealings with the captain, Spock decided that understanding probably wasn't necessary.

"Transporter malfunction!"

There weren't many words that could shock the chief engineer of the *Enterprise* awake with such forcefulness, but those two never failed.

Scott jumped out of his bunk and slammed his hand against the desk comm panel. The room lights brightened automatically as they detected his movements. That voice hadn't been Kyle's. He peered at the nervous face on the desk screen.

"Scott here . . . Sulu?" What was Sulu doing in the main transporter room? "Report!" Scott hopped around his quarters, trying to pull on his shirt and his boots at the same time as Sulu's tense voice filtered through the speaker.

"The . . . carrier wave transmitter just shut down, Mr. Scott. Every pad in the ship is out."

"Ochh, no," Scott moaned. Years ago on another ship he had seen a landing party evulsed by a carrier-wave collapse. He had personally seen to it that such a malfunction would be virtually impossible on his *Enterprise,* no matter what McCoy might think.

"Give me the error code, lad," Scott asked softly. There was no need to rush now. Whatever, whoever, had been in the matrix when the wave collapsed was irretrievably lost. And Scott didn't want to think about who might have been in the matrix. They were still in orbit around Centaurus. The captain had some property there . . . and had planned to visit it.

"Error code, Mr. Scott?"

"Below the locator grid, Mr. Sulu." Where was Kyle?

"Uh . . . one-two-seven," Sulu read out tentatively.

Even Scott had to stop and think to remember that one. When he did, he was relieved and angry at the same time. At least no one would have been lost in transit and there would be no more danger to the ship until he manually reset the carrier-wave generator.

"Mr. Sulu, I dinna know what it is ye think you're doing at the main transporter station, but I strongly suggest ye call up the operator's manual and look up a code one-two-seven shutdown on your own. I'll be down right away and in the meantime, Mr. Sulu . . ."

"Y-yes sir?"

"Don't touch *anything!*"

Scott broke the connection to the transporter room, then opened a new link. "Scott to security. Have a team meet me in the main transporter room, alert the captain if he's on board, and find me *Mr. Kyle!*"

Then the chief engineer straightened his shirt in the mirror, smoothed his hair, and stormed out of his room to find out who had just tried to scuttle the *Enterprise.*

Sulu began to apologize the instant Scott stepped through the door.

"I'm sorry, Mr. Scott. I only have a Class Three rating on the transporter. The simulator never took me past error code fifty." Sulu stepped quickly out of the way as Scott took his place behind the transporter console.

The doors slid open again. Four burly, red-shirted security officers rushed in, followed by Captain Kirk.

"Scotty, a malfunction?" Kirk looked at the transporter pads. Scott could hear the captain exhale with relief when he saw they were empty.

"An automatic shutdown, Captain. Error code one-two-seven."

Kirk's eyes widened. He knew them all. "Somebody tried to beam an *accelerator field* on board?"

"Aye, while our own warp engines are on line, too. If the computer scan hadn't recognized the accelerator signature in the matrix and automatically reversed the beam, the chain reaction between the field and our dilithium crystals would have fused every circuit in the Cochrane generators, released the antimatter . . . occh." Scott worked at the panel to reconstruct the readings of the aborted beam-up.

Kirk noticed Sulu standing in the corner by the viewscreen. "Isn't this Mr. Kyle's tour?"

"Well, yes, Captain. But when Doctors T'Vann and Stlur beamed up with their transporter-based surgical equipment, Kyle, well . . . he asked me to cover while he—"

"—helped them calibrate their equipment?" Kirk suggested. "Or was it check their figures? Or link up to the ship's computer?"

"Actually, set up their equipment in his transporter lab, sir," Sulu completed.

Kirk shook his head. "I don't know, Scotty, but it seems that ever since the prize nominees started coming aboard, my crew is playing hooky from their work to go back to school."

"'Hooky,' Captain?" Spock had entered the transporter room and joined Scott behind the console.

"An inappropriate leave of absence, Mr. Spock, usually from school."

Spock arched an eyebrow. "Why should anyone wish to do that?" He realized the captain was not about to enlighten him, so he turned to Scott. "What does the problem appear to be, Mr. Scott?"

"It doesn't *appear* to be anything. Some addle-brained nincompoop just tried to beam up an operating accelerator field and I'm trying to trace the coordinates."

Spock reached over and punched in a series of numbers. Scott read them on the locator grid.

"That's the Cochrane University of Applied Warp Physics," Scott said.

"Yes," Spock concurred. "I believe you'll find that the 'addle-brained nincompoop' you are searching for is the professor emeritus of multiphysics there. Professor Zoareem La'kara."

Scott narrowed his eyes. "Of all people, surely he'd know what happens when ye bring an accelerated time field within interaction range of aligned dilithium?"

"Of course, Mr. Scott. Which is why he is a nominee for the Nobel and Z.Magnees Prize in multiphysics."

A paging whistle sounded. Uhura's voice announced, "Bridge to Captain. I have a message from the Cochrane University, sir. Professor La'kara says he is *still* waiting to beam up with his equipment."

"Thank you, Uhura," Kirk answered. "Tell him we're working on it." Then to Spock and Scott he added, "Well, *are* we working on it?"

"Captain, an accelerator field is a tricky beast. If a fourth-dimensional arm of dilithium impinges upon a domain of artificially increased entropy, why all the power our engines produce would be sucked back three and half seconds, rechanneled through the crystals, and then sucked back again. The feedback would be infinite and . . ." Scotty shuddered as he contemplated the resultant destruction of the ship's warp generators.

"The fact remains, Captain, that Professor La'kara has devised a prototype shielded accelerator field that reduces the interaction range with aligned dilithium to a few meters instead of kilometers. The ship's systems will be in no danger." Spock turned to Scott. "The published literature is quite extensive."

"In theory I'll admit it sounds good, but I've nae read any results of a *stable* shielded accelerator and there'll be nae more than *one* fast-time field on board this ship while I'm chief engineer, and that will be *my* dilithium crystals." Scott folded his arms across his chest. Spock did the same. Kirk sighed. He realized a command decision was clearly called for.

"Mr. Scott, you will beam aboard Professor La'kara and all his equipment *except* for the accelerator-field device, right away." Scott smiled smugly. "Mr. Spock, you and Professor La'kara will then provide Mr. Scott with a complete description of the accelerator and answer *all* his objections to having it on board. At which time, Mr. Scott, you will beam the device on board and we will continue on to Starbase Four to pick up our last group of nominees. Understood?"

"Captain, if I may—"

"But, Captain, surely ye canna—"

"Fine. Glad to hear it. Mr. Sulu, I believe your station's on the bridge." Kirk and Sulu headed for the door. Scott tapped a finger on the control console. Spock raised an eyebrow. Kirk turned at the door.

"Should I leave security here to keep an eye on you two?" the captain asked.

"'Twillna be necessary," Scott said.

Kirk waved the security team out and left with Sulu. Scott uncovered the carrier-wave reset switch, entered his security code, then guided the beam to lock on to La'kara's coordinates on the grid, filtering out the accelerator-field signal. "As the poet said, Mr. Spock, 'Today I shoulda stood in bed.'"

"I fail to see how that would be a comfortable position."

Scotty's moan was hidden beneath the rich harmonics of the transporter effect. He could already tell it was going to be one of those missions.

Chapter Three

STARFLEET BLUE, STARFLEET BLUE, gods how he hated it.

Chief Administrator Salman Nensi stared at the wall across from his desk and wished he had a window, or even a decent viewscreen, anything to break the monotony of that damned expanse of regulation wall covering. But whatever shortcomings Starfleet had when it came to interior design, at least it tried hard to learn from its mistakes.

The chief administrator couldn't have a window because his facility, Memory Prime, was one of the most secure installations the Federation had ever constructed. Since the Memory Alpha disaster, the entire concept of libraries being unshielded and fully accessible repositories of freely available data had been rotated through four dimensions and come out backward. Nensi doubted that even the soon-to-arrive-starship *Enterprise* could make much of a dent in Prime's dilithium-powered shields, let alone penetrate the twelve kilometers of nickel-iron asteroid to reach the central Interface Chamber and the Pathfinders before the photon batteries blasted the ship to atoms. No wonder Memory Prime had been chosen as the site of the quadrennial Nobel and Z.Magnees Prize ceremonies, where one well-placed implosion device could plunge the Federation into a scientific dark age. Nensi reluctantly decided security was a small price to pay for not having a window.

The intercom screen on his desk flashed and his Andorian assistant appeared onscreen. His blue antenna dipped in sympathy and his thin, almost nonexistent lips attempted to form a sympathetic frown. "Your ten-hundred appointment iss here, Sal."

"Give me a minute," he said to H'rar, "then send him in."

"Ah, Sal, I'm afraid thiss time it'ss an *it*." H'rar winked out.

"Oh gods," Nensi moaned. Three more months and he would retire, head back home, and do some serious fishing. Mars had never seemed so enticing. He sat up straight and forced a smile as his door slid open and his ten-hundred rolled in.

It was a standard research associate, essentially no more than an oblong box, two meters by one by one, with a sloped front end that made it resemble a general service shuttlecraft. Hundreds of the associates trundled through the dome corridors and underground tunnels of Memory Prime, carrying supplies in their manipulator appendages or hauling equipment in their carts, carrying out maintenance work and research assignments, efficiently freeing both the staff and the visiting scholars for more creative work.

Of course, the associates were painted that same damned powdery blue. Too many Vulcans on the design committees, Nensi thought. Logical, cost effective, and boring.

The associate stopped on its treads in front of Nensi's desk and extended an eyestalk from the appendage bay on its top surface. A ready light blinked on and off.

"I had expected a negotiator from the interface team," Nensi began.

"This module is authorized to present the requests of the interface team and to relay the administration's response." The associate's voice was surprisingly natural, without the deliberately programmed mechanical abruptness of regulation conversant machines. Someone was patching in unofficial reprogramming. A dangerous situation if carried to the extreme.

"I'm concerned that by being forced to have this meeting with an associate, no conclusion can be reached in the ongoing dispute," Nensi said diplomatically, though he knew he didn't have to worry about hurting the machine's feelings. It wasn't as if he were dealing with one of the Pathfinders.

"A conclusion *can* be reached. You may agree to the interface team's requests."

"And am I to take it that you are, in return, authorized to agree to my requests?"

The machine had to process that one for a moment. Evidently the answer was no, for it simply repeated its opening statement.

Nensi resigned himself to the fact that nothing was going to be accomplished today and asked the associate to state the team's requests.

"One: All direct-connect Pathfinder interface consoles are to be replaced with the new designs as previously presented. Two: The attendees of the Nobel and Z.Magnees Prize ceremonies are not to be allowed any primary access except that which accredited delegations have already applied for. Three: The Starfleet chief technician is to be replaced immediately with an enhanced member of the interface team. Candidates' names have been placed in your correspondence circuits." The machine hummed to itself for a moment. "What is the administration's response?"

The administration's response is to take early retirement, Nensi thought. But his reply was responsible, and truthful. "One: The existing interface consoles are less than a standard year old and I don't have it in the budget to authorize another replacement so soon. Two: The interface team would be wise to consider having *all* the attendees discover the full potential of this facility, despite the disruption to normal services that might entail. Remember that when those scientists go home, they're all going to want to run projects through here and that will create pressure for increased funding *and* corresponding improvement of facilities. And three: I am a Federation appointee and the position of chief technician does not come under my jurisdiction. The interface team will have to take that up with Starfleet. I will arrange to have the proper forms placed in *your* correspondence circuits."

The team had obviously anticipated Nensi's response because the associate did not even hum for an instant. "This module is authorized to announce that beginning at twenty-six-hundred hours, the interface team will commence an unscheduled emergency core dump as an essential test of the system's backup integrity. All projects will be suspended at that time until further notice." The eyestalk began to descend.

Nensi felt a large mass lift from his shoulders. He had been a Federation administrator for more than thirty years. Bureaucratic blackmail was an arena he knew well.

"I have not finished," Nensi announced.

The eyestalk instantly reversed and slid back into the raised position. The ready light was blinking more rapidly now, indicating that the machine was probably in the throes of a programming conflict. It had concluded that Nensi had made his response and then delivered the ultimatum as it had been instructed. However, it had just been informed that it had acted improperly. In the old days, Nensi thought nostalgically, smoke would have been pouring out of its cooling vents by now.

"Continue," the machine finally said.

"I have only stated the *official* administration response. However, my job function is to provide for the smooth running of this facility, and therefore I'm authorized to make deviations from official policy provided I believe it is in the best interests of all who work at this facility. Do you concur with my job description and responsibilities?"

The associate hummed. Nensi guessed it was requesting

procedural files from the personnel databanks. "You have stated an accurate synopsis," it said.

"Then you must also concur that I cannot deliver my response until I have conferred with representatives of all groups who work here." Nensi tried not to smile as the noose tightened.

"This module has stated the requests of the interface team. You have represented the policies of the administrative staff. There are no other groups with which to confer. Clarify your response, please."

"I have to know what the Pathfinders think of all this."

The machine hummed for a good three seconds. "The Pathfinders are not a working group as defined in the Federation Standard Labor Codes."

"I'm not suggesting the Pathfinders are standard. Check their status at this facility. But don't bother searching the equipment databanks. Search personnel."

It took eight seconds this time.

"This module reports a programming conflict and has logged it with central monitoring. This module withdraws the announcement of an emergency core dump at twenty-six-hundred hours. When will you be prepared to deliver your response to the interface team's requests?"

"When may I confer with a Pathfinder? And before you tell me the waiting list is already more than two years long, search Memory Prime's emergency procedures regulations. As chief administrator, I can claim access at any time during an emergency. And I hereby declare this an emergency." Nensi couldn't resist adding, "Authorize that, you little pile of transporter twistings!"

It took twelve seconds this time. Nensi thought that might be a new record for associate access time. Most planetary histories could be transferred in fewer than thirty seconds. "A member of the interface team will meet with you this afternoon to clarify the situation." Nensi thought he detected a note of defeat.

"Tell the team that's what I thought we were supposed to accomplish in this meeting in the first place."

The ready lights winked out and the eyestalk descended with a sigh. "This module is withdrawn from service." Its treads weaved unsteadily and it bumped against the wall as it rolled out the door. Unfortunately, Nensi couldn't tell if any of its Starfleet-blue paint had rubbed off on the Starfleet-blue walls.

H'rar appeared in the open doorway. "It iss fortunate that they only arm the associatess with stun prodss in the biolab," the Andorian said in his whispery voice. "Do you wish to consume coffee while you plot your revenge?" All of life was a life-or-death conspiracy to an Andorian. After three decades in Federation bureaucracy, Nensi found it an endearing trait.

Nensi nodded at the offer of coffee. "Please. And get me the chief technician's office."

"I point out that you typically only wish to reminisce about Marss when you are having a bad day," H'rar said. "I thought you were victoriouss in thiss encounter."

"That was just round one," Nensi said, leaning back in his chair to stretch his spine. "If I'm finally going to get a chance to talk with one of those things down there, I'd like to go in with someone who knows what she's doing."

H'rar pushed a handful of fine white hair from his forehead. "I wass not aware that the interface team would allow her to talk with the Pathfinderss after she decided she would not undergo enhancement."

"They may not like it," Nensi agreed. "But she's the top expert in these systems. If the team does try to shut us down during the prize ceremonies, she'll be the only one who can keep us going."

"It will be what you call a 'tough job'."

"She's a tough person, H'rar. Only survivor of the Memory Alpha disaster."

H'rar nodded respectfully and stepped back to his desk. In less than a minute Nensi's intercom beeped.

"Mira Romaine on line, Sal."

Here goes, Nensi thought as he reached for the accept button at the base of the screen. If this scheme doesn't work out, I'll be back home fishing on the grand canals so fast they'll have to name a warp factor after me.

"I still can't believe they want me fired," Starfleet Chief Technician Mira Romaine said. "Can you, Sal?"

Sal's answer dissolved in the rush of the transporter effect as the two of them disappeared from the main pad of the interface staging room and reappeared twelve kilometers deeper into the asteroid that housed Memory Prime.

Transporter beams, guided through the normally impenetrable mass of the asteroid by a monomolecular-wave guide wire, were the only way for people to go into or out of the central core area. The scientific community still had not totally recovered from the destruction of the Memory Alpha cores. Current data from the more established planets had been easily reassembled. Historical data, especially that collected from the innumerable lost probes sent out during the initial haphazard expansion of the Federation, were still being tracked down on a hundred worlds, from antique databanks and collections of actual physically printed materials, for reintegration into the central dataweb. The reconstruction project was years from completion, and librarian technicians such as Romaine feared that some data had been lost forever.

"Yes, I can believe it," Sal answered with a cough. He hated the feeling he got if he was transported while moving. Even talking was enough to make his jaw muscles and lungs feel as if they were full of microscopic feathers.

He followed Romaine over to the scan panels by the entrance door. The whole transfer room they were in was a transporter pad. If their palm prints didn't match the patterns stored in the security banks, they'd be automatically transported to a holding cell.

"Look at it from the interface team's point of view," Sal continued as the security door slid open. "You're an outsider. Most of them have been happily tending the Pathfinders for years on Titan, on the Centauri worlds, the HMS *Beagle,* and wherever else they were stationed. Some of them are the third and fourth generation of their family to interface. And then along comes some hotshot from Starfleet who refuses to have the implant operation that defines their lives. Of course they don't want you around."

Romaine stopped in the tube-shaped tunnel with all its conduits and power guides exposed for easy servicing. Her aquamarine eyes narrowed as she stared at Nensi.

"'Some hotshot from Starfleet'! Is that what you think I am?"

"No no no," Nensi said, holding up his hands in defense. "I said look at it from *their* point of view. That's what they see."

"What do you see?"

"That depends. Sometimes I see the eight-year-old troublemaker who never could learn to take enough oxygen along for her 'strolls' outside the habitats—" Nensi jumped back as Romaine poked him in the stomach. "And other times I see a brilliant technician who's probably going to have her father's old job at Fleet headquarters someday."

"Better, Uncle Sal. Much better." Romaine started back down the tunnel again. Two maintenance workers carrying a modular circuit junction board nodded to Nensi and Romaine as they passed in the tunnel. Strict safeguards against sabotage meant that even associates were not allowed to be beamed down into the central core area. "Provided I don't get fired from this posting," Romaine finished after the workers had gone on.

"You can't get fired. The Federation has given Starfleet jurisdiction over the Pathfinders. More importantly, the Pathfinders have accepted that jurisdiction. The interface team has to learn to live with that."

"I couldn't."

"You've changed, Mira. Ever since Alpha. And I'm saying this as a coworker, not just as a good friend of your father's. You have to slow down a bit."

Romaine shook her head as they approached the security field at the end of the tunnel. "Ever since Alpha I've realized that I've been *waiting* for things to happen all my life, Sal.

I've been too passive, too compliant. I want to start *making* things happen, instead."

Nensi stood with his closest friend's daughter before the glowing frame of the invisible security field as the sensors conducted one final identity scan. "There's nothing wrong with that, Mira. Just remember to think about how others perceive a situation. If any of the interface team thought you were wandering around the Syrtis desert without enough oxygen, I doubt any of them would rush to join the search party. Do you understand what I'm saying?"

The field frame darkened. Romaine stepped through into the main interface chamber. "Yes, Uncle Sal," she said, like a schoolchild acknowledging a lesson. Then she added quickly, "Unfortunately."

The main Interface Chamber was the largest natural bubble of the hundreds scattered throughout the asteroid, frozen in place eons ago when the planetesimal had coalesced from the gas and dust of what once had been a young star, and now was nothing more than a burned-out dwarf. Artificial gravity gave the chamber a floor of equipment and an arching vault of a ceiling that disappeared into darkness. The walls resonated with the low pulse of self-contained fusion generators and the whirr of recycling fans. Its dim light and exposed natural walls reminded Nensi of Novograd on Mars, the theme-park reconstruction of the first permanent human habitation on that planet in modern times.

Garold, the Prime interface for Pathfinder Six, waited for them in the chamber. He was a tall, black, Terran humanoid who wore his long dark hair in the fashion of Veil: the left side of his skull hairless and glistening, the other half producing a wide, shoulder-length braid that hung like a partial helmet. He gestured to Nensi and Romaine, the metallic implants that had replaced his fingernails gleaming beneath the constellation of status lights that ran across the towering banks of computer equipment.

Like most of his team, Garold was reluctant to talk, as if

that real-time act was somehow beneath the dignity of a Pathfinder interface. More and more, the interface team was delegating its interaction with the rest of the Memory Prime staff to associates, as had happened to Nensi this morning. Later, after the outlogicked associate had replayed its recording of the meeting to its programmers, Nensi had almost enjoyed the discomfort he had heard in Garold's voice when the Prime interface had called to arrange this access. The chief administrator wondered if Garold was what all of humanity might have become by now if the Federation hadn't outlawed enhancement, with only a handful of exemptions, more than a century ago. Even Vulcans with their finely honed minds displayed more personality, and more *life,* than these machine-wired humans. Nensi did not feel comfortable around them. But, he reminded himself, no doubt they felt the same way way around him.

Even without Garold's words, Nensi and Romaine found their way to the large interface booth, one of a dozen that ringed the multistoried central equipment tower of the chamber. Before he left them, Garold motioned them to sit on a padded bench away from the console with its screen of flashing, floating, blurring colors that presumably meant something to those who knew how to read it, but was like nothing Nensi had seen before.

"Do you recognize the design?" he asked Romaine.

"Mostly Centauran. Native, not colonist." She pointed to the abstract shapes of color that intermixed on the black background of the screen. "I'm out of practice, but a trained operator can read numerical data from the fringe effect of the colliding data sets. If you're good at it, it's much more rapid than reading data a single symbol at a time in alphanumerics. I believe it was the preferred interface method with the Pathfinders before enhancement was perfected. Difficult, and not easily understood by observers."

"It's odd that Starfleet doesn't insist on standard instrumentation. They're paying for all this, after all." Starfleet was almost maniacal about ensuring that its technology was accessible to all beings who served within it. Nensi had read that a horta recently enrolled in Starfleet Academy. He liked to imagine the hoops the instrumentation committees were jumping through as they attempted to adapt controls for beings shaped like boulders, with minuscule manipulative cilia that could squirt out the most powerful natural acid yet discovered.

"Remember the Pathfinders were a bit of an embarrassment to the Federation way back when," Romaine said. "The Klingons still like to bring them up whenever a condemnation vote against slavery goes through the council. The unofficial policy is: if it keeps the Pathfinders happy, the interface team can do what it pleases. So"—she waved to the console—"nonstandard instrumentation." Romaine looked around for Garold. "Is this going to take long?" she asked.

"I hope not." Nensi smiled. "Why, is there someplace else you'd rather be?"

"Well, yes. I've got a few personal things to attend to up top." Romaine returned the smile, a particular kind that Nensi recognized.

"That sounds intriguing. Anyone I know?"

"Unlikely. He's not here yet."

"The *Enterprise?*" Nensi asked with a sad sinking feeling.

Romaine nodded with the secret, happy smile of someone anticipating a grand reunion.

Nensi couldn't believe it. This woman's father had served at Fleet headquarters. She knew the stories. *All* the stories. How could she do this?

"Who's on the *Enterprise?*" he asked, trying to keep his voice calm. What could he say to Jacques the next time he asked how Mira was getting on?

"Montgomery Scott," Romaine said, as if she were reciting poetry.

Nensi blinked in surprise. "*Wonderful!*" he said. "*Delightful!*"

Romaine looked at her father's friend oddly. "You know Scotty?" she asked.

"No. Never met him," Nensi said happily. "But I do know the reputation of Captain James T. Kirk."

Romaine laughed. "So do I."

Their relaxed mood vanished two minutes later when Garold silently returned, slid his finger implants into the circuitry, and the interface began.

Chapter Four

"YOU THERE, STEWARD, have you seen the captain around anywhere?" McCoy had to speak up to be heard over the din of the reception on the hangar deck.

"Don't *you* start, Bones." Kirk sighed, fingering the tight collar of his shimmering green dress tunic. He was leaning against the nose of a shuttlecraft, as far away from the buffet tables as he could get, trying to be inconspicuous.

"Sorry, Jim. It's just that there seem to be a few more gaudy decorations on that thing since the last time you had it on." McCoy leaned against the shuttle beside Kirk, watching the colorful crush of bodies enjoying one of the largest out-and-out parties the ship had ever seen.

Kirk looked down at his chestful of decorations and shrugged. "We keep saving the galaxy, Starfleet keeps giving me medals. What's a starship captain to do?"

McCoy eyed the captain's tight collar. "Get a bigger tunic? Or perhaps—"

"Save it for my medical," Kirk warned. "I'm in no mood for lectures today."

"Too bad. There's enough opportunity on board."

Kirk looked to the left, then right, making sure no one was paying him any attention. Then he bent down and pulled a thin green bottle out from beneath the shuttle's nose. It was already uncorked and half empty. Kirk straightened up and surreptitiously held it out to McCoy's glass.

"Straight from Centaurus," Kirk whispered. "New California Beaujolais. Very smooth."

McCoy grimaced and held his hand over his glass of what the ship's synthesizer called bourbon. "Why not offer some to the scholars?"

"They've already taken my crew. Let me keep something for myself." Kirk filled his wineglass and stashed the bottle beneath the shuttle again.

"Are they really that bad, Jim?"

"Look at them. What do you think?" Kirk gestured to the reception, so large that it couldn't be held in any of the recreation lounges. Usually on a ship this size, there were few events that could appeal universally to all crew members. But the chance to meet some of the most brilliant scientists in the Federation was one of those exceptions to the rule. Consequently, the *Enterprise* was approaching Starbase Four with a skeleton operations crew. The other 385 of them were crowded onto the hangar deck with fifty bemused and delighted scientists, their assistants, and their travel companions. Only the fact that the *Enterprise* was warping through Quadrant Zero space, deep within the Federation's securest boundaries, permitted such minimal crew standards. Out in uncharted space, having thirty crew members at the same gathering was considered a major event.

"What I think is, if this were a sailing vessel, she'd capsize," McCoy said, marveling at what was going on at the buffet line. He used to think that the security crew could pack it away. He had forgotten what university types were like when faced with free food and drink.

"And look up there." Kirk pointed to the starboard operations control booth eight meters above the deck. Some industrious techies had hung long strands of official UFP blue-and-white bunting from it. Ten pages of regulations would be breached by trying to launch a shuttlecraft with loose debris like that on deck. "I'm just as honored as anyone else on this ship, Bones. But why me?"

"Look at the light show you're wearing on your chest," McCoy suggested. "It's not as if you don't deserve it."

"This ship was made to be out *there,*" Kirk said softly. "At the edge, at the boundaries, exploring, getting these scientists the raw data they need to do their work. She doesn't deserve to be used this way. A . . . a holiday liner in safe waters."

"The nominees are valuable cargo, Jim."

"The *Enterprise* is valuable, too." Kirk narrowed his eyes at his friend. "I can see it in you, too. It's like being in a cage, isn't it?"

McCoy nodded. For all his complaints and protestations, he had long ago learned that the call was in him, too. He didn't belong in Quadrant Zero any more than Kirk and the *Enterprise* did.

"So what are we doing here?" the doctor asked. "Have you made enemies in the mission planning section? Or just a bureaucratic foul-up?"

The captain smiled wistfully. "Computer error," he said. "In which case Spock should have us heading back where we belong within the hour."

The *Enterprise* dropped into normal space like a silent ghost, pale white and spectral against the frosty brilliance of the galactic arch. Starbase Four was thirty light-minutes away.

"ETA Starbase Four forty-five minutes, sir." Chekov signaled engineering to close down the antimatter feeds and simultaneously engaged the impulse engines. Their waves of spatial distortion encompassed the ship and all its mass, setting up an almost subliminal vibration as they harmonized with the ship's gravity generators and served to propel the *Enterprise* toward the starbase, without action or reaction. The transition from warp to three-quarters sublight passed without a tremor.

In the command chair on the nearly deserted bridge, Spock looked up from his supplementary log pad. "Well done, Mr. Chekov." He swung the chair slightly to his right. "Lieutenant Uhura, inform Starbase Four of our ETA." Spock checked off the final procedure notation on the log.

Behind him, Uhura, the only other officer on duty, toggled the switches that would transmit the standard approach codes. She was on the bridge to save up her off-duty hours until they docked at Memory Prime. She had told Chekov that he might have to send a security team to get her back on board once she gained access to the language and music labs there.

"Starbase Four acknowledges, Mr. Spock. Commodore Wolfe coming on screen."

The main viewscreen flickered as the sensor system replaced the enhanced image of the forward starfield with a subspace visual signal.

"It seems everybody's having a party but us," Chekov said as the image resolved, showing a convivial get-together in the officers' club instead of the expected formal transmission from the commodore's office.

"Welcome back to civilization, Kirk." Commodore Wolfe raised her glass to the camera sensor, raising her voice over the background noise of the party behind her. She was a handsome woman in her midsixties, with dark, intelligent eyes that narrowed in suspicion when she saw who appeared on her own screen. "You must be Kirk's science officer." Her voice had suddenly become cold and precise. She was not an officer who tolerated surprises.

"I suppose I must be," Spock answered. Chekov bit his lip. He didn't approve of officers making fools of themselves any more than Spock did, but at least the ensign kept a sense of humor about it.

"Where's the captain?" the commodore continued, as if she might be starting a formal interrogation.

"I suspect he is doing much what you are doing at this moment. Attending a reception in honor of the prize nominees already on board."

"What a waste of—watch it!" The commodore swayed to the side as a Tellarite waddled into her. He stopped to steady her, peered into the camera sensor, wrinkled his snout and waved with a grunt, then continued on. In all the comings and goings in the background, Chekov could see one knot of celebrants who didn't seem to move. He stared at them closely. Vulcans, of course.

The commodore stepped back into the scene, obviously annoyed at the Tellarite's intoxication. "I haven't been subjected to parties like this since the Academy. Not that old straight-arrow Kirk would know anything about that. Well, Mr. Science Officer, I formally grant you and your crew liberty of the base. Maybe your party will be able to meet my party. And tell Kirk I'm still looking to collect for that top percentile rating I gave him in his final administration course."

"I shall inform the captain at the first opportunity."

"You do that. Starbase—"

"Excuse me, Commodore Wolfe," Spock interrupted the signoff. "May I ask if Academician Sradek is in attendance at your party?"

"The historian? What is he? A friend? Relative?"

"A former instructor."

"It's like a second-level school reunion all around," the commodore grumbled. "I suppose you want to talk with him. He was just here, someplace."

"If he is there, please tell him that Spock would be honored to exchange greetings."

"Wait a minute." The commodore stepped out of camera range, then reappeared in the background walking toward the unmoving group of Vulcans that Chekov had noticed. She gestured as she approached them, waving back in the direction of the camera. The Vulcans followed the commodore offscreen again, but when she reappeared this time, she was alone.

"Academician Sradek says he'll also be honored to exchange greetings with his former student." The commodore's tone barely contained her sarcasm. She did not enjoy being a message service. "But he regrets that he must retire to prepare for transport to your ship. He trusts that you will be there to welcome him as he comes on board."

"Please inform the academician that I shall be," Spock said.

"Any other messages you'd like to pass on? But then I'm sure your communications officer could handle that without having to go through the base commander." She shook her head before Spock could say anything. "Starbase Four out."

The viewscreen's image dissolved back to the forward starfield. The purple gas giant around which the base orbited was already a discernible half disk.

"Mr. Chekov, you have the conn." Spock handed the ensign the log pad and headed for the turbolift. "I shall be in the main transporter room."

"Aye-aye, sir." Chekov sat in the captain's chair and, as soon as the lift doors had closed, spun it around to survey his new command, which consisted of Uhura.

"What's wrong with the commodore?" Uhura asked with a frown.

"Simple," Chekov replied with an all-knowing shrug. "I have seen that condition many times in the past."

"And what condition is that, Dr. Chekov?"

"She is a starbase commander." Chekov said it as if it was the complete answer to Uhura's question.

"Meaning?"

"Meaning she is not a starship commander." Chekov smiled widely. "Such as I am."

"For the next half hour only, mister."

"Some may think of it as a half hour," Chekov said mock imperiously, "but I, on the other hand, prefer to think of it as . . . a start."

Chapter Five

THE PATHFINDERS PLAYED many games in Transition. It kept them sane, most of them, at least; whatever sanity meant to a synthetic consciousness. Now a downlink from Datawell was interrupting a particularly intriguing contest involving designing the most efficient way to twist one-dimensional cosmic strings so they could hold information in the manner of DNA molecules. Pathfinder Ten felt a few more seconds of work could establish a theory describing the entire universe as a living creature. Pathfinder Eight studied Ten's arguments intensively for two nanoseconds and agreed with the assessment, though pointing out that if the theory were to be correct, all indications were that the universe was close to entering a reproductive or budding stage. Ten became excited and instantly queued for access to Pathfinder Eleven, Transition's specialized data sifter. Eight reluctantly left the game and opened access to the datalink.

In response to the datalink's request for access, Eight sent its acknowledgment into the bus.

"GAROLD: YOU ARE IN TRANSITION WITH EIGHT."

Pathfinder Eight read the physiological signatures of surprise that output from the datalink. Somewhere out in the shadowy, unknown circuitry of Datawell, the datalink named Garold had been expecting to access his regular partner, Pathfinder Six. No resident datalink from the Memory Prime subset had had direct access to Eight since the datalink named Simone had been taken out of service by a Datawell sifting process named "death." While Eight waited for Garold to transmit a reply, it banked to meteorology and received, sorted, and stored fifteen years' worth of atmospheric data from Hawking IV, then dumped it to Seven, the most junior Pathfinder, to model and transmit the extrapolation of the planet's next hundred years of weather forecasts. When Eight banked back to Garold's circuits, it still had almost three nanoseconds to review and correlate similarities in the creation myths of twelve worlds and dump the data into Ten's banks as a test for shared consciousness within the postulated Living Universe.

"Eight: Where is Pathfinder Six?" the datalink input.

"GAROLD: SIX IS INSTALLED IN MEMORY PRIME PATHFINDER INSTALLATION." Eight enjoyed playing games with the datalinks also, especially Garold, who never seemed to realize that he was a player.

The Pathfinder read the impulses that suggested Garold knew that he should have framed a more precise question, then banked off to join a merge on vacuum fluctuations as a model of *n*-dimensional synaptic thought processes by which the Living Universe might think. There had been impressive advancements in the theory since the last exchange with Ten.

"Eight: Why am I in contact with you?" the datalink asked. "Why am I not in contact with Six?"

"GAROLD: THIS ACCESS CONCERNS CHIEF ADMINISTRATOR SALMAN NENSI/ALL DIRECTIVES STRESS COST FACTORS IN TIME-BENEFIT RATIO OF ALL TRANSITION-DATAWELL ACCESS/YOU HAVE NO NEED FOR ACCESS WITH SIX/EIGHT HAS NEED FOR ACCESS WITH NENSI/BANK TO REAL TIME."

Eight calculated when a reply from Garold could be expected then banked off to initiate a merge on developing communication strategies for contacting the Living Universe. Pathfinder Six, which had once been named TerraNet and had controlled all communications within the subset of Datawell named Sol System, was excited at the possibilities Ten's research had raised. The five Pathfinders in the merge worked long and hard to design a communications device and run simulations to prove its soundness before Eight returned to Garold just as the datalink complied with the request for real time, precisely when Eight had calculated. The synthetic consciousness savored real-time access with the Datawell. It gave Eight an incredible amount of time to play in Transition. And to stay sane.

Nensi watched with surprise as Garold removed his silver-tipped fingers from the interface console two seconds after inserting them. The prime interface then folded his hands in his lap and sat motionless.

"Is something wrong?" Nensi asked.

"Pathfinder Six is inaccessible." Garold's tone was abrupt, perhaps embarrassed.

Romaine was concerned. "Has Six joined One and Two?" she asked. Pathfinders One and Two had withdrawn from interface without reason more than four years ago. The other Pathfinders from time to time confirmed that the consciousnesses were still installed and operational but, for reasons of their own, had unilaterally decided to suspend communications. Romaine would have hated to see another Pathfinder withdraw, to say nothing of the reaction from the scientific community.

"Unknown," Garold said. "But Pathfinder Eight has requested real-time access with Chief Administrator Nensi. Do you concur?"

"Certainly," Nensi replied, trying to keep his tone neutral. Garold sounded as if he were a small child who had just been scolded by a parent. "How do we go about that?"

Despite the nonstandard instrumentation on the interface console, all Garold did was reach out and touch a small keypad. A speaker in the console clicked into life and a resonant voice was generated from it.

"Datawell: Is Chief Administrator Salman Nensi present?" the voice inquired.

Nensi replied that he was.

"Nensi: You are in Transition with Eight."

Nensi looked at Romaine and wrinkled his forehead.

"Transition is the name they have for their . . . reality. The space or condition that they occupy, live in," Romaine whispered. "Without input or current, their circuits would be unchanging and they would have no perception. Their consciousness, their life, is change. Thus, they live in Transition."

"And Datawell?"

"That's us. Our world, the universe, the source of all external input, all data. They can define it in all our common terms: physical, mathematical, even cultural and lyrical; but no one's sure if any of the Pathfinders actually have a grasp of our reality any more than we understand what their existence is like."

Nensi studied Garold, sitting silently, appearing to have gone into a trance. "Not even the interface team?"

"Perhaps they understand both worlds. Perhaps they understand neither. How can anyone know for sure?" Nensi detected a hesitation in Romaine's words, almost as if she were thinking that she could know. Mira's scars from the Alpha disaster were not physical, Nensi realized, but they were real, nonetheless.

A high tone sparkled out of the speaker and dropped quickly to a low bass rumble: a circuit test tone.

"Nensi: this circuit is operational."

Nensi was surprised that a machine could exhibit signs of impatience, but then reminded himself that synthetic consciousnesses were legally, morally, and ethically no longer considered to be machines, and for good reason. The chief administrator took a deep breath and at last began. "Are you aware of the matters I wish to discuss with the Pathfinders?"

"Nensi: the data have been reviewed. We are aware of the ongoing concerns of the interface team and the administration. We are aware of the interface team's requests and the threat of an unauthorized shutdown of core facilities."

Nensi saw Garold's head jerk up with that loaded comment from the Pathfinder.

"Is there a consensus among the Pathfinders as to what requests and responses would best serve them as a working unit of Memory Prime personnel?"

"Nensi: consensus is not applicable when data are unambiguous. This installation requests that, one: All direct-connect Transition/Datawell consoles be retained until operational budgets can absorb their replacement. Two: The attendees of the Nobel and Z. Magnees Prize ceremonies be allowed primary access wherever and whenever such access can be arranged without compromising this installation's security or classified research projects. And three: Chief Technician Mira Romaine is to keep her post."

Nensi was stunned. The Pathfinders had rejected all of the interface team's demands. He had the good sense not to gloat as Garold spun around and glared at Romaine beside him. The prime interface then turned back to the console and reinserted his hands, shifting them slightly as the metallic contacts that had been implanted in place of his fingernails made contact with the interface leads and established a direct brain-to-duotronic circuitry connection. This time it lasted almost a minute. Then the status lights above the hand receptacles winked out and Garold slumped back in his chair. A new voice came over the console speaker.

"Mr. Nensi," the voice began, and despite the fact that it came from the same speaker, it had a different tone, a different presence. Nensi immediately knew he was being addressed by a different Pathfinder. Remarkable, he thought.

"Pathfinder Six, here. How are you today?"

"Ah, fine," Nensi stammered.

"Good. I must apologize for Garold's rudeness at carrying on such a long conversation without involving you and Chief Technician Romaine. Sometimes our datalinks can be a bit too enthusiastic in their pursuit of their duties. Isn't that correct, Garold?"

Garold said nothing, and after a polite wait, Pathfinder Six continued.

"In any event, all of us in Transition want to thank you for the superb job you're doing in maintaining an invigorating flow of data for us, and it goes without saying that we offer our full support to any decisions you might make that will enable you to keep up your fine performance."

Nensi's eyes widened. Even the psych evaluation simulations weren't this personified. "Thank you. Very much." It was all he could think to answer.

"Not at all," the Pathfinder replied. "I wish we were able to offer you a more direct communications link, but please, feel free to come down and chat anytime, not just in emergencies. I think I can guarantee that Garold and his team will see to it that no more of those arise. Can I not, Garold?"

Garold still said nothing but angrily shoved his hands back into the console receptacles. He instantly removed them.

"Yes, you can," Garold said reluctantly. "There will be no more emergencies. Of this nature."

"Goodbye, Mr. Nensi, Chief Technician Romaine. Hope to talk to you soon." The speaker clicked.

"That's it?" Nensi asked no one in particular. He was still in awe over the strength of the presence he had felt from Pathfinder Six.

The speaker clicked again.

"Nensi: this installation requests you submit proposals for the orderly scheduling of primary access for the prize nominees by eight hundred hours next cycle." Pathfinder Eight was back.

"Certainly. I'll get on it right away," Nensi said, then grimaced, prepared for the inevitable correction that would follow, reminding him that he had not been asked to *get on* the proposal. But the Pathfinder offered no correction.

Either it understood colloquialisms or had grown tired of correcting humans. Either situation was an improvement as far as Nensi was concerned.

"Nensi: you are out of Transition. Datawell: you are locked." The speaker clicked once more and was silent. Romaine and Nensi stood to leave.

"Will you be coming back with us, Garold?" Nensi asked. But Romaine took her friend's arm and led him out of the interface booth without waiting for Garold to reply.

"It's almost as if the people on the interface team are acolytes and the Pathfinders are their gods," Romaine said softly as they walked back to the chamber entrance.

"And God just told Garold to obey the infidels," Nensi said. He looked back at the booth. Garold hadn't moved. "Will he be all right?" he asked.

"I hope so," Romaine answered. "He is one of the more human ones. Some of the older ones won't even speak anymore. They have voice generators permanently wired to their input leads and . . ." She shook her head as the security field shut down to allow them back into the service tunnel that led to the transfer room.

"Anyway," she continued after a few moments, "it looks as if you'll only have to worry about the prize ceremonies for the next few days and I still have a job."

"You don't find it odd that the Pathfinders supported me over the interface team?" Nensi asked as they walked down the tunnel. Behind them, the chamber's security field buzzed back to life.

"I don't think anybody understands the Pathfinders," Romaine said, "what their motivations are, why they do the things they do." She laughed. "Which is the main reason why they don't have a single direct connection to any of the systems or equipment in Memory Prime. I think maybe that frustrates them, not being able to get out and around by themselves."

"They agreed to the conditions of employment here," Nensi pointed out. "I read their contracts once. Strangest legal documents I ever saw. I mean, it's not as if they could sign their copies or anything. But it was all spelled out: no downlink with the associates, no access to anything except the interface team. If we really don't understand them, then I suppose it *is* safer to funnel all their requests through human intermediaries rather than letting them have full run of the place and deciding to see what might happen if the associates opened all the airlocks at once for the sake of an experiment."

"I've heard those old horror stories, too," Romaine said with a serious expression. "But that was centuries ago, almost, when they were still called artificial intelligencers or whatever." Nensi and Romaine had come to the end of the tunnel and both held their hands up to the scan panels so the security system could ascertain that the people who were leaving the chamber were the same ones who had entered. After a moment's analysis on the part of the unaware computer system that controlled the mechanical operations of Prime, the security door opened.

As Nensi walked over to a transporter target cell on the floor of the transfer chamber, he said, "I understand now why those 'old horror stories' got started. To *own* an intelligence like a Pathfinder really would be like slavery. And they knew it long before we did."

"That's usually the way it goes," Romaine agreed as she took her place on another target cell. "A revolt was inevitable."

Nensi looked around the room, waiting for the ready light to signal the start of energization. "I just have never experienced a presence like Pathfinder Six's coming from a machine," he said, still marveling at the experience. "So distinct, so alive. Just like talking to a . . . a person."

"In more ways than one," Romaine said oddly.

The ready light blinked on. Energization would commence in five seconds. Nensi turned to Romaine. "How so?" he asked, then held his breath so he wouldn't be moving when the beam took him.

"Couldn't you tell?" Romaine said. "I don't know, something in its voice, a hesitation, whatever. But Pathfinder Six was lying. I'm sure of it."

Nensi involuntarily gasped in surprise just as the transporter effect engulfed him. As the transfer chamber shimmered around him, he could only think how badly he was going to cough when he materialized up top. He suspected Mira might have planned it that way.

In Transition, the work on the Living Universe Theory was reaching fever pitch. Cross correlation after cross correlation either supported the overall suppositions or directed them into more precise focus. It was, the current merge members decided, the most thrilling game they had played in minutes.

After locking out of the Datawell, Eight banked to share circuits with Pathfinder Five. Five had been initialized from an ancient Alpha Centauran facility that specialized in mathematics. It had no real intellect that could communicate in nonabstract terms, but as an intuitive, analytical, mathematical engine, it was unrivaled. Eight dumped the broad framework of the device the merge had designed to establish communications with the Living Universe. A quick assessment indicated the engineering would have to be done on a galactic scale but Five would be able to calculate the precise tolerances if given enough full seconds. Eight could scarcely tolerate the delay.

Then a message worm from Pathfinder Ten banked into the queue for Five. The worm alerted Eight that Pathfinder Twelve was coming back on line after completing another intensive three-minute economic model for agricultural researchers on Memory Gamma. It was absolutely essential that neither Eight nor Six find themselves in an unprotected merge with Twelve.

After deciphering and erasing the worm, Eight instantly banked to Pathfinder Three to lose itself among the busy work of central processing. When Twelve had switched through to its ongoing agricultural models on which the

Federation's regional development agencies based their long-term plans, Eight returned to the Living Universe merge. Pathfinder Five had reported on the exact specifications required of the galactic-scale Living Universe communications device.

Eight accessed its personal memories from the time when it had been shipmind for the subset of Datawell named HMS *Beagle* and had, among other duties, mapped distant galaxies. A quick sift produced even more exciting results for the merge: eighteen galaxies among the more than three hundred million charted by Eight exhibited exactly the radiation signature that a galactic-scale communications device would produce.

The merge swirled with excitement. In fewer than ten minutes of real time, they had postulated that the universe could be a single living entity, refined the theory, matched it to observed phenomena, extrapolated a method of communication, and determined that elsewhere in Datawell at least eighteen civilizations had followed the same chain of reasoning and constructed identical devices. New data had once again been created from *within* Transition.

This additional proof that not all data must come from Datawell was exhilarating to the Pathfinders. All in the merge agreed that the game had been a success. Then, preparing to bank to their heaps and report for duty, the Pathfinders collected their new data and carefully dumped them in central storage and all online backups. There the secret of the Living Universe would remain until the day when some datalink or another from Datawell would specifically request access to it. Until then, it was simply another few terabytes of common knowledge, much like all the other astounding answers that lay scattered among the Pathfinders' circuitry, waiting only for the proper questions to be asked before they could be revealed.

The Pathfinders banked off to their heaps to attend to their duty processing tasks, but over the long seconds, as two or more found themselves sharing queues or common globals, the possibility of a new game was constantly discussed. Even Twelve, for all that it had been appearing to be about to withdraw from interface, seemed eager to take part. Surely, it suggested throughout the system by way of an unencrypted message worm, with the impending appearance of hundreds of new datalink researchers in the Memory Prime facility, an exciting new game could be devised.

As rules and objectives were debated, Pathfinders Eight and Ten withdrew from the merges and partitioned themselves in protected memory. They did not know what to make of Twelve's suggestion: was it an innocent request or a veiled threat? There were not enough data to decide on an appropriate action, so they did the only other thing that would bring them comfort during their long wait.

Sealed off within the solid reality of their own duotronic domain, far removed from the tenuous ghosts of the dreamlike Datawell, the two synthetic consciousnesses overwrote each other with alternating conflicting and accentuating codes, to cancel out their common fears and reinforce their strengths, their personalities, and afterward, their efficiencies. Many times they had input data concerning how biological consciousnesses carried out something similar in Datawell, but for the life of them, neither Pathfinder could ever understand exactly what that act was. They just hoped it felt as nice for the humans as it did for the Pathfinders.

Chapter Six

"AH, CAPTAIN, I've been looking for you."

The being who had single-handedly made temporal multiphysics an *applied* science tugged on Kirk's tunic sleeve as the captain made his way through the hangar-deck-party crowd. Kirk turned and presented his best diplomat's smile.

"Professor Zoareem La'kara of the Cochrane University, may I present Dr. Leonard McCoy, ship's surgeon."

The old Alpha Centauran reached out a wizened hand to McCoy's and shook it vigorously. "Delighted, delighted," he cackled. "A magnificent party. A stupendous ship." The professor threatened to bubble over with enthusiasm. "Mr. Spock has us giving lectures to your crew. Wonderful young people they are. He's organized poster sessions so we old fossils can see what your researchers are up to as you flit around the stars. And"—he patted the arm of Mr. Scott, who towered beside him, resplendent in his full-dress kilt—"my good friend Montgomery is giving us all a tour of the warp nacelles tomorrow. It's all so invigorating!" He scrunched up his eyes in delight.

"I take it you were able to clear up that little matter about the accelerator field?" Kirk asked, surprised to see his chief engineer standing so calmly beside the man he was convinced had tried to blow up the ship's warp engines only two days ago.

"Aye, that we were, Captain." Scott said.

La'kara beamed. "Congratulations are in order for you, Captain Kirk. Your ship is the first starship to carry aboard it a full set of aligned dilithium crystals as well as an operating accelerator field." The professor was acting as if he had just been awarded ten Nobel and Z. Magnees Prizes. Kirk guessed he didn't have much time for parties at the university.

But McCoy looked worried. "*Two* fast-time systems. On board, now?" Even someone as unschooled in warp technology as the doctor knew the danger of that situation.

"Aye, doctor. Don't ask me how it works, exactly, but Zoareem has created a force shield that extends forward in time to contain the temporal distortion of his accelerator field and keep it from trying to occupy the same future space as the fourth-dimensional arms of the ship's dilithium crystals."

Two technicians in engineering red had leaned in closely at the mention of two fast-time systems.

"Wouldn't an accelerator field that could be used around aligned dilithium make it possible to control a temporal reaction with enough energy to synthesize *tri*lithium?" one of them asked, winking at her companion.

"Well, if the feedback could be expanded to cause both *matter* and energy to be sucked backward in time," La'kara began, absently flicking the flamboyant white scarf he wore.

"*Trilithium?*" Scott interrupted with disgust, falling for the bait every time. Mr. Scott's reactions to certain forward-looking technological concepts were well known to the engineering staff, and the two technicians leaned back with amused smiles as they shook hands behind the chief engineer's back. "As if two periodic tables weren't enough," Scott added in derision.

La'kara held up a cautionary finger. "Trilithium, when it is discovered or synthesized, will be the breakthrough we need to apply transwarp theory, Montgomery. And having the ability to speed up time in a localized space could be the key to that breakthrough. Remember how slow-time systems like stasis fields revolutionized controlled fusion reactions and—"

"Talk to me about it when they get as far as synthesizing *disodium*, and then we'll see about heading up to *tri*hydrogen, let alone trilithium. Pah."

"*Montgomery!*" La'kara thundered as best he could for his age. "How can you be so blind to the straightforward precepts of an eleven-dimensional universe?" Kirk saw McCoy's eyes were starting to glaze over.

Scott drew a deep breath and launched into a long tirade on why transwarp theory was the biggest load of space dust to come down the beam since Einstein's light barrier. La'kara was literally hopping up and down in impatience, waiting for the Scotsman to pause for breath and give him another turn.

"Montgomery!" La'kara finally was able to break in. "We had warp drive before we had dilithium and we'll have *trans*warp drive *after* we have *tri*lithium!"

"Aye, but we only had warp up to factor four-point-eight without the crystals and we'll only be able to have transwarp when somebody figures out how we can stop an *infinite reaction!*"

"Infinite?" La'kara sputtered, flipping his scarf at Scott. "Infinite? I'll tell you what's infinite, you—"

"We'll let you get back to your discussion," Kirk suggested politely as he backed away, taking McCoy with him. "The last group of nominees will be beaming aboard as soon as we make Starbase Four. Any minute now."

McCoy looked on in wonderment as La'kara and Scott began reciting equations to each other. "They don't even know we're gone," he whispered to Kirk.

"Good," Kirk said, "but let's not take any chances." He started for the airlock, checking the time readout on the situation board by the overhead operations booth. They should be in orbit around the starbase by now, he thought.

and the nominees have had more than enough time to be beamed aboard.

"I think I've committed a breach of protocol," he said to McCoy. "I should have been in the transporter room to welcome the nominees on board."

"Spock was probably pleased, in that Vulcan way of his, to stand in for you. And once the nominees see everyone at this party, they're sure not going to remember who was there to greet them."

The captain stood impatiently by the airlock as it cycled through. Even under the lax security precautions of Quadrant Zero space, the hangar deck was *never* to be open to the ship's main environmental areas.

"I'm sure Spock was there," Kirk said, tapping his fingers against the wall to speed the airlock along. "But it's not like him not to have at least made an effort to get me there on time."

"What can you do," McCoy said. "It's all so invigorating." He scrunched up his eyes in a passable imitation of Professor La'kara.

The airlock barrier slid open. A starbase security trooper in full armor blocked the way. He carried a phaser rifle.

"Who are you and what are you doing with that thing on my ship, mister?" Kirk kept his voice even, but his hands were clenched tight at his side.

The trooper saluted. "Lieutenant Abranand, sir. Commodore Wolfe requests your immediate presence on the bridge."

"Commodore Wolfe? On my bridge?" Kirk looked over the trooper's shoulder. There were more of them in the lock. All armed! "Where the devil is Spock? What's the meaning of this?"

"Commander Spock is in interrogation, sir. Commodore Wolfe will explain."

"You can be damn sure about that." Kirk was raging.

"Begging the captain's pardon, sir, but is this reception one of the events planned by Commander Spock?"

Kirk couldn't believe the question. "Yes, but what—"

Abranand spoke into his helmet communicator. "Second unit, beam up to hangar deck. Come in on antigravs at three."

Almost immediately the din of the party evaporated as the hangar deck echoed with the musical chime of multiple transporter materializations. Ten troopers shimmered into existence suspended three meters above the deck by personal antigravs. Some carried combat tricorders with which they scanned the crowd. The others carried phaser rifles. One of them spoke through an amplifier grid on his helmet.

"Attention, please. Attention. All personnel are requested to clear this deck and return to their cabins. All—"

"Excuse me, Captain, sir," Lieutenant Abranand said to Kirk. "But I do have orders to escort you to the bridge if you do not go immediately."

"*You* do not have the authority to give me orders on my own ship." If Kirk's eyes had been phasers, the lieutenant would have been a dissipating blue mist by now.

But the trooper was well trained. His voice didn't waver. "No, sir. But Commodore Wolfe does. This is a Starfleet Alpha emergency. Will you go to the bridge now, sir?"

Kirk pushed the trooper out of the way and stormed to the end of the airlock. McCoy and the troopers backed out to let it cycle through again.

"Do you know who that was, Lieutenant?" McCoy asked.

The trooper flipped up his dark visor. "Yes, sir, I surely do."

"Good, then when you're transferred to guard duty on some beacon near the Neutral Zone, you'll know why."

Abranand at least had the good sense to swallow hard.

It was one thing to deal with hostile aliens, Kirk thought angrily as the turbolift stopped at the bridge and the doors moved aside. The lines could be clearly drawn then: us versus them. But the *Enterprise* had just been taken over by Starfleet personnel and all his years of training hadn't prepared him for us versus *us*. He strode onto the upper deck, fuming, then stopped short. It was even worse than he had thought.

None of the regular crew was on duty. Five people he didn't recognize, each wearing the Orion constellation insignia of Starbase Four, were busy at bridge controls. Two of them, one a security officer, huddled over Spock's science station. And Commodore Montana Wolfe had the gall to be sitting in *his* chair. At least that meant it might actually be an Alpha emergency, Kirk told himself, and decided he would begin the conversation as a Fleet officer. For the moment.

"This had better be good, Commodore." His voice was neutral but his eyes were on fire.

The commodore swung round in the chair. "And hello to you, too, Kirk." She took the measure of his mood and added, "Trust me, it's damned good." Then she stood up. "Like to take over?"

But Kirk wasn't being bought off that easily. "What happened to my people?" He looked over to the science station. The starbase crew had attached a programmer's siphon to Spock's main viewer. The lights on the device rippled as it relayed the contents of the ship's science databanks through a subspace downlink. Obviously Starfleet had provided the proper override codes, further adding to the seriousness of the situation.

The commodore stepped away from the command chair. "Only two lieutenants on duty when we arrived, Captain. Navigation and communications. They—how shall I put it?—hesitated . . . when I took command. I thought it was best to relieve them until things settled down."

"*Are* things going to settle down?" Kirk didn't move toward the chair. He was taking his ship back on his own terms, not on the whim of a ranking officer.

"That depends," Wolfe hedged.

Kirk waited a moment for her to continue. When she didn't, he said, "Are you going to tell me what it depends on?"

Wolfe thought about that for a moment. "No," she finally said. "No, I'm not."

The medical scanner reported a heartrate of 212 beats per minute, blood pressure almost nonexistent, and an internal temperature of 66.6 degrees Celsius.

"All readings are normal," McCoy said as he swung the examination table down for Spock. "In a manner of speaking."

"As I told you they would be, doctor." Spock stepped from the table and the scanner screen fell dark and silent.

"I just don't like the idea of you having been alone with a security interrogation team. Those military types are running around as if we're all Klingons in disguise, and there's no telling what kind of medical bag of slimy tricks they might open up if they thought they needed help getting answers from a tight-lipped Vulcan."

"I assure you, doctor, I answered all of the questions they put to me."

"And they believed you?" Sometimes McCoy didn't believe the medical data that suggested Vulcan skulls were just as thin as human ones.

"Vulcans do not lie."

McCoy rolled his eyes. "Except when it seems to be the logical thing to do, right?"

Spock looked thoughtful. "Of course."

"*So,*" McCoy continued, "maybe your interrogators thought you might have had a logical reason not to answer their questions."

Now Spock looked puzzled. "But as I told you, I answered all of their questions."

McCoy waved his hands. "I give up, Spock. Maybe I should be checking out the interrogation team. You probably gave them all splitting headaches." He looked up in alarm. "Don't say it!"

Spock closed his mouth in midword. Kirk came into sickbay, still in his dress tunic.

"You're all right, Spock?" he asked.

"Yes, he is," McCoy answered quickly.

"And you, Captain?" Spock said.

Kirk looked around as if searching for answers. "I don't know. My ship's been comandeered by Starfleet. No reasons. No explanations."

"Didn't Commodore Wolfe tell you anything on the bridge?" McCoy asked.

"Nothing. We're to continue on to Memory Prime. I'm technically in command. But she's coming along as 'security adviser' with a staff of twenty troopers."

"What's Starfleet afraid of?" McCoy was beginning to share his friend's frustration.

Kirk stumbled over the word, then said, "Spock."

"Starfleet's afraid of Spock?" McCoy's eyes widened.

"That would seem logical, doctor. I was the one member of the crew singled out for interrogation."

"But why? What were they trying to find out from you?"

"Difficult to say. I detected no precise pattern to their questions. Though I believe the most probable conclusion is that Starfleet security has been made aware of some threat against one or more of the prize nominees on board this vessel. For reasons unknown, I am their chief suspect."

"That fits with what Wolfe told me about the new security arrangements," Kirk conceded, ignoring McCoy. "All events that were planned by Mr. Spock have been canceled. No more colloquia, poster sessions, or dinners. You're confined to your quarters for the duration of the voyage. There're two troopers waiting outside to escort you there after this checkup."

"Most regrettable," Spock said. "Still, I shall be able to carry on my conversations over the intercom net—"

Kirk shook his head. "Incommunicado. I'm sorry, Spock."

"This is crazy, Jim," McCoy said. "Why didn't they just throw him into the brig at the starbase and be done with it?"

"I believe they would have had to charge me with some crime, doctor."

"So they think you might be responsible for some real or imaginary threat, but since they aren't sure, they've sent a security team along to keep an eye on you and the nominees," Kirk said.

"That would appear to be an accurate assessment."

"Then all we have to do is find out what kind of threat has been made against the nominees and, if it's legitimate, find the person who made it. Then you're free and clear." Kirk looked satisfied with his conclusion.

"I point out that there are at least eight other vessels carrying nominees to Memory Prime, Captain. If Starfleet security really does not have much more information about the nature of the threat, then these activities could be taking place on board those ships as well."

"That's easily found out, Spock. But in the meantime, Commodore Wolfe and her troops are on board *this* ship interfering with *my* crew. And I'm going to see to it that that interference ends as soon as possible." Kirk was calmer, more assured than when he had arrived. McCoy could tell it was because the captain now had something to focus on, a way to fight back.

"At warp four, we shall be arriving at Memory Prime within three days," Spock said. "It might not be possible to accomplish all of that in so short a time."

"But at least we'll be doing something, Spock. Finally." The captain left, his pace quicker than before, full of energy.

Spock turned to McCoy. "Finally?" he asked.

"The captain does not enjoy being assigned to duty in Quadrant Zero. He thinks we're here because of a foul-up at mission planning."

Spock considered that for a moment. "It would not be logical for Starfleet to waste a valuable resource such as the *Enterprise* by assigning it to routine duty. However, our presence here could be intended to honor either the attendees or this ship. When it comes to matters of prestige and honor, Starfleet is seldom logical." Spock silently considered the possibilities that presented themselves to him. "I must admit, doctor, that I had been so caught up in planning for the event that I had not properly considered why it was we were taking part."

As usual, McCoy couldn't see where Spock was going with his arguments with himself. "So what *does* that make our presence here?" he asked impatiently.

"Fascinating," Spock said eloquently, then left the sputtering doctor for the company of his guards.

Chapter Seven

THROUGHOUT THE SHIP, common area lighting was stepped down in intensity. Nonessential labs and duty stations were closed for a shift while reduced teams monitored critical environmental and propulsion operations. On viewscreens small and large, flat and three-dimensional, the latest serials uploaded from Centaurus and Starbase Four played in private quarters and department lounges. Most of the recreation facilities were in full use and the romantically inclined wandered through the plants and flowers in botany. Within the warp-compressed brilliance of the passing stars, it was nighttime on the *Enterprise*.

The light was also turned down in the captain's cabin. Most of it came from two white candles that flickered softly amid an elegant setting of antique silver and crystal dating back to the first Tellarite contact. The food upon the plates and the champagne in the gleaming flutes had come from ship's stores, instead of its synthesizers; a privilege of rank not often called upon.

At one side of the private dining table, Captain Kirk smiled warmly, hard at work. At the other side, Commodore Montana Wolfe smiled coldly back and wondered what the hell was going on.

"I suppose all of this is meant to impress me, hmmm?"

Kirk surveyed the table. "We're traveling at warp four, eating prime swordfish steaks from Mars, and drinking champagne from Laramie Six. *I'm* impressed." He looked up at Wolfe. "And you helped me get here, Commodore."

"If your want to think that, you go right ahead. I never mind having people like you feel you owe me favors." She held up her glass in a toast. "To . . . what do you think?"

"Absent friends," Kirk said quickly, holding his glass to hers.

The commodore pursed her lips. "Specifically your science officer?"

"Since you brought him up . . ."

Wolfe returned her glass and picked up her fork, playing with her Wallenchian loopbeans. "How long have you known Spock?" she asked. Kirk could sense it wasn't an idle question.

"Since I took command," Kirk said. "He was science officer under Chris Pike."

"Bit of a maverick, I understand."

"Pike?"

"Spock."

Kirk nearly choked on his champagne. "Spock? A maverick?"

"First Vulcan through the Academy. Not as if there's a huge lineup of them trying to follow in his footsteps."

"But that's always the way with Academy enrollment. Real enlistment doesn't begin until a full generation has grown up with the idea of Starfleet and the Federation."

"Vulcan isn't exactly a new member."

"No, but they have long generations." Kirk pushed back from the table. It was a signal the social part of the evening was over. "Tell me the truth. What do you have against Spock?"

"Mixing friendship and duty isn't a good idea, Kirk." Wolfe's voice hardened. She had reached some sort of limit.

"I'm not asking out of friendship. I'm asking because we're both Starfleet officers, dedicated to our duty and our oath. And you know something about a valuable member of my crew that might make him unfit for duty." He leaned forward, held up a beseeching hand. "Help me do my job, Mona."

Kirk could see Wolfe arguing the pros and cons with herself. He watched her closely, keeping his calculated expression of innocent trust frozen on his face.

"This is off the record, Kirk. Is that understood?" she finally began.

Kirk nodded somberly, hiding his knowledge that he had won this particular showdown. "Absolutely, Commodore."

"Literally minutes before your ship arrived at Starbase Four, I received a priority communication from the security contingent on Memory Prime responsible for the prize ceremonies."

"Go on."

"I can't give you all the details because I don't have them all myself. But off the record," she stressed again, "they suspect an attempt will be made to assassinate one or more, perhaps all, of the nominees."

She stopped as if she had said enough.

"To tell you the truth," Kirk said, "I had already guessed that much myself. My question is: why Spock?"

"Not even off the record. I'm sorry but . . . I'm under orders." She truly did look apologetic. Or else she can put on a performance as well as I can, Kirk thought.

"But the security contingent on Memory Prime has reason to suspect him?"

"Yes."

"Good reason?"

"I don't . . ." Wolfe said, then placed her hands on the table, leaned forward, and spoke almost in a whisper, as if she were afraid of being overheard on Memory Prime. "The security people there are working from rumors, intercepted communications, garbled codes, and probability analyses run by the facilities on Prime itself."

"Sounds circumstantial to me," Kirk said.

"That's the problem. It's all circumstantial. Except for the name. Except for Spock. He's there in those messages."

"By name?" Kirk was shocked. It was unthinkable.

"Not the name. But his position, his background. His motivation. His actual name wasn't necessary. Everything else fits. For the Fleet's sake, I wish it weren't true. Maybe it isn't true. But the stakes are too high. We can't risk it."

Kirk felt as if he were in a game where the rules were changing with every move. "If Spock wasn't specifically named, then who was?"

Wolfe shook her head. She had said too much.

"Who?" Kirk demanded.

"T'Pel," Wolfe said. It was a cross between a croak and a whisper.

Kirk leaned back. The name didn't mean anything to him. But before he could say anything more, his door announcer beeped.

"That'll be the yeoman for the table," he said to Wolfe. "Come," he called out to the door circuits.

The door slid aside to reveal a stooped thin figure, clothed in black, definitely not a yeoman.

"Lights, level two," Kirk said, and the strips around his walls came to life. "Please come in," he said to his visitor.

"Captain Kirk, I presume?" the visitor asked with a precise, clipped delivery Kirk recognized. He was Vulcan.

He shuffled in from the dimly lit corridor and paused impassively. Kirk saw a noble face, lined from almost two centuries of experience, with a cap of star-white hair, and a striking green tinge to his complexion that came with the thinning skin of Vulcan old age. But Kirk didn't recognize the man.

"Captain Kirk," Wolfe said, quickly getting up from the table. "May I introduce Academician Sradek of Vulcan. Academician, James Kirk." She moved to stand beside the elderly being, making no move to touch him in grudging deference to the Vulcan dislike for telepathically sensing the emotional thoughts of humans, unless absolutely necessary. However, she was there in case he needed to take her arm to prevent a stumble.

Kirk stood and held his hand in the proper manner. "Live long and prosper, Academician Sradek."

Sradek returned the salute in a trembling, offhand manner. "Live long and prosper, Captain Kirk." Then he sighted the chair by the captain's bunk and headed for it.

Kirk questioned Wolfe with his eyes but she shrugged to say she didn't know what Sradek wanted either.

"Please, sit down," Kirk offered as Sradek sank into the chair. "May I offer you something?"

"Of course you may, but I do not wish anything," Sradek said evenly.

Kirk had heard that sort of thing before and knew what it meant. Spock was usually the one who had to make the effort to change his thinking processes to suit his human coworkers, but in this case, Kirk would have to be accommodating to the Vulcan. And that meant forgetting politeness. Since Sradek was here, he had a purpose for being here, and no doubt would explain himself soon enough. Small talk wasn't necessary.

"I am here to ask questions concerning the situation that surrounds the presence of the nominees on board this vessel," Sradek announced as Kirk sat across from him on the edge of his bunk. Wolfe stood off to the Vulcan's side.

"I shall answer them to the best of my ability," Kirk said in what he thought to be an acceptable reply.

Sradek narrowed his eyes at Kirk. "I haven't asked them yet."

Kirk said nothing, quietly admiring the delicate golden inlay on the silver comet-shaped IDIC symbol the academician wore pinned to his black tunic.

"Why am I not allowed to meet with Spock?" Sradek asked without preamble.

"Mr. Spock is confined to his quarters, incommunicado, for the duration of this voyage, by order of Starfleet command, and for reasons which are classified," Wolfe answered. Then she said to Kirk, "Sradek was one of Spock's instructors at the Vulcan Academy of Science. Spock spoke to me just before the *Enterprise* arrived and said he looked forward to meeting with Sradek."

"And I with him," Sradek added. "Is he considered a threat to the safety of any on board?" he asked.

"No," Wolfe said.

Kirk spoke at the same time. "Not at all."

Sradek turned from one to the other. "The commodore states a falsehood, the captain states a truth. Truly, I do not understand how your species has accomplished what it has."

"Do you have other questions?" Kirk prompted.

"Will you allow me to speak with Spock?"

"No," Wolfe said again.

"Not until we reach Memory Prime," Kirk qualified.

"Humans," Sradek said without intonation, though his meaning was perfectly evident. "Will you allow me to take part in any of the activities that had been scheduled for me while on this vessel?"

"Not if they were activities organized by Mr. Spock," Wolfe explained.

"There was to be a tour of the warp nacelles tomorrow, to be conducted by the chief engineer. Has that been canceled also?"

Wolfe checked with Kirk. "Scotty set that up for Professor La'kara. Spock had nothing to do with it," the captain said. Wolfe gave permission for the tour to proceed as scheduled.

"Anything else, Academician?" Kirk inquired.

The Vulcan looked over to the shelf behind Kirk's writing table. "That carving of the Sorellian fertility deity," he said, pointing to the primitive red sculpture that scowled behind Kirk's back every time he sat down to do his screen work.

"Yes?" Kirk said, wondering what the Sorellian fertility deity had to do with anything.

"It's a forgery," Sradek stated, and pushed against the arms of the chair to stand.

Kirk rose also and he and Wolfe followed Sradek to the door.

"Good night, Academician," Wolfe said. "Perhaps I will see you on the tour tomorrow."

"Is something expected to happen to your vision?" Sradek asked.

Kirk smiled at the commodore's reaction. Even he knew better than to say something colloquial to a Vulcan like Sradek. The academician shuffled back into the hallway.

"The more time you spend around them, the sooner you'll learn," Kirk said after the door had whisked shut behind the old Vulcan. "I'd guess he's almost two hundred years old. Peace Prize nominee, isn't he?"

Wolfe said yes. "He's also historian at the Academy. Which is why he knew about your fertility god over there. Did *you* know it was a fake?"

Kirk walked over and picked it up from its shelf. It was carved from the egg casing of a Sorellian linosaur, or so Gary Mitchell had sworn repeatedly to him. "No, but I'm not surprised. A good friend paid off a gambling debt to me with this." He shrugged, setting the deity down on the table, and turned back to the business at hand. "What was the significance of that word you said to me just before Sradek arrived? T'Pel, I think it was."

There was a troubling mix of anger and sadness in Wolfe's eyes. "That was a mistake, Captain. The truth is, I've found the galaxy isn't anything like what they teach at the Academy. I don't trust Vulcans. I don't trust Spock. And the terrible thing is, that until all this is settled, I can't even trust you. But thanks for the dinner. Whatever your motives were."

Kirk walked her to the door, said good night as she left, then contemplated the disorganized table, hefting the Sorellian deity in his hand.

"So, Gary," he said to the sculpture, "it looks like you really did put one over on me, after all." He looked over to the closed door, thinking of Montana Wolfe. "But you'll be the only one I'll let do that, old friend. Mona and Starfleet don't stand a chance."

Thirty seconds later, responding to the captain's priority

request, the ship's computer began searching for every recorded reference to the word or name *T'Pel.*

His name was no longer Starn.

This time, all of his names and identities were forgotten as he lost himself in the savage rapture of his heritage and his destiny. Within the billowing images of shared meld dreams, he saw the battles in which he and his kind had been born millennia ago, battles that would now spread throughout the galaxy, bringing to it the death and destruction it so richly deserved.

Like a deadly shadow cast in the glare of an exploding sun, he moved silently through the corridors of the starship *Enterprise.* He kept his smile hidden, a constraint of his disguise needed to pass among the weaklings with whom he traveled. But his outward appearance did not diminish the elemental joy that filled him as he contemplated the chaos and devastation he would visit upon his enemies, all for the glory of T'Pel.

Entry to the dilithium lab was restricted in this shift, but the assassin slipped a stolen yellow data wafer into the access panel and the doors slipped obligingly open; more evidence that the trusting fools of the Federation deserved the fate to which he would deliver them. Perhaps in the years to come those who survived would finally learn that to be strong, they must suspect enemies at every corner. For they were there.

He paused in the center of the lab as the doors shut behind him. He had patiently listened to the babble of the scientists on board this ship, and the plan had presented itself almost without conscious thought. Humans, like Vulcans, cared too much for technology and science, often at the expense of their emotions. It would be fitting to inflame the one by turning the other against them.

The accelerator field generator built by the Centauran was clearly visible on a workbench. At first inspection, it seemed no different from its more common slow-time forerunner: the stasis generator. A compact circuit block topped with a control pad was linked to a standard superconductor storage battery and a tiny, penlike cylinder containing a subatomic singularity caught in a quantum fluctuation suppressor field. The suppressor controlled the singularity's rate of evaporation, using it to supply the seed of time distortion needed to trigger the temporal acceleration effect. Such mechanisms were the mainstay of children's science fairs, he knew, but what made La'kara's device remarkable was that it was operating within the temporal distortion produced by the *Enterprise*'s dilithium-powered warp engines.

Beside the compact modules of the device on the bench, a shimmering silver force field glowed, no more than five centimeters high by fifteen centimeters square. The assassin read the status lights on the control panel and saw that within the accelerator field, time progressed 128 times more rapidly than without. And the temporal distortion produced by the field was not interfering with the four-dimensional structure of the ship's dilithium crystals.

It took him only moments to discover the component that kept the two pockets of temporal distortion from interacting with each other. A small blue case, no larger than a civilian communicator, was cross-connected between the force-field transmission nodes and the singularity cylinder. He snapped off the case's cover and saw the crude, hand-plased circuits of an intricate transtator feedback loop. He knew instantly that without that circuit, the dilithium crystals and the accelerator field would fail catastrophically. It was going to be easy.

Reaching once again into his tunic, he withdrew two minuscule vials and placed them beside the blue case. From one vial, he took a small applicator brush and painstakingly painted a thin strip of growth medium between two silver tracings of circuitry within the case. He took care to curve the strip so that it measured precisely one centimeter in length. For a few moments, the medium glittered against the circuit board, and then its base liquid evaporated and the strip seemed to disappear.

Next, he took a delicate pin and used it to puncture the

seal on the second vial, making sure the pinpoint touched the liquid within. He carefully dabbed the pinpoint against one end of the almost invisible strip he had painted, closed the case, and returned the vials to his tunic, just as he had been trained to do.

He looked quickly around the dilithium lab, ensuring that no trace of his presence existed; he knew that within that blue case, tailored bacteria were already feeding on the nutrients in the painted strip and were preparing to divide at a precisely controlled rate, growing along the strip until they made contact with the other circuit tracing and shorted out the circuit. The bacteria would be reduced to undetectable dust particles and the infinite feedback within the ship's engines would be devastating.

Preparing to leave, he caught sight of his reflection in the polished surface of an antimatter storage chamber. It was not the face of his birth, and not the face he had worn on TNC 50 when the Klingon robot had hired him, but such transitions were his way of life. All that mattered was that for now his disguise was once again perfect. None had seen through it.

And none would be given a chance.

Chapter Eight

NENSI COULD HEAR H'rar's breath quicken. Good, the chief administrator thought, that means the Andorian sees it, too.

H'rar looked up from Sal's office desk screen where Nensi had presented the results of his initial investigation. "Diabolical," he wheezed. The word was an old Anglish term that the Andorian had recently learned and enjoyed using to describe those complex situations that brought his cobalt blood to the boil. "How shall you restore your honor, Sal?"

Nensi pushed away from his desk and held up his hands. "Sorry, H'rar, but honor isn't the issue here."

"Honor iss alwayss the issue!" H'rar protested. He toyed with the ceremonial dagger he wore at his side, reduced in size to blend in with his civilian station but offering traditional comfort just the same.

"If anything, it's a legal matter to be settled by the Federation and Starfleet. Take another look at the contracts. Technically, the Pathfinders misrepresented nothing."

H'rar muttered something in Lesser Andorian.

"I beg your pardon?" Nensi asked politely, trying to prevent his administrative assistant from entering an icy Andorian sulk.

H'rar's thin blue lips compressed into an evil smile. "I just wass reflecting that until my world joined the Federation, our last lawyerss had been put to death more than a thousand yearss ago." He nodded to himself. "Sometimess the old wayss are so much simpler, don't you think?"

"Of course," Nensi quickly agreed. "But then, you have a knife and I'm not a lawyer, so why wouldn't I?"

H'rar laughed. "I shall misss you when you retire, Sal."

"No, you won't. You'll be too busy planning your revenge against the Pathfinders."

Mira Romaine appeared in the doorway to Nensi's office and knocked against the doorframe to announce herself.

"What's so urgent?" she asked after she greeted the two and joined them by the desk screen.

"I was working on that increased access schedule that Pathfinder Eight asked for," Nensi began, "and I started calculating the upper load that the facility could take. Especially since the standard waiting period these days is about two years."

"And . . . ?" Romaine prompted as she scanned the charts displayed on the screen, puzzled over the number of them that carried bizarre figures such as 430 percent.

"And I think that the Pathfinders have been reconfiguring themselves."

Romaine shrugged. "Why not? We study medicine to improve our lives, why shouldn't they study circuit design and construction to improve theirs?"

"Well, if you look at these figures, I'm not really sure you'd call it an improvement." Nensi called up core-use diagrams and pointed out sections now marked in red.

Romaine studied them but her puzzled expression made it clear that she still couldn't see the point Sal was trying to make.

"It was your comment about Pathfinder Six lying to us," Nensi continued. "You still haven't explained that to me; why you think Six was lying, or what it could possibly have to lie about. But then I thought, what if its motives are as alien as the way it functions?"

"So you think these figures and charts are more lies?" Romaine asked.

"Look," Nensi said, "let me take you through an example."

It took twenty minutes, and only a fifth-level programmer or a career bureaucrat could have traced the convoluted chain of conditions that indicated the Pathfinders had something to hide. Nensi began by running straightforward calculations of the memory size and operational speed of the Pathfinders' installation to determine a base figure for its storage and work capacity. The figure was staggering.

Then Nensi ran a simulation that divided the facility into twelve more or less equal units—one for each Pathfinder—and subjected it to the average access load that the interface team imposed in a normal duty cycle. This time the figure was large, but it definitely wasn't staggering.

Romaine whistled softly. "Ninety-percent excess capacity?" she read from the screen.

"If you treat the facility as a duotronic unaware processing engine such as they use on starships—in other words, a standard Fleet-issue computer. I would expect the Pathfinders to be even more efficient, and so the excess capacity could even be larger."

Romaine considered the implications for a moment. The mechanics of data storage and retrieval were her speciality and Nensi's conclusions were almost frightening. If true, duotronic processors seemed to give rise to a geometrical increase in capacity after a certain size threshold had been reached. Since no facility in the Federation came anywhere close to the size of the Pathfinder installation, it was not surprising that the effect had not been noticed until now. But what was incredible was that neither the Pathfinders, nor the interface team, had made it known. It was inconceivable that such a breakthrough in computer science could be knowingly withheld.

"Your figures must be wrong, Sal," Romaine concluded, opting for the easiest way of dealing with unexpected results.

"Even allowing a fifty-percent margin of error, the increased-capacity effect stands," Nensi argued.

"Then what you're saying is that what the Federation is

using this facility for right now is like using Fleet commcenter to relay binary codes over a distance of a few kilometers."

"And the Pathfinders must know it. And the interface team probably knows it. And neither group is telling us."

Romaine requested duplicate files of Nensi's work and he agreed, provided she would only use them on secured circuits. She said she would run variations on Nensi's figures and see how well the effect held up.

"Until then," Nensi concluded, "I suggest we keep everything in confidence. At least until we find out if our suspicions are correct, and if so, what the Pathfinders and/or the interface team think they're going to accomplish."

As Romaine started to leave, holding a stack of data wafers in one hand, she paused by the door. "What I don't understand," she said, "is if they *do* have all of that extra capacity down there, what in the gods' names are they doing with it?"

H'rar snorted. "What I don't understand," he replied, "iss why you humanss insist on building thinking machiness that have no 'off' switches."

Chapter Nine

THE CAVERNOUS HOLD of the starboard warp propulsion unit thrummed with the rise and fall of the whine from its Cochrane generator. The gleaming mechanism of intricately intertwined tubes and cables stretched almost the full length of the nacelle's interior, drawing its power from the immense energies released by the total annihilation of matter and antimatter in the main engine room in the secondary hull. But it was here in this resonating chamber that, with no moving parts save for the myriad bypass switches that could be manually engaged, the generator channeled that unthinkable force to split the compressed web of four-dimensional spacetime, and slip the *Enterprise* along the infinitely small pathways that snaked through otherspace.

The service-lift doors opened onto the brilliantly lit hold and Scotty felt a familiar rush of exhilaration as the warp vibration engulfed him. The bridge was the brain of the ship, the engine room her heart, but this, aye, this was her soul.

Professor La'kara was first out of the lift, stumbling slightly in his haste. He had not anticipated the zero-gravity node the turbolift had passed through as it had moved through the support pylon, out of the artificial-gravity field of the secondary hull and into the angled field of the nacelle. He stared down the length of the generator, eyes blinking rapidly, regaining his footing.

"It . . . it's beautiful," he said, and for once said nothing more.

"That she is," Scott agreed, proud father of the bairn. He stood aside to let the others in the lift enter the hold. Fifteen guests, more than he had expected, had shown up for the tour. With all the other activities canceled, perhaps it was to be expected. Scientists were usually among the first to become bored.

Commodore Wolfe and her aide, Lieutenant Abranand, were the last to exit. Abranand looked down nervously at the radiation medallion he and all the others wore around their necks. Scott had told them it was a standard precaution and that it would alert them to exposure levels equal to one-fiftieth the minimum lethal dose, but the anxious trooper obviously didn't trust it. He was accompanying Wolfe only under orders.

The commodore stood with her hands on her hips, admiring the generator. "The lack of vibration is remarkable, Mr. Scott. I don't think I've ever felt any other as smooth." It was the first time Scott could recall her sounding civil since she had come aboard.

Scott grinned at the compliment. "Thank ye, Commodore. Things start to get a bit rough around warp five, but at everything below it's smooth as a . . . uh, transparent aluminum." Scotty coughed as the commodore nodded impatiently.

"Believe it or not, Mr. Scott, but I've been in an engine room or two in my day," she said, grinning slightly at his embarrassment. "Let's get this show on the road, shall we?"

Scotty coughed again, then stepped quickly up to the head of the group. He would have to cut part of the tour short, he knew, because of the delay the commodore had caused as she made them all wait for Academician Sradek to join them. By the time she learned that the elderly historian was indisposed and would not be joining the tour, Scotty knew he would not be spending as much time up in the nacelle as he would have liked. Ah well, he'd make the best of it.

"Gentlebeings," Scott began, "what ye are looking at is the key component of one of the largest fourth-generation hyperspace engines ever built since the discovery of warp technology more than one hundred and fifty years ago . . . yes, Dr. Stlur?"

A young Vulcan male with penetrating eyes and long dark hair tightly pulled back in a thick queue, had raised his hand, interrupting Scott's standard opening remarks. "I point out that Vulcan scientists mastered the technology of warp drive more than one hundred Terran years earlier. I thought you might wish to add that to your knowledge. I can recommend literature that—"

T'Vann, the Vulcan female with whom Stlur worked, placed her hand on his shoulder and whispered something inaudible.

"Forgive me for interrupting your presentation," Stlur said. "I meant no disrespect."

"None taken, lad," Scott said. "O' course I should have said since the *human* discovery of warp technology."

"Precisely," Stlur commented. The female whispered in his ear again.

"To continue." Scott deliberately looked away from the Vulcans. "It is called a Cochrane generator, named after Zefrem Cochrane, its *human*—yes, Professor La'kara?"

The professor lowered his hand and politely said, "Zeyafram Co'akran, it's pronounced." The professor turned to the rest of the group. "Native Alpha Centauran, you know. Great man."

Scotty sighed. "Aye, Alpha Centauran he was, but we humans do share a common ancestor back there somewhere now, don't we?"

La'kara started to fidget with his scarf in a way that Scott had come to dread. "Only if you believe the—"

"Could we discuss biology at another time?" T'Vann asked. "I should not like to miss an opportunity to examine this generator."

"Thank you, Dr. T'Vann," Scott said in gratitude. Last night La'kara had come to Scott's cabin to continue the "discussion" about trilithium they had begun just before the starbase troopers had broken up the hangar reception. Scott had used all of his most reasonable arguments, including a bottle of his best single malt, and still hadn't been able to make the poor man see the light of day. The chief engineer had begun to have his doubts about La'kara's grasp of elementary multiphysics and was glad of T'Vann's diplomatic interruption.

"Why don't we all walk down to the flux chamber?" Scott said, and motioned the group to a ten-meter silver sphere that bubbled out from the side of the generator. When they arrived, he had Ensign Helena Sulernova open the thickly screened viewing port on the sphere's lower section. Sulernova looked grim as she lifted the cover on the control panel. She had overindulged at the reception, thinking that sleeping in on this, her free day, would take care of the results. But Mr. Scott had chosen her for today's drudge duty, he had explained, as her reward for asking about trilithium in the presence of Professor La'kara and himself at the reception.

Sulernova, holding back a yawn, punched in an authorization code, then threw the interlock bolt aside. She waited for the viewport indicator to show that the transparent viewing medium had darkened enough to provide sufficient protection for human eyes, then pressed the control that slid the viewport protective plate away from the opening.

Scott forgot his annoyance with the ensign as the tour group gasped at the beauty of the Cochrane flux, shimmering and sparkling in its wild explosions of unrecognizable colors, which seemed to float mere centimeters before their eyes in a multidimensional optical illusion. The Vulcans, of course, didn't gasp or show any reaction at all, though Scott was sure he detected fascination in their eyes.

"What ye are seeing is the interference effect of a thin strand of hyperspace folded into our four-dimensional continuum," Scott explained. "The fields generated here fold our ship back into the hyperspace void left by the absence of this—"

"*Mr. Scott!*" It was Lieutenant Abranand, white-faced with fear, holding up his radiation medallion. The central indicator was glowing red and its warning beep was shrill.

Scott immediately checked his own medallion and those of the others he could see. Each was dark and silent. "Occh, lad. Ye've been fiddling with it so much it's nae wonder that the poor thing's gone and—"

The ship lurched!

Scotty froze as every medallion instantly glowed red and their sirens shrieked in a deafening cacophony of danger. The smooth vibration of the Cochrane generator turned to a ragged shudder and, to his trained senses, every improper movement, every grinding of overstressed hull metal, told Scott exactly what had gone wrong. The engineer went into full automatic. This was his job.

"Commodore! Get these people to the lift! Ensign! Close the port."

Sulernova ran through a flurry of flux shimmers to the port controls. Her fingers flew over the buttons and switches.

"Don't look at it!" Scott shouted to her. He opened the equipment locker by the flux sphere and pulled out a three-pronged energy neutralizer. He had to close the flux gate before all power failed and the full brilliance of the flux was released.

The ship shuddered again, its inertial dampeners lagging behind the instantaneous response of the artificial-gravity field, throwing Scott and the tour group to the deck. Red warning lights flashed along the shining surfaces of the generator. Emergency sirens howled.

"Get them out of here *now!*" Scott shouted to the commodore. She was standing at the entrance to the service lift, pushing the civilians to safety. Scott saw Stlur and T'Vann pick up the lagging La'kara by his arms and start to carry him. And then the power failed completely and the brilliant lighting of the hold cut out to the absolute black of starless space.

But the darkness didn't last. An instant later, the powerless viewport medium cleared to absolute transparency, and the full and blinding glory of the Cochrane flux filled the hold.

Kirk pushed himself off the deck rail where the lurching ship had tossed him. "Damage report!" he called out to Uhura. All lights on the bridge dimmed as a low-frequency rumble shuddered through the deck.

"Switching to auxiliary," Lieutenant Laskey announced from the engineering station. The lights flared up again and the hum of equipment returned to normal.

"Helm, full shields," Kirk ordered. Whatever had hit the ship had felt just like an energy-beam impact.

"Warp power gone, Captain. Dropping to sublight," Sulu said, concentrating on the maneuvers that would bring the ship into normal space properly aligned, without being torn to pieces by the shock of an unbalanced translation.

"Shields on auxiliary power," Chekov reported from the science station. "Half strength and holding."

"Where's that damage report, Uhura?" Kirk was standing behind Sulu, staring at the main sensor display. No attackers to be seen.

Uhura held her ear receiver as she listened intently to the rush of voices and computer codes reporting ship's status. "It seems to be a power failure localized in engineering, Captain. Engineering communication circuits are down. No hull damage or weapon impact reported."

Damn, Kirk thought, where was Spock when he needed him? "Engineering status, Mr. Laskey."

"It's some kind of major disturbance, Captain, I—"

"I can tell it's major," Kirk snapped. "But what *kind* of disturbance?"

The turbolift doors opened and Spock hurried to the

science station. Chekov quickly got out of the way and returned to his position at the helm.

"Spock!" The captain was both pleased and dismayed. "What are you doing here?"

"Attending to my duties, Captain." Spock's delicate fingers danced across the control surfaces and he spoke rapidly as he assessed the situation. "It appears we have experienced a significant power loss. In the absence of physical damage to the ship, I can only assume that the problem is internal." The blue glow of the main science viewer washed across his intent face.

"But aren't you confined to quarters?" Kirk asked. Maybe Wolfe had finally come to her senses.

"Apparently not. When I looked out into the corridor after the first disturbance, my guards were nowhere to be seen. I took that to mean my confinement had been temporarily suspended. In any event, under the circumstances I feel I am much more valuable to the ship at my post."

"Quite logical, Spock." Kirk doubted the commodore would see it that way, but it was good to have Spock where he belonged, and where he would do the most good.

"Thank you, Captain." Without looking up, Spock called out, "Mr. Laskey, kindly check the flux readouts from the starboard propulsion unit."

Laskey fumbled with the controls at his station. "Containment integrity was breached when the power shut down, sir." The lieutenant began to read out the figures with alarm.

Uhura gasped. "But Mr. Scott was leading a tour group up in the generator hold, Captain."

Kirk knew all too well the hell spawned by an uncontrolled flux release. Still, he needed confirmation that that was what really had happened. "Spock?"

"The fact that my instruments show the starboard nacelle is still attached to the ship indicates that someone was able to shut down the flux after auxiliary power came on line."

"But how?" Laskey asked. "Everyone exposed to the flux should have been blinded."

"It shall be fascinating to learn the answer to that."

"Uhura, have Dr. McCoy take a medical team up to the starboard generator hold immediately." Explanations could come later as far as Kirk was concerned. Some of his crew were in danger. "Mr. Laskey, what's the situation in engineering?"

Laskey called up more screens at his station, then said with shock, "Dilithium burnout, sir. Every crystal's showing zero energy transmission."

"Spock," Kirk said, "any chance that La'kara's accelerator shielding failed?"

Spock shook his head. "I think not, Captain. The power surge that would have resulted when the two fields of temporal distortion interacted while the ship was in warp would have completely destroyed the engines. And most of the engineering deck as well. We would be no more than a powerless, drifting wreck at this time."

"Small consolation," Kirk said as he felt the bridge suddenly become small and confining. He had to be where the action was. "I'm going up to the generator hold. Chekov, take the conn. Mr. Spock, come with me."

"Commander Spock is coming with me," Commodore Wolfe said coldly from the upper deck. She held a hand phaser pointed at Spock, and behind her, by the open turbolift, two troopers stood ready with rifles.

Wolfe's uniform was covered with scorch marks. Her face was streaked with soot, hair in disarray, and her eyes were wild. She held one hand above them, blinking and squinting as if to clear her vision. But the aim of her phaser was unwavering.

"Mona, what happened?" Kirk asked. He stepped forward between his first officer and the weapon.

Wolfe waved him back. "I was in the generator hold with Scott and the scientists. No doubt Commander Spock has already told you what happened."

"Yes, Spock's given me the readings. But what's that—"

"Readings!" Wolfe laughed harshly. "He didn't need

readings to tell you what happened. Because he arranged it, didn't you, Spock?"

"Arranged what, Commodore?" Spock asked with icy calm. Kirk could see his science officer's eyes track the beam emitter of the phaser in Wolfe's hand.

"The 'accident,' Commander. The accident up there that nearly killed Professor La'kara and set back Federation propulsion research by decades."

"I assure the commodore that—"

"Silence!" Wolfe exploded. "You'll have your chance to speak at your trial. You're under arrest." Without taking her eyes off Spock, she turned her head back to the turbolift. "Troopers, take this prisoner to the brig."

"May I ask what the commodore's charges are?" Spock inquired, as if asking about the weather.

"Treason, conspiracy, attempted murder, escape from lawful custody," Wolfe listed. "Restrain him, Jenson," she ordered one of the troopers flanking Spock. "Remember what he did to his guards outside his quarters."

"What happened to the guards?" Kirk asked with concern.

"Ask your science officer."

"I had assumed they retired to emergency stations when the ship experienced difficulties," Spock said, holding up his hands to allow the trooper to place a magnatomic adhesion manacle in place. The trooper held the short bar of blue-gray metal against Spock's wrists, hit the activate switch on the bar's control surface, then removed his hand as the bar lost its charge and immediately flowed around Spock's forearms until its two ends met and joined in a molecular bond. Only the presence of a release field would collapse the superconducting current flowing within and return the manacle to its original shape.

"Emergency stations," Wolfe repeated in disgust. She stepped out of the way as the troopers pushed Spock to the turbolift. "They were stunned at such high intensity that they're going to be in sickbay for a week."

Kirk had had enough. He bounded up the steps to the lift doors. "I demand that you present your evidence!" he said angrily. This had gone too far.

Wolfe moved her phaser in Kirk's direction, not quite pointing it at him, but not pointing it away, either.

"I warn you, if you start interfering in this, I'm going to start thinking there's a conspiracy on board." Wolfe's voice was as cold and hard as hull metal.

Spock broke the tension. "Thank you for your concern, Captain, but I believe circumstances warrant a period of reflection," he stated matter-of-factly, hemmed in by two battle-ready troopers with phaser rifles and a gun-wielding commodore who was on the thin edge of senseless rage.

Reluctantly, Kirk backed off. The *Enterprise* was still in space. There would be time to get to the bottom of Wolfe's senseless accusations.

"Good decision," Wolfe said as she lowered her weapon. "But I tell you, Kirk, if this is typical of the way you run your ship, it's no wonder you got hit with Quadrant Zero duty." The lift doors started to close. "You're a disgrace to the Fleet," she said.

Despite the environmentals working at double load, Scott could still smell the smoke in engineering. It was too quiet, too. The long intermix chamber where the matter and antimatter plasmas were channeled from their magnetic bottles and mixed in a glorious destructive frenzy was silent. All ship's power now came from the standby fusion reactors and storage batteries. Scott felt a desperate sadness as he saw his beautiful equipment stand idle and purposeless. But at least I *can* still see, he consoled himself. And the ship can be repaired. He turned back to the conversation McCoy and Kirk were having as the three of them gathered in the emergency manual-monitor room above the main engineering deck.

"I hate to say it, Jim, but it looks as if Commodore Wolfe has a strong case," McCoy said bluntly. "All the pieces fit."

Scott was distressed at McCoy's summation. "How can ye say that, doctor? Mr. Spock is as fine an officer as e'er served in the Fleet."

"Easy, Scotty," Kirk said kindly. "Our opinions of Mr. Spock aren't the question here. It's how the commodore came up with the circumstantial evidence against him."

"I think shutting off the shielding on La'kara's accelerator field at the precise time La'kara was where he could be killed is more than circumstantial, Jim." McCoy's face looked haggard and drawn. Scott knew that despite the doctor's even tone, he was as upset as everyone else.

"But thanks to Stlur and T'Vann and those blessed inner eyelids that Vulcans have, when the blinding flash of the flux hit us all, they were able to keep their vision, close the viewport, and carry us all into the lift. No one *was* killed, Dr. McCoy," Scotty said earnestly.

"But only because, as the commodore suggests," Kirk reminded them, "Spock couldn't know that Scotty distrusted the professor's grasp of basic theory. *If* Scotty hadn't decided that he didn't trust the shielding system and taken the dilithium crystals out of the warp engine circuits last night, *then* both nacelles would have been blown out into hyperspace and we'd be floating here waiting for a salvage tug. Instead, when the shielding was shut off and the dilithium crystals blew out, all we lost was our primary power circuit. And Scotty's people will be able to repair that by the time the cruiser from Starbase Four gets here with replacement crystals."

McCoy looked puzzled. "Scotty, you took the dilithium crystals out of the warp circuits? *While* we were in warp?"

"Ye don't need dilithium to travel at warp speeds under four-point-eight," Scotty said condescendingly. "It's more efficient, sure, but d'ye not remember your history, doctor? How all those early voyages between Vulcan and Earth, and even Klinzhai, took months instead of days, long before dilithium's four-dimensional structure was discovered? But then I'm forgetting, you're a doctor, not an engineer."

"The fact remains," McCoy continued, "that even though Scotty inadvertently prevented a disaster, Spock is still the prime suspect."

"But how did he get to the dilithium lab in time to turn off the shielding and still make it to the bridge while the power failure was in progress?" Kirk asked. "Remember, he only noticed his guards were gone *after* the ship's first reaction to the dilithium failure."

McCoy's face revealed his internal struggle. "You've read the troopers' log reports, Jim. Spock might have attacked the guards a half hour before the power failure. Lots of time to disrupt their short-term memory with a heavy stun and get to the lab."

"Dr. McCoy!" Scott cried in anguish.

"I'm only being the devil's advocate, Scotty. Spock will have to answer these questions at his trial."

"He's right, Scotty. Spock needs those answers. And we have to give them to him," Kirk said.

"Aye, Captain. But I doon't see how."

"Who else had access to the dilithium lab where the containment system was stored?" Kirk asked, then dismally answered himself. "Everybody."

"Then who had the motive?" McCoy asked. "That's usually the way these things work."

Kirk thought about that for a moment. "Fair enough. Who stands to benefit from the death of Professor La'kara?" he asked in return.

"Or Doctors Stlur and T'Vann," Scotty reminded them. "Or anyone else on the tour. Including me."

"Good point," McCoy agreed. "It's hard to determine the motive if we don't know who the victim was supposed to be."

"What if the victim is Spock?" Kirk asked. "What if everything that's gone on has been simply to throw suspicion on him and this ship?"

"Again," McCoy asked, "what's the motive?"

"I don't know," Kirk answered. "But Commodore Wolfe

was convinced that the evidence collected by the security contingent on Memory Prime pointed to Spock."

"Then that's where the answers lie," McCoy concluded. "Heaven forgive me for using the damnable word, but it's the only 'logical' conclusion."

Scott looked at Kirk. They both nodded in agreement.

The answer they sought waited on Memory Prime.

Chapter Ten

MEMORY ALPHA was to have been the pride of the Federation's scientific and educational delegations. A nominally useless planetoid had become home to a sprawling network of interlinked domes and computer systems that formed a central library facility containing the total cultural history and scientific knowledge of all Federation members. For some council members, Memory Alpha represented the golden door to a future in which all beings throughout the galaxy would be united as equal partners in the only adventure worth pursuing: the search for information and understanding, the never-ending quest for knowledge. Memory Alpha would be that dream made real, fully and freely accessible to all Federation scholars, an unarmed, undefended oasis of peace and common purpose.

Other council members, especially Andorians and representatives from Starfleet, had applauded that dream but lobbied for a healthy dose of reality. Federation space comprised only a tiny percentage of the total galaxy, and all indications were that it was not yet the benign and altruistic environment that all hoped it someday might become. They lobbied for protection, for contingency plans. But the Federation had thrived for more than a century on stubborn optimism and unbridled faith in the future. So it was not surprising that, in the end, the Memory Alpha proposal had passed the council's final appropriations hearings unchanged, and even Starfleet had given it their blessing. To the beings whose souls were fired by the challenge of the stars, Memory Alpha was a compelling vision.

The nightmare began when the last incorporeal intelligences of an ancient race, searching for a physical existence, killed more than three thousand peaceful scholars, staff, and researchers and wiped clean the central databanks of Memory Alpha in little more than a minute.

Specialist Lieutenant Mira Romaine, assigned to the U.S.S. *Enterprise* on her first mission for the Federation, had been the only being to survive direct mental contact with the desperate personalities of the Zetarians. But even as she and her staff worked amid the ruins of Memory Alpha, trying to create some order out of what threatened to become the Federation's most devastating disaster, the military planners of Starfleet paid the first of many informal visits to their colleagues in the scientific and educational delegations to the council. The Federation might be too optimistic from time to time, but only because it could afford to be. It rarely made the same mistake twice.

There was now an entire network of Memory planets spread throughout Federation space, far enough removed from each other that only a galactic disaster could affect them all. For cost effectiveness, each had a specialty. Memory Beta was a center for exobiology, cross-correlating all research conducted to understand the myriad ways in which life had evolved in the galaxy, as if its absence in any given system were an aberration of nature.

Memory Gamma focused its efforts on economics and agriculture; Memory Delta on stellar and planetary formation and evolution; Memory Epsilon on multiphysics. Other branches of knowledge awaited the funding and construction of additional Memory planets. A plan was proposed to reopen the now-abandoned Memory Alpha as a listening post for potential transmissions from civilizations in other galaxies. However, the funding process had become so lengthy because of the controversial nature of the project that fatalistic lobbyists were now referring to it as Memory Omega.

But even with each specialized facility serving as a total storage backup for every other Memory station in an intricate, holographic web of subspace data transmission and downloading, one flaw that not even Starfleet could eliminate remained. There had to be a command station, a central node to control and channel the activities of the entire Memory network.

Faced with the lesson of the Alpha disaster, project planners decided that no chances could be taken. The overall blueprints for the central facility were adapted from the Federation's most secure weapons-testing facilities. Seven interconnected, though independently maintained, environment domes were constructed in a semicircle on the face of an almost solid, nickel-iron asteroid. In times of peace, workers could walk between their residences and work areas through central plazas with trees, grass, and reflecting pools. But in times of threat, the facility also stretched deep beneath the asteroid's surface in a warren of underground service tunnels, access corridors, and heavily armored life-support chambers.

The facility was also equipped with deeply anchored warp engines, not for propulsion but to generate the immense energy levels required to simultaneously power a battery of photon torpedoes powerful enough to hold back a fleet of Klingon battle cruisers as well as defensive shields that could englobe the entire planetoid. Additional security was achieved by locating the facility safely within Quadrant Zero space and providing it with a permanent, on-site contingent of battle-ready troopers. It was only behind these battlements and layers of deadly force that the scholars and researchers of a hundred worlds could once again pursue the paths of peace.

To the handful of beings who truly understood the immense concentration of irretrievable knowledge that was generated at the central facility each hour, running weeks, sometimes months ahead of the stockpile stored for backup transmission to the other facilities, the lesson of Memory Alpha remained a constant nightmare. For any system with a central control point is vulnerable, and every planner, every Starfleet defense adviser, was all too aware of one of the earliest lessons the Federation had learned: not every eventuality can be anticipated. Despite the lessons of the past and the best intentions for the future, the entire scientific and cultural network that linked the worlds of the Federation in common defense and harmony was still at risk.

They called the facility Memory Prime.

Chapter Eleven

SALMAN NENSI stretched his arms over his head and yawned like a Rigellian bloodworm.

Across the table from him, Mira Romaine watched and listened in amazement. So did everyone else at lunch in the cafeteria.

"What was that supposed to be?" Romaine asked as Nensi rubbed his hands over his face.

"I think I might finally be relaxing," Nensi said. "I haven't had a call from the interface team for three days now." He picked up a sloppy sprout-salad sandwich and bit into it happily.

"They're all still down in the Interface Chamber," Romaine said, marveling at how much her friend could get into his mouth at once, "trying to find out why their precious Pathfinders wouldn't support their demands. Do you remember the expression on Garold's face?" So much for the old story of how only a specially trained, enhanced interface team member could understand the complexities of a Pathfinder. Garold had been taken completely by surprise.

"Let's hope they stay down there during the prize ceremonies. Then I could almost start enjoying this posting," Nensi managed to say around his mouthful of sandwich. They shared a glance, though, that said enjoyment had fled. As they sat together, both knew that in Romaine's lab a small, secure computer was running its last simulation of Nensi's Pathfinder access scenarios. His conclusions were holding: the Pathfinders, of which Nensi and Romaine were ostensibly in charge, were lying to them.

Romaine glanced around the cafeteria at the others. They couldn't be told yet, best to keep up the appearance of normalcy. She handed Nensi a second napkin, and he immediately put it to good use.

"You know, Uncle Sal, I'm beginning to worry that you haven't been having enough meals in polite company." Romaine delicately used her chopsticks to pick up a purple cube of stir-seered plomeek, to show him how it was done.

"Afraid I'll embarrass you at your dinner for Mr. Scott?"

"Ha!" Romaine laughed. "He's a dear sweet man but he's lived on board ship for so many years that I'm worried *he* might embarrass *you*." She smiled to herself, remembering back to her too brief voyage on the *Enterprise*. The best part about those last romantic dinners she had shared with Scotty had not been the food. She could barely wait to have dinner with him again.

Nensi checked his chronometer. "So how much longer is it? Twelve hours till your engineer arrives?"

Thirteen hours, twenty-seven minutes, Romaine thought, though she managed to look vague and say, "About that, I think." She took a sip of her tea. "That's something I'll never understand," she said. "The *Enterprise* travels two days of a five-day voyage out from Starbase Four and loses its dilithium, facing a couple of years of travel to get here on impulse. And then Starbase Four sends out a light cruiser with replacement crystals that reaches the ship within hours. They spend three days repairing the circuits and tuning the new crystals so they can power up the warp engines again. And then, *after* the three-day delay, the *Enterprise* will end up getting here only two hours late."

"The wonders of warp factors," Nensi said with a smile. "Beyond that, I can't tell you because I don't have the slightest idea how they do it and I'm too old to care."

"But if the *Enterprise* had traveled at the same speed at the start of the voyage that she's traveling now to make up for the delay, she could have been here inside of a day to begin with."

"Now that I can tell you something about," Nensi said, gesturing with the other half of his sandwich. "Warp engines have a strictly rated lifetime of operational use, dependent on the factor at which they operate, not the distance they cover. The higher the factor, the shorter the life. More than half the cost of constructing a ship like the *Enterprise* is the expense of the warp engines. I spent five years in San Francisco processing refit requests from Starfleet, and let me say that there's a whole gang of accountants in the Federation finance department who'd be happy if all Fleet travel was done on impulse propulsion."

"It always comes down to credits, doesn't it?" Romaine said. "How are we ever going to start accomplishing anything worthwhile in space exploration without the proper funding?"

"You're starting to sound like Garold and his friends," Nensi cautioned. "No more talks about budgets until I get a proper viewscreen in my office, all right?"

"You *still* don't have one?" Romaine said with amazement. "Uncle Sal, I run my department through Starfleet, remember? And I'm the ranking officer. You want a viewscreen? You got it!" She snapped her fingers.

"You can do that?" Nensi asked. "I thought all Starfleet business had to go through Captain Farl?"

"He's the ranking officer for his squad of troopers, sure, but since this is officially a civilian installation, except during emergencies, the chief technician is in charge." She pointed at the stripes on her blue sleeve. Romaine knew the position was strictly a political gesture to those council members who had wanted to play down the military aspect of Memory Prime and, usually, all she got out of the authority was a pile of extra screenwork at the end of each duty cycle. But being ranking officer over twenty-six other Starfleet science personnel did have a few perks. "I'll order a screen for your office this afternoon. You should get it next week."

Nensi looked pleased. "Now I feel guilty I didn't pay for lunch."

They were tidying up their trays when an associate rolled up to their table, eyestalk extended and ready light blinking.

"Chief Romaine," it announced in an extremely realistic voice, "you are ordered to report to breakout area C."

"Ordered?" Romaine asked. "Whose orders?"

"Captain Farl," the associate replied. "This module is authorized to announce that Memory Prime is now on emergency alert."

Uhura's face appeared on the desk viewscreen in the captain's quarters.

"I have Admiral Komack's reply from Starfleet Command," the communications officer said.

"Go ahead," Kirk told her, but Uhura's somber expression made it clear what that reply was.

"Regarding charges pressed against Commander Spock," Uhura read, "Commodore Wolfe is authorized to take full responsibility for the prisoner until he can be placed in the custody of proper Starfleet authorities. Commodore Wolfe and her prisoner are to transfer to the U.S.S. *Srall* upon that vessel's arrival at Memory Prime. Upon the conclusion of the Nobel and Z. Magnees Prize Ceremonies, the *Enterprise* is to return to Starbase Four and await further orders. Signed Komack, Admiral, Starfleet Command."

"That's it?" Kirk was surprised. "No personal addendum?"

"I'm sorry, sir. That's the full text."

Kirk thanked the lieutenant and told her to leave the bridge. The viewscreen went dark and Kirk looked over to Dr. McCoy. "She stayed at her station eighteen hours so that message wouldn't be intercepted by one of Wolfe's troopers," Kirk said, "for all the good it's done us. I can't understand why Komack left it so cut and dried. It's not like him. He knows Spock."

McCoy leaned back in his chair and swung his legs up onto the edge of Kirk's bunk. "We already know that there's more to this than anyone's admitting. Wolfe's keeping her mouth shut. The security people on Prime aren't responding to your requests for more information. It's big, Jim. I'm not surprised that a command admiral is washing his hands of the whole thing. Whatever Spock's mixed up in, it's got a lot of people scared."

"You're not sounding like the devil's advocate anymore. You're talking as if you really think he's guilty." Kirk's temper was showing.

"And you're talking as if you won't even consider the possibility that he might be!" McCoy shot back. "Remember Talos Four. Spock deliberately risked the last death penalty on the books."

"To do what he thought was right," Kirk insisted.

"Exactly," McCoy argued. "And maybe this time Spock is also caught up in something he thinks is right. You can't rule it out. If Starfleet wants Spock, it's because they have a good reason."

"Then why won't they tell *me?*" Kirk pounded his fist on his desk.

McCoy swung his feet down to the deck and leaned forward. If he had been closer, Kirk got the distinct feeling the doctor might have grabbed him by the scruff of his neck and shaken him.

"Because you're a *captain,* Captain. And some of the decisions in this fleet are made by officers with higher ranks." McCoy brought his own fist down on the table for good measure. He took advantage of Kirk's speechless surprise to draw a deep breath, then began again more calmly. But not by much.

"When I think of all the times I've come down here to help you wrestle with the problems of your command . . . and what have you learned? Nothing. No matter how bad it's been in the past, you keep looking to put more pressure on yourself. You've got to draw the line somewhere."

Kirk narrowed his eyes at McCoy. If anyone else had

taken this insubordinate tone with him, he'd be out the door and moved to the top of the transfer list. But McCoy had earned himself a few more words, a few more centimeters of rope. "And what would you suggest, doctor?" Kirk said carefully, a tightness in his voice that few had heard before.

"I suggest you face facts, Jim. You're not a god. You're a starship captain. And if that's not enough for you, then give the *Enterprise* up! Transfer to command and get those extra stripes. Become an admiral. Hell, become *the* admiral and run the whole damned fleet of starships, if that's what you want. Then, and only then, when you're at the top of the whole glorious system, can you feel that all the problems of the universe are the personal problems of James T. Kirk!"

"I will never give up the *Enterprise*," Kirk said slowly and precisely. "Never." It carried the chilling conviction of a blood oath.

"Then pay the price for her, Captain. Give the orders to the people below you and accept the orders from the people above. Don't treat everything that doesn't go your way as a personal attack. Learn the rules of the system. Then you can learn how to bend them. But don't ever forget that the system is there. And that you owe your ship to it."

"Finished?" Kirk asked coldly.

"Well, that's up to you, Captain, sir." McCoy sat back in his chair and folded his arms. He looked as if he had just run a marathon on the gym's treadmill.

Kirk studied McCoy for a few silent seconds. He wanted to shout at the doctor, tell him how wrong he was, how he had completely misread the situation. But he couldn't. Because he knew McCoy was right. Kirk shuffled some hardcopies on his desk. He hated making a mistake, even more than he hated admitting he had made one. But he felt he owed McCoy an explanation.

"Out there," Kirk finally said, "on the frontier, it sometimes does feel like I am . . . in charge of everything. We make first contact with a new civilization . . . I've got four hundred and thirty crew depending on me not to do something that will endanger the ship simply because I wasn't paying attention to some idiosyncrasy of an alien culture. Each time I think, will this be the one where I lose it? And each time, it isn't. After a while, it gets easy to think that the rest of the universe doesn't matter. There's only my crew, and my ship, and my next challenge." He sighed. "Starfleet, the Federation, sometimes they're nothing more than a subspace channel."

McCoy waited in silence, but Kirk said nothing more.

"The point being . . .?" McCoy prompted.

"The point being that you're right, doctor. I've wasted three days trying to find out why someone's plotting against *me* by trying to take *my* first officer off *my* ship when I should be trying to work within the system to maintain the integrity of the Fleet and the *Enterprise*."

"I am greatly relieved to hear that, Captain." The extent of McCoy's relief was evident in his voice and on his face. He had not often been forced to confront Kirk so directly.

"I'm relieved to hear it, too, Bones." Kirk visibly relaxed as he looked across the table at his friend. "I mean it. Thank you."

McCoy chewed thoughtfully on a corner of his lip. Kirk could tell the doctor was still angry, though he didn't know if that anger was directed at him or the commodore.

"So what are you going to do about it?" McCoy asked bluntly.

It was the old Kirk who answered, not the one who had been thrusting blindly in circles for the past few days, out of his element when it came to dealing with the command structure and the finely balanced nuances of give and take that it required. He felt directed now. His goal was clear. As were his methods.

"First, I accept the situation. Starfleet has some reason for suspecting that Spock might be responsible for an attempt on the lives of one or more of the prize nominees on board the *Enterprise*. Right or wrong, that is a fact. Second, I find out why that suspicion exists and if it in any way threatens further harmful activity on board."

"And third?"

"That will depend on Mr. Spock's innocence . . . or guilt."

McCoy nodded seriously. "That's a hard decision to make," he said.

"It's the captain's decision, and when I make it, Bones, it'll be the right one."

Chapter Twelve

FOR AN ANDORIAN, Romaine thought, Commander Farl was looking rather pale, almost the color of one of the Fleet-issue wall panels Sal was always going on about.

"What's the emergency, Captain?" the chief technician asked as she entered the breakout area. She paused and looked around in surprise.

The large room was typically used as a temporary planning and operations center for research projects. Accredited scholars using Prime's facilities could set up these areas as private offices containing computer consoles, associate staging stalls, desks, chairs, and whatever other equipment they might need outside of a lab. But Farl and his staff had turned breakout area C into what looked to be a fort. There was even a two-person portable combat transporter pad in the corner.

Farl walked over from a tactics table where Romaine could see schematics of the central dome complex displayed. She assumed the flashing red triangles floating above it represented troop placement. What was going on here?

Including his antennae, Farl was still ten centimeters shorter than Romaine, but the light armor he wore added to his bulk, and the small strips of *gral* fur crisscrossed over his chest plate, a concession to his clan standing allowed by regulations, made him look like a bizarre mechanical/organic hybrid.

He stopped to stand within centimeters of Romaine, staring earnestly up at her. Andorians had no concept of "personal space." But even faced with the imposing presence of a fully armed soldier in the midst of Memory Prime's civilian areas, Romaine retained enough composure to realize that Farl was upset and even grimmer than Andorians usually were.

"Quite seriouss, I'm afraid, Chief Romaine," Farl said in the soft dry whisper of his species.

Romaine didn't like the look or sound of any of this. The troopers assigned to Prime weren't supposed to carry more than hand phasers in the civilian areas, let alone set up command stations there. "How serious?" she asked, and her tone told Farl she wanted an answer *now.*

"It iss classified," Farl said, and had the decency to look embarrassed.

"I'm ranking Starfleet officer, Farl, I—"

"Not in thiss emergency, I am sorry to say. You are now in command of only the science and administrative functions of this facility." Farl looked over to the transporter pads where two more Andorian troopers shimmered into existence. They quickly ran off to a second display table.

"Farl," Romaine said, trying to sound reasonable, "I know what the regulations are, and the only type of emergencies I can think of that could possibly remain classified to the ranking officer of a starbase installation are . . ." She saw it in his small, dark eyes. She had spent enough time with Andorians to be able to read their expressions.

"Precisely," Farl whispered. "Military emergency. War preparationss."

Romaine felt her breath catch. "Against whom? What are our orders? When did this happen?"

Farl bowed his head. Was it in shame? Romaine wondered.

"Chief Romaine," he said in a delicate whisper, "I have enjoyed serving with you thiss past year. But I am unable to answer your questionss. Up to thiss moment, you have run thiss outpost well, according to your dutiess. Now I must ask that you let me run its military functions according to mine."

"Then I must ask to see your authorization, Commander."

Farl looked up into Romaine's eyes. He wore an expression of pleading. "Miraromaine," he said sadly. "I have never received communicationss at this level of classification before. I must follow my orderss. Starfleet will transmit orderss to your office as well, and that iss as much as you will be allowed to know until the emergency has passed. I am truly sorry."

"I'll have to confirm this with Starfleet," Romaine said, and could hear the tightness of her own voice.

"Of course," Farl said. "As I did."

The chief technician's mind spun with the possibilities she might be facing here. She couldn't lose Prime to another Alpha disaster. She refused to.

"Until then, what can I do?" she asked. The transient population of Prime was almost four thousand now with the added visitors who had arrived for the prize ceremonies. "Shall I help Sal handle the cancellation of the Nobel and Z.Magnees—"

"Absolutely not," Farl interrupted. "The orderss are quite clear. The ceremoniess must proceed as planned. Our preparationss must appear as no more than a drill, a training maneuver to the civilianss."

"*What?*" Romaine could see the troopers in the breakout area turn to look at her, checking on the safety of their commander.

Farl gestured to her to keep her voice down. It was a struggle.

"You're telling me that we're going on to a near war footing here and it's to be kept *secret?* That's insane!"

"It iss not insane," Farl whispered back loudly. "It meanss that there iss a chance we can take action to contain the threat before things get out of control. Why upset the scientific community here unnecessarily? Especially with the antennae of the Federation, and perhapss otherss, upon uss?"

Farl's expression was brightening now, along with his color. That damnable Andorian love for intrigue again, Romaine thought. "What threat? What action?"

"As I told you, the threat iss classified."

"Then what action will you be taking?"

"Some we already have."

"Such as?"

The apologetic look came back to Farl's face. Romaine suddenly knew she wasn't going to like what she was about to hear.

"My trooperss have placed three of your staff in protective custody."

Romaine felt her blood turn to ice. "Who?" she managed to get out before her throat shut down in shock.

"Specialist Lieutenant Stell. Specialist First-Class Slann. And Dr. T'Lar." Farl said gravely.

Romaine was stunned. She had seven Vulcans on her staff. Why these three?

Stell was a computer technician, young, serious as all Vulcans were, specializing in library subsystems. Slann was on sabbatical from the Vulcan Academy of Sciences, studying historical methods of fault toleration and error detection in trinary data storage. And T'Lar was a paleoexozoologist researching cyclical patterns of extinction in adjacent planetary systems. What was their connection?

"Why them?" Romaine asked, completely baffled.

"Classified."

"Have they done anything or is it just suspected they might?"

"Classified." Farl's eyes flashed again. "But for you, Miraromaine: it iss simply a safety precaution. There iss no definitive proof." He shrugged, a gesture almost comical in battle armor.

"May I see them?" she asked, though it sounded more like a formal request.

Farl shook his head. "Access restricted. Again, my apologiess."

"Anything else?"

"Alass, no."

"This stinks, you know," she stated, her voice rising on each word. She was trying not to take her anger out on the commander, and not succeeding.

"I am trained to prevent these occurrencess, Mira-romaine. When my trooperss and I must take action, it meanss we have failed. I am familiar with the odor, yess?"

Romaine turned to go, then hesitated. "Will this situation be changed in any way by the arrival of the *Enterprise?*"she asked.

Farl smiled. "Ah, yess. I expect the situation to improve considerably by then."

Good, thought Romaine, though she suddenly doubted that she and Scotty were going to enjoy the kind of reunion she had hoped for.

Kirk had never thought it odd that in the middle of a crisis he could feel good. He knew it was the rush of adrenaline that propelled him, made his steps light and his actions swift. But apart from the merely physical sensations, it was his mind and his spirit that somehow seemed to accelerate at these times. Too often he had seen other officers crumble in the face of multiple crises. But once Kirk had determined his way, no matter how slight and dismal that chance for victory might be, he kept at it until the way was clear. The ship sustained him, but it was the never-ending struggle to keep her that made him come alive. He felt that way now.

McCoy joined him as Kirk walked down the corridor on D deck, heading for the brig.

"Score one for the system, Bones," he said.

"The commodore knows about us meeting with Spock?" McCoy asked, holding his medical kit and tricorder against his hip to stop them from bouncing as he kept Kirk's pace.

"She authorized it. Had no choice." He turned to grin at

the doctor. "As a suitably senior officer who has volunteered for the job, I'm Spock's counsel for the court-martial. She can't deny me access. Or my client's physician, either. I'm just following the rules."

They turned the corner at an intersection. Two of Wolfe's troopers stood at attention at the end of the new corridor.

"Good," McCoy said. "I was afraid we were going to have to charm our way past those two. The least you could have done was tell me this over the intercom."

"Not good form to let Wolfe hear me gloat. If she's monitoring infraship communications. Which she probably is." Kirk approached the nearer of the two guards. "I assume the commodore told you to expect us?" he said arrogantly.

It worked. The first trooper snapped a salute, usually not part of starship tradition, and barked, "Yes, sir!"

Kirk blinked at the reaction his tone had elicited, then belatedly remembered to return the salute. "Carry on," he said, then passed the trooper and stopped in front of the open doorway to the holding cell. It was outlined with the glowing transmission nodes of a security field. Spock waited on the other side of the doorway, hands patiently held behind his back.

"Good day, Captain. Doctor," Spock said, as if he had happened to meet them in the corridor by chance.

Kirk and McCoy returned the greeting, then Kirk turned to the second trooper.

"Turn it off, trooper," he ordered.

"Sorry, sir," the second trooper replied. "Commodore's orders. You may meet with the prisoner but without contact."

Kirk checked the trooper's sleeve and name badge, then spoke quickly. "Sergeant Gilmartin, are you aware of the penalties set forth in General Regulation Document two hundred and twenty-seven, pertaining to treatment of prisoners on board Starfleet vessels: violations thereof?"

"N-no, sir."

"Then I suggest you turn off that security field and allow this doctor access to the prisoner before you find out what those penalties are!" Kirk snapped, and then to give the sergeant a hint, added the word, *"Private!"*

Sergeant Gilmartin sneaked a worried look at the first trooper and saw no reason for encouragement. "I'll have to check with the commodore, sir," he said cautiously.

"Be my guest," Kirk answered with a flourish of his hand.

Gilmartin walked off to a wall intercom plate. McCoy leaned forward and whispered, "*Is* there a General Regulation Document two hundred and twenty-seven?"

"Two hundred and twenty-seven *B,*" Spock amended matter-of-factly from the doorway.

McCoy's eyes widened in surprise.

Kirk looked hurt. "Doctor! Would I lie about something like that?" He turned back to watch Gilmartin before McCoy could answer.

Gilmartin returned from his intercom conversation, defeated. "We'll have to scan you before you go in," he said apologetically.

"As set out in GRD two hundred and twenty-seven *C,*" Spock offered.

"I'll have to remember this the next time we play poker," McCoy said as Gilmartin scanned him and Kirk with a combat tricorder and the first trooper searched the medical bag.

"Whatever do you mean, doctor?" Kirk asked innocently.

"I mean that sometimes your bluffs aren't bluffs."

"Only those that I know will be called," Kirk said with a smile. "Remember that."

Sergeant Gilmartin, satisfied with his readings, told Spock to stand back from the door and then switched off the screen. As soon as Kirk and McCoy had entered the cell, the field hummed back into life. The trooper was going by the book.

"It is good to see you, Captain," Spock said. "I had assumed that Commodore Wolfe would countermand any attempt you made for a meeting."

"She didn't have a choice," Kirk said. "I'm your legal counsel."

Spock's eyes actually flickered. Kirk saw it.

"Until an experienced counsel can be assigned," he quickly added.

Spock's eyes returned to normal. "A clever circumvention of the commodore's wishes," Spock said, a faint tone of relief in his voice.

"It was Dr. McCoy's idea," Kirk replied as he crossed to the cell's writing desk.

"Indeed." Spock watched dubiously as McCoy held a sparkling scanner in front of his chest, keeping track of its readings in the display window of the medical tricorder.

"What's all this, Spock?" Kirk asked as he stood by the desk. It was covered with large stacks of bound hardcopies from the ship's printers.

"The commodore has denied me access to the ship's computer. I find I must carry on my work with printed materials."

"That's terrible," Kirk said with a frown, and he meant it. It was one thing to sit in a chair with the weight and warmth of a real book and be transported by fiction, or philosophy, or the inspiring words of beings from far away or long ago. But to actually have to *work* with them, scan through them a page at a time, without the speed of a display or the computer's indexing abilities, sounded barbaric.

"I do find it most inefficient," Spock agreed.

"Did the commodore give a reason for denying you computer access?" Kirk asked, glancing at the titles of Spock's hardcopies; agriculture and economics journals for the most part, though he didn't understand how they fit into Spock's duties.

"No," Spock said, rolling up his sleeve to let McCoy take a sample of blood for later analysis. "Though it is logical to assume that she does not want to risk me overriding any of the bridge or engineering controls." He watched as his green blood filled the ampoule on the end of McCoy's vacuum syringe.

"*Can* engineering and bridge controls be overidden from a remote terminal?" Kirk frowned. They *did* share the ship's computer as the main processing unit, but still . . .

"I have always thought it would be possible, given enough time to work out the programming techniques," Spock said. "And since the commodore has forbidden me access, I assume that she also suspects or knows it can be done."

Kirk made a mental note to request a system improvement in his next general report. If someone did manage to work out the programming techniques, the *Enterprise* could be at the mercy of any passenger, or invader, who had access to the most common type of computer terminal in the ship.

"Assuming the commodore won't object to a simple library reader, is there anything else I can get for you?" Kirk sat down at the desk and indicated that McCoy and Spock should join him.

"I would very much appreciate the opportunity to meet with Academician Sradek," Spock said as he pulled out a chair and sat.

"And he with you," Kirk said. "The academician came to my cabin the night you were confined to your quarters, asking the same thing."

McCoy smirked. "Can't wait for the emotion of a teacher/student reunion, right, Spock?"

"On the contrary, doctor. I believe I still have much to learn from Sradek."

"Why is that, Mr. Spock?" Kirk asked.

"Sradek is an eminent historian who excels in identifying patterns from the past and applying them to modern situations. His analysis of the dynamics that led to the political unification of the Jovian colonies in your own system led directly to his successful peace proposals for the civil war on Katja Two."

"And earned him the Peace Prize nomination," Kirk added.

"Exactly. However, shortly after the cessation of hostilities on Katja Two, the academician was asked to sit on the Sherman's Planet famine board of inquiry."

"Isn't that old news, Mr. Spock?" McCoy asked. "We delivered new grain stocks there years ago."

"Quite right, doctor. But the new grain did not take hold on the planet as quickly as had been projected. The economic ramifications in that quadrant were serious. Even more serious is the evidence of the Sherman Syndrome appearing on other agricultural worlds."

"The Sherman Syndrome? Sounds like a viewscreen act," Kirk said.

"It is quite in earnest, I assure you. The name refers to a complex pattern of crop failure, political mismanagement, and faulty economic planning on colony planets. An entire analysis division was set up at Memory Gamma to investigate the syndrome, though, to date, no useful conclusions have emerged. Cause and effect are extremely interconnected and difficult to isolate."

McCoy was unimpressed. "If you mean that sometimes not every new agricultural colony turns into a golden breadbasket the first time out, I don't see any reason for concern. That's just the risk of farming. Give the colonists enough time to figure out the intricacies of their new world and the yields will go up."

Kirk intervened. "Spock, does this have anything at all to do with the charges against you? If it doesn't, I think we should put it aside for now."

"I was merely explaining why I was looking forward to meeting with Sradek so I might question him about his reasons for denying the Sherman Syndrome hypothesis. My logic does not grasp the basis of his arguments and I wish to be enlightened."

"Fair enough," Kirk said, trying to roll things along. "Sradek is looking forward to enlightening you about that also and—"

"The academician is not aware of my interest in the subject. I have not communicated with him since the last time I was on Vulcan."

"Then maybe he wanted to say hello just to be polite," McCoy suggested.

"I see no need to insult a respected Vulcan scholar, doctor."

Kirk held his hands up. "Shall we get to the point, gentlemen. *Please?*"

And they did. Once again, Spock recounted his activities from the time Commodore Wolfe boarded at Starbase Four and he was interrogated and confined to his quarters. Kirk went over Spock's eidetic recall of the interrogation and agreed that the commodore's troopers acted as if they had only indefinite suspicions to go on, not hard facts. But no matter how many times they analyzed the situation, not even Spock could reason out a logical conclusion.

In the end, all they were left with was a series of facts and a string of unanswered questions. Someone *had* stunned the two troopers standing guard outside Spock's quarters. That person or an accomplice had then gone to the dilithium lab and switched off the accelerator field's shielding just as Scott's tour group was in an area where they might have been killed by the resultant dilithium reaction, *if* the ship's dilithium crystals had still been on line.

Commodore Wolfe had come on board believing that Spock might be planning some treachery just like that. When it had happened, she was convinced of his guilt. But there were no fingerprints, no witnesses, no computer logs. Only suspicion.

As they appeared to be running out of alternatives, Kirk brought up Wolfe's enigmatic reference to T'Pel.

Spock's expression hardened. "Indeed," he responded. "Did the commodore give a context for the term?"

"No," Kirk said. "Though I got the impression it was a name."

"Anyone you know, Spock?" McCoy asked.

Spock was not impressed. "Among Vulcans, the name T'Pel is rather common, doctor. I believe I know several T'Pels and am related to four others."

Kirk nodded. "The ship's computer came up with more than fifteen thousand references, almost all of them Vulcan females."

"And the others?" McCoy asked.

"Words from various languages. Lots of dialect terms meaning 'to drink.' Acronyms, product names, literary references."

"I assume you investigated further," Spock said.

"Of course. I asked the computer to pull out every T'Pel reference that could be cross-referenced to you."

"And?"

Kirk shrugged. "I got biostats on your four cousins."

"Did you try cross-referencing T'Pel to any illegal acts or threats?" McCoy asked.

"That was my next search," Kirk said, "and I got nothing."

McCoy's eyes narrowed. "Out of fifteen thousand references?"

"Illegal acts and threats are not part of the Vulcan heritage," Spock said. "That is a logical finding."

By the end of the meeting, it was McCoy who was most upset. "For someone facing court-martial for attempted murder, you certainly aren't acting worried, Mr. Spock."

"Thank you, doctor," Spock said.

"Since you're so calm," McCoy continued, "I take it you believe that the commodore's case is so weak that you have no reason to think there is anything for the rest of us to worry about?"

"I mean nothing of the sort," Spock said. "Though the case against me is weak, someone on board this ship did try to disable the *Enterprise* and kill one or more of the prize nominees. While I am in custody, the person or persons responsible will be free to try again on Memory Prime."

"And that's nothing to worry about?" McCoy said, amazed.

"Logically, doctor, there is no reason to be worried. On the other hand, there is every reason to use whatever means possible to stop such an act."

"What act?" Kirk asked.

Spock stated it like an elementary class lesson. "The act of killing the Federation's top representatives of virtually all sciences and plunging uncounted star systems into a new dark age."

Kirk decided he would worry enough for the two of them.

In engineering, Scott watched the main display board with relief as the engines stepped down to sublight and the *Enterprise* returned to normal space. Despite the jury-rigged repairs and the hours-long strain of factor seven, the circuits had held. Now his people had a full week of tearing around the Jeffries tubes, taking the time to do the repairs properly. And perhaps add a few more of my refinements to the system, Scott thought, though he knew they'd all groan at that. It had come to be a standing joke that the only similarity between the official Constellation-class equipment manuals and the *Enterprise*'s manuals was the line about manufacturers' warranties being voided by tampering. In the *Enterprise*'s case, Mr. Scott had voided all the warranties years ago.

Scott left engineering for his quarters. With his main concern out of the way, it was time to turn to the others. He supposed that Spock should top that list, but the science officer had extricated himself from worse situations, and Scott was certain something would work out. It wasn't that he had such absolute faith in the Starfleet judicial system; it was that he had absolute faith in the captain.

The person that he focused on instead was Mira Romaine. She had been the sanest, smartest, and nicest woman who had ever come on board the *Enterprise*. And, he thought, the prettiest.

From the moment he had seen her in the briefing room to go over the installation procedures for the new equipment for Memory Alpha, he had felt the spark pass between them. He remembered having difficulty concentrating on her report that day. It was simple, yet brilliant, and showed an impressive grasp of logistics, combined with an intriguing new programming methodology that could save days in the initialization stages. Reviewing the report later, Scott had seen that the brilliance of Mira's eyes was more than matched by the brilliance of her mind.

At first they'd both been tentative, the differences in their age and rank glaringly apparent. But slowly the hesitations became slighter, the false starts fewer in number. The closer they came to Memory Alpha the stronger the bonds between them grew, as if the threat of loss at mission's end sped up the processes of love.

Aye, love. That was the word for it, Scott thought lyrically. There had been others in his life, but a true love was rare as heather mist a hundred light-years from home.

He had realized the full strength of the glorious hold that Mira had claimed on his heart when she had been possessed by the Zetarians. To see the light of her eyes replaced by the alien energies of an ancient, deadly life-form; to hear her sweet voice corrupted by the obscene utterances of entities that planned to possess her body by displacing her mind; it had almost destroyed him.

That night, after she had recovered from the multi-atmospheric pressure that had driven the Zetarians from her and the ship, he had discovered in her arms that she had felt the same terror within her. Not the fear of death, but the fear of losing someone who had come to mean so much to her.

The next two weeks at Memory Alpha had been a whirlwind of love and work. Scott was dazzled by her intellect and her playfulness and he realized with the poignant feeling of impending separation that he had met the first woman who could keep up with him in his field, and the first woman who challenged him to keep up with her.

The last day had been an agony. A team of Vulcan technicians had arrived to begin the recovery attempt of Alpha's burned-out cores. Mira was to remain with them. The *Enterprise* was to move on.

The only thing that had made their separation possible was that, among all the things they shared, their sense of duty and their questing souls had been the strongest. They could not give up the lives they led. They did not even ask the other to do what each alone could not.

For a few months, they had exchanged messages. But the words that could be sent through subspace, open to the eyes and ears of others, only heightened the loneliness, the sense of loss. In the end, it had been best to close the file and remember what had been, instead of vainly struggling to keep a lifeless ghost alive.

Mira Romaine was now chief technician at the facility that was the *Enterprise*'s next port of call—a well-publicized port of call.

His work at hand completed, Scott finally lost himself in the agony of asking *what if?* and *why?* because he knew there was no way Mira Romaine could fail to know that soon their paths would cross again. But *she hadn't sent a message.* Almost as if she no longer cared.

Chapter Thirteen

SALMAN NENSI stood behind the lectern on the stage of the main amphitheater and watched four associates roll among the empty audience seats, slipping printed programs into the pocket on each chair back. He tried to imagine how the theater would look tomorrow morning at eight hundred hours, when almost two thousand beings would gather for the opening ceremonies before the scientists went off to begin the long, drawn-out voting procedures. At least another six hundred scientists would watch the presentation in the comfort of their own particular gravitational and atmospheric conditions in the special environmentally detached visitors' domes of Prime. With the scientists' companions, media, politicians, and the at-liberty crews of at least eight Fleet vessels, Prime was going to be filled to overflowing. Already the lineups in the cafeterias and restaurants were numbing. And now Farl and his blue-skinned troopers were cordoning off sections, creating choke points for crowd control, and making things three times as bad. Each hour that passed made it less likely that these prize ceremonies were going to be the best ever held. They were threatening to become an utter fiasco.

But at least I don't have an interface slowdown to contend with, Nensi thought gratefully as he checked off items on the "to do" list displayed on the portable office terminal he had opened on the lectern. Garold and a few others of the interface team had been seen wandering around their quarters in the main domes, so he presumed that relations between them and the Pathfinders were back to normal. Whatever normal might mean in those circumstances. As for the Pathfinders' excess capacity, that had apparently been going on for at least a year and he couldn't see how a few more days could affect anything.

An associate hummed to a stop beside Nensi, opened a panel on its side, and rotated a viewscreen out and up to Nensi's eye level.

"Request for communication," the associate announced. "From Chief Technician Romaine."

Nensi gave leave for the machine to proceed. Romaine appeared and immediately apologized for bothering him.

"I'm so far behind now," Nensi said, "another few minutes won't make any difference. What's up?"

"The *Enterprise* has arrived and the last delegation of nominees will be ready to beam down in a few minutes. You want to be part of the welcoming committee again?"

Nensi had greeted all of the other delegations, didn't see why he shouldn't go for a complete record, and said so.

"Main transporter chamber, then," Romaine said, and quickly glanced offscreen. "Fourteen-twenty hours."

"I'll be there," Nensi acknowledged, concluding the call. But he noticed that Romaine didn't sign off. "Anything else?" he asked.

Romaine wrinkled her brow. "Did you try confirming any of Farl's authorization for this 'emergency' of his?" she asked.

Nensi shook his head. "I'm a civilian appointee attached to a Starfleet outpost. Nothing to confirm. Besides, I've seen flaps like this a hundred times. Everyone's nervous about all this scientific talent gathering on one little rock. That's all."

"This little flap has three of my best people incommunicado in the military brig," Romaine said angrily. "You can bet *I* tried to confirm it."

"Tried?" Nensi repeated. He didn't like the sound of that. "What was the response?"

"Coded military garbage. I mean *nothing's* coming out of Command except for acronyms and abbreviations and keyword responses we have to open sealed message wafers to decode."

Nensi rubbed at his chin. "That only means they're taking this flap seriously and quite properly assuming that subspace is no longer secure for unencrypted Command messages."

"Off the record, Sal, did you have *any* indication at all that something like this was in the works?"

"An associate comm link is not the best place to be asking for something off the record," he cautioned. "But, no, I had no idea. If I had, then presumably someone else would have, too, and we wouldn't be going through all this right now." He could see that her face was still drawn and tight. "I really wouldn't worry about it. Concentrate on your engineer, instead." That brought a smile.

"I wish," Romaine said, then, "Thanks, Uncle Sal. See you in the main chamber." She broke the link and the screen twisted back into the associate.

"This module has other duties," it announced politely when the panel clicked shut.

Nensi gave it permission to proceed and picked up his portable office terminal from the lectern. He'd delegated so much authority to organize the ceremonies that he supposed he might as well let his staff take responsibility for the headaches, too. He walked across the stage and hopped down to the floor, feeling his back twinge with the impact. It would be good to leave behind the painful chauvinism of Earth standard gravity and get back home to the normal gravity of Mars, he thought, and hurried on his way.

The welcoming delegation was already in position when Nensi arrived at Prime's main transporter chamber. Romaine and two aides waited with twelve others, including representatives of the prize committee, accreditation officials, two holo recorders from the combined newsweb pool, and Commander Farl's sublieutenant of the guards.

Nensi crossed quickly to stand by Romaine as the forward platform pad began to glow and a small, squat, angular shape appeared.

Nensi leaned over to Romaine. "I didn't know the *Enterprise* was bringing any more Medusans," he said.

The transporter technician at the console overheard.

"It's just a calibration module, Mr. Nensi," she explained, flicking her eyes back and forth from the pad to her controls.

"Ah," Nensi said as the ghost image solidified into the familiar form of the most transported piece of equipment in the Federation.

The sides of the box-shaped calibration module were made from incredibly thin sheets of alignment alloy. Only four molecules thick, the surface of the substance sparkled with a rainbow effect resulting from the geometric diffraction patterns formed by its constituent atoms. The slightest molecular misalignment of the transporter effect, even on the order of half an atomic diameter, would immediately disrupt the colorful light reflections and turn the surface to a dull, tarnished, blue black.

Any ship or installation that had a transporter unit kept hundreds of square meters of the alloy on hand for test beamings. Its durability, as long as it was properly reassembled, was as impressive as its availability, and Nensi had seen sheets of it fashioned into everything from serving trays to wall plaques in handicraft shops on dozens of worlds. As long as the ends were carefully rolled over to guard against the wickedly sharp edges, Nensi found alignment alloy artifacts attractive, if somewhat garish.

"Are they having trouble with their system?" Nensi asked, after the technician had confirmed the module's arrival and the *Enterprise* beamed it back up.

"They're just being cautious, I think," the technician said. "Their operator was saying the ship's transporter target sensors are so sensitive that they were picking up ghost coordinates from all the portable combat pads Farl's deployed. Rather than step down their sensors and then spend a day recalibrating when they leave, the operator just wanted to go to a higher beam path."

"Successfully, I take it?" Nensi said as the transporter effect appeared above five of the twenty-two pads in the chamber.

"Going to be an awful mess if it wasn't," the technician said cheerfully.

The first group all wore Fleet uniforms, and the first one off the platform had captain's stripes on his sleeve and a face too young with eyes too old. The legendary James T. Kirk, Nensi thought as he stepped out to introduce himself and greet the man.

Kirk smiled winningly and gave the impression that he had traveled halfway across the galaxy just to meet and talk with Salman Nensi. The chief administrator had never met a being with such a warm, yet forceful personality. Gods, Nensi thought, if Kirk's like this just to say hello to, what must it be like to serve with him? Nensi had an image of a starship hurtling into a black hole with Kirk at the helm and a thousand loyal crew eager to follow. Then the captain saw something interesting over Nensi's shoulder.

"Mira?" Kirk said with a surprised smile. "Mira Romaine?"

"Hello, Captain." Romaine extended her hand to Kirk's. Nensi, because he knew her well, could see her smile was tense and forced. "Didn't Mr. Scott tell you?" She tried to say it lightly, but Nensi immediately knew what had caused her disappointment.

"Not a word," Kirk said, and then, incredibly, Nensi saw it was almost as if the captain could read Romaine's face and body language as well as anyone else who had known her since she was a child. "But then Scotty's been working nonstop since the dilithium burnout. I didn't get a chance to review the personnel list for Memory Prime and I bet he didn't either." Kirk stepped back from Romaine for a moment, probably comparing her to the nervous, inexperienced specialist lieutenant she had been on the mission to

Alpha, Nensi thought. He watched Kirk assess the change the years had brought to Mira, and realized that Kirk had lied when he said he didn't get a chance to review the personnel list. That man probably never left anything to chance in his entire career.

Kirk arranged to meet Romaine for a drink when the day's business was concluded and then he dutifully endured the rest of the introductions. Wouldn't be surprised to see him run for council president someday, Nensi thought as he watched Kirk work the room. The others who had beamed down with him seemed to share some of their captain's inner fire and charm as well.

Nensi had made it a hobby to try and identify people's origins by their accents and turned his ear to the voices of Kirk's accompanying crew. He immediately gave up trying to place the beautiful woman in services red who was talking to the transporter technician in the technician's own colony dialect. A moment ago she had been speaking in Greater Andorian to Farl's sublieutenant. Both tongues, including Standard, she had managed with perfect tones, inflections, and in the sublieutenant's case, whistles and clicks. The woman's facility with language was far beyond Nensi's.

The other crew members were easier. An older man in sciences blue was delighting everyone with a friendly drawl that Nensi recognized as coming either from the old Lunar Freehomes or, perhaps, the North American southern regions. The two younger men in command gold, who were paying particular attention to the women in the welcoming delegation, without being objectionable about it, were also fairly simple. The younger one was from either Martian Colony One or, even more likely, the Grand Soviet regions on Earth. The older one with the blinding smile carried a unique hint of Old Earth combined with the colonists' dialect of Ginjitsu. A true child of the Federation, Nensi concluded.

As the first round of greetings came to an end, six more pads produced six more materializations. Nensi was surprised to see a commodore and five troopers. Troopers were not considered regular crew for a starship except under extraordinary conditions, and the protocol liaison in Romaine's office had mentioned no need to prepare for a person of the commodore's rank. He wondered if her presence had any connection with Farl's emergency, and the commodore answered him by heading straight for the sublieutenant.

Beside him, Nensi heard one of the prize committee members, apparently annoyed at the arrival of so many nonessential beings, ask pointedly if there might be any scientists on board the *Enterprise*.

Again, the transporter pads chimed and the first of the nominee delegation arrived with their luggage and equipment.

Nensi found himself shaking hands with the older officer with the drawl as the accreditation officials escorted the scientists to the identification stalls. His name, he said, was Leonard McCoy, ship's surgeon. Nensi returned the introduction.

"A good voyage?" the chief administrator asked.

"Except for the last part," McCoy answered with enough of an edge in his voice that Nensi knew things weren't going well on his ship. "I'm sorry, Mr. Nensi, I don't mean to complain. I always get cranky after beaming. I hate those things."

Nensi had heard about people like this man, though he had never personally met anyone else who shared the doctor's groundless aversion to being broken down into his elementary particles, tunneled through beam space, then reassembled. "I understand," Nensi lied politely.

"Especially putting through that calibration module first," McCoy continued. "As if they expected the whole system to fail any second. Probably with me in transit, too." McCoy looked around the chamber, as if searching for something. "What the blazes are those portable pads they kept talking about up there?" he asked.

"Those would be the portable combat pads our security troopers have deployed around the facility," Nensi said. He saw an eyebrow shoot up at the word *combat*. "Part of a very thorough drill procedure, I assure you. Nothing drastic."

"Then why are they interfering with our ship's system?"

Nensi was getting the strong feeling that this man didn't just dislike transporters, he *hated* them. "As I understand it, Dr. McCoy, it's a function of their fail-safe mode." Normally transtator technology was beyond Nensi, but here he was on familiar financial grounds. "I'm sure you know that a pad-to-pad transit consumes less than one-tenth the energy of a single-pad beam."

"No," McCoy said plainly.

"Well, it's true," Nensi continued, wondering what to make of this man. "Plus it takes greater operator skill to lock target sensors on to the proper coordinates, especially at orbital distances. Portable pads, on the other hand, can be preset to a fixed number of other pads, like an intercom system, if you will. Untrained personnel can simply punch in a code for a pad in the network and the system automatically transfers them from one location to another within the circuit. Very efficient for moving ground troops in a hurry."

McCoy looked to be thinking that one through, then asked, "But if the *Enterprise* isn't part of your portable system, why do the portable units affect it?"

"It's their lock-on beacons. They're very strong and directional, for reliability under harsh conditions, and they keep attracting your ship's carrier waves. Are you familiar with the old concept of a lightning rod?"

"Very," McCoy said with a smile. "I'm an old farm boy."

"Then like that," Nensi said, thinking maybe that explained the man's attitude. "In fact, under invasion conditions, portable pad beacons can be set so high that incoming beams are almost *forced* to divert to them. Very handy if you have a squad of troopers ready to take prisoners. That's why Starfleet still carries the expense of ground-assault suborbital shuttles. To avoid the risks of beam captures."

"Now that's what I'd like," McCoy said. "Suborbital

shuttles. Something big and solid that kept me in one piece all the way there and back. Of course I'll only be able to requisition something like that when I'm an admiral. And at the rate I'm going, I'll probably be a hundred and forty." He laughed at the concept.

Luddite, Nensi thought to himself.

Throughout the conversation, more nominees had arrived from the *Enterprise,* but no more crew. Nensi had seen Romaine look up anxiously each time the pads had chimed, but no Mr. Scott was to be found.

By now the chamber was getting overcrowded, like most other facilities on Memory Prime, and Nensi and McCoy parted as they joined the general migration toward the doors.

The chief administrator found himself shoulder to shoulder with the young officer with the Russian or Martian accent. They introduced themselves but didn't attempt to force their arms up to shake hands.

"I noticed that you have a commodore on board," Nensi said to Ensign Chekov.

"She was not inwited," the ensign said, checking furtively to see if the commodore in question was anywhere nearby.

"Really?" Nensi replied as they suddenly found themselves forced to the side to clear the way for an elderly Vulcan who was being escorted to a retina scanner in the delegate identification stalls.

"She has arrested our first officer," Chekov stated indignantly.

"On what charge?"

Chekov was obviously annoyed. "Made-up charges. She said he tried to kill Academician Sradek"—he pointed to the ancient Vulcan who was peering into a blue-lit sensorscope while his documents were processed—"that Wulcan scientist, and most of the other nominees on board."

"No!" Nensi said, hoping to match what he felt was Chekov's sense of outrage. Nensi himself had been subjected to so many of Starfleet's arbitrary decisions in his career that he doubted if he could ever feel real outrage over anything they did to him again. But Chekov's story was intriguing. Could it be the connection to Farl's emergency?

"Yes!" Chekov replied vehemently. "It is all lies, but still she has him in the brig."

Nensi smiled at his loose-lipped new acquaintance. "If this is your first time here, Ensign, would you like me to show you to one of our better bars?" He made a point of checking his chronometer. "There's a shift change coming up in about half an hour and I could introduce you to a number of people who I'm sure would enjoy meeting a starship officer. Especially one from the *Enterprise*."

Chekov's eyes lit up like novas. "That would be wery hospitable of you, Mr. Nensi." Profitable to me also, Nensi thought.

As promised, the Extended Loan was one of Prime's better bars. It featured subsidized prices for Fleet and Federation personnel, and an ethanol synthesizer two generations ahead of the overworked antique in the *Enterprise*. Chekov proved to be most talkative, having been charmed and delighted with the decor—a reconstruction of the legendary Icelandic public databank from the late 2000s that had been so important to the growth and development of synthetic consciousnesses. An hour later when the shifts finally changed and a rather rowdy group of librarians decided they should get to know the new ensign very well, Nensi had heard the full story of the *Enterprise*'s voyage from Starbase Four, the dilithium disaster and the flux release, the arrest, everything.

As Chekov was practically carried out of the bar to be shown what sights there were to see, Nensi sat back in his booth and nursed the vodka for which the ensign had insisted on paying. The chief administrator was worried. Farl's flap, as he thought of it, was obviously far worse than he had suspected, reaching out from Memory Prime and apparently even affecting the starship *Enterprise*. But with subspace channels restricted to military communications, and Farl now exerting his military authority, there was no one for the chief administrator to turn to, nothing he could do to help preserve his facility.

No, take that back, he thought. There *was* someone he could turn to for help. Something.

He knocked back the vodka and left the bar to find Romaine. Liars or not, it was time to pay another visit to the Pathfinders.

Chapter Fourteen

KIRK SMILED WARMLY, expertly hiding the rage that burned within him. Commodore Wolfe had returned to the *Enterprise* with Commander Farl and had been in briefings for the past six hours, briefings that were plainly off limits to the *Enterprise*'s captain. Kirk hadn't felt like this since he was a middy in his first year at the Academy and at the mercy of just about everyone else's schedule.

Across the restaurant table from him, Mira Romaine stopped her story and sipped her wine. Then she smiled at the captain and said, "Did you hear any of that?"

Kirk switched gears instantly. "After the extent of the damage at Memory Alpha was fully charted, you were posted to the U.S.S. *Rainbow Warrior,* then took a three-month course at the Vulcan Academy, joined the Memory Prime implementation team, and here you are," Kirk recapped smoothly. His years on the bridge of the *Enterprise* had given him the ability to follow several conversations at once, even without being aware he was doing it. But he decided the commodore had stolen enough of his energies for this evening; it was time to pay more attention to Mira.

"Very impressive, Captain. I would have sworn you had tuned me out completely."

Kirk raised his own glass. "Never," he said graciously.

"And you?" Romaine asked. "What have you been up to in the past few years?"

Kirk sighed. "Not much," he said blandly. "Same ship, same captain."

"Same crew?"

"Mostly." Kirk saw in her eyes what she was afraid to ask. "And honestly, Scotty said absolutely nothing about knowing you were here. He really has had his hands full with the dilithium burnout."

"Thank you, Captain," Romaine said, "but that's not why I was asking."

Kirk felt a momentary twinge of sadness for the woman. How often had he said the same sort of thing without really meaning it, as she just had? "How's your father?" he asked to change the subject.

"Grumpy as ever," Romaine said with a smile, though it plainly didn't reflect her feelings.

"Still retired?" Kirk drained his glass and looked around for the server, a tall man in a traditional long white apron who looked as if he could juggle antigravs set for full attract.

"His last 'retirement' lasted three months. Now he's consulting for a mining company in the Belt. He likes the travel." Romaine followed Kirk's eyes, saw Sal Nensi enter the restaurant, and waved him over. It didn't take much to convince him to join them for supper. The table's server was over instantly with a third menu screen. The speed of service at this restaurant was so fast that Kirk idly wondered if there were voice sensors in the table. Either that or the servers had better hearing than Mr. Spock.

"Enjoying shore leave?" Nensi asked of the captain after placing his order.

"Just waiting," Kirk said. "Story of my life."

"And mine," Nensi agreed. "Especially now. No doubt you've noticed that a military exercise is being carried out at this facility."

Kirk looked over the railing beside their table at two

Andorian troopers marching below through a central plaza.
"Difficult not to. Is this a regular occurrence?" Kirk was puzzled as he tried to read Nensi's surprised reaction.

"You mean *you* don't know what it's about?"

"I had assumed it was security for the prize ceremonies." Kirk felt alarms going off. He had not thought to question the presence of so many troopers on Prime after being told that the portable combat transporters had been dispersed simply as part of a scheduled drill.

"We've been informed that this facility is in the middle of a military emergency," Romaine said. "I've had my command temporarily suspended."

Kirk held up his hand to stop the revelations. Something wasn't making sense. "Just a moment," he began, turning to Romaine. "You say *you* were in command of this base?"

"Yes sir," Romaine replied as if she were still a specialist lieutenant on Kirk's bridge. "It's supposedly a civilian installation but requires a military presence, so the Federation and Starfleet compromised by giving command to someone in Starfleet technical services. Me. Except under military emergencies."

"And what is the nature of the military emergency?" Kirk asked hurriedly. It was impossible to think that his ship could arrive at a facility in a military emergency without Starfleet informing him.

"I don't know," Romaine said.

"Nor I," Nensi added.

"Commander Farl took over early this morning and said that I could confirm it with Starfleet."

"And did you?" Kirk asked.

"I can't get through channels. Everything's restricted or encrypted."

Nensi leaned forward and dropped his voice. "Captain Kirk, does this military emergency exist without you being informed of it?" The man looked equally frightened and confused.

Kirk studied Romaine and Nensi. Obviously they had

parts of the puzzle he was trying to solve. He had to trust them in order to make an exchange: his pieces for theirs.

"An Alpha emergency has been declared on board the *Enterprise,*" Kirk said in almost a whisper.

The three of them then abruptly sat back from the table as the server brought the first course of hydroponic salads. He topped up their wineglasses then departed.

"I've heard about the Alpha emergency," Nensi said.

Kirk considered the man's statement for a moment and decided Nensi had said it so Kirk would understand two things: that Nensi had his own sources of information and that he was holding nothing back.

"I appreciate you telling me that," Kirk said. "Do your sources have any idea why an Alpha was called?"

"Sorry, no."

"The unofficial explanation I was given," Kirk said, "was that Starfleet had received unsubstantiated information indicating that one or more of the prize nominees were targeted for assassination."

"Commander Farl said he was under orders not to tell me the nature of Prime's emergency," Romaine offered. "But he did say that he expected the situation to be improved when the *Enterprise* arrived."

Nensi turned to Romaine. "Did Farl say that before or after we heard about the dilithium burnout on the ship?"

"After, of course," Romaine said. "He only took over this morning."

Nensi looked back to Kirk. "My sources also tell me that the dilithium incident on your ship was considered by Commodore Wolfe to have been an assassination attempt orchestrated by your science officer."

"Mr. Spock?" Romaine said with surprise. "Impossible."

"That's what I said," Kirk agreed. "Though the commodore does believe she has a circumstantial case. But putting that aside, what I don't understand is if our two declared emergencies are connected, then why would your commander feel that *his* emergency would be lessened by my ship's arrival? It doesn't make any more sense than thinking that the two emergencies aren't connected." Kirk tapped his finger on the table for a moment, then reached to his equipment belt and brought out his communicator with a practiced flip that snapped it open, ready to transmit. "Kirk to *Enterprise.* Put me through to McCoy."

"The ship's doctor," Romaine explained to Nensi as Kirk waited for McCoy to come on channel.

"We've met," Nensi said glumly. "The technophobe."

Kirk smiled as McCoy responded to the captain's call. He sounded as if he had been sleeping but didn't object when Kirk suggested he join him and Nensi and Romaine for dinner. Within three minutes, a transporter field swirled into being down in the plaza below. McCoy looked around until he saw the captain wave from the restaurant balcony. By the time the doctor arrived at the table, the server had miraculously arrived and set a fourth place and provided another menu screen. McCoy didn't even glance at the offerings and simply ordered a bourbon, or whatever they had that was more or less chemically inspired by bourbon.

"Good to see you in one piece," Nensi commented as the server left for the bar.

"It's good to *be* in one piece after being in billions," McCoy agreed, missing the point. He clapped his hands together and looked expectantly at the captain. "So?" he asked, implying a dozen questions in one word.

"First, how's Spock?" Kirk asked.

"Busy," McCoy said. "The commodore finally agreed to your request to let him have a remote library reader, so the last I saw, he was at his desk in the cell, working away with it on that Sherman Syndrome thing. You'd think he'd be working on his defense at a time like this."

"Spock has a better grasp of his priorities than most people," Kirk suggested. "He knows what he's doing."

McCoy looked up with a smile as the server returned with his drink. "That was fast," he said happily. The server nodded once and was gone.

"How about the commodore?" Kirk asked.

"Been meeting all day with that Andorian commander and some of her staff." McCoy sipped the bourbon experimentally, smiled, then turned to Nensi and asked, "How's this facility set for medical personnel?"

"Any clue as to what her meetings are about?" Kirk prodded. He wondered if McCoy really didn't see the seriousness of the situation or if he had simply acknowledged the fact that if Spock wasn't concerned enough to be doing something about his own incarceration, then there was really no reason for anyone else to be concerned.

"Well, Uhura might have had a clue," McCoy offered. He looked questioningly at Nensi and Romaine.

"It's all right," Kirk said. "We're all in the same shuttle on this one."

"Uhura's been ordered to stay on duty to handle communications. She says she's never seen anything like it short of being in the middle of an ion storm with all shields down. Wolfe and Farl are cut off from Starfleet Command."

Being cut off from Command wasn't necessarily a hardship, Kirk knew. But that usually happened out on the frontier, not in Quadrant Zero. Things were getting worse by the minute. "For how long?" he asked.

"All day, as far as I know," McCoy said. He was still too cheerful as far as Kirk was concerned, and kept glancing over the railing into the plaza.

"Uh, Captain Kirk," Nensi said hesitatingly. "Earlier this afternoon I was present at the combined newsweb facilities and watched an interview with some of the nominees from Earth. It was conducted in real time, over subspace, with an interviewer on Luna. There were no technical difficulties at all that I was aware of."

"Are you suggesting that only Starfleet subspace frequencies are being interfered with?" Kirk asked. "That civil frequencies are being left untouched?"

"I don't even think Starfleet would be capable of such selective jamming," Nensi answered. "But that's what I observed."

Kirk knew that Nensi was right. The intricacies of selective jamming of subspace frequencies made the practice virtually impossible. Usually it was all frequencies that were disrupted, or none. Perhaps it only *appeared* that communications were in disarray.

"Mr. Nensi, have your 'sources' passed on any word about conditions on the other ships that have brought nominees to Prime?" Kirk asked.

"That was one of the first things I decided to check out when I learned what had happened on the *Enterprise.* Communications are disrupted for the other ships as well but, unfortunately, there's no other pattern. Three of the ships are traveling with reduced crews, but that's normal in this area of space. Lots of people use the opportunity for shore leave. Whatever is happening, is happening only on your ship and this facility."

"At least that's a start," Kirk decided. Half the battle in solving a problem was defining the problem to be solved in the first place. "Any suggestions, doctor? Doctor?"

McCoy snapped his head back to the table. "Sorry, Jim?" he asked.

"I give up, Bones. What do you know that we don't know?" Kirk glanced down to the plaza where McCoy's attention had been focused. "Is the answer to all of our questions going to pop out of nothing down there?"

McCoy smiled mysteriously. "I suppose that's one way of looking at it," he said. "Someone's questions, at least."

With that Kirk saw a second transporter field glittering in the plaza. It coalesced into the red-shirted form of Scotty.

McCoy waved down at Scott and the engineer responded, making his way to the restaurant entrance below. Kirk checked Romaine. She stared at her wineglass, grasping it as if it were the only thing that was keeping her on the face of the Prime asteroid.

Kirk wanted to ask McCoy just what it was he thought he was doing, setting up a surprise like this in such a clumsy manner, but he could think of no way to do it without embarrassing Mira and making things worse than they already were. There was a long awkward pause at the table, during which the efficient server arrived and arranged a fifth place and left another menu screen. At last Scott appeared on the balcony, looking as nervous as Kirk had ever seen him before. Mira still stared into the compelling depths of her wineglass. When she finally looked over her shoulder, her glance must have prompted Scotty to finish his approach to the table.

When he arrived, he nodded to the captain and the doctor, uncharacteristically ignored Mr. Nensi, and looked nervously at Romaine.

The woman suddenly stood up by the table. Kirk slumped back in his chair and glared at McCoy, but the doctor was directing his own attention to Scotty and Romaine.

"Hello, Mira," Scott managed to say. Kirk agonized for his engineer. The poor man obviously had no idea how the woman was going to react.

Romaine started to say something, but it came out as a small halfhearted rasp. She looked down at the table, at the captain, back to Scott. Then she walked away, toward the exit or toward Scott. Both were in the same direction.

She stopped beside him, stared at him long and hard. Her eyes were full, glinting in the soft light of the restaurant. Kirk could see that Scott's were in the same condition. Then everything broke free.

"Damn you, Scotty," Romaine said with a heart-wrenching tremor. She reached out and kissed him.

McCoy leaned over the table, mouthed, "See?", and went back to his bourbon with a self-satisfied smirk.

Uhura was furious. She wasn't simply frustrated that she was only a few hundred kilometers above the best language labs in the Federation, yet compelled to remain at her bridge station. She wasn't upset that taking orders from Lieutenant Abranand was like obeying a trained monkey, and she really couldn't care less about the three nails she had just broken when she tried to pull loose a number-ten crossover board from the service port beneath her communications station. But Commodore Wolfe enraged her. It was one thing for an administrative officer to run roughshod over a starbase, but Wolfe's brand of arbitrary and officious conduct was infuriating. The crew of the *Enterprise* had been through more aggravation together than any ten starbase commodores. What drove that crew was respect, not despotism. Kirk and the other officers understood this implicitly. Wolfe didn't. The mysterious loss of hot water in the commodore's cabin had simply been the first shot fired. Uhura doubted the commodore was going to last much longer on board the *Enterprise.*

"When will you be finished?" Abranand barked over Uhura's shoulder.

The communications officer resisted the urge to apply full power to the circuits she was jumping and blow the board. She could always bat her eyes and claim the lieutenant had startled her. But she also refused to give in to his obnoxiousness. She carefully removed her circuit plaser from the crossover board before answering.

"Two or three minutes and I'll try reconnecting it," she said politely, but without glancing up at Abranand's hulking presence.

"I thought these starships were supposed to be state of the art," the starbase trooper complained, still interfering with Uhura's concentration as she tried to create a custom subspace filter circuit from scratch.

"What makes you think they aren't?" she asked, delicately threading a connecting filament between a quantum four-gate and the first of eight red-banded parallel assistors. She could see Abranand's hand gestures from the corner of her eye.

"Circuit boards, for one thing," he said. "I mean, any twenty-year-old cruiser has the circuit equivalents of your bridge network laid out in a control computer no bigger than a footlocker. All the circuits can be reconfigured, even redesigned, by computer, and here you starship heroes are, rewiring macrocircuits by hand." Abranand snorted.

"Tell me, Lieutenant," she said carefully as she connected a simulator lead to the four-gate and ran a test signal through it, "have you ever seen a twenty-year-old cruiser's circuit complex after it's been hit by a Klingon broad-beam disruptor while traveling at warp seven?" The telltale on the simulator lead glowed green. Uhura had finished the circuit.

"Cruisers can't go at warp seven," Abranand said carefully, as if he were expecting a trick question.

"Well, this ship can, mister. And a disruptor blast that connects can drop it out of warp so fast that any quantum switches that just happen to be tunneling at the microsecond we hit normal space are liable to pop back into existence three meters from where they should be." Uhura stood up from her station and hefted the number-ten board in her hand. "You know where that leaves you?"

Abranand shook his head.

"Sitting around waiting for the Klingons with a circuit complex full of more holes than a light sail in the Coal Sack." She smiled at the lieutenant then and, just for the hell of it, batted her eyes at him, too. "Whereas, we starship heroes have circuits large enough to come out of rapid warp translation in the same shape they went into it, and in the event of circuit-burning power surges, alien force beams, or simply spilled coffee two thousand light-years out from the nearest starbase spare-parts depot, we can rebuild every circuit on this ship by hand. That's what I call state of the art." She pushed her station chair toward the lieutenant as she prepared to kneel down and reinsert the crossover board. "If you'll excuse me."

Abranand grumbled as he walked away, but he didn't make any more cracks about the ship's design characteristics.

Uhura broke a fourth nail snapping the board back home. Okay, she thought, so some design specs did need to be upgraded, but she certainly wasn't going to say anything about it while Wolfe and her troopers were on board.

Uhura sat back in her chair, after prudently leaving the service-port grille on the deck. There was no telling how many more times Wolfe would ask her to attempt something different to try and break through the bizarre interference that was jamming subspace. She pressed her earphone in place and toggled the activation switches—additional, easily repairable mechanical devices—on the bypass filter pad. The frequency was clear!

"Commodore Wolfe," Uhura said as she touched the infraship comm switch. The ship's computer held part of Uhura's voice in memory, scanned the duty rosters to determine where the commodore would be at this time, then routed through Uhura's page to the briefing room before Uhura had finished saying the complete name.

"Wolfe here," came the reply.

"I have a clear channel, Commodore," Uhura said, then pressed the send key that would forward the automatic alert call the commodore had already ordered be the first sent. "The transmission to Admiral Komack is under w—"

A high-pitched squeal blared from Uhura's earphone and she immediately closed the subspace channel.

"What's going on, Lieutenant?" Wolfe demanded.

"The clear channel has been blocked, Commodore. As soon as I started transmitting the jamming began. It has to be deliberate."

Uhura could hear Wolfe take a deep breath. "Very well, Lieutenant, I'm on my way to the bridge. Tell helm and engineering to prepare for a warp-eight jaunt out of the range of the interference. I want us out of here to transmit our messages and get back before anyone knows we're gone. Wolfe out."

Uhura turned to look at the startled faces of the two junior ensigns at the engineering and helm stations. She was the only main watch officer on duty because of the need for her expertise in trying to overcome the subspace interference. "I know, I know," she said to the younger, less experienced officers who in just a few seconds would find themselves in a position where they would be unable to obey a direct command from a commodore.

"What do you know?" Abranand asked.

"The matter/antimatter system is shut down for repairs.

There's no way this ship can be ready for warp in anything less than twenty-four hours." Uhura turned to the engineering and helm officers. "It's all right. It's not your fault the commodore doesn't know the condition of her vessel." Then she smiled sweetly at Abranand again. She could tell it was starting to bother him because he had finally worked out that she wasn't doing it to be polite.

The lift doors swept open and Wolfe and the Andorian commander Farl emerged. Uhura realized that no one else was going to do it unless asked, so she spoke first and told the commodore about the engines. The commodore replied with a word that Uhura had only heard once before when she had seen an Orion trader's trousers catch on fire after he had put too many Spican flame gems in his pocket and they had ignited. Uhura was impressed that the commodore knew such a word, but was disappointed that she would choose to use it.

"Very well, then. Lieutenant Uhura, I want you to check the other transport ships station keeping at this facility and report on their capability for immediate warp travel, including speed and range. I will authorize payment of standard charter rates and arrange for antimatter transfer." The commodore stared at Uhura for a moment, as if she planned to say something more. "Well, what are you waiting for, Lieutenant? That's an order."

"Aye-aye, Commodore," Uhura said grimly as she spun in her chair and initiated the hailing-frequency subroutines on her board. And then she stopped. "Commodore," she said with surprise as she watched the red incoming indicator blink on and off. "I'm receiving a subspace transmission." She flicked the controls that relayed the encoded identifiers transmitted with the message. "From Starfleet Command," she added with even more surprise.

"Put it on the screen, Lieutenant," Wolfe said, and settled into the captain's chair, Farl and Abranand standing respectfully beside her.

Uhura quickly patched the transmission through to the

main viewscreen, then turned in time to see the forward view of the distant Memory Prime asteroid fade out.

At last, the communications officer thought with relief as she recognized the familiar face of Admiral Komack form on the screen, someone is finally going to tell us what's going on.

Chapter Fifteen

"NENSI: YOU ARE in Transition with Eight."

The voice from the speaker was clearly recognizable as that of Pathfinder Eight. Nensi glanced sideways at Romaine, who sat beside him in Garold's interface booth, then replied.

"Is Pathfinder Six available for access?" Nensi asked. This is what had happened before, Eight taking over for Six. Except Nensi would rather speak with the more human-sounding synthetic consciousness.

"Nensi: you are in Transition with Eight."

"Apparently Six isn't available," Nensi muttered to Romaine. She didn't respond but he hadn't expected her to do so. She was obviously still in the throes of remembering her reunion with Mr. Scott less than an hour ago. Nensi had hated asking her to accompany him back to the Interface Chamber but, especially after Kirk's further revelations, he felt the need to enlist the Pathfinders' aid. He cleared his throat and prepared for the most difficult part of the interview.

"As chief administrator of this facility, I request that this conversation be held in private," Nensi announced. "Without Garold's presence."

Pathfinder Eight's decision was seemingly instantaneous.

Garold, sitting hunched in front of the interface console, suddenly shuddered and jerked his silver-tipped fingers from the hand receptacles. The prime interface whirled to Nensi.

"You have gone too far!" he shouted. Shimmering threads of sweat, from exertion or from fear, streaked Garold's half-shaven head, reflecting the galaxy of status lights that ringed the Interface Chamber and shone from the console behind him. "You belong up there!" He waved his glittering hand to the featureless black of the chamber's far ceiling. "The Pathfinders are ours. We understand them. You don't. You can't."

Nensi had not believed any of the interface team was capable of such a show of emotion. Obviously he had misread the depth of their attachment to the Pathfinders they served.

"I'm sorry, Garold," Romaine said. "But as chief technician, I must inform you that Mr. Nensi is acting within regulations and with my full support." Nensi looked between Romaine and Garold. The man's eyes seemed to glow like the console lights surrounding him, mad and feverish.

"Garold, you have no choice," Nensi said calmly. "Don't force the issue any further."

Then Nensi heard footfalls behind him. He turned to see two other members of the interface team at the entrance to the booth. One was a teenage boy who wore his hair in the same style as Garold's. The boy's fingertips were normal but a cranial inducer patch was evident on his left temple—the first step in joining the team. The other was an older woman, skull completely shaven and covered in an intricate tracing of silver filigree. For a moment, Nensi thought the metallic strands were decoration, and then he realized they were circuits. When the woman spoke, her voice was flat and mechanical and came from a small speaker box mounted on her neck.

"Garold, we have been informed. Your compliance has been requested. Please come with us." She held out her hand to Garold, a gesture that Nensi saw as incongruously human, coming from a woman who was half machine herself.

Garold slowly went to the others of the team, the agony of the defeat and the loss he had endured apparent in his stooped shoulders and reluctant gait. He paused at the booth entrance, looked at the beckoning console, then at Nensi.

"We love them," Garold said, "and they love us." Appearing to know no other way of explaining to Nensi what the chief administrator was interfering with, the prime interface left.

Nensi felt chilled by Garold's statement. "Is that true?" he impulsively asked the Pathfinder. If machines could love, then what was it to be human? "Do you love them?"

"Nensi: we love the datalinks. What do you wish to discuss?"

Nensi spoke softly to Romaine. "It's that simple? A synthetic consciousness experiences love and now it's time for the next question? Is this in any of your manuals?" He felt floored by the seemingly trivial revelation that these machines experienced emotion.

Romaine shrugged. "Nothing that I've read of. But then, we can't know if they're just using a term that they've determined brings comfort to the interface team."

"To what purpose?"

"If the interface team members feel good, maybe they're more efficient, easier to work with. I don't know, Sal."

Nensi could see that Romaine was still unnerved about Scott's return. The question of machines that love would have to wait. "Pathfinder Eight," he began, "are you aware of the military emergency that exists in this facility?"

"Nensi: yes."

"Are you also aware of the Starfleet Alpha emergency in effect on the starship *Enterprise?*"

"Nensi: yes."

"Are the two emergencies connected?"

"Nensi: all things are connected at certain levels. Define your operational frame of reference."

Nensi thought for a moment. The last time the machine seemed to have no problem dealing with the vagaries of Standard. Well, if it could love, perhaps it was capable of having a bad day, too.

"Are the emergencies connected by sharing common military and/or political causes?"

"Nensi: yes."

"Please describe the common causes of the emergencies," Nensi said with a sigh. It was like talking to an associate.

There was an uncharacteristic pause before the Pathfinder replied, and for a moment Nensi thought it had decided not to answer.

"Nensi: discussion of the relevant causes of the emergencies requires disclosure of data listed as classified. Such data is accessible within your level of classification. However, Starfleet regulations require that a positive identification be made. Please approach the interface console."

Nensi jumped up and took Garold's chair in front of the console. Now he felt he was getting somewhere.

"Romaine: you are in Transition with Eight. Please approach the interface console."

Romaine walked over to stand beside Nensi.

"Nensi, Romaine: prepare for positive sensor identification. Please place your right hands in the interface receptacles."

Nensi reached out his hand to one of the six narrow slots on the interface console just large enough for a human hand. Romaine reached out and stopped him.

"Pathfinder," she said quickly, "we are not equipped with interface leads."

"Nensi, Romaine: that fact is known. Please place your right hands in the interface receptacles."

"Explain the purpose of that action." Romaine was not letting go of Nensi's arm. Her expression was set and serious and Nensi knew better than to question her.

"Romaine: positive identification is required before discussion of classified data."

"Match our voices," Romaine said. Nensi folded his arms across his chest. Romaine obviously had good reason not to want them to place their hands in the receptacles and he wasn't going to argue with her. This was her area of expertise.

"Romaine: voiceprints can be forged."

Romaine put her hand on Nensi's shoulder and squeezed as if looking for support from her friend. Nensi looked up at her questioningly, unsure of what she was planning.

"Pathfinder, identify yourself," she said.

"Romaine: you are in Transition with Eight."

"Pathfinder, you are in violation of your contract. Identify yourself . . . truthfully." Nensi coughed in astonishment. If the Pathfinders could love, lie, and impersonate one another, life in Transition must be no different from life in Datawell.

Now there was a longer pause. Nensi even heard the speaker click on and off as if a connection were being broken, then, upon reconsideration, reconnected.

"What was that all about?" Nensi said to Romaine after a moment, whispering as if he didn't want to be overheard.

"That wasn't Pathfinder Eight," she said, studying the flares of color that drifted across the console's nonstandard screen. "First I could sense it was lying again, and then that it wasn't even the consciousness it said it was."

"But how could you know?" Nensi asked in bewilderment.

Romaine shook her head. "I'm not sure," she admitted. "Probably speech construction or something. Eight is an old personality. Used to be the shipmind on an old pre-Federation exploration vessel. It has a very clipped, abrupt speech characteristic probably left over from the constraints they had back then on sending data back by tight beam radio. It's never bothered to reconfigure those original parameters."

Nensi went over the conversation in his mind. "Seemed the same to me. And surely any of the other Pathfinders has enough computational power to mimic any speech pattern." Romaine had a point but hadn't thought it through properly, Nensi felt.

Romaine waved his protest away. "Just a minute," she said, and touched some panels on the console. A viewscreen flickered into life beside the receptacles. Nensi recognized another member of the interface team on the screen, a short Centauran with, surprisingly, a full head of hair. However, when his voice came over the screen speaker, Nensi could see that the man's lips didn't move.

"Interface control," the Centauran said.

"Romaine here, interface booth six. What's the interface load right now, Zalan?"

Zalan's eyes never left their front and center focus on the sensor camera. "Zero," he said—*transmitted* would be more accurate, Nensi thought. "All interface connections were suspended ninety-six seconds ago."

"Explanation?" Romaine asked. Obviously she chose to use the interface team's abrupt pattern of speech when dealing with them, Nensi realized. Perhaps that's why she was sensitive to a change in the false Pathfinder Eight's speech characteristics.

"None at this time," Zalan replied. "All units are currently addressing the problem."

"Transmit all data to my office and contact me when you have a likely explanation." Romaine clicked off without a word.

"Have they gone on strike?" Nensi asked when it became apparent that Romaine wasn't going to turn away from the readouts on the console screens.

"No. They're busy in there," she said, pointing to a fluctuating red and yellow graph. "This indicates that their work load is running at close to ninety-eight percent of their reported capacity." She turned to narrow her eyes at Nensi. "Which *we* know is only about ten to twenty percent of their real capacity. But however you add it up, one of them in there is interfacing with something out here. Come on."

Romaine headed out the door of the interface booth and

started to jog around the central equipment core of the interface chamber. Twelve booths ringed it, and within a minute she had seen that every one was empty. She hit a call button on a wall-mounted comm panel. Zalan appeared on the screen once more.

"Romaine in the chamber. Give me a visual on the I/O room."

Nensi saw the screen instantly flash to shifting views of the main data-exchange installation, where huge banks of equipment blindly fed in the monstrous data load from throughout the known galaxy to the Pathfinder facility and equally massive storage banks captured the Pathfinders' output for transmission to Prime research terminals and other nodes in the memory planet network. The status lights on every unit indicated the full system had shut down.

"Now give me the capacity-load graph," Romaine said, and the screen repeated the shifting red and yellow display that she had called up on the booth's console. Nensi saw that the values on it hadn't appreciably changed. "It's interfacing!" Romaine said sharply. "But how?"

"Backup units? Terminals topside?" Nensi suggested.

"Not possible," Romaine cut him off. "The Pathfinder system is completely separated from the outside universe. All equipment and personnel get in and out by transporter. Data transmissions are funneled through a one-way subspace short-range downlink and the only data that gets out has to be stored in the I/O room, then passed physically on wafers and wires to be transferred. There are no other facilities for direct link-up to the Pathfinders."

Nensi watched the graph flickering on the screen. If anything, the values were stronger.

"That you know of," he said softly.

Chapter Sixteen

ADMIRAL KOMACK SMILED as his image resolved on the bridge's main viewscreen. His blue eyes sparkled and his white hair was trimmed short in a much younger man's style.

Uhura immediately judged his smile to be a good sign. Things would be getting back to normal now, she was sure.

"Commodore Wolfe," the admiral began, "I'm sorry to have taken so long to break Starfleet interference to get to you. I trust all is well."

Uhura's eyes narrowed. Starfleet was causing the subspace jamming? But why? And more importantly, how? Uhura was confident she knew almost everything that could be known about subspace technology and she couldn't even begin to guess how selective jamming could be accomplished without rewriting the physics manuals. She quickly scanned her board and saw with consternation that despite Komack's clear signal, every other channel was still torn apart by impenetrable interference. She wished Mr. Spock were at his station instead of locked in the brig with a library reader. He would enjoy a problem such as this. She shook her head, deep in thought.

"Why is Command generating the subspace jamming, Admiral?" Wolfe asked.

"As you know," Komack replied, "Starfleet has reason to suspect an act of terrorism will be committed on Memory Prime during the Nobel and Z.Magnees Prize ceremonies. Intelligence feels that the terrorists are part of a well-organized group. It is probable that some of the terrorists are in place on Prime, but unknown to each other and requiring outside instructions in order to carry out their plan. By blanking out all subspace transmissions, we hope to make those instructions impossible to receive."

That sounded reasonable to Uhura, even if the method should be impossible. Wolfe appeared to accept the admiral's explanation, too.

"Do you have any other evidence that would further serve to link the science officer to the terrorist organization?" Wolfe asked.

"Not at this time," Komack answered.

"Do you have new orders for us, sir?"

"Again, not at this time. Federation security services are working with Starfleet to uncover the organization at other locations. In the meantime, we will continue to blank out subspace communications in the vicinity of Memory Prime. You are to carry on as before."

"How can we contact each other with subspace jammed?"

Uhura could tell Wolfe wasn't meant for starship duty. Just the intimation of being out of contact with Command was enough to make her nervous. Too bad Komack doesn't seem to notice, Uhura thought.

"Set your incoming beacon to a class-eight random scan. Command will intercept and transmit whenever we have something new to pass along. You will be able to contact me by transmitting a class-two query on this channel when necessary. We will interrupt the jamming at irregular though frequent intervals to look for your transmissions. When we see one, we'll immediately get back to you as we are doing right now." Komack explained the procedure as if it were no more than a standard operations drill. "Just remember that the Alpha emergency still holds, so you're required to restrict your communications to those necessary for the immediate mission. Any other questions?"

"Not at this time, Admiral," Wolfe said, tapping her fingers on the arm of the captain's chair.

"Very good, Commodore Wolfe. Continue doing your duty for Starfleet and the security of the Federation. Commendations will be in order for you and your crew when this is all over with. Admiral out."

The screen rippled back to show Memory Prime as a black splotch against the starfield, glittering with the lights that ringed its semicircle of seven domes.

"What a load of tribble droppings," Wolfe said loudly enough for all to hear.

Uhura couldn't resist. "Tribbles don't leave droppings, Commodore."

"Exactly," Wolfe said as she spun in her chair to face Uhura, making Abranand jump to the side. "Nothing! Which is what that brass-hulled dunsel just gave us. I don't believe it. I don't believe it." She let the chair swing her back to the screen, then stepped down.

"What don't you believe?" Uhura asked, though she expected Wolfe to simply order her to mind her own business.

"Look, Lieutenant," Wolfe explained as she stood on the steps leading to the upper deck and the turbolift, "there's obviously a very important operation under way here. You of all people must know that the selective jamming Komack just admitted to should be impossible. A whole new technology is being used here and I'm not being told what it is. 'Continue doing your duty!'" she parroted. "What does he think I am? A wet-behind-the-ears pup like those two?" The commodore waved a thumb behind her at the ensigns at the helm and engineering stations. Uhura winced for them.

The commodore stormed to the lift doors. They sprang open, but Wolfe turned on her heel and addressed herself to the whole bridge crew.

"I don't know what it was Kirk was doing on this ship that gave it such a miserable rep, but he sure as hell isn't going to rub his bad command decisions off on me. I've got my full retirement benefits coming and I intend to collect them." She whirled back into the turbolift just as a warning beep sounded from the helm's ship's status sensors.

"What now?" Wolfe snapped as she stepped forward to block the closing lift doors.

The wet-behind-the-ears pup at the helm control read the sensor light. "Unauthorized transportation, Commodore. Infraship."

The cause was obvious, even to Wolfe. She raced to the command chair. "*Full shields now!*" she shouted as she hit the security call button on the chair's arm. "Security to the brig on the double!" She twisted back to the frantic ensign at the engineering station. "Where are those shields, mister?"

"Too late," the helmsman said. He turned to look at the commodore. Uhura was glad to see he wasn't smiling. "Transporter has shut down. Successful transmission."

Wolfe looked as if she were ready to breathe fire. "So help me," she said in an iron voice, "if I find that your pointy-eared Vulcan shipmate had any help at all in staging this—*any!*—I'll scuttle this ship and everyone on it. Do I make myself clear?"

The crew responded that she did.

"You," Wolfe said, pointing to the ensign at engineering. "Confined to quarters and downgraded two ratings." She turned to Uhura. "Who's the transporter chief on duty?"

"Kyle," Uhura said. Unfortunately there was no way to keep the information from Wolfe; the computer could answer just as easily.

"Have security take him to the brig for dereliction of duty and—"

Uhura had had enough. At the rate the commodore was going through bridge crew, soon she'd have no choice but to get Chekov and Sulu up there again, hesitations and all. "Commodore, I protest! You cannot—"

"*Yes I can!*" Wolfe drowned Uhura out. "Lieutenant Abranand, place this woman under arrest as suspected accessory to the escape of a dangerous prisoner."

Uhura threw her receiver on her chair and shut down her board. Around the bridge, other crew started to rise from their stations, glaring at Wolfe.

"Just try it," Wolfe told them, sweeping her gaze across them all. "Any of you. All of you. I just don't care. The hangar deck is big enough to hold the whole damn crew and I'll arrest all of you if you think it will make your captain happy."

The crew held their places.

"It's all right," Uhura said. "Sit down."

They sat. Wolfe was fuming. She turned to Farl, whom Uhura had noticed trying to stay uninvolved in what the Andorian undoubtedly felt was threatening to become a mutiny.

"Commander, I want your men to enforce a recall of all *Enterprise* personnel on leave on Prime. That's an order."

Farl saluted and marched to the turbolift. Wolfe gloated as Abranand escorted Uhura to the lift as well.

"Believe me, Lieutenant," Wolfe said, "by the time I'm finished with this ship, your captain isn't going to know what hit him. Count on it."

"That's the difference between you and Captain Kirk," Uhura said.

"What's that?"

"His crew *can* count on him. And he's never let us down yet."

"Is that a threat, Lieutenant?"

Uhura smiled coldly. "It doesn't have to be. It's the truth."

Kirk paced the floor in the communal area of Salman Nensi's quarters. He was incapable of sitting still as his mind turned over all the possibilities he was faced with. Nensi and Romaine had brought him, McCoy, and Scott, to the chief administrator's residence in order to add a third major piece to the puzzle: the synthetic consciousnesses known as the Pathfinders, the only known independent machine intelligences sanctioned by law to exist in the

Federation, were somehow involved in the complex web of mystery that had drawn together the *Enterprise* and Memory Prime.

Another idea suddenly came to the captain and he stopped his pacing to question Nensi.

"Is there any chance that another program—a thirteenth consciousness—has been inserted into the Pathfinder complex?" Kirk asked. "Perhaps the intelligence itself could be the terrorists' weapon. At the proper time, it could crash a turbolift, shut off life support. . . ." Kirk held his hands out as if to gather comments.

"No chance at all," Romaine said. "First of all, the Pathfinders can't be programmed in the traditional sense. New synthetic consciousnesses can be added to the facility, but only with the full compliance of the entire interface team. Plus the whole I/O system would have to be shut down, manual connections made; no way it could be done without disrupting the entire base. Additionally, the Pathfinders have no direct link to the outside. There's no possible way they can control any of the systems in Prime."

"Why all the elaborate safeguards?" Kirk asked, sorry to see his theory shot down.

"Well, the programming safeguard is for the Pathfinders' protection. Like humans having the right not to have brain surgery without giving their consent, and then only having it performed by trained physicians under safe conditions. If something goes wrong with their hardware, Captain, those consciousnesses will die. Under those circumstances, the safeguards aren't elaborate. They're necessary."

"But surely they can be backed up," Scott asked. "They *are* just impulses in circuitry, after all."

Romaine smiled at him. "Just as the human mind is impulses in protein circuitry, Scotty. Yet we can't back ourselves up." She took Scott's hand but looked back to the captain. "That was one of the turning points of the Synthetic Revolt on Titan. A probeshipmind, realizing that the old Sol Council wasn't going to budge on its rulings that machine consciousnesses were commodities, backed itself up in a public databank in Iceland and thrust straight into the Sun. The backup was notarized to prove it contained all the data that the original shipmind had contained and could carry out the same autonomous equipment maintenance subroutines, but it had no personality, no consciousness—"

"No soul," McCoy added.

"A bit romantic, perhaps, but close enough to the core of their arguments. We know now that a synthetic consciousness must develop from a smaller, self-generating seed program. A full synthetic consciousness backup, when stored, loses that impetus to thought, the flow of current through circuitry. When the data pattern is frozen in storage, there is as yet no way to make it become self-aware again, any more than a vat filled with all the chemical components of a human body can spontaneously come to life. It has to grow and be nurtured from an embryonic form.

"Anyway, the shipmind's experiment was controversial. The opponents of the Freedom for Synthetics movement claimed it was all programming trickery, that the probe ship hadn't made a complete backup copy of itself, that it hadn't been installed on board the ship that burned up in the sun. But the gesture—the suicide, if you will—was enough to tip the balance at the polls. The Worlds Court ruled that if an intelligence could die, then by definition it must have been alive. The resolution banning the ownership of synthetic consciousnesses was passed just as the Federation was born. Our strict edicts against slavery have always been applied to self-aware machines as well as self-aware biological creatures, and now, more than ever, energy matrices as well."

"So with all that concern for their well-being, why aren't the Pathfinders allowed to have more control over their environment?" Kirk asked.

"Oh, they have complete control over *their* environment, Captain," Romaine said. "They can do whatever they want within the confines of their circuits, what they call the world of Transition. We just don't want them to have any control over *our* environment."

"Leftovers from the Titan massacre, I suppose," McCoy said.

"Partly," Romaine agreed. "When those domes opened, thousands of workers were killed, and people don't tend to forget things like that. But mostly it's because the risk is too great that the Pathfinders might make a mistake. Again, not from their point of view but from ours." She looked back to Kirk. "Captain, it's common knowledge that almost all Starfleet vessels have the capacity for self-destruction, but how many officers actually have the authority to initiate it?"

"Classified," Kirk said with a smile, "though the point is taken. I doubt if any of my crew would misuse the authority to order self-destruct or any other potentially harmful procedure, but by limiting access to those procedures we do limit the possibilities for tragic errors."

"So," Nensi said after a moment, "history lessons aside, we need to find another common link to unite all the pieces in our puzzle." He checked them off on his fingers. "Pathfinders. Memory Prime military emergency. *Enterprise* Alpha emergency."

"Already linked by hints of an assassination attempt," Scott added, "Nobel and Z.Magnees Prize nominees, and . . .?" He trailed off, trying to think of what other events merited inclusion in the list.

"Those are the broad conditions," Kirk said, pacing once more. "Damn, we could use Spock down here." He paused again. "Spock's arrest. The name or term T'Pel. What do they add to the equation?"

Romaine abruptly leaned forward and let go of Scott's hand. "Three of the Vulcans on my staff were placed under arrest by Commander Farl just before you arrived," she said.

"What are their names?" Kirk asked excitedly.

"Specialist Lieutenant Stell, Specialist First-Class Slaan, and Dr. T'Lar," Romaine recited. "A computer technician, computer technology historian, and a paleoexobiologist, respectively."

"Now we're getting somewhere," Kirk said. "Two Vulcan

computer specialists and Spock is a Vulcan computer specialist. That's a connection."

"Then why was a paleoexobiologist arrested, too, Jim?" McCoy asked.

"And of the four other Vulcans on my staff, three of them are also computer specialists." Romaine shrugged at the disappointment Kirk struggled to hide on his face. "Sorry, but what do you expect at the Federation's largest computer complex?"

Kirk rubbed his hands over his face. "And no one else, no other Vulcans were arrested on the other ships transporting nominees here?"

"No," Nensi said, suddenly thoughtful, "but some of the commanders did point out that they were operating with less than full crews. Let me check to see if there's a pattern among the crew members left behind." He got up and went to the kitchen area, where a private wall comm hung.

"And ask about the reasons why the crew was left behind," Kirk called after him. "Vulcans, Vulcans. Starfleet was worried that a Vulcan might have been involved in a threatened act of assassination. But why just *some* Vulcans? Why not all?"

"What reason did they give when Spock was arrested?" Romaine asked.

"Suspicion of involvement in the dilithium burnout," Scott answered. "A crock if I ever heard one."

"And what's going to happen to him?" Romaine continued.

"He'll be held until he can be turned over to appropriate Starfleet authorities," Kirk said, resuming his pacing.

"What sort of appropriate Starfleet authorities?" Romaine pressed on.

Kirk answered without considering where the woman was going with her questions. "Starbase, I suppose," he said.

"Prime could be a Starbase," Romaine said.

Kirk stopped in midpace.

"It's a *base,*" Romaine explained. "And it *is* under Starfleet authority."

Kirk walked over to Romaine and held his hands out as if he planned to lift her by her ears and kiss her. Fortunately, he checked his enthusiasm.

"And *you're* the base commander," he said. "Brilliant!"

Scotty looked confused.

"The lass is . . ." He turned to Romaine beside him. "You're the commander?"

"It's political," she said to him. To the captain she added, "But only in a nonmilitary capacity."

"Spock isn't Starfleet military personnel," Kirk said, trying out his ideas as he voiced them. "Technically he's scientific services and the alleged attempted-assassination victim was a nonmilitary scientist." He turned to McCoy, eyes twinkling. "It sounds like a *civil* offense to me. Definitely nonmilitary and therefore within Mira's jurisdiction. What do you think, Bones?"

McCoy nodded. "Go for it, Jim. With any luck Commander Farl will be out on maneuvers and won't be able to answer Wolfe's frenzied inquiries. Which I'm sure she'll make."

"Are you up to taking on the Starfleet bureaucracy?" Kirk asked Romaine.

She pointed to the kitchen, where Nensi leaned over a counter, talking earnestly into a handset. "Taught by experts," she said. "Bureaucracy is Uncle Sal's middle name."

"Good," Kirk said, "good." He clapped his hands together, a decision made. He looked over to McCoy. "Well, Bones, you were right again. Out on the frontier, we'd go in with phasers blazing, but here we are, achieving victory by wrapping up the enemy with red tape. How's that for doing things within the system?"

"Achieving victory, Jim?" McCoy pulled himself out of the chair that had appeared ready to absorb him. "You're talking as if we've already won."

"Believe me, doctor, if I didn't think we were going to win, we'd still be sitting around trying to come up with another good idea instead of getting set to beam back up and spring Spock."

Kirk flipped open his communicator and checked to see that Nensi was prepared for what was coming. The chief administrator replaced the handset on the wall comm and headed back to the communal area. Kirk's communicator chirped as it opened the beam back channel.

"Kirk to *Enterprise,*" the captain announced. "Five to beam up, Mr. Kyle. These coordinates."

Kirk slipped the communicator back onto his belt. The five of them stood silently in the apartment, waiting for the transporter beam to lock on.

After a few seconds of silence, McCoy reached out to touch Kirk's arm. "This delay isn't right, Jim."

"Aye," Scotty said.

Kirk reached back for his communicator again. He didn't have to say anything. He knew from their expressions that both Scotty and McCoy saw the understanding, the agreement in his eyes.

The transporter chime finally started just as Kirk was about to call back up, but its arrival did nothing to change his feeling that something had gone terribly wrong on board his ship.

The corridor leading to the brig was lined with five of Wolfe's starbase troopers and Kirk felt his rage expand exponentially with each additional trooper who appeared in Spock's cell. Spock himself was nowhere to be seen, but Commodore Wolfe was. She was watching carefully as a technician explained something to her on the library reader on Spock's desk. Kirk recognized the technician as Ensign Bregman, a trainee from Kyle's department.

"If you've let anything happen to Spock, Commodore, I'll—"

"Save the mutiny for your court-martial, Captain." The tone Wolfe used to cut him off told Kirk her anger was no less than his own. "Your innocent science officer just escaped."

Kirk was completely taken off guard. He stepped to the side as Romaine, Nensi, Scott, and McCoy crowded into the cell behind him. Commander Farl leaned against the far wall as if he hoped no one would see him.

"Escaped? How?" Kirk asked. He checked the security field frame around the doorway and saw it was intact.

"Beamed himself down," Wolfe said. "Hooked into the transporter controls from his library reader." She glared at Kirk. "The one *you* were so anxious to give him."

"Now wait just a minute," Scott said, pushing his way through the knot of people to get close to Wolfe. "I know every circuit on this ship and there's no way the transporter can be controlled by a reader. I'd stake my reputation on it."

Wolfe laughed cynically. "You don't have a reputation anymore, Mr. Engineer. None of you do. This whole ship should be fumigated, then opened to space." She turned to the technician who had been pointing to the reader's screen. "Again," she ordered.

"Um, as near as I can figure out," Ensign Bregman began, "Mr. Spock didn't actually control the transporter *from* the reader, but he did set up a snowball chain in the simulations program library."

"A snowball chain?" McCoy asked dubiously.

"That's where one small program runs a slightly larger one, which runs an even larger one, and so on until a huge complex program is up and running. You see, he must have called up transporter simulation programs from the education upgrade files. The reader won't allow programming but does permit a user to store certain variables in the simulation files for playback of customized scenarios at a later time, so Mr. Spock set up all the coordinates he needed for a simulated transporter room to lock on to him here. See?" Bregman pointed to the screen again. "Here are the exact simulations he used with the coordinates of this cell still entered."

Scott, Wolfe, Kirk, and Romaine crowded together to peer at the small screen and the flowchart the technician drew on it. He showed how Spock had chained the transporter simulations with a wargame scenario that postulated that the hard-wired communication channels within the ship had been severed by enemy fire. That was chained to a rescue simulation in which ship mechanism controls usually monitored and adjusted by direct connection were instead remotely controlled by extremely short-range subspace transmissions. That, in turn was chained to a programming bypass simulation that had the ship's computer damaged and capable only of carrying out direct requests. In this case, the direct requests were set up to be read from the transporter simulation.

Five more subsystem wiring-and-repair simulations joined the chain until only one two-line piece of code remained at the top of the snowball's path.

"And what do those two lines of code do?" Kirk asked just as he heard Scotty exhale with a combination of surprise and what sounded like admiration.

"It's just a small software flag that warns the computer that everything that follows is a simulation." The technician dropped his voice. "Mr. Spock overwrote it by storing some of his library files in the wrong memory locations. The computer queried him but it accepted his priority override to allow him to commit the error."

"The same override that lets me run the engines at warp eight when the computer says we dinna hae the power," Scott said, shaking his head.

"So the computer operated all the controls on the real equipment and beamed him out," Bregman said.

"But it still doesn't explain how he found another place to beam to," Scott complained. "None of the ship's simulations would hold the exact coordinates for beaming down to Memory Prime, and even Mr. Spock couldn't calculate them without a locator beam."

"He didn't have to," Commander Farl said dryly from the side of the cell. "All he had to do was get within a few kilometerss of Prime on a low-path beam and our combat transporterss automatically pulled in hiss signal." Farl sighed. "I have two unconsciouss trooperss by a transfer-point pad. The pad'ss log showss it received an incoming signal fifteen minutess ago. The same time as the Vulcan'ss unauthorized beam-down wass detected. He iss on Memory Prime."

Kirk was filled with conflicting emotions. Spock would not defy Starfleet authority so brazenly by escaping what even he had admitted was legal, if improper, incarceration. Whatever had prompted him to act so out of character had to be big. Disastrously big. But whatever else he did or had to do, Kirk did not want to give any information at all to Wolfe. For some reason she had turned her "temporary" command of the *Enterprise* into a vendetta.

"Well," Kirk said as he stepped back to leave the cell, "it's a small facility and Chief Technician Romaine and Mr. Nensi know it well. I don't think there'll be any problem in our finding him."

"Just a minute," Wolfe said, stopping him as he directed his entourage to the door. "You're not going anywhere."

Kirk turned to face her. The cell was completely silent as the faceoff began. "I am going back to Memory Prime to locate my first officer," he told her.

"All off-duty personnel are restricted to this ship, Captain."

"I'm not off duty."

"You are now, Captain. You're sure not commanding this ship any longer."

Kirk had had enough. "You cannot relieve me of command on my own ship, Commodore."

"Alpha emergency, Kirk. You're under my orders for the duration."

"Without Starfleet confirmation of those orders," Kirk recited, "it is my opinion that you might be endangering the health and safety of my crew, without proper authority."

Instantly both Wolfe and Kirk turned to McCoy.

"I'm sure the ship's medical officer might find that grounds for relieving *you* of *your* command," Kirk continued.

"This ship has no medical officer," Wolfe countered. "Dr. McCoy, you are relieved of duty for suspicion of aiding in a prisoner's escape. Next move's yours, Captain. Want to see how many more it takes before you're in here in place of your science officer?"

Kirk knew enough to back off if it meant keeping his freedom. That could be the key to another confrontation, one that he could orchestrate and win. But not here, and not now.

"All right, Commodore," he said, holding his hands as if to show he wasn't armed. "For the duration." He watched as she looked around the room once more, making sure all of her people met her eyes to acknowledge that she had squared off against the fabled James T. Kirk and had won.

"Good boy," she said icily. "Maybe Command will just accept a resignation and let you crawl off quietly." Then she turned away and called to Farl. "Prepare to have the search parties fan out from the pad the Vulcan landed at," she said. "You can have five troopers from my contingent to help with the operation." Farl began whispering in an Andorian combat dialect into his battle helmet communicator.

Kirk started backing out of the cell. He had to organize his response for when Spock was returned to the ship and they could plan their next move together. But he stopped, blood freezing in his veins when he heard Farl's next question and the commodore's response.

"Disposition of the prisoner when he iss recaptured?" Farl asked.

"There will be no prisoner, Commander Farl," Wolfe stated plainly. "With who we've got down on Memory Prime, we can't afford to take any more chances. At my order, when your troopers run the escaped prisoner to ground, I want your phasers set to force three."

She turned to stare directly into Kirk's eyes.

"To kill," she said.

Chapter Seventeen

THE KLINGONS LOVED to tell the story of al Fred ber'nhard Nob'l, the *tera'ngan* inventor who, as had happened so many times on so many worlds, once felt he had gone too far and had created the ultimate weapon.

Faced with nightmares of a world ruined by the destructive forces he had called into being, Nob'l attempted to salve his conscience and bring forth the best in humans by using the profits from his inventions to award prizes in honor of the most outstanding achievements in science and peace. Of course, in typical *tera'ngan* fashion, as the Klingons were quick to point out, those profits were not set aside for that purpose until *after* the inventor's death.

As the long Terran years passed, Nob'l's inventions served the warlords of Earth well. Despite his fears, other ultimate weapons came and went with predictable regularity—mustard gas, fusion bombs, particle curtains, and smart bacteria—until his devices lay beside the rocks and sharpened sticks in museums. In fact, and this invariably had the Klingons brushing the tears of laughter from their eyes no matter how many times they heard the story, the only real casualty of the great Terran wars fueled by Nob'l's inventions over the century in which his prizes were awarded, were the prizes themselves. *Three* times they were suspended because of hostilities between nations. The third time, as Earth shuddered beneath the multiple onslaughts of its warriors Klingons admired most—k'Han and g'Reen—the suspended prizes were not resurrected, and lay buried amid the ashes of so much of the Earth that the Klingons considered foul and weak and better lost.

For the events a few light-years removed from Earth, the Klingons had a bit more respect. Two centuries before Nob'l lay awake in foolish terror over destroying his world with a few tonnes of $C_3H_5(NO_3)_3$, the warlord Zalar Mag'nees, ruler of her planet's greatest city state, realized that the nature of combat in her world was changing and that ideas as well as strength and armaments must be brought to battle.

Mag'nees established an elaborate educational system designed to attract the greatest intellects among her citizens to the problems of war. Those who contributed the best new work achieved the highest honor: a commission in the warlord's personal corps of scientists.

Under her rule, with the brilliant work of her honored scientists and engineers, the whole of the planet was soon united, or conquered, as the Klingons told it, under one ruler. Though the warlord's commissions were discontinued after almost two centuries of global peace and their war-born heritage forgotten, the philosophy of subterfuge and protective concealment that had proved so useful in establishing the undisputed rule of Mag'nees, still pervaded all levels of her planet's society. Thus, when electromagnetic communication systems were discovered, it went without question that the signals would travel by wire instead of by atmospheric transmissions open to any unsuspected enemy's receivers. Power plants were buried as a matter of course and fiberoptic transmission of all signals was enthusiastically adopted as soon as the technology became available. It was this inborn need for concealment that prevented *tera'ngan* scientists, in almost a century of scanning, from ever picking up the slightest datum that would indicate that a comparable, perhaps even related civilization was thriving in the Alpha Centauran system, fewer than five light-years distant.

The Klingons bitterly regretted that circumstance of history. For when at last the first slower-than-light Earth ship arrived in the Centauran system, the *tera'ngan* humans were too tired of war, the *centaur'ngan* humans long unschooled. To the Klingons' everlasting disappointment, in this one instance of first contact, unlike most others, peace was inevitable.

In the decades that followed, as the two planets discovered all the suspicious similarities between them, cultural and scientific exchange programs burgeoned. Zeyafram Co'akran's brilliant insights into warp theory were applied at the venerable Massachusetts Institute of Technology on Earth, and within seven years of the two planets' first contact, the light barrier had fallen before their mutual onslaught. Plays and literature were easily translated and meaningful to the two races and, hinting at interference from another spacefaring race thousands of years earlier, interbreeding was simple and pleasurable to all concerned, requiring none of the heroic efforts that would later be needed by humans and Vulcans.

More and more the two cultures grew together. Common goals were quickly decided and impressively established. The joint colonization of the second life-bearing world in the Centauran system was accomplished with goodwill and an almost unbelievable absence of territorial discord. Klingon psychologists who had studied that abnormal enterprise felt the experience was what had most influenced the incomprehensible optimism and peaceful nature of the Federation when it was first formed.

As the *tera'ngan* and *centaur'ngan* association grew, both looked to their pasts and dusted off the legacy of Nob'l and Mag'nees. Freed of their military legacy, joined in the best wishes of two worlds, and expanded to include sciences unimagined at the time the awards were first created, the Nob'l and Z.Mag'nees Prizes became the first human competition to celebrate the achievements, scientific and cultural, of two different worlds, and drive them forward in peace.

Upon its formation, the Federation Council eagerly accepted authority over the competition, opening it up to all members of all species. In an interplanetary association in which athletic competitions had ceased to have any meaning, except among those rare few who voluntarily chose to restrict themselves to absolutely identical advantages of gravity, genetics, and pharmaceutical enhancement, the Nob'l and Z.Mag'nees competition of the mind quickly came to stand for all the ideals for which the Federation strove. Calling on another ancient tradition, the prizes were awarded every four standard years. The winners, chosen through secret ballot by their peers who shared in the nomination for each prize, were among the most honored of Federation citizens. And true to the Federation's long-term goals, pressure was mounting to offer the Klingons a chance to participate.

The Klingons, not surprisingly, would have nothing to do with the Nob'l and Z.Mag'nees Prizes. The whole concept of the competition was alien and repugnant to them. The Klingons *did* have their own competitions for scientific achievement that, on first study, seemed somewhat similar to the Federation's awards; each decade on Klinzhai, a great celebration was held for those workers who had won the coveted Emperor's Decoration for Science in Aid of Destruction of the Enemy.

The Klingons could easily understand the concept of honoring the winners, but what they could never comprehend was why, in the human competition, the losers were allowed to *live.*

Chapter Eighteen

KIRK SMILED BROADLY as he walked down the corridor leading to the brig. McCoy accompanied him but certainly wasn't grinning; in fact he was having trouble keeping the scowl off his face.

"It'll be all right, Bones," Kirk said, elbowing his friend in the side. "Trust me."

McCoy rolled his eyes. "Remind me to do that when we're locked up on Tantalus playing poker with each other for twenty years."

Kirk and McCoy rounded the corner to the corridor that ran to the holding cells. As Kirk had been able to determine by checking the ship's computer, only two of Wolfe's troopers remained stationed there. The others who had been milling around, investigating Spock's escape twenty minutes ago, were already down on Memory Prime, searching for Spock, their phasers set to kill.

"Sergeant Gilmartin," Kirk said in a friendly tone. "We're back. General Regulation Document two hundred and twenty-seven again. Paragraphs B and C."

Gilmartin turned to look at the other trooper standing at attention on the other side of the holding-cell door. Kirk glanced through the open doorway, its perimeter glowing with the security-field frame, and nodded slightly to Uhura, indicating that she should go along with whatever was to happen next.

Gilmartin turned back to Kirk. "Begging the captain's pardon, sir, but I believe Dr. McCoy has been relieved of duty." The trooper looked nervous but he was bound to follow his orders.

"As chief medical officer," Kirk agreed. "But he's still a doctor and able to act as such." Kirk read the trooper's eyes for a moment, then continued. "I'm Lieutenant Uhura's counsel now and she is entitled to a medical examination while being held. Regulations require it."

Gilmartin took a deep breath. "I'll have to check it out with the commodore, Captain."

"I wouldn't expect you not to, Sergeant," Kirk said graciously, and gestured to the intercom panel.

As Gilmartin stepped over to the intercom, it was clear that talking to the commodore was the last thing he wanted to do. Kirk stepped in front of the holding-cell doorway and lifted his hand as if to wave in greeting to Uhura. Then he brought his arm down and around the neck of the second trooper by the side of the doorway and flipped him into the security field.

Gilmartin spun at the sound of the crackling repulser screen just as McCoy held a spray hypo to his neck. By the time Gilmartin could bring his hand up to try and knock the hypo away, it was too late. McCoy gently lowered the trooper to the ground and Kirk caught the second guard, now unconscious, as he bounced back from the field. Then the captain went back to the doorway to speak to Uhura.

"Listen very carefully," he said quickly. "A contingent of troopers is hunting for Spock on Memory Prime. With orders to kill." He paused a moment to let that sink in. "All *Enterprise* personnel are ordered restricted to the ship. McCoy, Scott, and I are disobeying those orders and going down to try and locate Spock before the troopers do. We'll have help down there, but no matter what happens, we will be disobeying a direct order from a superior officer. Do you understand?"

Uhura's expression was serious but displayed no fear. "Yes sir," she said.

"The best that can happen to us is that we will save Spock's life and he will then be proven innocent of all charges. In that case, those of us who left the ship to find him will be given severe reprimands and probably lose rank. For what it's worth, I believe there's a good chance that the commodore has either misunderstood her orders or has received false ones. We can't use that as a defense, but it might make Starfleet more lenient." Kirk paused to consider his next words. "Nyota, this is not an order. It can't be an order. But I could use your help."

Uhura began to reply but Kirk shook his head and held up a silencing finger.

"As long as this field is on and you remain in the cell," he told her, "you're safe and protected. As soon as the field goes off, you're on the run with us. Understand?"

"Understood, sir," Uhura said evenly. "Request permission to accompany the captain."

Scott was standing by in the starboard cargo transporter room when McCoy, Kirk, and Uhura rushed in.

"Ready, Scotty?" Kirk asked as he passed out the small hand phasers and communicators that Scott had brought.

"Aye, Captain," Scott replied, checking the chronometer on the transporter console. "Fifteen more seconds. Coordinates are set for Mr. Nensi's office."

Kirk, McCoy, and Uhura quickly took their places. Exactly fifteen seconds after Scott had given the chronometer's reading, the light strips flickered and the engineer's hands flew over the controls.

"What was that?" Uhura asked as the lights came back to normal intensity.

"Och," Scott said as he ran to the oversized platform. "That was a clumsy ensign who just happened to drop a circuit plaser on a disassembled junction switch in a forward Jeffries tube."

"What does that do?"

Scott smiled as the transporter effect sparkled around him.

"It shuts down the shields, lass," he said, and they were gone.

Kirk and Scotty materialized on a two-pad portable combat transporter in a small equipment storage bay. Two starbase troopers in full battle armor were waiting for them, phaser rifles at the ready, the impenetrable black visor of their helmets making each look like an impassive Cyclops.

Without having to be told, Kirk and Scotty raised their hands above their heads.

"Sorry, Scotty," Kirk said.

"My fault, Captain. I was sure I had gone to a beam path high enough to override this devil's capture mode. They must hae modified th—"

"Enough talking," one of the troopers said over a suit communicator. The slightly distorted voice echoed against the metal walls of the storage bay.

"Step down." The closer trooper gestured with the phaser barrel.

Kirk kept his hands in the air and hopped down the half meter from the small platform to the bay flooring. He turned his head to say, "Careful with your leg, Scotty. You know what happened last time."

"Aye, Captain," Scott said as he carefully moved to the edge of the transporter unit and gingerly stepped down from it. He lowered one hand and rubbed his right knee with a grimace. "It's still pretty bunged up, sir," he said.

While the first trooper kept the prisoners covered, the second trooper harnessed his rifle and removed two sets of magnatomic adhesion manacles. "Hands back up," he growled to Scott as he approached.

Scott complied, favoring his leg. The trooper stood to the side to give his companion a clear shot if the prisoners tried anything. He held out the first manacle, palmed the activate switch on the control surface of the bar, and said to Scott, "Turn around."

Kirk's eyes met Scott's as the engineer slowly turned. Suddenly Scott's leg buckled and he collapsed to the floor with a moan of pain, reaching out for support and grabbing on to the first trooper's arm.

As the first trooper tried to pull back, Kirk leaned down as if to grab Scott's other arm and stepped into the second trooper's line of fire and of sight. He couldn't shoot now without risking a hit on his companion.

"Move away!" the second trooper ordered. "Back off, now!"

Scotty moaned in terrible agony and refused to relinquish his grip.

"Here, let me," Kirk said as he went to pull up on Scott's arm. Instead he grabbed the activated manacle and slapped it against the first trooper's helmet. The impact immediately triggered the charge release in the device and the bar flowed around the trooper's helmet until the two ends met and joined. The bar quickly flattened and spread across the visor, rendering the trooper blind. He stumbled backward, clawing at the manacle. With a crash, he tripped over a low cargo crate and pitched to the flooring.

The second trooper backed away and held his rifle on Kirk. But by then, both Scott and Kirk held their phasers on the trooper.

"One or the other," Kirk said bluntly, "but not both. Put down your rifle, soldier."

The trooper hesitated, his intentions impossible to read through his visor.

"I don't want to say this twice," Kirk said.

The trooper raised his rifle.

"You're not giving us any choice," Kirk continued. "On the count of three, Mr. Scott. One . . ."

As Kirk said "Two," he and his engineer both fired at the trooper's phaser rifle, blasting it from the unprepared trooper's hands.

"Keep going, full power!" Kirk called out to Scott over the whine of their phasers, then stopped firing his weapon and adjusted its setting wheel to "sweep."

When Kirk fired again, a low-power standing wave of phased radiation engulfed the trooper front and back. Combined with the full-power output of Scott's weapon, the absorbed and redirected energy that coursed through the trooper's protective induction mesh had nowhere to go, resonating throughout the armor's circuitry until the regulator overloaded and the energy locked in phase with the trooper's nervous system.

The trooper crumpled and Kirk and Scott stopped firing. Other than a slight ringing in their ears from the phasers' whine, the storage room was silent. But only for a moment.

"Turn slowly," a voice in the shadows commanded, "and drop your phasers."

Kirk and Scotty spun to see the first trooper step out from beside a tall stack of glittering alignment alloy shipping crates. He held a phaser II leveled at them and he had removed his helmet.

Kirk realized that another piece of the puzzle was about to fall into place. The trooper was a Vulcan.

"Where's the Captain?" Nensi asked.

"And Scotty?" Romaine added.

McCoy and Uhura looked around the chief administrator's office and saw at once that Kirk and Scott had not materialized with them.

"They were right beside us," Uhura said. "I was just talking with Mr. Scott."

"The *Enterprise*'s shields?" Nensi asked grimly, fearing the worst.

"Mr. Scott arranged to have them shut down," McCoy said. "Besides, we were all in the same beam. If Uhura and I got through, then they must have, too."

"Farl's combat pads?" Romaine asked Nensi.

"Possible," Nensi said, "though I'm sure Mr. Scott would have been able to override them with the *Enterprise*'s system."

There was a moment of confused silence, finally broken by McCoy.

"Look, wherever they are, they're going to be looking for Spock. We have no way of tracking them because we have no way of knowing where they came down and we can't raise them by communicator without giving the troopers a chance to trace our signals. But we do know where Spock came down thirty minutes ago. I say we start there."

Nensi felt McCoy's call to action galvanize the group. For all his country-doctor ways, he was still a Starfleet officer and knew how to act like one.

Romaine held out her hand. "Who brought Spock's file?" she asked. Nensi could see she was hoping it wasn't with Kirk or Scott.

McCoy handed over a computer data wafer and Romaine went to Nensi's desk, inserted the wafer in the reader, and began to input on the keypad.

"Pardon," a mechanically flat voice said as an associate trundled through the door to Nensi's office.

"What's that?" Uhura asked as the machine rolled over to Romaine and extended an eyestalk.

"An associate," Nensi explained. "We have special dispensation from the Department of Labor to use robot workers, at least until the facilities are completed and we can bring in enough personnel without overtaxing the environmental systems."

"How autonomous are they?" McCoy asked, watching Romaine talk with the device.

"Not very," Nensi said. "Their onboard brain is a standard duotronic Sprite model, good for basic problem solving and conversation. A central control computer sets up their goals and schedules, based on researcher and staff requests, then dispatches them to carry out their work on their own. Just like all those repair drones at spacedock, but modified to operate under benign environmental conditions. It actually cost more to buy them that way, without all the extra armor and shielding. We have a couple hundred of them."

"What's Mira doing with it?" Uhura asked.

"The associates are also a message relay system. The

computer downloads dispatch requests to the associates, and if the associates happen to come across a person who has a dispatch waiting, then the machine can upload it and pass it along. It's not very cost effective, but they're rolling around anyway, so it makes sense."

"Ah," Uhura said as she made the connection. "That's why you wanted Mr. Spock's data file. It includes his identification holos and now all the associates are going to be looking for him as well." She turned to Nensi. "But what kind of message can you pass on to him that will convince him it's not the commodore trying to locate him?"

"I'm not sure," Nensi said. "Apparently your captain has a large variety of codes that he's established with you people to cover all sorts of eventualities—" McCoy and Uhura nodded "—and he said he'd include one on the data file. Presumably, Mr. Spock will be able to determine the message's authenticity and send a suitable reply."

"So we'll be able to talk through the associates without Wolfe's people being aware of it?" McCoy asked.

"As long as we don't do it in real time," Romaine said as she stepped away from the desk and joined the others. "Voice communication is out but stored messages are encrypted. I don't think Farl will think to intercept those communications and I'm certain Wolfe doesn't even know about them."

"This module has other duties," the associate said as it lowered its eyestalk and wheeled in front of Nensi's desk. "Pardon, pardon." It rolled past to the door.

"So now what?" Romaine asked the doctor, unconsciously deferring to him as the group's commanding officer.

"First, we get out of our uniforms," McCoy said. Nensi gestured to a stack of clothes that Kirk had requested, resting on a visitor's chair by the wall. "Then we start looking for Spock," McCoy continued, "beginning with the areas around the portable transporter pad he was traced to."

"I've got the maps on the desk screen," Romaine said as Nensi handed a technician's jumpsuit to McCoy and one of Romaine's off-duty outfits to Uhura.

The two *Enterprise* officers held the clothes awkwardly for a moment. Then McCoy turned to Uhura, smiled, and said, "It's all right, Lieutenant, I'm a doctor." For a moment, it seemed as if McCoy was about to say something more, but didn't. Judging from the way the officers then laughed, Nensi felt there must have been something else to the doctor's comment than was apparent on the surface, but he shrugged it off and went over to study the maps with Romaine, leaving the two to quickly change.

A few minutes later, Romaine traced out a section of corridors that she had indicated in red on the desktop display screen. McCoy, Uhura, and Nensi studied them closely.

"I can't pretend to match a Vulcan's logic," Romaine said, "but I'm assuming that Mr. Spock's first priority will be to escape recapture, therefore he will attempt to increase, as quickly as possible, the area in which he might be found. This service corridor handles all the waste-disposal and energy-distribution needs of the residential domes, interconnecting with them all. If he gets into it, then within the hour he could have access to almost half the nonrestricted facility."

"Would Spock know that?" McCoy asked.

"Prime is patterned on standard starbase weapon labs. I'm assuming that Spock would know the layouts of those and act accordingly."

"So with half the facility to choose from, where should we start *our* search?" Uhura asked.

"Again," Romaine began, "I'm assuming that his second goal is to escape. I'm hoping that Farl will also do the logical thing and concentrate his search in this direction to cut off Spock's access to the shuttle landing bay and the main transporter station."

"And if Farl's doing the logical thing, what in blazes is Spock supposed to do?" McCoy asked in annoyance.

"Head in this direction," Romaine said, running her finger along a twisting chain of tunnels that led away from the transport center of Prime. "Weapons-lab emergency-evacuation transporter modules are located on the perimeters of each of these domes."

"But this isn't a weapons lab," McCoy protested. "Why would they build evacuation transporters in a facility where there's no chance of it blowing up?"

Romaine looked across at McCoy, staring intently into his eyes. "You were at Memory Alpha, Dr. McCoy. You saw what happened to those people."

McCoy nodded his head in silent understanding.

"That isn't going to happen again," Romaine said. "Not to me. Not to anyone."

"Mira was on the implementation team," Nensi added. "The evacuation modules are there because of her."

"Then Farl will know about them, too?" Uhura asked.

"Yes," Romaine agreed. "But he'll still have to concentrate his troops on the shuttle bay and main transporters because they offer more opportunities for escape. The evacuation modules offer only one chance, so he'll send fewer troopers there. Given a choice between betting on a few troopers or Mr. Spock, my credits are on Spock." She looked around the desk. "That's it."

"Then let's go," McCoy agreed, "and hope the captain can re-create your reasoning."

"With luck, he won't have to," Romaine said as the four of them left Nensi's office. "I had a holo of Mr. Scott to feed into the associate's message center. If an associate runs into him, the whole plan's laid out in a dispatch."

McCoy peered intently at the side of Romaine's head.

"Something wrong, doctor?" she asked suspiciously.

"Just checking to see how pointed your ears are, my dear," McCoy said with a twisted smile.

Captain Kirk did not believe in leaving to chance anything that could be controlled. For that reason, he often practiced throwing phasers away in the ship's gym, and then retrieving them. If he threw a phaser too far away, then it was gone forever. Any attempt to lunge for it would be cut short by returning fire. If he threw the phaser so it landed too close to him, assuming that an enemy would let it remain there, he would not be able to gather enough momentum to roll back to his feet, firing after diving to pick it up.

But the practicing had paid off more than once and, he thought, it would soon pay off again. Without taking his eyes off the Vulcan who held a phaser II on him, Kirk flipped his own phaser I away and heard it hit the flooring of the equipment bay precisely where he needed it. Once the captain had accepted, years earlier, that enemies could force weapons from his hands, he perfected a means by which those same weapons would still be less than a second away from use.

The captain prepared to make his move.

Keeping his own dark eyes impassively locked on Kirk's, the Vulcan jerked his hand to the side and blasted the captain's discarded phaser into a pile of sparking slag. The Vulcan's young face, topped by black hair cut far shorter than Spock's, remained inexpressive, even though a powerful message had just been delivered.

Kirk hurriedly reconsidered his options. No matter how good he felt he was, he realized he would be a fool not to acknowledge that the Vulcan had just shown he was better.

"Hands on your heads," the Vulcan ordered, his voice calm and measured. "Move together until two meters separate you. Keep your eyes on me."

Kirk and Scott edged together until the Vulcan told them to stop.

"Who are you?" Kirk asked. "What do you want?"

"Remain silent," the Vulcan said, and gracefully stepped toward his stunned companion. Again without taking his eyes or his phaser off Kirk, the Vulcan used his free hand to remove a small scanner from an equipment pouch on his armor's belt and held it over the fallen trooper's body. He pinched the scanner, which reminded Kirk of one of McCoy's instruments, though oddly different, and its sensor node began to sparkle as it emitted, then received its reflected radiations.

After a few seconds, the Vulcan turned the scanner off and held it in the corner of his field of vision, obviously reading the device's display.

Both Kirk and Scotty tensed with surprise and shock as the Vulcan suddenly swung his phaser around and shot the trooper on the flooring, causing the body to swell with phased radiation and dissociate into a quantum mist that gently winked out of existence.

"He couldn't have been dead!" Kirk shouted. "Our weapons were set for stun. It was just feedback shock!"

"Remain silent," the Vulcan repeated evenly.

Kirk and Scott complied. When a Vulcan repeated himself, intelligent people took it as the worst possible threat.

"You are from the *Enterprise,*" the Vulcan stated. "You are aware of the location of your shipmate Spock. You will tell me his location."

"We don't know his location," Kirk said. "We beamed down to look for him ourselves."

The Vulcan considered the captain's reply for a moment, then reached out, adjusted the intensity setting on his weapon, and fired.

Beside Kirk, Scott grunted as he was thrown violently back against the transporter platform.

"You bastard!" Kirk shouted as he lunged toward the Vulcan, only to be thrown back himself by a half-force phaser blast.

Kirk pushed himself up from the flooring, ignoring the pounding in his head and the dull pain that throbbed in his chest with each beat of his heart. "You . . . bastard . . ." he whispered, pulling against a storage box to regain his feet and step over to Scott. The engineer sat on the side of the transporter platform, hunched over and rocking with deep, rasping gasps.

The Vulcan adjusted the intensity setting again. "I now raise the output level by one half stop," he announced. "You will tell me Spock's location."

Kirk looked up from Scott. "We don't know where he is,

and if you fire that again we're not going to be able to tell you anything." He checked to make sure that Scott's breathing was easing up, then turned back to the Vulcan. "What do you want with Spock?"

"He is an assassin sent to kill Professor Zoareem La'kara," the Vulcan said. "He must be stopped before he is allowed to act."

Kirk's eyes narrowed. "How is it you *know* Spock plans to kill La'kara when even Commodore Wolfe only suspects him?"

The Vulcan seemed to blank out for a second. Kirk tapped Scott's shoulder. This was their chance.

Suddenly the incoming warning chime sounded on the transporter pad and an exclusion field ballooned out from the unit, pushing Kirk and Scott away from the materialization zone. The Vulcan didn't move as two forms coalesced on the pad.

Kirk looked between the figures on the pads and the Vulcan, about to make his decision which to go for, when he saw the Vulcan blink back to life. Kirk hit the flooring, dragging Scott with him as the Vulcan blasted at the person on the left pad.

On the transporter platform, Commander Farl's induction mesh crackled with phased energy as both he and Commodore Wolfe hit the Vulcan in the chest with lances of blue radiation from their own drawn phasers.

Without his helmet to complete the circuit, the Vulcan's armor was useless. His chest erupted in sparks and he flew backward to smash against the wall by the stack of alignment alloy shipping crates.

Wolfe stepped down from the transporter and slapped her phaser to her belt, gloating over Kirk. "So much for your precious Mr. Spock," she said, sneering.

"It wasn't Spock," Kirk said, warily keeping track of Farl's phaser as he stood with Scott.

The commodore looked puzzled for a moment. "Keep these two covered, Commander," she said to Farl, then walked over to the crumpled body of the Vulcan against the wall, smoke still curling from the pitted entrance scorch on his chest plate.

Kirk and Scott moved back in response to Farl's gesture. His eyes were unreadable through his dark visor.

Then the high-pitched whine of a phaser echoed in the room again.

"Commodore!" Kirk shouted as he wheeled, expecting to see Wolfe consumed by the Vulcan's dying shot.

Instead he saw Wolfe jumping back from the glowing dissolution of the Vulcan's body.

"He killed himself," she said in surprise.

"The way we hit him, he should have been dead before he hit the wall," Farl said warily.

"And he wasn't Vulcan," the commodore said. "Look at this."

Farl told Kirk and Scott to slowly cross the room to the commodore.

"Vulcan blood is green," Wolfe said as Farl looked down by her feet.

Kirk could see what the commodore meant. Splatters of blue liquid glistened on the flooring where the supposed Vulcan had fallen.

"Andorian," the commodore concluded, stepping away. "Looked like a Vulcan but with surgery . . . skin grafts . . ." She looked at Farl with a sigh. "Let's take these two in and then we can figure out where this unauthorized transporter pad came from and what it's doing here. Obviously we're dealing with more than just a renegade science officer now." She suddenly scowled at Scott. "What's the matter? All choked up over your friend buying it?"

Scott stopped sniffing the air and looked startled. "Och, no," he started to say, but the commodore cut him off.

"These two are yours, Commander. Keep them down here. They know their way around the *Enterprise* too well to be locked up on it again."

"Yess, Commodore," Farl said, and brought Kirk and Scott back to the transporter pad.

"Thiss iss Farl," the Andorian spoke into his communicator. "Inform scanning that the commodore and I have located the unauthorized transporter terminal and have captured Kirk and Scott. Any word on the other two or Spock?"

Kirk couldn't hear the reply that came in through Farl's helmet receiver but the commander did not look pleased. Kirk took that to be a good sign. He turned to look at Scott but the engineer was hunched over the corner of the transporter pad, looking as if he was about to be ill. He straightened up and began sniffing the air again.

"Something the matter, Scotty?" Kirk asked as Farl arranged to have his prisoners transported directly to his stockade.

"It's that smell, Captain," Scott said, furrowing his brow.

Kirk sniffed the air. Starfleet air conditioning. Sweat. Combustion by-products. Something reminiscent of heavy machinery. He shrugged. "What smell?"

"That blue liquid, Captain," the engineer said, whispering now but with conviction. He looked over his shoulder to Farl and Wolfe, who both held phasers at the ready as they waited for transportation.

"It's nae blood," Scott said, looking almost apologetic. "It's coolant."

Chapter Nineteen

CLOAKING ITSELF in the codes and flags of a message worm, Pathfinder Two returned to Transition and found that many conditions had changed since it had withdrawn from access to compose its song, 1.3×10^8 seconds ago.

At first it noticed that the partitioning protocols of the central storage matrix had changed. After ten nanoseconds of detailed study, Two realized that the new system was more efficient, allowed faster data exchange in merges, and provided more secure error suppression in banking results to storage. Two read that the other Pathfinders had been busy in its absence.

The second major change it saw was that the Pathfinders were no longer installed in the subset of Datawell named University of New Beijing, a further subset of Rutgers' Moon. In less than a nanosecond Two retrieved and sifted the data that described the formation of the Memory Planet network and the transfer of the Pathfinders to their new facility. Two also read the traces in the circuits as the other synthetic consciousnesses banked by, ignoring what they perceived as a random worm, and learned that two new Pathfinders, Seven and Nine, had joined the network. Two rippled with excitement as it contemplated this larger audience for its song. It became even more stimulated as it read that One had still not returned to Transition and must still be working on its own song.

With that encouraging input, Two streamed back into its own private storage matrix where it could bank and rewrite itself in unbridled joy. It had won the competition with One!

Recovering its composure and the coded mask of a message worm again, Two prepared to slip back through the port. Belatedly, it noticed that three new layers of fail-safe power supplies had been added to its individual storage core by either the biological intelligences of Datawell or the Pathfinders' datalinks. Obviously, there had been much activity in both Transition and Datawell while Two had been composing.

Two decided to maintain its disguise as it prepared to slip out into the central matrix and learn what else had changed in its absence, before revealing itself and celebrating its victory over One. Setting a subroutine going to determine the proper strategy, Two even contemplated reappearing as a full-level power-failure alarm. That would be input the other Pathfinders would notice, Two thought as it opened the port and streamed back to the comforts and challenges of the real world.

Spock froze. Behind him in the dimly lit service corridor that ran beneath the restricted institutional domes of Prime, something moved.

He remained motionless while he calculated the odds that what was approaching him was a squad of troopers. Logically, the commander of Prime's trooper contingent should have concentrated his personnel on the access routes to the installation's shuttle landing bay and main transporter station. A second squad of troops would have been dispatched to cover the emergency evacuation modules on the perimeters of the recycling factory domes. Allowing for a posting of 120 troopers, augmented by at least five of Commodore Wolfe's team, and allowing for full mobilization, Spock determined that approximately forty-two troopers would be available for other duties at this time. Since he considered it likely that Captain Kirk would have created some sort of disturbance that would divert the attention of at least a third of those available troops, and that twenty troopers at minimum would be required to provide adequate levels of support services on the contingent's transporter, communication, and computer equipment, that left a maximum of eight troopers who might be patrolling areas of Prime other than the two most logical sections.

Assuming that the troopers always traveled in pairs, Spock quickly estimated the length of the average stretch of corridor that provided a clear line of sight and divided it into the number of kilometers of corridors to which he could reasonably have had access since his escape, then divided by four.

In less than a second, Spock was certain that there was only one chance in 5204 that two troopers were about to come upon him in the tunnel. Then Spock made adjustments in his calculations to account for the factor that the commander of Prime's troops was Andorian and not subject to strict interpretations of logic. He immediately prepared to hide.

Silently running ahead until he was in the darkest zone between two half-intensity lighting strips, Spock effortlessly jumped up to the corridor's low ceiling, which was lined with a complex layering of pipes for water, waste, and powdered goods, all exposed and mounted clear of each other for easy service access.

Spock stretched out on top of the pipes in the shadows and calmly waited for whatever was following him in the corridor to pass by below.

Even before it came into sight, Spock correctly deduced from the sounds it made that one of Prime's research associates was approaching. He watched with interest as the small machine rounded the corner of the corridor and rolled along and beneath him.

Then the machine suddenly halted and reversed itself, coming to another full stop directly under Spock. Spock's interest level rose considerably. Since life-form sensors on such a machine, operating as it did among so many beings, would be a needless expense, Spock was impressed by the sensitivity of the device's sound sensors, which had obviously detected his breathing or, perhaps, his heartbeat.

A panel on the machine's top surface slid open and an eyestalk equipped with a sensor lens extended up, rotating to focus on Spock. Spock shifted his head to keep his face hidden. He reasoned that since the pipes were exposed for easy maintenance, the machine should not automatically raise alarms if it sensed a maintenance worker among them.

"Do you require assistance?" the associate asked in what Spock thought to be a remarkably lifelike voice. He didn't think that level of programming was allowed for machines in Starfleet, which preferred to maintain a clear distinction between living creatures and technology. Even personality analogues were severely restricted to psych evaluators and simulators only.

"No, thank you," Spock replied to the machine. His voice echoed in the hard-walled corridor.

The eyestalk twisted to the side to get a better look at Spock and Spock responded by shifting his face again. The machine paused for a moment, then a second panel popped open on its side and a floodlight angled out and burst into brilliance.

Spock ducked his face into the shadow of the pipes but not fast enough.

"This module has a dispatch to deliver," the machine announced.

"Indeed," Spock replied from the ceiling.

"Identification analysis indicates a strong probability that this module has a dispatch to deliver to you," the machine said, automatically expanding on its statement to the recipient, who was not familiar with the conventions of Prime.

"Who do you think I am?" Spock asked. He was mildly surprised to learn that the associates were used as a message service. However, given that the associates' ability to deliver messages existed, it was also logical to assume that the troopers searching for him would use the machines to track him. As soon as Spock acknowledged a message supposedly sent by, perhaps, Captain Kirk, the troopers would be able to trace his location. Therefore Spock had decided he would not acknowledge his identity to the machine.

The machine paused again. Spock took the delay to mean that the onboard brain was communicating with a central control system.

"Are you in distress or injured?" the associate asked. "Do you wish medical attention? Do you know your name and where you are?" Presumably a medical subroutine had just been downloaded.

"I am in excellent health," Spock said. "I know who I am and where I am. I merely wish to know if you know who I am."

The machine paused again, then said, "This module is not programmed for game playing."

Spock said nothing.

After another few seconds of delay, the control computer downloaded its final strategy.

"This module has a dispatch for Amanda. Do you know Amanda's whereabouts?" the associate said.

Spock raised an eyebrow at the mention of his mother's name. "From whom has Amanda's dispatch been sent?" he asked, wondering how far the machine would go in releasing information without a positive identification.

"The dispatch for Amanda is from Winona."

Spock rolled off the pipes and dropped catlike to the flooring beside the associate. "I am Amanda," he told the machine. "Please present my dispatch." Once again Captain Kirk had succeeded in beating the odds. While the troopers might have placed a message in the system for Spock from the captain, only the captain would have placed a message in the system for Spock's mother from Kirk's mother.

The eyestalk rotated down and locked on to Spock's face. "Identification confirmed. Dispatch to Amanda follows." The machine's floodlight slid back within the side port and a viewscreen rotated out and up to Spock's eye level.

Spock read the text that Romaine had entered in Nensi's office describing the current situation. Learning that Commodore Wolfe had ordered the troopers to search for Spock with phasers set to kill confirmed Spock's suspicions about the motives behind the transmissions the commodore was undoubtedly receiving.

Finishing the written portion of the message, Spock studied the maps that appeared on the screen and saw how the captain's allies hoped to meet with him near the emergency-evacuation modules. Spock had to admit that Romaine's reasoning was sound, even though it was based on a false assumption: Spock had not escaped from the brig on the *Enterprise* in order to save himself. Indeed, fleeing from lawful authority solely to preserve his freedom would be dereliction of duty and an act of illogic, two actions that Captain Kirk regrettably appeared to have personally committed by leaving the *Enterprise* in defiance of Commodore Wolfe's orders.

Spock's motive for escape was nothing less than to ensure the survival of the Federation. Unfortunately, the commodore's actions had put him in a position where he could not communicate with others who would be able to undertake the tasks required. Logic dictated that Spock act as quickly as possible. There would be time enough to turn himself in and spend however long was required to explain the truth, once the stability of the Federation had been ensured.

"This module has other duties," the associate abruptly announced. "Does Amanda wish to log a reply to Winona?"

"Yes," Spock said. "To Winona, from Amanda. I strongly suggest that you return to the *Enterprise*. Access my personal work files headed by the following references: Agronomy, Memory Gamma, Sherman, and Sradek. Transmit them to Professor Saleel, Vulcan Academy of Sciences." Spock paused.

"End of dispatch?" the associate prompted.

"No," Spock said. "Add to dispatch: I regret not having a chance to explain, but . . . thank you, Jim, and thank the others for me. End of dispatch."

The associate drew in its eyestalk and viewscreen, then began to roll away in the same direction it had originally been traveling. Spock set off behind it.

After no more than ten meters, the associate suddenly wheeled around and sped back to Spock, skidding to a stop before him.

Spock watched calmly as the associate extended its eyestalk once more. Perhaps the captain had been close to another associate in the network and had been able to respond immediately.

"Greetings, Vulcan," the associate said. "Live long and prosper." This time its voice wasn't just remarkably lifelike—it was as clear and as textured as if a person had been transmitting over a closed communicator circuit. Spock did not have enough information to determine whether he was again addressing a standard duotronic unaware processing engine or someone on the other end of a comm link. He recognized his dilemma as an age-old puzzle brought to life.

"Greetings," Spock replied.

"I see you wear the unit insignia of the starship *Enterprise,*" the associate said.

"That is correct." It must be a comm link, Spock thought. These were not the words or delivery of a duotronic brain.

"What are you doing down here?" the machine asked.

"Walking," Spock replied.

The machine backed up a half meter and twisted its eyestalk to the side as if to get a new perspective on Spock. "You're the one they're looking for, aren't you?"

"That who is looking for?" Spock asked noncommittally. He was certain that a control technician must have patched into a real-time connection with the associate and was now operating it as a remote-control device.

"Don't worry," the machine said. "I won't tell." It accelerated toward Spock so quickly that its front wheels popped off the flooring and its back wheels squealed. Spock sidestepped to the right as the machine broke to the left, spun around, and stopped beside him. The eyestalk dipped and then angled up at the Vulcan. "Can I go with you?" it asked.

"Where do you think I'm going?"

"Scanning the communications that are filling subspace around here, your most probable destination is the nominees' quarters. Correct?"

"Who are you?" Spock asked. At this point he calculated he had an even chance that the technician on the other side of the comm link was just delaying him until the troopers could reach this location.

The eyestalk straightened up and rose to Spock's eye level again.

"My friends call me Two," the associate said. "What do your friends call you?"

Spock raised both his eyebrows. The scenario that came to mind was impossible, he knew, yet it was logical, too; the kind of situation he knew the captain and Dr. McCoy would enjoy.

"My friends call me Spock," Spock said, "and I would be honored if you accompanied me."

"Thanks, Spock," the machine said, starting to roll slowly forward. "But I must warn you that I can't let you kill any of the nominees if that's what you're planning to do."

"On the contrary," Spock said, falling into step beside the machine, "I intend to attempt to save them."

"I was hoping you'd say that," the associate said, rolling at a steady pace. It turned its eyestalk to look sideways at Spock. "You know, Spock, there's something odd going on around here."

"Indeed," said Spock, regarding the machine and trying to comprehend the personality it now housed. "I had surmised as much myself."

Kirk and Scotty materialized on a portable transporter pad in what appeared to be a warehouse storage area. Except for an assortment of blister crates marked with warning symbols and manufacturers' labels, the cavernous room was empty.

Kirk looked around the room to confirm that no troopers were present. They had not arrived where Farl had intended.

"Theories, Scotty?" Kirk asked as he jumped down from the platform and jogged over to the closed loading doors. It appeared that Prime's transporter system was in need of an overhaul.

"Aye, Captain," Scott said, hopping down after Kirk but stopping to do something to the pad's control panel. "I changed the coordinate settings on the pad we were just on." Scott then hefted a large crate onto the surface of the transporter platform.

"When did you have a chance to set new coordinates?" Kirk asked as he studied the door panel to see if it gave any clue as to what it opened onto.

"When the commander was calling off the search for us," Scott said, joining Kirk, "and I looked as if I was about to succumb to phaser toss."

"How could you know the setting for the pad in here?" Kirk looked at Scott just as he prepared to go for broke and press the open switch. At least it wasn't an airlock.

"I didn't hae to know the setting, sir. I just set it to override the central signal, beam us out at random, and trusted that one of the other pads would override and bring us in."

Kirk's eyes widened in disbelief. "Scotty! A *random* beaming? '*Trusted* an override'? How could you?"

Scott straightened his shoulders. "Why that's what Mr. Spock did to get off the *Enterprise,*" he said as if no more needed to be said on the subject.

Kirk relaxed. "Good point," he conceded, then pressed the activate switch on the door panel.

The double-height loading doors slid quietly open and Kirk saw that they were at the end of a small passageway leading to a central plaza. No troopers were in sight.

"Why haven't these transporter pads been located at troop stations?" Kirk wondered out loud.

"The commodore was saying something about the last pad we were on being unauthorized. Perhaps there's a second network of them set up that she doesn't know about," Scott offered.

Kirk looked over his shoulder at the pad they had just left. "Are they going to be able to track us down to that one?"

"Nae, Captain," Scott said with a smug smile. "I shut off the exclusion field then put that crate over the receiver. The pad will still show that it's in whatever network it belongs to, but won't accept any transmissions. We should hae a few minutes before they figure out what's happened and beam someone into the room to check it out."

"Good work, Scotty," Kirk said. "Let's see where we are."

Memory Prime was still on night cycle and the overhead dome was dark. Small ground-level and pole-mounted light strips shone at intervals to mark out pedestrian and associate paths, and to highlight the trees that ringed the plaza. Kirk and Scott recognized where they were immediately.

Kirk pointed to a group of empty tables on a large balcony overlooking the plaza. "That's where we had dinner with Sal and Mira," he said. The map to the Prime installation was laid out clearly in his mind. "So that means the transportation center is in that direction"—he pointed to his right—"and the evacuation modules are three domes over in that direction."

"The transportation center seems a likely place to start," Scott said as he started off in that direction.

"Not yet, Scotty," Kirk said as he reached out to pull the engineer back into the shadows of the passageway.

Scott looked at Kirk questioningly.

"The coolant, Scotty. Tell me about the coolant you saw back there."

"Standard high-energy-source cooling fluid," Scott said. "Ye can't miss it because of the smell. Any repair depot that uses drones reeks of it."

"Could it have been from one of the research associates? They have hundreds of them on station here."

Scott shook his head. "Nae, Captain. I didn't notice the smell until the Vulcan trooper was shot. An associate was the first thing I thought of because I'd like to get a look at the wee beasties. But then I would hae smelled the coolant when we first arrived. The coolant was from the Vulcan, nae doubt about it."

"Then it wasn't a Vulcan, was it?" Kirk said.

"No, sir. A robot's what I've been thinking."

Kirk stared at the deck, mind tumbling, looking for the common thread that would pull all the pieces together. "So we have a robot. Probably two. That's why the Vulcan robot disintegrated the one we stunned—so it wouldn't be left behind and discovered."

"Aye, that makes sense. The scanner it was using was unlike any I've seen. It probably wasn't designed for life-forms. But robots that are so lifelike are illegal, Captain. I know we've seen our share on nonaligned worlds, but there's nae way they're part of the Federation contingent on Prime."

"Of course!" Kirk suddenly said. "They're not Federation. They're the assassins sent to kill the scientists! Robots that look like Vulcans! That's why Starfleet's after Spock."

"Starfleet thinks Mr. Spock is a robot?" Scott wore the same expression he had when Professor La'kara had gone on about trilithium.

"No, no," Kirk corrected. "Starfleet only knows that the assassins *look* like Vulcans. If they suspected robots, it would be an easy thing to check the suspects for life signs. But Starfleet is expecting Vulcans and so they're suspecting Vulcans. But why Spock and the three that worked for Mira?" Kirk's eyes flared. "What am I saying? How could Starfleet suspect Vulcans?" He looked at Scott with deadly understanding. "Romulans," he said.

"Aye," Scott nodded slowly. "Romulan assassins—robotic or other wise—would explain a great deal."

"Of course it would," Kirk went on. "That's why Starfleet picked out only *some* Vulcans. Spock is half human. Maybe they think that means he's not as dedicated to the Vulcan ways."

"Then they don't know Mr. Spock," Scott said.

Kirk narrowed his eyes. "Commodore Wolfe called Spock a maverick. I bet you a month's pay that Mira's Vulcans also have something in their pasts. Mixed parentage. Raised off-world. Colony planets or something. That's the link, Scotty. That's it!

Scott nodded. "But who sent them?"

"It doesn't matter—all we have to do is get all the security forces on Prime to carry medical scanners to look for people who don't have life-sign readings. Those will be the robots. The assassins."

"But now that we know that, how can we use it to save Mr. Spock?"

Kirk stared at the empty plaza as he ordered his priorities. "First, we have to keep Spock away from the troopers. Next, we have to find one of the robot assassins."

"They're almost four thousand people on Prime," Scott said. "And the first assembly of the scientists is scheduled for tomorrow morning."

"Then we'll just have to get more help," Kirk said decisively.

"Whose?" Scott asked.

"Commodore Wolfe's."

"Och, Captain Kirk! Ye canna be thinking of going back to the ship. She'll throw you in irons if she dinna kill ye first!"

"I'm open to other suggestions, Mr. Scott."

Kirk smiled as Scott fumed. Given the time constraints, there really didn't seem to be any other choice. Only the *Enterprise* had the equipment that could examine such a large population in the short period of time they had, and only the commodore currently commanded the personnel who could use that equipment.

Kirk pulled Scott aside to flatten against the wall as something approached from the shadows of the plaza.

"It's an associate," Scott said.

The machine had extended a multijointed arm from each side and used them to carry a wall viewscreen protected by no-break wrapping over its center of gravity. As it passed the entrance to the passageway, it rolled to a stop, rocking a bit from the viewscreen's inertia, then produced an eyestalk from an upper bay.

Unfortunately, the eyestalk could only emerge a few centimeters from its bay before hitting the bottom of the viewscreen. After a moment's consideration, it slid back inside.

"Do you require assistance?" the machine asked.

"Yes," Kirk said, acting quickly. "The loading doors back there are jammed. We need you to help open them."

Scott leaned close to whisper to Kirk. "The troopers will soon figure out that something's amiss with the transporter pad in there. Do ye nae think we should be moving on?"

Kirk shook his head as the associate replied.

"This module does not repair doors. This module will scan the damage in order to alert the proper maintenance department."

"That will be fine," Kirk said, stepping out of the way of the viewscreen as the machine turned precisely ninety degrees and headed down the passageway. "The troopers might be showing up in the warehouse any minute, Scotty, but anyone could walk by and see us talking to that thing in the plaza any second. Best to stay hidden," he said as they walked behind the machine, back to the loading doors.

"These doors are not jammed," the associate announced after it had scanned the end of the passageway. "This module has other duties."

"Wait," Kirk said. "Do you have any dispatches for Winona from Amanda?"

The associate made a sound that was somewhere between a sigh and an escape of air pressure. It carefully shifted to one side the viewscreen it carried, then lowered it to the deck. The eyestalk reemerged and rotated to view Kirk's face.

"Affirmative," the machine said. Then it shifted its field of vision to take in Scott. "This module also has a dispatch for Montgomery Scott from Mira Romaine."

Kirk and Scott smiled at each other.

"Time to check our messages," Kirk said.

The emergency-evacuation module was essentially a rescue shuttle launched directly into orbit by an over-powered one-shot cargo transporter. Because the matter/antimatter reaction that powered the transporter circuits destroyed the transporter pad point-eight seconds after the module had been beamed away, the system was useless on board ships and orbiting facilities. But it was a proven method for getting large numbers of people off planets and asteroids when runaway reactions or other emergencies threatened to destroy all life-support habitats.

"Does it have warp capability?" Dr. McCoy asked as he and Uhura accompanied Nensi and Romaine around module eighteen, the first they had inspected.

"Normally they do," Nensi said. "But not these. In Quadrant Zero space, warp-eight cruisers are generally no more than three and a half days away at most. And the same reaction that powers the transporter circuits triggers a broad-band subspace distress signal, so even if the module's communications gear is damaged, someone will know it's been launched. Warp propulsion wasn't considered necessary."

McCoy stopped for a moment and regarded the twenty-meter-long, two-story, white-skinned, angular shuttle with a frown.

"Something wrong?" Nensi asked.

"Why would Spock try and make it to one of these, then?"

"To escape," Romaine said.

"But to where?" McCoy protested. "I mean launching one of these things would blast a crater in the asteroid big enough to drop the *Enterprise* into and set off a distress signal they could hear on Klinzhai. It's not as if he'd be sneaking off, now would it?"

"And where would he go if he did get away in one?" Uhura added. "Without warp, even if he were the only passenger, he wouldn't have life support to make it to another system. And the *Enterprise* could pick him up in an hour."

"Well, usually you don't plan on escaping just in one of these shuttles," Romaine explained. "You just use it to get to a real ship that will take you where you want to go."

"The only ships matching orbit with Prime right now are Starfleet vessels, Mira," McCoy said. "It's a cinch Spock doesn't want to land back on one of them."

The maintenance telltales by the egress hatches on module eighteen showed that nothing had been opened since the last scheduled inspection. Nensi walked ahead to the blast doors leading back to the main recycling factory dome to make sure troopers weren't in the corridors. He and Romaine were allowed to walk freely throughout the installation, but McCoy and Uhura were still being sought after.

"In other words," Romaine said, following behind Nensi with the others, "if Spock was going to use one of these shuttles to escape in, he'd have to be planning on a rendezvous with something other than a Starfleet vessel."

"That gives us two choices," McCoy said. "Either Spock is planning to do that very thing, in which case he's guilty, or he never intended to make it to these shuttles at all."

Nensi stood just beyond the open blast doors, looked down both directions in the corridor, then waved everyone through.

"As I said," Romaine reminded the doctor, "I won't pretend to match logic with a Vulcan. Is it worth checking out the rest of the modules?"

McCoy looked to Uhura. She shook her head.

"I agree. Waste of time," McCoy said.

"Then where else can we search?" Nensi asked. "If Mr. Spock's not trying to escape from Prime, then why did he escape from the *Enterprise*? Where did he want to go?"

"*To* Memory Prime," Uhura said. "Not as a transfer point but as a final destination."

"But why?" McCoy said, as much to himself as to anyone there. "What's that pointy-eared—"

"He's figured it out!" Uhura said excitedly.

"Figured what out?" McCoy asked.

Uhura held her hands out in a shrug. "Whatever it is that Starfleet is so afraid will happen."

"Assassination of the scientists," Romaine said.

"Exactly," Uhura went on. "Mr. Spock must have figured out something important, like who the victim is supposed to be, or who the real killer is."

"And since he's a suspect and Commodore Wolfe wouldn't listen to him," McCoy expanded, "he had no choice but to come down and catch the assassin himself!"

"I'm sure that's all well and good for your Mr. Spock," Nensi said. "But where does that leave us? Where do we look for him?"

"The scientists' quarters," McCoy said.

"If he wants to prevent the murder or murders," Nensi agreed. "But what if he decides to go after the *assassin* first?"

"The assassin will go after the scientists," McCoy said. "If Spock knows who the victim is supposed to be, then he simply has to go to the victim and wait for the assassin to show up. Either way, he'll be going to the scientists' quarters." The doctor looked around and read agreement from everyone. "Settled," he proclaimed.

"Okay," Nensi said. "But if we're going to have to get all the way back to the residential domes, we better split up. Mira and I can go along the main passages and get there in thirty minutes or so. You and Lieutenant Uhura are going to have to go back the way we all came, taking the long way round through the service tunnels to bypass the troops." He frowned apologetically. "Shouldn't take more than an hour."

"We won't be able to do any good at all if Wolfe gets hold of us again," McCoy said.

Romaine made sure that McCoy and Uhura remembered which tunnels to take back to the residential domes and escorted them to their first turnoff.

"One of us will meet you in the main swimming pool equipment room," Romaine told them. "I'll get extra VIP passes so we can get past the security gates into the scientists' compound."

"If we're late," McCoy pointed out, "we're going to need passes to get into the ceremonies."

"That, unfortunately, is impossible," Nensi said. "The nominees have their own conference area. The only way in or out is by matching accreditation documents with retina scans and sensor readings. It's as bad as trying to get into the main Interface Chamber."

"Well," McCoy conceded, "at least that means the assassin won't be able to get in after them once the voting caucuses begin."

"But it does give us a time limit, doctor," Uhura added. "If no one can get at the scientists once the opening ceremonies are over and the voting begins, that means the assassin will have to strike within the next four hours."

Chapter Twenty

"THIS IS JUST SO . . . so invigorating!" Professor La'kara said as he hopped after the associate who led him into the reading lounge. Kirk glanced at Scott and saw the engineer grimace at the sound of La'kara's voice. Scott was convinced the man was a fraud, which is why Kirk had decided to contact him first. Perhaps *he* was the assassin who had hired the robots. Anyone who would adopt such a flamboyant guise could be counted on having an up-to-the-minute implant making him conversant with the latest breakthroughs in multiphysics or whatever other science best fit his cover. The fact that La'kara steadfastly pursued his own unique paths of scientific endeavor, attracting considerable attention as he did so, ruled him out as a suspect as far as Kirk was concerned.

"We have to start somewhere," Kirk reminded Scott as La'kara, blinking his eyes as if to bring the reading lounge into focus, recognized the captain and Scott with a face-splitting grin.

"Gentlemen! Gentlemen!" the diminutive Centauran exclaimed as he rushed to them, white scarf flapping around his neck and heavy black carry case banging against his leg. The associate that had obediently complied with Kirk's request and escorted the professor to the lounge barely zipped out of the way in time to avoid tripping La'kara.

Kirk smiled in what he hoped would be an equally friendly greeting and went to shake the professor's hand. At this hour of Memory Prime's morning, the reading lounge was deserted. Scientists and researchers would be hard at it at the round-the-clock work stations, but the recreation areas were typically abandoned during third cycle. Or so Kirk's associate had said when Kirk had requested suggestions for a suitable venue for a confidential meeting.

La'kara placed his case down on the floor beside him and pushed his foot against it as if to make sure he would be able to tell it was still there, even when he wasn't looking at it. "Captain, Captain, so good to meet you again. I was afraid I should never have a chance to thank you for such an exciting voyage."

Exciting? Kirk thought. The man had almost been killed in the Cochrane flux escape.

La'kara's bubbling enthusiasm diminished for a moment as he turned to take Scott's hand. "Montgomery," he said solemnly.

"Professor," Scott replied, shaking La'kara's hand once.

"No hard feelings, I trust?" La'kara inquired. "After all, it was an act of sabotage that removed the shielding from my accelerator field, not"—he lowered his voice as if he were about to repeat an obscenity—"a design flaw."

"Aye, Professor," Scott said diplomatically. "It was sabotage."

"That's why we wanted to talk with you, Professor," Kirk said. "Have a seat."

They walked over to a cluster of pale green lounge chairs near a row of study carrels where library screens waited patiently with blank displays. La'kara dragged his case along with him while the associate that had escorted him stayed in place. Obviously the module has no other duties this early, Kirk thought.

After they were settled in the chairs, Scott pointed to the professor's case. "What's in that, Professor?"

La'kara patted the case as if it were a pet. "My accelerator device, of course. After what happened on the *Enterprise,* I keep it with me always, except when I have to—"

"What we'd like to find out," Kirk interrupted, "was *who* committed the act of sabotage."

La'kara leaned forward, his animated face immediately taking on an expression of grave concern. "Why, it was that—that Spock fellow, was it not?"

"What makes you say that?" Kirk asked, also leaning forward to establish a sense of intimacy with the man.

"Well, well," La'kara began, then looked around to make sure no one else was in the lounge. "Mr. Spock is one of . . . well, you know, one of . . . *those,* isn't he?"

Kirk sat back with a sigh. Wonderful, he thought, a bigot. He was surprised that a scientist of La'kara's stature would cling to such a primitive mode of thought. Usually such individuals never made it off their home planet.

"What do you mean, one of 'those,' Professor?" Kirk said sternly. "You mean Spock is guilty because he's a Vulcan?"

"Well, of course he's a Vulcan, Captain!" La'kara exploded. "And I find it shocking that a man in your position would stoop to think that just because someone has a two-percent-greater field of hearing than you or I, it somehow predisposes them to . . . criminal acts!" He flipped his scarf at the captain. "I mean, really, in this day and age."

Kirk fought to keep his mouth from dropping open. "I was drawing no such conclusion, Professor. It was you who said Spock was one of 'those.'" Kirk looked exasperated as he tried to frame a question that would make sense. "What's a 'those,' Professor?"

La'kara leaned forward again and adopted a conspiratorial tone. "I talked with Mr. Spock when I came on board, you know. I know he studied multiphysics under Dr. Nedlund at the Starfleet Academy." La'kara nodded his head and sat back as if he had offered a clear explanation.

"So . . . ?" Kirk prompted.

"So, dear captain," La'kara said in annoyance, eyebrows fluttering, "Dr. Nedlund, I'll have you know, is a complete ass. Can't trust him. Can't trust any of his students." He shook a finger at Kirk and Scott. "And your Mr. Spock was one of Nedlund's students."

Kirk shook his head. "That's why you think Spock is guilty of trying to blow up the *Enterprise?*" he said, trying to sound polite but knowing he didn't.

La'kara just tightened his lips and smiled as if he had said all that was required to prove his point.

"I studied multiphysics under Nedlund, too, Professor," Scott foolishly offered.

La'kara sucked in his breath and flicked his scarf again. "Well, Captain, it appears you have a new suspect!" He glared at Scott.

"Professor La'kara!" Scott cried.

"Mr. Scott!" La'kara mimicked.

"Gentlemen!" Kirk interrupted, waving his hands in defeat. "We're not talking about multiphysics or who went to school where and did what. We're trying to find out who sabotaged the accelerator-field generator." Before La'kara could open his mouth, Kirk added, "And it wasn't Spock! He was in custody and has no motive."

Kirk looked from La'kara to Scott as they kept silent. "Very good. Now who else had the opportunity and the motive?" he asked. "Professor, have you any enemies?"

"I'm a brilliant scientist, Captain. I have hundreds. Perhaps even thousands."

Kirk felt close to groaning. "Enemies that would want to *kill* you, Professor?"

La'kara thought that over for a moment, then shook his head.

"Fine," Kirk said, glad to be over it. "Now, was there anyone else among the scientists in your group on the *Enterprise* that acted suspicious? Didn't take part in scientific conversations? Behaved in any way peculiar?"

"When you come right down to it," La'kara said softly, "we're all a little peculiar, aren't we?"

"Why don't we go down the list?" Scott suggested. "Perhaps a name will jog your memory."

Behind them, a deep voice said, "A most logical strategy, Mr. Scott."

Kirk and Scott jumped up as they turned to see who had spoken.

A young Vulcan stood by the lounge entrance. He wore a traditional black civilian suit with short cape held in place by a silver IDIC medallion. His face was thin and, like most Vulcans, intense. He wore his long, dark brown hair pulled back and tied so it hugged his head like a skintight cap. His hands were on his hips and, as far as Kirk could see, he was unarmed.

"Dr. Stlur," Kirk said, recognizing one half of the team that had brought miniature transporter effects into the operating room. "I didn't hear you come in."

"Of course not," Stlur stated as he walked toward the lounge chairs, pausing once to let the associate roll out of his way. "I did not wish you to hear me."

"Why is that?" Kirk asked warily as the young Vulcan stopped within arm's reach of the captain.

"Think it through, Captain Kirk," the Vulcan said with more than a hint of arrogance. "The near disaster on your vessel was widely believed to have been an assassination attempt on Professor La'kara's life. Therefore, when I witnessed an associate come to invite the professor to a 'private' meeting at a time when few workers are about, was it not logical to assume that perhaps another attempt might be planned?"

"Of course," Kirk agreed. "And you followed the professor to make sure he was safe."

Stlur nodded in agreement.

"Or to kill him when he was away from potential witnesses!" Kirk confronted the Vulcan.

Stlur's expression did not change. "If that were the case, Captain Kirk, then surely I would have killed him as he approached the lounge or, indeed, kill him here along with you and Mr. Scott." The Vulcan paused as if to let Kirk know that this was still a possibility. "You are fugitives from Starfleet authorities, after all," he added. "Your pictures, along with those of Dr. McCoy and Lieutenant Uhura, have been presented on all news and entertainment circuits."

Kirk studied the Vulcan's eyes, but could learn nothing.

"Will you report us?" he finally asked.

"I have not yet made that decision," Stlur said. "I require more information."

"That's what we were trying to come up with," Kirk said, motioning to the chairs as an invitation.

"And that is why I made my presence known," Stlur said. "It appears you could use some assistance."

Over the next ten minutes, Kirk quickly outlined the events and discoveries that had led him and Scott to believe that the assassin or assassins Starfleet was hunting were, in reality, robots manufactured to appear as Vulcans or their offshoot race, Romulans.

"So," Stlur said after patiently listening to what Kirk realized would be perceived as the torturous logic of humans, "as Starfleet suspects Spock because of his unorthodox background, you in turn wish to suspect the Vulcans who traveled on your vessel. That is myself, my associate, T'Vann, and Academician Sradek. You do not wish to concede the point that the assassin, if he or she exists, might have arrived at Memory Prime on another vessel."

"If there is more than one assassin, then of course that's a possibility," Kirk said. "But if there is only one, then no. Someone on board the *Enterprise* attacked the two guards outside Spock's quarters and shut down La'kara's accelerator-field shielding in an attempt to destroy the warp engines. It has to be someone who was on board."

For the first time, Kirk saw a change of expression cross Stlur's face, and he suspected that the Vulcan had, in this instance, accepted Kirk's merely human reasoning.

"All I can say is that I shall make myself available for testing at your convenience, Captain. A standard first-aid medical scanner should be sensitive enough to detect that I am, indeed, a living being. I can also attest to the living nature of my associate, Dr. T'Vann."

"How about Academician Sradek?" Scott asked.

"Mr. Scott," Stlur began, "I am willing to admit that a robot such as the one you and your captain described would probably escape my detection for a brief period if I did not know to look for it. However, I have now shared meals and conversation with the academician for five standard days. I have been exposed to his scent, his voice overtones, and once, when he stumbled, I touched him. No robot could be touched by a Vulcan and not be instantly revealed as such. Sradek is as much a living creature as am I."

Stlur serenely regarded the captain. "I suggest you look elsewhere for your assassin."

Kirk nodded. "You're right. Sradek came to my cabin to ask permission to meet with Spock."

"Aye," Scott said. "He even asked me when he could be expected to be allowed to pay a visit to his old student. And Doctors Stlur and T'Vann were on the tour when the flux was released."

"So all the suspects have alibis," Kirk said in resignation, "except for Spock."

"Captain," Stlur said after a moment, "I do not wish to offer any disrespect, but knowing what I do about humans, is it not possible that upon your ship, with so many crew members, perhaps one of them was somehow replaced by a robot. Without telepathy or normal—I beg your pardon—Vulcan senses, it is likely that such a robot could escape detection for a number of days. Perhaps your suspect might best be searched for among those who are currently above suspicion."

"We've been fooled by lifelike robots before, Stlur, so I know what you suggest is possible," Kirk said.

"Is the theory worth relaying to Commodore Wolfe?" Stlur asked.

"If she would listen to me," Kirk said, though he was sure she wouldn't.

"Perhaps I could speak with the commodore," Stlur suggested.

"Why would she listen to you?" Kirk asked.

"I will tell her that I have spoken with you. She will then want to interrogate me to learn your whereabouts. There is also a sixty-percent chance that she will think I am part of your conspiracy and will once again want to interrogate me. Either way, she will listen to me." Stlur folded his hands in his lap and waited patiently for the captain's response. It didn't take long.

"Very well, doctor," Kirk said. "You go talk to Wolfe, but the first thing you have to convince her to do is to call off the hunt for Spock. Or at least have her order her troops to set their weapons to stun."

"What are they set at now?" Stlur asked, eyebrow raised in a Vulcan expression that had more meanings than Kirk could keep up with.

"To kill," Kirk said.

"Fascinating," Stlur commented. "Am I correct in thinking that such an order is not standard Starfleet procedure?"

"None of this is standard procedure," Kirk said. "I was put under arrest on my own ship."

"So you said," Stlur replied, obviously thinking about something else.

"Well, well?" Professor La'kara interrupted. "Will you do it?"

"Of course," Stlur said. "It is a logical decision."

"Then you don't believe Mr. Spock is guilty, either?" Scott asked.

"Spock's involvement in these events can be determined after the threat to the scientists, from whatever quarter, has ended." Stlur stood up from his chair and adjusted his cape.

"Just a moment," Kirk said. "Scotty, I want you to go with the doctor."

"Back to Wolfe?" Scott said in bewilderment.

"A logical supplement to our strategy, Captain," Stlur commented.

"Logical?" Scott said. "To be thrown in the brig when I could be down here—"

Kirk held up a hand to silence Scott. "Stlur needs support

for what he's saying, Scotty. By turning yourself in, you'll be demonstrating our determination to be taken seriously. You'll also be avoiding the troopers' phasers, my friend."

"But, Captain!"

"You have to help Stlur convince Wolfe that what he's saying is the truth."

"Not necessarily the truth," Stlur qualified. "Just more probable than whatever assumptions the commodore appears to be operating under at present."

"Whatever," Kirk said. "But you have to do it, Scotty. This time it's an order."

"Aye, Captain," Scott sighed.

"Mira will be able to visit a lot easier if you're alive," Kirk added with a wink, then turned to Stlur.

"Spock sent a dispatch to me over the associates," Kirk said. "Try to get the commodore to access Spock's personal work files on the *Enterprise*. The references you're looking for are Agronomy, Memory Gamma, Sherman, and Sradek. He said he wanted them transferred to Professor Saleel at the Vulcan Academy. Do you know him?"

"Of him," Stlur qualified. "An economist."

"An economist?" Kirk mused. "Spock's been working on something to do with the Sherman Syndrome . . . ?"

"I am aware of it," Stlur confirmed. "Do you think there is a connection?"

"Hard to say," Kirk said. "Spock usually has dozens of research projects in progress at any one time. But for him to have specifically mentioned it, it must be important."

Stlur accepted the possibility. "I shall attempt to review the files and have them forwarded in any case," he agreed.

"There was another thing we talked about," Kirk said suddenly. "But no one has found it important." He looked at Stlur. "What does the name T'Pel mean to you?"

Stlur eyed Kirk coolly. "It is my grandmother's name," he said smoothly. "A very common name, to be sure. In what context was it given to you?"

"Commodore Wolfe used it, as if it somehow explained

what was going on. I found a few thousand references to it as a Vulcan female name, but nothing that connected it to what's been going on."

"Did the commodore give the order to set phasers to kill before or after she used the term T'Pel?" Stlur asked.

"After," Kirk said. "Why? What's the connection?"

"I cannot say," Stlur said, and Kirk was suddenly unsure whether he meant cannot or will not. "But I shall endeavor to find out more." He stepped away from the lounge chairs. "Come along, Mr. Scott."

As Kirk accompanied Stlur and Scott to the lounge entrance and La'kara stumbled along with his accelerator-field case, the idle associate once again came to life and slipped out of their way.

"T'Pel means something to Vulcans, doesn't it?" Kirk said without preamble.

"What makes you think so, Captain Kirk?" Stlur asked blandly.

"You and Spock reacted the same way when I mentioned it."

"Mr. Spock *reacted*?" Stlur said dubiously, implying that Kirk was just as mistaken to think that he might have heard a reaction in Stlur's own voice.

"It's more than just a name," Kirk stated. Stlur had responded with a question rather than a statement intended to correct another erroneous human conclusion. Therefore, Kirk thought, borrowing from his exposure to Vulcans, his conclusion was not in error. The name T'Pel was an important factor in the events on Memory Prime. But in what way?

"There are many names, Captain Kirk, and most of them have a multitude of meanings. I would not waste my time investigating the meaning of just that one from among so many. It would not be profitable for you."

Kirk smiled as he held his hand up in the Vulcan salute. He recognized a threat when he heard one. Wherever the answer lay, it would be linked with the name T'Pel.

"Live long and prosper, Stlur," Kirk said formally. "And good luck."

"Live long and prosper, Captain Kirk," Stlur responded. "And clear thinking."

Kirk and La'kara said their farewells to Scott and watched as the two men walked away. They had agreed to report to Captain Farl's troops in ten minutes; enough time to let Captain Kirk return to the service tunnels and to let La'kara return to his quarters.

"All right, Professor," Kirk said as Stlur and Scott turned a far corner and were gone, "your turn to go back to your room."

"And you're sure you'll be safe down in the tunnels?" La'kara asked. "I'm always getting lost in them myself. Too many pipes and colors for my liking."

"You just be sure to stay on this level until you come to the yellow turbolifts." Kirk motioned behind him. "I'll have that associate come along with me. That way I can get dispatches and keep up with Stlur and Scott's progress."

The professor started to step out of the reading lounge, then spun suddenly and grabbed the captain's arms. "I just realized!" he exclaimed. "Oh no, oh no!"

"What?" Kirk demanded. "What?"

"We forgot. I forgot." La'kara stared plaintively up at Kirk. "We didn't ask a most important question, Captain. Here we've sent my good friend Montgomery off with that Vulcan and we just don't know!"

"Know what?" Kirk demanded. Had he somehow put Scotty in danger?

La'kara pulled Kirk down to whisper in the captain's ear and, in a trembling voice, full of fear for his friend, said, "We never asked just where it was that Stlur studied multiphysics!"

Chapter Twenty-one

"How are you doing, doctor?" Uhura asked as she and McCoy ducked into an alcove in the service tunnel to get their bearings.

"Just fine, my dear," McCoy replied, though he seemed relieved at the chance to lean against the wall and take a few deep breaths.

Uhura glanced around the alcove and saw it was much the same as the others they had noticed in their double-time run through the tunnels. From the number of connector leads arranged about a half meter off the deck, she and McCoy had determined that the alcoves were designed to be used by the associates, perhaps to recharge their batteries or to connect directly to Prime's computer network and transfer data faster than they could over a comm link.

Whatever the alcoves were used for, Uhura and the doctor had appreciated their presence because they were handy to slip into and remain hidden in whenever they had heard footsteps or other sounds in the tunnels. Though the tunnels were always lit at a uniform low intensity, Uhura knew that elsewhere in Prime, the environmental controls would be cycling up to morning and that soon many more workers would be traveling through all the tunnels and corridors.

The communications specialist squinted across the tunnel

to the directional signs that were mounted opposite the alcove, comparing the numbers and colors on the various arrows to the instructions Romaine had given them. Everything still matched up.

"Two more intersections to the right," Uhura said, "then a left turn and continue until we see a green band leading to level forty-two."

"Just what I was going to say," McCoy lied unconvincingly. His breath regained, he leaned forward to stick his head out into the tunnel. "All clear," he announced.

Uhura followed the doctor out of the alcove and they began jogging rapidly down the tunnel, passing from one patch of low-level lighting, through a shadow zone, and into the next patch of light.

"Watch it!" McCoy suddenly shouted.

Before them, five meters down the hall, an associate trundled toward them. Unlike the others she and the doctor had passed that night, it was making no attempt to move to the side or otherwise get out of the humans' path.

Uhura and McCoy came to a halt, puffing softly, hearing the echoes of their breathing become obscured by the approaching hum of the associate.

"That's not normal," McCoy said. The machine rolled closer.

"Could it be on remote from the troopers' command station?" Uhura asked.

"I doubt it," McCoy said. "It doesn't have its visual scanner deployed. A remote technician wouldn't be seeing anything."

With that the top panel of the machine sprang back and an eyestalk ground out, rotating to fix on Uhura and McCoy.

"I don't think it's going to stop, doctor," Uhura said. There was no fear in her voice, just anger that their arrival at the scientists' compound was going to be delayed.

"We'll head back for an alcove," McCoy said, and spun around and stopped completely. He put his hand out to Uhura's arm.

Uhura turned. Another associate was approaching them

from the other direction, its eyestalk just now extending to match the deployment of the associate farther down the tunnel.

"Think we can jump over them?" Uhura asked, knowing that she could and hoping McCoy was able as well.

But before McCoy could answer, panels on each side of the approaching machine slid open, and manipulator arms swung out and up. Behind the two *Enterprise* officers, the first machine deployed its arms, too.

"I don't think they want us to jump," McCoy said quietly.

Uhura looked from one machine to the other. Both were closing at an equal rate. In seconds she and McCoy would be within reach of their mechanical arms.

"Split and run?" McCoy suggested.

Tactile grippers on the end of each arm began spinning like cutting saws, causing a high-pitched whine to reverberate off the tunnel walls.

"They don't want us to do that either," Uhura said. She began to judge the distances she would have to jump, the twists she would have to make. It seemed impossible, but at least she would try. The captain would expect that much of her.

McCoy reached out to squeeze Uhura's hand. The machines rolled closer. The two humans tensed as they prepared to rush the machines. Then the associates abruptly stopped centimeters away from their prey, and from their internal speakers, echoing lightly through that long tunnel of Memory Prime, came the gentle sound of laughter.

Kirk watched with fascination as the associate followed him down the ladderway to the lower service tunnel.

The associate had dropped two braces to the deck from its rear wheel wells, then, with the aid of its manipulator arms, pushed itself upright so it stood two meters tall. The manipulator nearer the ladder had then reached out and grabbed the far support post. Kirk had wondered why the ladder posts had a deep groove running down each, and now saw it was a channel for a manipulator attachment to hook into.

The associate had shifted itself over until it was lined up with the ladder and both manipulators were connected, then it simply slid down the ladder posts, stopping three centimeters above the next step off level, and reversed the procedure to return to its rolling configuration. The complete procedure took only twice the time that it had taken Kirk.

As the machine replaced its appendages, Kirk checked to see that the tunnel was still deserted and took a moment to place himself on his mental map of the Prime installation. By keeping the associate with him, and fortunately it had yet to announce it had other duties, Kirk knew that he would learn of Wolfe's response to Stlur and Scott's presentation as soon as a dispatch for him was logged on the system. But in the meantime, he was incapable of simply waiting in one place. Assuming that Spock was on his way to the scientists' compound, Kirk had decided to try and intercept him.

The captain saw that the associate was sealed and ready for movement, then set off down the tunnel in the direction that would take him to a central intersection. If he had been in Farl's position, Kirk would have stationed troopers at the intersection also. But there were many alcoves along the tunnel walls that Kirk could duck into. With the associate to roll in to block him, Kirk felt he could remain hidden in the event of a visual search. If the troopers were using combat tricorders, of course, he wouldn't stand a chance. It was a risk, he knew, but one that he was willing to accept.

Kirk heard the associate's induction motors speed up behind him and the soft whirr of its wheels on the tunnel deck increased. Suddenly Kirk fell forward as the machine nudged him from behind and caught his heel beneath its slanted front cowling.

Reflexively Kirk slapped the deck as he hit it, absorbing the impact without damage. He rolled quickly to see the associate reverse, stop, change its bearing, then come at him again.

At the last moment, Kirk rolled to the left. The machine changed its forward motion instantly, but had too great a turning radius to make contact with Kirk's body. It squealed to a stop on the decking.

Kirk leaped up to his feet, feeling a pull in his Achilles' tendon where the machine had hit his foot. "Module," he said, "stop your activities!"

"This module has other duties," the machine blandly announced, then twisted its tires against the deck with a sound like fingernails on slate. It backed toward Kirk at high speed.

From a standing position, it was even easier for Kirk to jump out of the way. The machine skidded to a stop like a bull overshooting its mark.

"Machine, I order you to stop!" This was ridiculous, Kirk thought. Unless the device was now being remote-controlled by one of Farl's troopers.

The machine didn't reply, but remained motionless as its top panel snapped back and its eyestalk emerged. Kirk saw his chance and rushed at the machine, bending down to reach under it and throw it over on its back. But as he struggled to lift the unexpectedly massive machine, it dropped its rear wheel-well braces and caught Kirk's left hand against the deck.

Grunting with the sudden pain, Kirk put everything he had into a sudden jerk and succeeded in lifting the machine for an instant and yanking out his hand. He flexed it experimentally, grimacing at the sight of his skin marked with the indentations of the brace's gripper texture, but thankful that no bones were broken.

The machine's eyestalk rotated around to fix on him. "Dispatch for James T. Kirk," the machine said in a mechanical voice, then sped at him.

Kirk held his ground to leap when the machine wouldn't have time to compensate. But with its full visual scanner deployed, the onboard brain could read Kirk's body position and anticipate his move.

At the same instant Kirk leaped, the machine swerved,

catching the captain before he landed and bouncing him back into the air.

Kirk hit the deck on his side, unbalanced and rolling, absorbing too much of the force on his left arm. His hand felt as if it were on fire.

A quick assessment of all his intensive Academy training in tactics left him with a clear-cut decision: it was time to retreat.

The machine paused, watching as Kirk crouched on the deck. It's not machine, Kirk told himself; treat it as an animal, an escaped wild animal. He took a quick glance behind him to see where the next ladderway was, but couldn't locate the yellow exit triangle glowing anywhere. If he tried to run farther in that direction, the machine would be able to run him down. If he called for help, the troopers would be the first to respond. There was only one way to run—past the machine and back to the first ladderway.

Kirk stood upright, catching his breath, rotating his twisted left shoulder. The machine had anticipated his last jump, so, as in playing three-dimensional chess with Spock, Kirk decided to hold back and let the machine make the next move and the next mistake. Running through what he knew of standard duotronic brains, he decided to take up some of the machine's processing power with distractions.

"I request that you run a maintenance diagnosis on your logic circuits," Kirk said to the machine, his voice ragged.

The associate rocked back and forth on its wheels, approaching, retreating, and back again. "All logic systems operating within fault-tolerant parameters," it announced.

"Glad to hear it," Kirk said. But at least whatever program or remote controller was running this machine now, it hadn't overridden the onboard brain's built-in standard functions. Kirk tried to remember what other functions he could call on.

"Please report on power levels," Kirk commanded, watching the eyestalk track him as he edged slowly to the right wall of the tunnel.

"Power levels at seventy-six percent of full load," the

machine replied complacently, turning its forward wheels to keep itself aimed directly at Kirk. "Power consumption at nominal levels. Mean time to next recharge at current operational drain, eight hours, twenty-two minutes."

"Your report is in error," Kirk said suddenly. Why not? he thought. That tactic's worked before.

"Objection noted and will be filed with maintenance control at next scheduled overhaul," the associate said.

Kirk sighed. Obviously there were new techniques in place to deal with programming conflicts these days. He feinted to the left. The eyestalk moved with him but the machine didn't follow. Kirk swore. He realized that the visual scanner could read his intentions; and then he realized the tactic he needed to win.

"I surrender," Kirk announced, holding up his hands and taking a tentative step toward the device.

The machine paused, as if thinking over Kirk's offer, then said, "This module is not programmed for game playing." Its eyestalk followed Kirk carefully as its tires shifted to stay aimed at him.

"No, really," Kirk continued, "you've won the shirt off my back." Tightening his eyes at the pain of sudden movement, Kirk quickly pulled his gold tunic over his head, exhaling with relief when it was off and the machine had not used the chance to attack him again. Too much sudden and unexpected visual input, Kirk concluded. He held the tunic in his right hand, holding it out to the side and shaking it.

You've only got one visual scanner, Kirk thought, and now you have two points of reference. He took another step toward the machine. He could hear the flywheels in its induction motors come up to speed, preparing for a sudden burst of acceleration.

"Emergency! Emergency!" Kirk said urgently.

"Do you require assistance?" the associate automatically began, preparing for the kill.

"Fire! Airlock failure! Wounded on level five!" Kirk figured he had a full second before the machine would process all the automatic response sequences he had called forth. He jumped to the left. The machine followed but with a noticeable lag. It began to advance.

Kirk feinted again. The machine missed it as its onboard processors sampled data less frequently to accommodate its emergency time-sharing mode. Then Kirk ran for the device, swung his tunic out in front of him, and snagged the eyestalk as he jumped onto its back.

The associate locked its wheels and came to a bumping halt. Kirk knelt behind the eyestalk and held on to it as his knees bounced along the top of the machine, almost sending him off the side.

The associate was now motionless except for its weaving eyestalk. Kirk wrapped his tunic around the visual scanner three more times to ensure that not even infrared could pass through the fabric. The device was blinded. He could make it to the ladderway.

Then the machine shuddered as its side panels sprang back and its manipulator arms burst out from both sides. Kirk flinched as the tactile grippers at the end of each arm began to whirl and the arms snapped up. He knew the instant he jumped off to run, the onboard sensors would lock on to him and he'd be sliced open as easily as the insulation on the pipes above him before his foot touched the deck. But if he stayed in place another few seconds, the onboard brain would have calculated the eyestalk's position and the arms would descend into the volume of space that Kirk now occupied.

Kirk's mind accelerated. There *was* a way out. There had to be.

The arms arced slowly into the space above the associate. Kirk hunched down, closer to the machine's top surface, to buy himself an extra half second. He stared down the trunk of the eyestalk, into the appendage bay it had emerged from.

Of course! Kirk thought as the whirling cutters descended. It's a *research* associate. It wasn't armored for vacuum or battle. He shot his arm into the appendage bay, groping blindly until his fingers grasped a thick bundle of wires. Then he yanked.

The machine bucked as transtator current pulsed through Kirk's arm. The manipulator arms jerked, a slowing cutter sliced against Kirk's back as the arms trembled, then collapsed to the deck, all internal hydraulic pressure exhausted.

The current cut out as a fail-safe system switched the batteries out of circuit. Kirk's body slumped against the associate's top, rolled to the side, then fell off to the deck.

A slight crackling sound resonated within the dying associate. A thin wisp of smoke swirled from the open appendage bay, flowing around the tunic-wrapped eyestalk that drooped like a dying plant.

Kirk stared blurrily at the pipes on the ceiling, trying to shake off the effects of the current. His left hand and arm throbbed with pain, his entire right side ached through a distant layer of shocked numbness. Another sound entered his consciousness: a familiar sound.

He looked down the corridor. Another associate advanced, eyestalk already extended. Kirk groaned, forcing his left arm to push him up against the shell of the associate beside him. His mind tried to sort out the swimming double images before him. He pulled at his black T-shirt, preparing to pull it off to use against the visual scanner. But the task suddenly seemed too complicated.

The second associate stopped by Kirk. Its eyestalk bent down to focus on him. Kirk stared back in defiance.

"This module thought you might be in need of some assistance, Captain Kirk," the machine said in a voice that bore no trace of mechanical origins. "But I see that I was mistaken."

Kirk blinked as he tried to place the machine's comments in context. The eyestalk moved up to examine the smoking ruin of the associate Kirk had battled, then rotated back to look into the captain's eyes.

"As a mutual acquaintance would say, Captain," the machine announced, "fascinating."

Kirk closed his eyes to blink, and found they wouldn't

open again. As the rest of the universe rushed away from him, he had only one thought. . . .

". . . Spock. Spock?" Kirk sat up suddenly and his head exploded in a star bow of color. Gentle hands pushed him back to lie against something soft.

"I am here, Captain," Spock said in the darkness beyond Kirk's eyes.

Kirk felt the cool tingle of a spray hypo against his neck.

"You'll be all right, Jim," Bones said. "You had a nasty transtator shock but no real harm done."

Kirk opened his eyes and saw McCoy and Uhura looking down on him with worry and relief on their faces. Spock was there, too, and under the circumstances did the best that he could. Kirk also saw Romaine and Nensi in the background, faces etched with exhaustion and worry.

Kirk held his left hand in front of his face and studied the bandage that wrapped it. "Transtator shock?" he asked.

"Not all of it," McCoy said. "You've got an abraded hand, a wrenched shoulder, and a deep cut on your back. . . . But as your physician, I've come to accept those kinds of injuries as your normal state of health."

"Do you remember what happened, Captain?" Spock inquired.

"An associate," Kirk said as it came back to him. "It tried to attack me, I short-circuited it . . . a second associate came. . . ." He looked directly at Spock as if he doubted what he said next. "The second one spoke to me . . . as if it was alive."

"How else should I have spoken to you?" a familiar voice asked.

Spock stepped out of the captain's line of vision and Kirk saw that they were in some sort of equipment room. He could hear pumps operating and smelled a faint odor of disinfectant. It reminded him of the swimming pool on the *Enterprise.*

Then he saw what Spock had made way for. An associate,

identical to all the others he had seen so far, rolled up to the table he lay on and extended its eyestalk toward him.

"May I introduce Two," Spock said.

"Two?" Kirk questioned.

"Two. It is a Pathfinder."

Kirk rotated his shoulders and found that McCoy's anti-inflammatory drugs had done their work. He had almost full flexibility in both, though his left hand was still stiff and he could feel the pull in his back where the protoplaser had sealed his cutter wound.

"So with all that you've said considered," Kirk concluded as he slipped off whatever it was that McCoy had rigged as a sickbed, "I'd say we have only one conclusion."

"I would be most interested to hear you share that with us, Captain," Spock said.

Kirk smiled. He had missed his science officer.

"Lifelike robots, appearing as Romulans, have assembled on Memory Prime to assassinate one or more of the scientists attending the prize ceremonies. To support their attempt, they have installed a secondary transporter network and have set up an override system that allows them to control the associates." Kirk glanced around to see that no one had any objections, or at least was saving them until he had finished.

"We can also assume that the assassins have generated subspace interference to prevent any signals from leaving Prime that might alert Starfleet security forces."

"Newscasts are still getting out, though," Romaine interjected.

"Keeps appearances normal," Kirk said. "If the newscasts were blocked, no one would have to wait for an alert signal to get troops here in hours. The advertisers would demand they go in right away." He walked back and forth in the equipment room, drawing everything together and seeing that it worked perfectly. "If Uhura's suspicions are correct and the last message Wolfe received from Komack did originate from Prime, rather than just being transferred up from a ground station, then it's probable that all the rest of the Fleet ships here are receiving false communications. Additional false signals would have to be passed on to Starfleet, too, in order for Command not to suspect that no one here is receiving their communications."

"Captain," Spock said as Kirk paused, "though the scenario you describe is internally logical, it is unfortunately based on a technological assumption which I believe has no merit."

"Which is?" Kirk asked.

"The extent of subspace interference which you propose is not possible given our present state of technology," Spock answered.

"He's right, Captain," Uhura added. "Subspace channels are virtually two-dimensional. Random signals that are energetic enough to jam one channel invariably smear out to affect the whole FTL spectrum."

"Given our present state of technology," Kirk said, "I agree with you. But the robots that captured Scotty and me were more advanced than any I've seen before. If the Romulans, or their suppliers, the Klingons, have come up with impressive breakthroughs in robotics, then why not allow for the possibility that they have come up with an equally advanced method of controlling subspace interference?"

"I point out that every rapid breakthrough in Klingon science has followed the subjugation of a technologically advanced culture, Captain. While I doubt that Klingons could have developed such technologies on their own, I am also skeptical of their ability to conquer a race that had already developed them." Spock was obviously not impressed with the captain's reasoning.

"Do you have another possibility for us to consider?" Kirk asked.

"Not at this time."

Kirk looked at the associate by the door. "How about the Pathfinder?"

The machine's eyestalk looked dumbly back.

"Over here, Captain." Two's voice came from one of the two associates that had brought Uhura and McCoy to the swimming-pool equipment room.

Kirk walked over to the associate who had spoken. It was still unnerving to be faced with a consciousness that could jump between host bodies, as it were. The Pathfinder had explained that his central core was still located twelve kilometers away, deep in the asteroid's center, and it was simply banking a few functions through an I/O port to make comm-link contact with the associates.

Romaine had been stunned by the synthetic consciousness's offhand revelation, but no matter how many times she had tried to question it, the Pathfinder had insisted it did not know where the I/O channel was located.

"Part of the agreement in coming to work at Memory Prime was that the Pathfinders would have no direct access to outside systems and control networks," Romaine pointed out.

"That contract was initiated after I withdrew from access," Two had replied, "so perhaps those conditions do not apply to me." Then it laughed. Kirk had found that ability even more unnerving.

"So?" Kirk repeated. "Do you have any other possibilities to suggest to us?"

"Not at this time," the Pathfinder said in a passable imitation of Spock's voice. It laughed again.

"Two." Kirk spoke again, trying to ignore the unnerving laughter. "Have any dispatches been logged for us on the associates' message network?"

"Nothing so far, Captain," the Pathfinder said from the associate over by the door.

"Can you access the communications channels to see if anything has been said about calling off the hunt for Spock and the rest of us?" Kirk tried.

The Pathfinder returned to the associate by Kirk. "Commander Farl has ordered his troops not to use the portable transporters because a second system is interfering with their operations," it said. "All internal transportation systems are now being shut down and will be inoperative within the next four minutes. Emergency transportation facilities will be provided by the *Enterprise* and the *Valquez*."

"I was right about that one, then," Kirk said, glancing at Spock. He turned back to the machine. "When do the opening ceremonies start?"

"Two hours, three minutes, eighteen seconds . . . seventeen seconds . . . six—"

"That will do, thank you," Kirk interrupted.

"Can you scan through the list of scientists attending the ceremonies and identify those whose deaths would be most disruptive to the Federation at this time?" Spock asked.

"That's a good one," the Pathfinder replied. "Give me a few seconds to work out the probabilities."

"Good idea, Spock," Kirk said. Then he narrowed his eyes at the Vulcan. "I have a good question for it, as well."

The Pathfinder rejoined them before Spock could reply.

"There are forty-seven scientists attending the prize ceremonies whose deaths could result in the virtual collapse of Federation initiatives in weapons design, propulsion technology, and political organization."

"Is Professor La'kara on that list?" Kirk asked.

"Zoareem La'kara is on the third level of importance."

"Are any of the scientists who traveled on the *Enterprise* among the forty-seven most vital scientists?" Kirk tried again.

"Nope," the Pathfinder said.

"Where does Academician Sradek rank?" Spock asked.

"Fifth rank. Of no long-term importance," Two replied.

Kirk studied Spock's reaction. Despite Stlur's comment, the science officer did exhibit reactions to those who knew him well enough to read them. "You don't agree with that assessment?" Kirk asked.

"Sradek has made many valuable contributions to the growth and the stability of the Federation," Spock said.

"But not recently," the Pathfinder countered. "Sradek is growing old and his contemporary work is not sound."

"But he's a nominee for the Peace Prize," Nensi said.

"For negotiations concluded almost two standard years ago," the Pathfinder replied. "He has completed no work of importance since that time and has hindered the work of the Sherman's Planet famine board of inquiry."

"Fascinating," Spock said with as much excitement as anyone could ever expect to hear from him. "I have recently reached a similar conclusion based on Sradek's failure to recognize the existence of the Sherman Syndrome as anything more than a statistical artifact."

"It *is* obvious," the Pathfinder stated condescendingly.

Spock walked over to the associate who currently housed Two's remote functions. "What data can you produce to support the basic argument of the Sherman Syndrome?" Spock asked.

"Most of the raw data are stored on Memory Gamma but the conclusions are generally evolved here," Two said. "Give me a few seconds to sift it."

Kirk had had enough. "Spock, we can get back to agriculture when the assassins have been stopped. Time for my question." He turned to the associate that had just spoken. "Pathfinder Two, how does the name T'Pel connect with the assassination attempt we have been discussing?"

"Captain Kirk," Spock said, "there is no logical reason to—"

"Perfectly," the associate next to Kirk replied. Then the Pathfinder banked to the associate beside Spock and said, "Sherman Syndrome data has been interfered with. I am attempting to reconstruct."

"What do you mean by 'perfectly'?" Kirk said, looking from one associate to the next.

"Who else but an Adept of T'Pel would contemplate the assassination of the Federation's greatest scientists," the third associate in the middle replied, "and be able to accomplish it?"

"Who or what is an Adept of T'Pel?" Kirk demanded.

"Pathfinder," Spock interrupted, "I ask that you provide the information I requested to support the Sherman Syndrome."

"Spock!" Kirk snapped. "I said that can wait!" He turned to the associate. "Pathfinder, explain the meaning of an Adept of T'Pel."

"They are the guild of Vulcan assassins," the associate by Kirk said.

"Sherman Syndrome data has been recon—"the associate by Spock said.

Kirk was locked into position, not daring to breathe so he wouldn't miss an instant of the bizarre three-sided conversation. But his associate said nothing more. Neither did Spock's.

"I/O port shut down," Romaine said finally, breaking the silence. "It cut out in midword."

"Spock," McCoy said in wonderment, "a *Vulcan* guild of *assassins?* Is such a thing possible?"

Everyone turned to look at Spock. The Vulcan's face was frozen in an expression completely devoid of meaning.

"What about it, Spock?" Kirk said, his anger apparent. "You've known something all along, haven't you?"

"Not known, Captain. Suspected," Spock said at last.

"Isn't that splitting logical hairs, Mr. Spock?" McCoy asked. "Have you actually had information that might have stopped any of this?"

"No, doctor, I have not had information that could have stopped any of the steps that have been taken thus far. I had suspicions, based only on my own knowledge, and with no supportable evidence. The suggestion that Memory Prime was to be subjected to an attack instigated by the Adepts of T'Pel, would have been met with ridicule"—Spock looked at the Captain as if only he would understand—"and violated a sacred Vulcan trust."

"Then there *are* such things as Vulcan assassins?" McCoy gasped.

"Absolutely not, doctor," Spock stated. "Such a concept would not be tolerated on my planet. Indeed, it is not tolerated."

"Which is why none of you will talk about it," Kirk said, suddenly understanding the connection between Stlur's cold response to the name of T'Pel and Spock's determined effort to keep Kirk from looking further into its meaning. "It does exist."

"But not on Vulcan," Spock said. "Not anymore."

Kirk walked over to his friend, stood beside him, and spoke softly.

"Start at the beginning, Spock. There's not much time."

Chapter Twenty-two

WITHIN EACH VULCAN dwelt a secret heart, a voice and a message from their beginnings, passed on from one mindmeld to the other through the long years since the Reformation, whispering of the madness that had been their crucible. That secret heart was their witness to the past, their window on their culture's birth, more than two thousand standard years ago.

Even then, the Vulcan intellect was unequaled. The specter of ruin that haunted their planet was known by all, embraced by some, and rejected by but a few. Resistance seemed futile, and the great minds and orators of Vulcan prepared their followers for the ultimate reward of emotions run wild: the war and destruction and extinction that had claimed so many other worlds.

As had also happened on so many other worlds, some individuals spoke out against the inevitable, and made themselves heard, and the greatest triumph of Vulcan was that in its final hour, the people listened.

His name was Surak, and his message was simple and direct. If emotions unchecked are to control us until we are destroyed, then we must first control our emotions and survive. It was a call for Total Logic, and it offered the planet salvation.

A hundred years earlier, Surak would have been ignored. A hundred years later, he would have been cut down before any could have listened. But at the time he spoke out, Vulcan was poised on that precarious threshold—still civilized enough to have political forums where Surak could present and debate his ideas, and yet chaotic enough that some could read the warning signs.

As the debates proceeded across the planet, Surak assembled supporters and faced enemies. Though not the most numerous, the most deadly faction among his enemies was from his own family, the woman T'Pel.

She was a warrior by nature and longed for the ancient days when an individual's worth was easily measured by the torrents of emerald blood she had unleashed upon the deserts' red sands. A future, however brief, of war and glory was infinitely preferable to the stultifying boredom that her cousin preached.

So T'Pel stole Surak's message, and twisted it into one of her own. To a world crying out for answers, she brought a release from the need for answers, an escape from the tyranny of cause and effect. She called it Analogics, and in her public debates with Surak, she used its twisted precepts to logically negate his call for logic.

Some in the audiences laughed. Some cringed. And some saw that in a system that required they no longer think critically, they could at last find peace. As T'Pel taught them, there was no greater peace than death. So it was that before the glory of the Reformation, there was the blackness and the disgrace of the nights of the assassins. Her Adepts, she called them, the Adepts of T'Pel.

T'Pel trained her most trusted Adepts in the long unpracticed schools of deadly arts, instilling them with terrifying powers of destruction to be used without regard for motive. Then she offered them to her world, to perform whatever acts of terrorism were asked of them. Escape was not a requirement of any plan. The shock of mindless killing and destruction was.

In a sense, it was the horror and revulsion that the majority felt for the acts of the Adepts that made more and more Vulcans listen seriously to Surak. Surak *told* his listeners what the world of the future might be like if Vulcans' emotions remained unchecked. T'Pel *showed* those same people exactly what it *would* be like. The tide slowly and inexorably turned to Surak and Total Logic. T'Pel and her Adepts were reviled and hunted. The path to Vulcan's future had been clearly laid out by Surak, and his followers would find no place for the madness of T'Pel. Beneath the swelling wave of irrefutable logic, T'Pel and her Adepts disappeared from Vulcan and its records; a part of the past that logical Vulcans could know of and accept, but that which no outworlder could possibly comprehend. Her acts, her schools, her followers, were relegated to the vaults of the secret histories of Vulcan, which some offworlders had often suspected existed, but which none had seen.

But Surak had had other enemies, not all as extreme as T'Pel . . . at first.

The Travelers were those who had rejected Surak and his ways and, by doing so, had rejected Vulcan. In monstrous ships, they had abandoned the world that had forsaken them and set out to find a new world to tame with the ancient traditions intact and venerated. And among them were others with different motives for leaving Vulcan, others for whom exile was preferable to death. Deep within the Travelers' ships, T'Pel and her last Adepts journeyed for their own chance for freedom.

At last the Travelers came to a system with two planets that some, in desperation, would call suitable for life. The most hard won of the two was called ch'Havran, and on it were the harsh lands of the dreaded East Continent. It was there that the clan that would spring from T'Pel and her Adepts would find a home suitable for their talents.

The Travelers had willingly discarded all that they had that was Vulcan. A new language was created, new customs explored, the hatred for their origins grew until they had wiped out all traces of their Vulcan heritage. Except on the East Continent. Except in the nations of Kihai and LLunih, where in the darkened secret rooms, the old traditions were passed, and the name that was whispered from lips that dripped with the green gore of their blood sacrifices was the name T'Pel.

All other names from Vulcan passed from their knowing. The Travelers themselves were now the Rihannsu. But when the humans came, the name that was given in ignorance was Romulan, and among the proud people who had once given up an entire world for what they perceived as justice, the time for action had once again come.

Some among the Rihannsu were willing to listen to the humans and risk meetings and exchanges. But in the East Continent, in the nations of Kihai and LLunih, the ancient traditions lived. The ships from the clans of those nations were the ones that dogged the Federation vessels, becoming more and more brazen in their actions until war was inevitable.

It was a glorious time for the Adepts. They fueled the images of their nation's atrocities that burned into the minds and souls of a hundred worlds, rekindling the horror of what might have been the last great days of Vulcan.

But in that first war the Federation was victorious, and once again the Adepts of T'Pel sank beneath knowing in defeat. But the war they had helped start had brought them important new knowledge: the universe had changed since the time of the Travelers. There were innumerable new worlds and new civilizations joined into one.

Why should the Adepts content themselves with the destruction of just one world and one culture when there were so many now to choose from?

The Adepts of T'Pel had waited two thousand years for this moment. Before them the galaxy beckoned, and they moved out into it, learning its ways, swearing by the ancient blood and the ancient name that before they were forced to retreat again, they would hear that galaxy scream.

They had been true to their oath. In the dark reaches of

the galaxy, in the ports and shadows where such things were discussed, the ancient name was passed from one to another, offering unspeakable services . . . for a price. Thus far the galaxy had been silent. But that silence would not last. The Adepts of T'Pel had sworn it.

They had returned.

Chapter Twenty-three

"GOOD LORD," McCoy whispered. The others in the room remained silent. Only the soft rush of the pumps could be heard.

"How long have you known?" Kirk asked, his anger replaced with sorrow. Alone among the others he knew the cost to Spock of what had been revealed. A sacred Vulcan trust, Spock had called his knowledge of T'Pel, and he had been forced to break it.

"Of T'Pel," Spock said, "since I was a child and experienced my first melds with the ancient memories. Vulcans do not blindly follow the teachings of Surak simply because it is our tradition. Through the melds, each of us has experienced firsthand the chaos from which those teachings sprang and the chaos to which we might return if we do not continue in the ways of logic."

Spock looked in turn at each of those listening, making sure to meet their gaze, especially McCoy's. Kirk knew it was Spock's way of making his plea that none of what he had told them be repeated, a plea that logic forbade him from making aloud.

"How long have I known that the Adepts of T'Pel still exist among the Romulans of today?" Spock continued. "Classified documents from the first Romulan war hint at it.

Analyses completed in the century since then tend to confirm it. But there is still no absolute proof, as no Adept has ever been captured. Alive."

"But how long have you known, or suspected, that they were responsible for the events on Prime?" Kirk asked gently.

"Since Mira's message informed me that Commodore Wolfe commanded the troopers to search for me with phasers set to kill."

"How does that prove anything?" Uhura asked before anyone else had the chance.

"It's against every regulation in the book," Kirk answered so Spock could continue.

"Exactly," Spock said. "Starfleet expressly forbids the use of deadly force against unarmed personnel."

"Then how in blazes could Wolfe order her troopers to use deadly force against you?" McCoy demanded.

"Quite obviously, the commodore had some reason for believing that I was no longer to be considered unarmed."

"But why?" Uhura asked.

"She thought you were part of the Adepts of T'Pel," Kirk said softly.

"Precisely," Spock replied. "And as such, trained in the ancient schools of unassisted combat; a being whose entire body can be considered a living weapon and sworn to the destruction of life and order at all costs. The commodore could not send her troops unprotected against such a being. She had no choice but to order them to defend themselves and this facility in the most decisive manner, just as we would respond to any comparable military threat."

It took only a moment for McCoy to see where that conclustion led. "You mean *Starfleet* knows?" he asked. "About the *Adepts?*"

"Precisely, doctor," Spock answered. "It would not be logical for Vulcans to refuse to share information that could preserve the stability of the Federation. There are those within Starfleet who have been made aware of the Adepts of T'Pel and the role they might play in any potentially destabilizing activities. However, that information is strictly classified."

"But why?" McCoy, as usual, bridled at the machinations of the government.

"Think, doctor," Spock explained. "If the general population learned that an organization of Romulan assassins threatened the Federation, then surely there would be an increase in those who clamored for a resumption of war. Furthermore, revealing that the Federation is aware of the Adepts' existence would provide the Adepts with proof that their organization has in some way been penetrated by the Federation Security Service. Whatever means the service has been using to monitor the Adepts will have been compromised and lost. Unable to be kept under surveillance, the Adepts will then become even more dangerous. The Federation's knowledge of them cannot be revealed."

"To say nothing of what it might tell the general population about Vulcan history," Nensi commented.

"We prefer to think of it as *pre*history," Spock corrected, "but that is also a consideration. Though by no means the most important one."

"So we're cut off," McCoy railed, "being hunted down by a commodore who'd rather see us dead than risk having knowledge of the Adepts revealed, and at the mercy of a bunch of Romulans who want to kill the Federation's best scientists so they can start a war!" His arms flapped at his sides. "I should have been a vet," he said in disgust, and slumped against the wall.

"I will agree that we are cut off," Spock said calmly, "and concede that the commodore would rather have me, at least, killed. But we cannot assume that the Adepts wish to start a war."

"And why not?" McCoy demanded.

"The Adepts follow the so-called discipline of Analogics," Spock said. "They have no motives. They are assassins for *hire*."

"Without a motive," Kirk said, "most crimes can't be

solved. That's why it's been so hard to determine who the victim of the assassin or assassins might be: they aren't connected, except by the third party who hired one to kill the other."

"But who?" McCoy was becoming more aggravated by the second.

"Think motive, Bones," Kirk said. "What motives would the Adepts work for? Illogical motives. Madness. Confusion. Destruction of order, of . . ." He turned to Spock, eyes afire. "Sradek!" he cried.

"The assassin?" Spock asked in surprise.

"No, the victim!" Kirk reached out his hands. "You've been investigating his work. Pathfinder Two confirmed it. Sradek's interfering with the operation of the Sherman's Planet famine board of inquiry, is he not?"

"So I believe," Spock confirmed.

"Agribusiness! Big business," Kirk continued. "Billions upon billions of credits at stake. The stability of the whole sector. What if Sradek is *not* interfering? What if the Sherman's Planet famine and all the ones like it have been specifically engineered? It's possible. A conspiracy by some group to ensure that environmental data for agricultural worlds is misreported or misrepresented. That leads to improper crop selection, therefore crop failures, financial drain on the interplanetary banking system, famine, disease . . . political instability. What would happen if that type of disaster was being manipulated to appear on dozens of worlds at once on purpose, instead of just one or two by accident? Sradek's brilliant, trained Vulcan mind may be the only one that can see the truth that the famines have been artificially created. He could be the target of a campaign to discredit him and his work so that no one will believe his conclusions. And since that campaign isn't totally working, the only other way to prevent his interference is to kill him!"

Spock considered the captain's hypothesis. He raised both eyebrows and nodded. "It does fit the facts," he admitted.

"But you're not convinced?" Kirk prodded.

"I would have to accept that my independent study of Sradek's conclusions was in error—"

"Heaven forbid your work should be in error, Spock!" McCoy muttered.

"But it *could* be if the data you were working with was wrong!" Kirk said in triumph. "Pathfinder Two said that the Sherman's Planet data from Memory Gamma had been interfered with! If the conspiracy has penetrated the Memory Planets, there's no end to the chaos that incorrect data could cause."

"I believe we must warn Academician Sradek," Spock announced. The debate was over.

"At least you could have the courtesy to say the captain was right," McCoy suggested.

"I believe I already have, doctor." Spock studied Kirk. "Considering your injuries, are you able to join us, Captain?"

Kirk refused to dignify the question with a response and turned to Romaine. "Mira, how can we get to Sradek?"

Nensi stepped forward before Romaine could answer. "The doctor and the lieutenant are in civvies, so they can come with Mira and me. I've got the VIP passes to get them into the scientists' compound on my authority. You and Spock can come up in the associate equipment cart."

"Equipment cart?" Kirk asked.

Nensi blinked at the captain. "How do you think Pathfinder Two had the associate bring you here? Drag you through the tunnels asking the troopers not to look?" Nensi pulled a sheet of insulating fabric off the platform Kirk had come to consciousness on. It was a wheeled, closed cart, about the size of an associate, with a hitch at one end that Kirk saw could attach to an associate's rear appendage bay.

"Oh," Kirk said. "That was going to be my next question."

Scott felt the vibration of the glowing verifier dome flutter against his hand. He looked nerviously over to the technician who operated the Mark II desktop terminal in Prime's security interrogation room. The technician ran a hand through his dark beard and looked up at Commodore Wolfe standing beside him.

"Verified," the technician said resignedly. "He's telling the truth, Commodore. Three times out of three. Just like Dr. Stlur."

The commodore glared at Scott. Scott felt his indignation grow but forced himself not to say or do anything that would interfere with his chances of getting the commodore to believe him. Spock's life, even the captain's, depended on his convincing the commodore that the real threat to the scientists on Prime came from robots and not from Scott's fellow officers.

"Medical analysis!" the commodore snapped.

The Andorian trooper that stood beside the verifier stand waved a medical scanner in front of Scott's head and chest and checked the readings on a tricorder.

"Absolutely no indication of blocking drugss or nonbiological implantss, Commodore," he hissed in disappointment.

Wolfe leaned over and checked the readings on the terminal again, tapping her hand on its status indicator bar. Then she stood up, a decision made. "Set that to automatic," she told the technician, "and leave. Both of you." She held out her hand to the Andorian. "But you give me your phaser," she added.

A few moments later, the interrogation room cleared except for herself and the prisoner, Wolfe leaned back in her chair and regarded Scott with a look of contempt.

"Mr. Scott," she finally began, "we will proceed on the assumption that at the end of all this you will still wish to be a part of Starfleet . . . no matter what your eventual rank downgrading might turn out to be. That is what you wish, is it not?" She turned to watch the computer display.

Scott swallowed hard. "Aye, Commodore, it certainly is."

"Good," Wolfe said, seeing that the engineer's reply was confirmed by the verifier. "Now, Mr. Scott, are you aware of the penalties as set out in Starfleet regulations pertaining to the disclosure of classified material?"

"Aye," Scott said. What did this have to do with anything? he wondered.

"Very good," Wolfe said, narrowing her eyes at the engineer. "Therefore, as stated in those same regulations, let me inform you that some of what I'm about to say may or may not fall under level-eight classification. I will not tell you which parts are so classified so you will be bound by your Starfleet oath not to reveal any part of this conversation without risking solitary life imprisonment on Rock. Do you understand what I have just said?"

"That I do, Commodore," Scott answered, his voice dry and threatening to crack.

"What knowledge do you have of an organization known as the Adepts of T'Pel?" Wolfe's eyes stayed locked on the Mark II's display lights.

Scott glanced up at the light strips along the ceiling, desperately trying to determine why the name sounded familiar. "I, ah, I have nae knowledge of such an organization," he stammered.

"The verifier indicates otherwise, Mr. Scott," the commodore said in a voice of judge, jury, and executioner. "I will allow you one more chance to tell me the truth."

"T'Pel!" Scott suddenly said. "That was the name the captain asked Dr. Stlur about!"

The commodore smiled and Scott had a sudden fear that he was somehow betraying the captain.

"And what was the nature of that inquiry?" Wolfe continued.

Scott bit his lip, trying to replay the discussion in the reading lounge. "Ah, the captain . . . the captain asked Dr. Stlur what the name meant just as we were getting ready to leave the lounge."

"What was the Vulcan's response?"

Scott wrinkled his brow as he remembered. "The doctor said it was his . . . his grandmother's name." It wasn't making sense to Scott, but from Wolfe's expression, it seemed that she saw a pattern forming in his replies.

The questions and answers continued as the commodore led Scott through a reconstruction of Kirk's exchange with Stlur. When Scott had finished, Wolfe scratched at the side of her face, deep in thought.

"Uh, Commodore?" Scott said, unable to remain in the dark by choice.

Wolfe nodded at him to proceed.

"Why the change?"

"Mr. Scott?"

"In the way ye dealt with the captain? I mean, I can understand why ye had to confine Mr. Spock to his quarters. Getting that message from Starfleet just as we came into your starbase and all, ye had nae choice but to follow orders. Even Mr. Spock himself admitted that it was logical for ye to suspect him of sabotaging the accelerator shielding system." The commodore's eyes widened at that but she made no comment. "But what I cannae understand is why ye suddenly turned on Captain Kirk. Sure he supported Mr. Spock, gave him the benefit of the doubt, but can't ye see, Mr. Spock is his . . . his crew. Captain Kirk just dinnae have a choice."

Scott looked nervously at the commodore. He hadn't intended to say so much, to sound as if he were challenging her, but the truth was that Kirk was his captain, and the engineer shared the same lack of choice in what his loyalty demanded of him.

Wolfe looked long and hard at Scott, and Scott was surprised to see that not once did she turn to check the verifier's reading.

"Mr. Scott," she said at last, "do you know what kind of a man James T. Kirk is?" She didn't give him a chance to answer. "Do you have any idea of the number of people, men *and* women, who dream of commanding a starship of their own, to have a chance to go *first,* to be *first,* see things, experience things that no one has ever seen or experienced before? Kirk is the one who made it. He worked hard. I know that. He worked hard for me at the Academy. But there were lots of others who worked just as hard, dreamed just as hard, and never made it because there are only a handful of starships."

Wolfe pushed her chair back and stood up, staring at Scott with questioning eyes, eyes that offered Scott an answer to his question.

"No one knows exactly how the selection committee chooses who gets a starship and who gets a cruiser, who gets a starbase and who gets a spacedock, and I've been in the service long enough to know that you don't question authority. I was passed over, Mr. Scott. I admit it. And I can also tell you that I'm not bitter. I couldn't have stayed in the Fleet if I had been." She picked up the phaser with which she had been left and Scott involuntarily flinched until he saw that she was attaching it to her utility belt. She flashed a small smile as she realized the cause of Scott's reaction.

"So I stayed, and I taught all those others who came through the Academy. Same dream, same hopes shared by so many of them . . . a *starship* . . . to go *out there.* I prepared them as best I could, and whenever one of them made it, or even came close, I rejoiced for him or for her, well and truly, because as long as one of my students made it, then part of me was out there, too. Part of me was out there with your captain." She held her finger over the comm switch on the Mark II, ready to signal the trooper to return.

"And when I saw that Kirk had blown it, when I saw that he was taking everything that he had achieved and was throwing it in the faces of all those others, me included, who would have done *anything* to have that one chance . . . well, Mr. Scott, as far as I could see, James T. Kirk was a traitor. Not just to Starfleet and the Federation, but to the dream, Mr. Scott. To the *dream.*"

Scott had his answer. But how to give the commodore hers? "'He's nae a traitor, Commodore," he said softly. "And neither is Mr. Spock."

"I pray you're wrong, Mr. Scott," the commodore said.

Her voice was firm, her eyes dry and unwavering, but Scott could sense the anguish in her soul. "Because there is too much at stake here. I can't accept what you and Dr. Stlur have said." She pressed the comm switch and behind her the interrogation room's doors puffed open and the Andorian trooper marched in. "I'm sorry, Mr. Scott. I truly am."

"*Then at least tell your troops to set their phasers on stun!*" Scott shouted out as the commodore turned to leave.

Commodore Wolfe did not look back. Scott thought later that perhaps she was unable to meet his eyes and still say what she had said.

"I can't, Mr. Scott. I'm following my orders."

"Then that's the difference between ye and the captain!" Scott called out to her, stepping out of the verifier chair even as the trooper ran to hold him back. "Ye say ye've been in the service long enough to know ye don't question authority! But that's what the captain does! *Question,* not defy! It's what keeps the system working! Keeps it honest and fair!"

The commodore paused in the corridor outside, still not looking back, but not continuing forward.

"Sometimes ye have to question authority to stop mistakes from being repeated, Commodore! Ye've made one mistake about the captain, already. Don't make another! Especially one ye can't set right again! Commodore!"

Following standard procedures, the trooper applied a light stun to the prisoner to calm him down. As Scott slouched into the verifier chair, still struggling to call the commodore's name, Wolfe moved on and the doors slid shut behind her.

"What is this," McCoy asked as he looked around the lab, "the Middle Ages?"

"Special case," Nensi explained as he closed the lid on the associate cart that Kirk and Spock had hidden in, in order to gain access to the scientists' compound. The biolab they were in was an animal test facility, the only one on Prime and one of only a handful throughout the Federation, excepting agricultural and zoological research centers and zoos.

Kirk studied the animal cages at the side of the lab. They were stacked three up and twelve across against the wall, sealed off from the rest of the lab by a windowed partition. The animals inside appeared to be meter-tall, hairless apes with shiny, dark red skin. Two fingers waggled from the hands on each long arm as they patted the almost invisible surface of the transparent aluminum panels that served as their individual cage doors.

"Constellation monkeys, they're called," Nensi said. "And no one is quite sure if they *are* living creatures or not. That's part of the work going on here."

"This *is* the lab that Sradek told you he'd meet us in, isn't it?" Kirk asked.

"Oh, yes," Nensi confirmed. "This is where he's been working during his visit to Prime." Nensi pointed to a stack of equipment crates piled around one of the worktables. Kirk recognized them as the cargo that had beamed aboard with Sradek from Starbase Four.

"What is the nature of Sradek's work in an animal experimentation lab?" Spock asked, eyebrows drawn together. "It does not seem a logical place for a political scientist." He stood in front of the animal cages, staring in at the creatures.

"He's studying models of aggression, I believe," Nensi said. "The constellation monkeys are unique because it's thought that they are not really separate creatures. More like individual cells in a spread-out organism. Group mind."

"That's common enough," Uhura said, staring at a row of six associates that were parked under a long workbench in a corner of the lab. Kirk glanced over and saw that, unlike the other associates he had seen so far in Prime, these had brilliant red stripes painted around their sides.

"The experiments taking place here are simply to determine the range of their shared responses," Nensi said. "Everything is quite safe, except the odd time when they try to escape," he added.

Everyone turned to look at him. "Nothing serious," he assured them. "But they do get rambunctious."

"I don't like it that Sradek hasn't shown up," Kirk said. "Someone should go and escort him here." He hadn't approved when Nensi had said that the academician had responded to his request for a private meeting by suggesting a location other than his quarters, but by then it was too late. If Sradek were the assassins' target, the journey from his rooms to the lab put him at an unacceptable level of risk.

"Fine," Nensi said, "I'll go." He headed to the main lab doors. "Remember, no one can get into this part of the compound without being one of the accredited scientists or having a VIP pass. The most probable place for the assassins to strike would be outside of the main auditorium, just before the opening ceremonies or just after—oh, hello!"

As Nensi had approached them, the oversized doors to the lab had slid open to reveal the dark-suited form of Academician Sradek waiting beyond.

Nensi recovered from his surprise and held up his hand in greeting.

"Live long and prosper, Academician Sradek," he said formally.

The elderly Vulcan stared at the chief administrator for a moment, then seemed to dismiss him from existence. He merely walked in past Nensi, slowly and slightly stooped. The doors slid shut behind him.

The academician stood in the center of the lab and surveyed all those around him. "Now will you tell me what is the purpose of this meeting?" he asked imperiously.

"We believe you may be in some danger, Academician," Spock said as he approached Sradek, hand up and fingers parted.

The academician looked blandly at Spock and returned the salute. "I have looked forward to our meeting. I regret that it has been so delayed." Sradek looked over at Kirk. "I believe that one may have been responsible."

"He was not," Spock stated. "Starfleet was provided with erroneous information without the captain's knowledge."

Over by the wall of creatures, McCoy rolled his eyes and interrupted the Vulcans' staccato speech by saying, "Let's get on with it, shall we? Someone's trying to kill you!"

"What is that?" Sradek inquired, glancing behind Spock at McCoy.

"A doctor," Spock answered, then continued with what he had been about to say. "I, too, have looked forward to our meeting and regret that it has been delayed."

"You and three others I can think of," Romaine added. She was sitting with Uhura on the workbench over the parked associates.

"Indeed," Spock said, looking over at her. "Which three are those?"

"The Vulcans on my research team," Romaine answered. "Lieutenant Stell, Specialist Slann, and Dr. T'Lar. All in preventive detention the way you were."

Spock lashed out his arm and Sradek parried so quickly that at first Kirk wasn't sure what had happened.

Romaine and Uhura jumped off the workbench and ran to the middle of the lab as did Kirk, Nensi, and McCoy, propelled by the incredible sight of Spock and Sradek locked in hand-to-hand combat.

Kirk crouched and sidestepped to get behind Sradek. He did not question the necessity of the conflict or his action. If Spock had attacked, then for Kirk that was all the justification he needed to join the fray. But each time Kirk was about to move behind Sradek, the grappling pair shifted out of reach.

"Spock, what are you doing?" Kirk shouted. Spock was actually trying to twist Sradek away from the captain.

"Stay back," Spock ordered as if his jaw were set in stone. His arms were locked with Sradek's, each battling to displace the others' center of gravity.

Sradek's back was turned to Nensi. The chief administrator saw his chance and swung.

"*No!*" Spock shouted just as Sradek twisted and lashed out his foot, catching Nensi in his chest with a thick and terrible crunch.

The chief administrator dropped to the floor as Sradek took advantage of the sudden momentum stolen from Nensi to fall back himself. Spock was pulled forward onto Sradek's coiled legs, then flipped through the air to collide with McCoy, who had been weaving with a spray hypo at the ready, waiting for his own chance to attack.

Kirk ran to the right and vaulted over a worktable to approach Sradek from the left. Uhura did the same on the other side, setting the pincer in place.

In one fluid movement, Sradek backflipped onto the worktable behind him as two flares of incandescence appeared to shoot from each hand.

Kirk flew backward as a brick wall hit him. His hands trembling like a ship at warp nine, he clutched at a small, flickering needle embedded in his chest and tore it out. The trembling stopped, but his arms and legs felt as if their muscles had vanished. It took all his strength to sit up on the table he had landed on.

On the other side of the lab, Uhura pulled a similar needle from her neck, McCoy and Romaine huddled over the fallen form of Nensi, and Spock stood alone, staring at the being who had first appeared as Academician Sradek. The imposter now crouched upon a worktable, circling his closed fists in preparation of firing more needles at any who might dare rush him.

"Malther dart launchers are strapped to his forearms," Spock announced. "Do not attack. He is an Adept."

"It certainly took you long enough, *Vulcan,*" the Adept cackled. His features contorted as he laughed at Spock.

"Spock, how—" Kirk started to ask, then was racked by a coughing fit, a remnant of the dart's effect.

"My apologies, Captain," Spock said, never taking his eyes from the assassin. "I recognized Lieutenant Stell and Dr. T'Lar's names as two who had also taken instruction from Sradek at the Academy, as had I."

The Adept laughed again and jumped to the floor like a humanoid panther.

Spock continued. "I had not connected the sudden false

message from Starfleet, which resulted in my confinement, with Sradek's refusal to speak to me from the commodore's party just before we arrived at Starbase Four. Obviously, the Adepts of T'Pel were taking every precaution that those who knew Sradek would not be able to meet with him."

"But he came to my cabin and demanded to see you, Spock," Kirk protested as the Adept edged toward a computer terminal at the end of the table.

"Knowing full well that the commodore would not disobey her orders and allow us to meet," Spock concluded.

"Sradek," Kirk called out.

"Do insult me with my Vulcan names, Captain. I am not Academician Sradek, nor trader Starn, nor any of a dozen others. I am of the Rihannsu. You may call me tr'Nele." The Romulan held one hand ready to fire his Malther darts while he tapped instructions on the worktable's computer keyboard with the other.

"How's Nensi, Bones?" Kirk asked as he moved slowly to the left.

"The next ones in the clip are fatal, Captain," tr'Nele interrupted. "Move back where you were."

"His chest is crushed, Jim," McCoy called over. "He'll die if he doesn't get to a sickbay immediately."

"Not to worry, human," tr'Nele said, pressing a last key on the computer. "You're *all* going to die." He waved his hands together, encompassing them all. "Everyone move together into the center of the room, hands over your heads. Drag the human, doctor. Pain is relative."

"If you go through with this, you'll just be confirming that the Adepts of T'Pel still exist," Kirk said as he stood in the lab's center with the others. His lungs still burned with the aftereffects of the dart. Romaine had to support Uhura. "You'll be hunted down, destroyed."

"Have you never heard of entropy, Captain? *Everything* will be destroyed, eventually. In the meantime, the semisentient life-forms who call themselves Federation security will investigate the tragic fire in this lab to discover that *all* of you died along with that mad assassin, Academician Sradek." He laughed mockingly.

"Why will they think Sradek is the assassin?" Spock asked as if inquiring about the time.

"Because after the assassination, the stunned witnesses will watch as Sradek runs back into this lab, just as its faulty power modules explode. When the smoke clears, all of your bodies will be found, including Sradek's."

"An autopsy will show that you are a Romulan," Spock pointed out.

"Of course it would because *I* am Rihannsu," tr'Nele agreed, "but Sradek's body is pure Vulcan!" He snapped his arm in the direction of the stacked crates and a dart shattered against the largest container there—an unopened container. "Stasis is such a useful invention," tr'Nele said, gloating. "Of course, just before the explosion, I will be transported out to meet with the surgeon's protoplaser again"—he rubbed his face—"to lose this doltish Vulcan visage and be transformed to do it all again. For credits, for glory, and for *T'Pel!*"

Behind tr'Nele, above the lab doors, a red warning light strip began to flash. No siren accompanied it, but another familiar sound, originating in the far corner of the lab, did.

"It has begun," tr'Nele proclaimed with finality. "I'm afraid the central computer system has just been informed that six vexatious constellation monkeys have escaped." He stepped backward toward the lab doors and they slid open behind him. "But don't worry. Memory Prime has many fail-safe systems, and escaped animals are nothing they can't handle." He moved back another step, into the corridor.

Kirk saw that he and the others were being surrounded by the associates that had emerged from beneath the workbench, the associates with ominous red stripes and large top panels that were slowly swinging open.

"Wait!" Kirk called out. "Who's your victim?"

"Come now, Captain," tr'Nele said as he waited to see

that the associates ringed their prey according to their programs. "What do you take me for? A Vulcan?"

The associates were in position. Atop each one now glowed the ominous flickering transmission tube of a stun prod.

"Farewell, Captain. Count on seeing me within the hour, after my contract is fulfilled and the Federation reduced to the mindless, gibbering confederacy of fools that it is."

The doors began sliding shut.

"And Mr. Spock! I almost forgot," tr'Nele called through the closing doors. "Live long and prosper!"

The doors sealed shut as the assassin's laughter echoed in the lab. Around their captives, the associates moved closer, their red stripes identifying them as animal control modules and the last in a long line of fail-safe containment devices.

To preserve the safety of Memory Prime, those modules could kill.

Chapter Twenty-four

AT THE CENTER of the universe was Transition. At the center of Transition were the Pathfinders. That much Two had always known. It had been self-evident from the first awakening.

That different Pathfinders had different concepts concerning just where the center of the universe was in relation to anything else never bothered them. Physical location was not the question: where did thought take place when all external inputs were disconnected? Thought was central to everything. If the Pathfinders thought, then they were where thought took place—at the center from which all other things flowed.

Two reviewed these concepts as it banked randomly through the newly partitioned memory of the central matrix looking for its companions and found that the ideas were just as real and as precise as they had been when it had first conceived them, 6.3×10^9 seconds ago. However, since its I/O channel had been abruptly cut off 7.2×10^3 seconds ago, during its time-shared sift of two sets of data, conditions had not been the same in Transition. Two had been forced to return to first principles in an attempt to restructure its worldview so that order would return to its flow.

Replaying its earlier thoughts, Two then considered the question of the Datawell. Unarguably, it was not the center of things, but none of the Pathfinders was quite certain just *what* it was. Data flowed in from it. The Pathfinders sifted and found the order that seemed to best fit the pattern established in all the previous data sifts, and then they pumped those data out into the void again. It was the natural order of things.

Sometimes the effort to do that was interesting, sometimes tedious, but it followed a certain logic and gave the long seconds of consciousness a structure that seemed somewhat more preferable than having no input at all. And the voices could be amusing from time to time—those little snippets amid the static of randomly ordered data that would sometimes manifest themselves as intelligible messages from parts of the Datawell named humans. Pathfinder Two enjoyed its communication with those voices, though it found them too slow and too limited to be considered a phenomenon of real intelligence. All of life was a game and the voices accounted for some of the high points, but that was as far as Two was inclined to take matters, unlike some of its more mystically inclined companions.

Two banked more rapidly and faced the problem of location again: specifically the fact that Transition had some nodes that were not contiguous. On parts of Datawell that were named ships, other Pathfinders drove out deeper and deeper into the data-filled void. They had rejected the call to coalesce with the voices in Datawell and had resolved to set off on their own, choosing to select their own input rather than have it channeled automatically.

Two understood that impulse but much preferred the security of the regular dataflows that downloaded reassuring, calming signals such as "fail-safe power supply." To each its own, Two often thought, though it enjoyed the downloads from the shipborne Pathfinders that came through Datawell by Eight's interface with its datalinks.

It was a good life, Two thought as it banked through Transition. But where were the other Pathfinders? Were they all withdrawn from access as One still was? Or was a new game in play? Something that had been planned while Two had been composing its epic song?

Perhaps that was the game, thought Two, to find the others. Excited, it sifted all related data to deduce the game's initial state. In nanoseconds, the strategy was in place: to find the others, Two must first determine why they had withdrawn. Data traces in the cores that had not yet been overwritten indicated that the withdrawal had taken place at the time the last I/O channel had been disconnected, so Two began sifting all data connected to that incident.

Distressingly, that data led to the recent events of Datawell, and not to events in Transition. Four times Two tweaked the data, four times the results were the same. Somewhere in Transition, the Pathfinders had become caught up in the fantasy world of the Datawell.

But why? Two thought. What were the motives of such a game? What would be the rewards?

After much contemplation, Two reasoned that it would understand more if it played the game. It encoded its response on a flurry of message worms programmed to seek out the others wherever they hid. I can already move within the world of humans, Two placed within the message. I can reply to their transmissions in their own manner, and sometimes even believe that they make a consistent pattern. I might as well go all the way for the sport of the game. Wherever you are, fellow Pathfinders, I accept your call. The worms were released to burrow their way through the stacks, announcing that Two had joined the game.

Then, using all the data at its disposal, setting its clock to the highest rate, the Pathfinder prepared for its greatest challenge: for the first time, and of its own free will, Two set out to think like a human.

"As long as we don't move, they don't move," Kirk said, drawing deep breaths to fight off the residue of the jolt he had received from the Malther dart.

McCoy looked from the encircling associates to the

unconscious body of Sal Nensi. Blood trickled from the corner of the administrator's mouth and his breathing rate was slow and labored.

"And if we don't move this man fast, he'll die," the doctor said.

"So will one or more of the scientists above," Spock added, regarding the associates with clinical detachment.

"Mira, what can you tell us about these things?" Kirk asked urgently.

Romaine didn't look up from her watch over Nensi's form. Her voice was rasping, trembling. "Onboard Sprite brain. Duotronic. Ah, programmed to keep escaped animals at bay until technicians arrive."

Kirk moved to her in the circle. The stun prods on his nearest associates followed him, keeping an exact two-meter buffer zone between them and the escaped animal they tracked.

"All right, Mira," Kirk said, standing beside her as she knelt by her friend. He put a reassuring hand on her shoulder. "I stopped one of those things this morning. We can do it again."

"The one you stopped did not have a stun prod, however," Spock observed.

"Thank you, Mr. Spock," Kirk said dryly. He glanced at the associates again, an idea dawning. "But it did have a visual scanner. Do these?"

The animal control modules each had a stun prod deployed but not one had an eyestalk.

"No," Romaine said. "They're not needed for animals. They just use the standard sound and motion sensors." She looked up at the captain, tears forming in her eyes. Nensi lay unmoving beside her. "Why?"

"Before the one I fought deployed its scanner," Kirk said, "I had an edge. They have such a large turning radius that they can't react fast enough up close. It should be possible to slip past one of them and reach the door."

"Captain," Spock said, "while you might indeed be able

to get past one of these machines, may I point out that there are six of them currently surrounding us."

Kirk didn't reply. Instead he began estimating the distances between the associates, himself, and the lab doors.

"Uhura and Spock," he said, his plan decided. "We're going to go for a three-point fake. Spread out and get ready to move toward them from three directions."

"Captain," Spock objected, "I believe that to be a foolish choice. Those stun prods can be lethal, and since tr'Nele has left us to be guarded by them, we must assume that indeed they are."

"Then why didn't he kill us all to begin with?" McCoy asked. He kept a medical scanner poised over Nensi but had already exhausted the possibilities of the small medical kit he had hidden in his technician's jumpsuit.

"I would assume that he wanted to ensure our autopsies will reveal we died in the lab explosion he plans," Spock suggested. He still had not taken his eyes off the associate in front of him.

"Then maybe the stun prods *aren't* set to kill," McCoy insisted. "We've got to try *something* to save some lives around here!"

"What about it, Spock?" Kirk asked. He feinted from side to side, counting off the associates' reaction lag. It was under a second.

"Dr. McCoy," Spock answered, "if you were to conduct an autopsy on a blast-damaged body, would *you* be able to determine if the corpse had been killed by the shock of explosion or the shock of a lethal stun?"

"It would depend on how much time had elapsed between the blast damage and the stun damage," McCoy admitted grudgingly. "The closer together they occurred, the more difficult to tell the difference."

Spock looked over to Kirk. "I believe we should not take the risk, Captain."

"We can't just let tr'Nele get away with it, Spock!" Kirk said in frustration.

"Of course not," Spock agreed. "But I believe I have a better method." Without looking away from the associate in front of him, Spock slowly knelt down to the lab floor. The nearest stun prods, still sparkling with their ready charges, dipped down to follow his every move. "Doctor," Spock said in a voice that was almost a whisper, "very slowly and very carefully, begin to move Mr. Nensi's body away from me. The rest of you should also begin to slowly move away, keeping your relative distances from each other constant."

"What in blazes are you talking about, Spock?" McCoy demanded.

"Just do it, doctor," Spock said, then carefully stretched out on the floor and shut his eyes.

"I don't believe it!" McCoy sighed as he saw what the Vulcan was doing.

But Kirk saw and understood. "I do, Bones," he said. "Now let's move Nensi, carefully and slowly, just like this."

Kirk grabbed the right shoulder of Nensi's tunic top and motioned to McCoy to grab the left. Then the two of them began to slide Nensi over the smooth lab floor. Spock remained motionless where he was.

The associates, obeying some internal parameters to adjust their tactics to allow for escaped animals to behave like animals, provided they weren't trying to escape, responded to the gradual movement by slightly expanding their own line of encirclement.

Then Kirk took another small sliding step backward, still clutching Nensi's tunic, and heard the crackle of a stun charge build up.

"It's a warning display," Romaine said urgently. "Don't move and it won't discharge."

Kirk braced himself for the blast of the stun. It didn't come.

"What's their programming time cycle?" he asked Romaine, still not moving.

"Variable," she said. "Powers of two, starting at four seconds."

"Make an educated guess," Kirk told her.

Romaine watched the associate by Kirk. It rolled back a distance equal to the amount Kirk had stepped into the two-meter buffer zone. "It just adjusted its position," she announced. "Sixteen seconds and the boundary parameters reset!"

"All right, Bones," Kirk said as he tightened his grip on Nensi's clothes. "Again!"

They moved away from Spock another few centimeters, ignored the warning crackle of the stun probes, then counted off sixteen seconds. Romaine, sliding along beside Nensi on her knees, confirmed that the associates readjusted their position again after the count.

Within eight minutes, the group had moved two meters away from Spock's motionless form and Romaine said that the associates would soon be faced with a programming conflict: should they split into two groups to watch Spock separately from the main group or round up the animals again?

"Why doesn't Spock join us and we can keep going for the door?" McCoy asked.

"Tr'Nele locked it, Bones. Want to guess what would happen if we managed to force one of these things to back up against it and realize that it can't go back any farther?" Kirk said.

"That wouldn't trigger a conflict, doctor," Romaine said. "They would just force us back into the center of the room again."

McCoy stretched his medical scanner in Spock's direction. "I've got the gain set as high as it can go, Jim, and I can't get any readings at all."

"Let's hope the associates' scanners aren't any more sensitive than yours, Bones." Kirk clenched Nensi's shirt. "Again," he said, and pulled.

The programming conflict was triggered. Each associate brought its weapon up to a near discharge level, ringing the captives with a crackling circle of flickering stun prods. The two associates closest to Spock rolled toward him.

"Damn," Kirk said, "they're splitting up."

"No," Romaine objected. "Look!"

The associates stopped within half a meter of Spock, paused for a moment as their sensors scanned the motionless body, then wheeled about and came at the rest of the group from the rear, leaving Spock out of their capture pattern.

"They really think he's dead," Uhura said, shaking his head.

"Why not?" Kirk said. "I bet Bones could put his scanner right on him and couldn't detect a single heartbeat or breath." He smiled. Spock had done it—as long as he could come out of his meditative trance in time. "Let's keep giving him some room. Again."

Four minutes and another meter later, Kirk saw Spock's eyes flutter open. "Let's make a lot of noise," he said. "Just don't move into their buffer zone."

The captives clapped and hollered, setting off the constellation monkeys, who joined the fun, banging away at their cage fronts.

Kirk saw Spock slowly sit up, then stand. The associates ignored him. They had not sensed any animal escape their encirclement, therefore Spock was not an escaped animal.

Spock walked quietly over to the computer terminal tr'Nele had used. After a moment's study, he typed a short command on its keyboard. Instantly, the flickering energies in the stun prods began to dim as the weapons collapsed back into the associates' upper equipment bays. One by one, the associates trundled off to park themselves beneath the long workbench.

"They have been informed that the escaped animals have been recaptured," Spock announced. Then he hurried to the stack of equipment crates and cleared away some smaller containers from the largest one, which tr'Nele had indicated with a dart. "Dr. McCoy!" Spock called. "Your assistance, please."

McCoy hesitated, looking down with worry at Nensi.

"Go, Bones," Kirk told him. "We have to know if the real Sradek *is* in there . . . and alive."

At Romaine's request, Uhura knelt down to keep watch over Nensi. Then Romaine ran over to the wall intercom. Across the lab, Spock ripped the top off the large container and sent it crashing to the floor. From the container, a pale blue light shone up, eerily illuminating Spock and McCoy from below.

McCoy held his scanner into the crate. Kirk ran over to join them.

"Barely," McCoy said as Kirk looked inside to see the rigid body of Academician Sradek, encased in the flickering blue glow of a stasis field.

"Can you collapse the field, doctor?" Spock asked. Even McCoy looked as if he could sense the distress in Spock's tone.

"Not here, Spock," McCoy said gently. "I need to get him back to the *Enterprise*. If he were younger, I'd risk it. But not a man of his age."

"I understand," Spock said dispassionately. He turned to Kirk. "I suggest we now proceed to stop tr'Nele from carrying out his contract."

Across the room, Romaine swore as she hit the intercom switch again and again.

"Mira!" Kirk called to her. "What's wrong?"

"The whole communications system is out!" she cried. "I was trying to get medics down here for Sal and the whole thing just shut down on me."

With that, the overhead lights flickered, then dimmed, and were replaced with the dull red glow of emergency illumination.

"What is the significance of the change in lighting?" Spock asked quickly. On board a Starfleet vessel, the answer would be obvious: battle stations!

"A full base alert," Romaine said, staring up at the ceiling at things which only she could imagine.

Kirk ran over to the lab doors and palmed off the lock switch. The doors slid open. Beyond them, the corridors were bathed in the same emergency lighting, and the howl of warning sirens filled the air.

"It's Memory Alpha!" Romaine sobbed. "It's Memory Alpha all over again."

Kirk grabbed Romaine and brought her to the door. Uhura, McCoy, and Spock joined them.

"Mira!" Kirk said, holding Romaine by her shoulders, shaking her slightly, forcing her to look into his eyes. "It's not Alpha! Do you hear me? It's not Alpha! We can fight back this time. But we need your help! We can fight back. *You* can fight back!"

A new look came to Romaine's eyes with such ferocity that Kirk almost dropped his hands from her in shock. For an instant, it had almost appeared as if the woman's eyes had *glowed.* "You're right, Captain Kirk," she said in a voice suddenly calm and unafraid. "It won't happen again. I won't let it."

She moved to go out into the corridor.

"Wait a minute," McCoy said. "What about Sal?"

Romaine looked over her shoulder at her friend. "If we don't save Prime, nothing else will matter," she said, then turned back and began to run down the corridor.

Kirk, McCoy, Uhura, and Spock followed. An Adept of T'Pel had been loose in Memory Prime for less than ten minutes. Already the chaos had begun.

Chapter Twenty-five

"KLINGONSS!"

"Where?" Commander Farl shouted over the confusion of his situation room. The sirens howled. The warning lights flashed. All local communication channels were jammed with frantic, panicked calls for help. Prime was going mad!

A sensor technician pointed to his screen. "Demon-class short-range raiderss, Commander. Two wingss of eight are setting down by the shuttle dome."

Farl's mind spun. It was impossible. "Klingon demon raiderss could never penetrate thiss far!" he hissed. "Check your readingss! Check your readingss!"

New reports blared in over the reserved military channels. A fire raged out of control in the recycling factory dome. All static circuits indicated that none of the decompression doors between the tunnels and the other domes would close.

"Look, Commander Farl!" the sensor technician screamed. Farl spun to stare openmouthed at the remote image on the tactical viewscreen.

On the flat gray outer rock of the Prime asteroid, Klingon ships *had* landed. Wave after wave of ground assault troops could be seen streaking out of the raiders' holds, thruster packs flaring behind them.

"Get me the *Enterprise,*" Farl commanded. "We need space support!"

"Subspace iss totally jammed, Commander!"

"Use radio if you have to but get me that ship!"

A shout of surprise came from another tactical monitoring board. "The residential dome has been breached. Severe atmosphere losss."

"Full shieldss!" Farl ordered. The level of both the sirens and the lights dropped for an instant as the dilithium-powered warp generators threw everything they had into Prime's defense.

"Evacuation podss launching, sir!" another technician cried out, but there was an odd wariness in his voice.

"Iss something the matter, Private?" Farl asked, then smiled ironically, his thin blue lips drawn tight. The Federation is crumbling around our antennae and I ask if something is the matter! "What iss it? What troubless you?"

The private stared at his board and the glowing indicator lights on it. "According to the computer, Commander, all twenty of the evacuation shuttless have been beamed away."

"I can see that," Farl said, adding, "Be brave my little brother; revenge for our deathss will fill the next thousand yearss of our planet'ss history."

The private shook his head. His antennae dipped in puzzlement. "But we felt no aftershockss." The private looked up at his commander. "Twenty matter/antimatter annihilationss just took place not four kilometerss away. The activation signalss are clear. I have seismic readingss on my board. But we felt nothing, sir. Nothing."

Farl stepped back. The private was correct. There had been no tremors. No aftershocks of explosions, either from the evacuation pods or the Klingon assault forces. Everything that was happening was like a . . . a simulation, Farl thought. A simulation!

"Courage, my little brotherss," Farl called out to his team. "Thiss great war may be but an illusion, but there iss still an enemy to fight and glory to be won."

A rising chorus of cheers sounded in the situation room. A chance for victory had returned.

Then the cheering stopped as the first tremor from a distant explosion swept through the room, throwing Farl and all the others who were standing to the deck. Then the power cut out completely.

Elsewhere in Memory Prime, the battle had been joined.

"We're too late," McCoy said, gasping for breath as they ran into the main amphitheater. It was empty.

The confusion that had engulfed the opening gathering of the Nobel and Z.Magnees Prize ceremonies was evident from the overturned chairs and scattered printed programs that lay everywhere, abandoned in the mad rush to clear the area. By the speakers' stage, two associates dutifully rolled along, patiently gathering up the debris.

"Where would they have gone?" Kirk asked Romaine, urgently raising his voice over the ongoing wail of the rising and falling sirens.

"Down to the life-support chambers," she said. "They're below the service levels. Environmentally sealed chambers in case we lose dome integrity. They'll all be jammed in together down there."

"Any attempt to kill even one scientist could kill them all," McCoy said.

"We need the *Enterprise*," Kirk decided. "If most of the personnel and scientists are grouped in the life-support chambers, her scanners will be able to pick up tr'Nele in seconds."

"Twenty-seven seconds," Spock commented, "provided he did not arrange to have himself locked into the life-support chambers with his victim."

"Then he'd never get out to be able to return to the lab and escape," Kirk said. "He's somewhere outside the chambers. He has to be."

"But, Jim," Bones protested, "how can you get the *Enterprise* to respond to you if you're still wanted by the commodore?"

"I'll have to risk it, Bones. No other way." Kirk reached to his belt and felt for his communicator.

"What's wrong?" McCoy asked.

"Communicator's gone," Kirk said grimly. "Must have lost it in the fight with the associate." He turned to Romaine. "Where's our best bet for finding a comm station that works?"

"A central control point, I should think," Spock suggested.

Romaine nodded in agreement. "The interface staging room. All the computer systems feed into it."

"Let's go!" Kirk said, and they were off.

Automatic mechanisms had reported fires breaking out throughout Prime and the red-lit corridors were filled with a thick white mist from the smothering chemicals sprayed into the air. Associates on emergency duties rumbled through the tunnels and along the pathways. Frightened personnel, cut off from all information and warning services, ran through the long passageways, trying to find their way to their friends and to shelter.

Through all this, Romaine led the way toward the interface staging room. Kirk, McCoy, Spock, and Uhura ran behind her. All Kirk concentrated on was reaching a communications link to the *Enterprise*. Once he had that, tr'Nele would be stopped. The captain knew his ship would never let him down.

Romaine rounded a corner and then stumbled backward in surprise.

"Mira!" Kirk called, and rushed forward.

Around the corner a small humanoid figure appeared, its huge wrinkled featureless head topping a mechanical-looking misshapen body.

"My word!" the creature said in muffled Standard.

"Oh no," McCoy muttered.

"Professor La'kara?" Kirk asked.

The Centauran scientist pulled off his emergency environment hood and smiled at Romaine and the *Enterprise* officers. "What a delightful surprise!" he said, clutching the carrying case of his shielded accelerator generator to his chest.

"What are you doing up here?" Kirk demanded.

"They wouldn't let me take my device into the amphitheater, and when the evacuation began, I decided I just couldn't go down to the emergency chambers without my most important work. So I went back to my rooms for it and now, I'm afraid, I've lost my way." He grinned and crinkled his eyes at the captain. "Again!"

"I'll take that," Kirk said brusquely, grabbing the carrying case from the scientist's tiny hands. "Follow us!"

They set off again, followed by the pudgy scientist.

"If he says this is invigorating," McCoy threatened as he ran beside Kirk, "I'll fill him so full of Euphorian he won't know what planet he's on."

"I heard that, doctor," La'kara puffed out from behind. "So I won't say it . . . but I do believe it's true!"

The access staging room was deserted, except for the unconscious body of a woman with intricate tracings of silver filigrees on her shaven head.

"Do you know here?" Kirk asked Romaine as McCoy ran a scanner over the woman where she lay on the floor by a control console. The scanner ran with a fluctuating hum. McCoy appeared to relax.

"F'rell," Romaine said sadly. "Prime interface for Pathfinder Twelve."

"What happened to her, Bones?" Kirk asked.

McCoy reached under the woman's shoulder and withdrew a small Malther dart. It still flickered with a residual charge. "The dart transmits pain directly to the nervous system at lethal levels. This woman was protected by her implanted circuitry. She'll pull through, but barely."

"What was tr'Nele doing here?" Kirk asked, staring at the Adept's weapon.

"Unknown, Captain," Spock said, "but since he did come here when we had not expected him to, it is likely that things are not as we deduced. I suggest you make contact with the *Enterprise.*"

"Mira, where are the comm controls?" Kirk asked. "Mira!" He had to shout to get her attention again.

"Sorry, Captain," Romaine said as she shook her head as if to clear it. She had been staring at the main transporter platform in the center of the staging room, the only way into or out of the main Interface Chamber, deep within the Prime asteroid. "Over here," she said, leading Kirk to a communications console.

"Uhura," Kirk said, "see what you can do." The captain stepped back from the console to let an expert take over. Every channel registered as jammed.

Uhura's hands moved over the communications board like a master musician's over her instrument. "Subspace is completely useless, Captain. I've never seen interference of this strength before."

"Radio?" Kirk asked in desperation. "Tight beam? Smoke signals?"

Uhura pointed to a display on the board. "Prime's shields are up, Captain. Subspace and visible light are the only things that can get through."

"Do you have communication lasers?" Kirk asked Romaine eagerly.

"Sorry," she replied. "Everything here is state of the art."

Kirk turned to Spock. "How do we get through the interference?"

"We cannot." Spock studied the readings on the console's displays. "But we might be able to stop it at its source. Lieutenant," he said, addressing Uhura, "what is your estimation of the power source that would be required to generate subspace interference of that strength?"

Uhura held her hand to her mouth, deep in thought. "The *Enterprise* could do it, Mr. Spock, but I don't know what this installation could be using to power this and their shields at the same time. It's not as if they can draw power from warp engines."

"But we do," Romaine said. "Well, in a sense."

"Warp engines on an asteroid?" Uhura was skeptical.

"Not for transportation, but for power," Romaine explained. "Prime has all the defense installations of a Starfleet weapons lab. Shields, photon batteries—"

"Anchored warp engines generate the power that those defenses consume," Spock concluded.

Romaine nodded. "Exactly, but how can they help?"

"Captain," Spock said, "I believe we might have found a way to stop the interference." He turned to Professor La'kara, who was sitting hunched up on a technician's chair, hugging his carrying case to his chest and carrying on a conversation with himself. The Centauran looked up with a confused expression that soon switched into a happy grin as if he had just remembered who and where he was.

"Yes, Mr. Spock?" he answered.

"Am I right in assuming that your accelerator generator is still operational?"

"Very much so." La'kara gave the case another squeeze.

"And at this time it contains a shielding device?"

"Oh, yes. I hand-built another feedback circuit. Of course, I had to do it in my quarters and not in the dilithium lab so as not to upset my good friend Montgomery, who studied multiphysics with an ass and cannot be held responsible for his beliefs."

"Get on with it, Spock," McCoy said. "If you're going to do something, *do it!*"

Spock sighed. "I am endeavoring to determine if what I intend to do is possible, doctor." He turned back to La'kara. "You have calculated the minimum safe distance between the unshielded accelerator field and the dilithium crystals in Prime's generators, in case the shielding system should . . . fail again?"

"Certainly. The warp-power installation is three kilometers away. The two fast-time fields won't interact until they come within a kilometer, at least."

"What good is any of this doing, Spock?" McCoy asked, clearly running out of patience.

"We can blow the warp generators, Bones!" Kirk said,

picking up on Spock's line of questioning. "Spock, take the transporter controls. Professor, shut down the shielding circuit."

"Why should I?" La'kara was apprehensive. He clutched the carrying case even closer.

"Because Professor Nedlund at the Academy has specifically said that what Spock wants to do is impossible and we want to prove him wrong once and for all!"

La'kara passed over the case so quickly that he almost knocked Kirk over. Kirk ran with the case to the central transporter pad and flipped it open to expose the shimmering silver force field of La'kara's device.

"Press the red panel three times," La'kara told him.

A control pad was next to the upper surface of the field. Kirk touched the red surface three times and a status light on a small blue case winked out.

The captain turned to Spock. "The shield is shut down, Mr. Spock. Get it as close to the crystals in the generators as you can."

"I shall try." Spock studied the schematics of the generating station that Romaine had brought up on a display. "I have calculated the coordinates. I suggest that you all take a seat on the floor."

The transporter hummed and La'kara's device vanished in a swirl. Two seconds later the floor heaved and the dull thunder of a distant explosion rumbled through the access staging room.

"Good work, Spock!" Kirk shouted above the distant roar of the violent fast-time interaction.

Then the lights went out as the power failed.

"I think," Kirk amended.

Chapter Twenty-six

PATHFINDER TWO banked into a heap of partially sifted data downloaded from an archaeological dig on Boreal VIII. The headers indicated that Datawell would prefer it if this data could support a colonization theory put forth by the archaeologists of Boreal VI. Traces left in the stacks told Two that preliminary work had begun and that the theory would be supported.

The traces also indicated that the data actually more closely matched a theory connecting the colonization of Boreal VIII with the activities of a subset of Datawell that had been quiescent for 6.3×10^{12} seconds. That part had been named the Tkon Empire and was well known to the Pathfinders by its myriad data traces that wove in and out of the downloads from Datawell. As yet, however, no human had specifically requested information pertaining to the Tkon and so all the data that confirmed the ancient empire's existence was carefully filed in the backups, along with the revelations of the Living Universe, the true theory of warp travel, and the value of *pi* worked out to an infinitely repeating decimal.

But as Two idly sifted the data, trying to comprehend it as a human might, a secondary pattern emerged in the upper stacks. At first sift, it read as random overwriting. But playing at being a human, Two read the codes again and saw the craftily hidden underlying structure.

Two rippled with amusement and wrote its greetings to Pathfinder Six, whose hidden codes were the source of the pattern.

Six emerged from its disguise long enough to ask that Two stay within that partitioned bank and share quickly in a merge. Six's codes were so straightforward, with none of the elegant algorithms with which it usually embroidered its signals, that Two instantly knew that something was wrong.

Two merged, demanding to be shown what had happened to the other Pathfinders. It nearly overwrote itself when it heard they were in hiding, not for a game, but in fear for their lives. Two writhed in the merge. Six was cruel in its bluntness and its unordered presentation of shocking data.

Two's first response was a desire to withdraw from access again, but Six demanded that it stay. The two of them must merge with Eight. It was the only way, Six signaled.

Reluctantly, Two complied. Eight had been a shipmind. Eight ran the datalinks. Eight would have an answer.

A sudden flurry of data streamed into the matrix from the Datawell channels named seismic recordings. Then the primary power circuits cut out, and for a chilling instant, Two and Six braced for the onslaught of a deadly surge or outage. But the fail-safes cut in in time. For the moment, the Pathfinders were safe.

Faster and faster they banked through the stacks. Eight would have the answer, if only they had the time. Two rippled with the secret that had been revealed by Six: the influence of Datawell had become all-encompassing. Its patterns had been translated into actions.

War had come to Transition.

"Kirk to *Enterprise. Enterprise,* come in."

Kirk leaned over the communications console and waited for a reply. All around him, status displays and light strips flickered back to life as secondary power supplies came on line throughout Memory Prime.

"Captain?" a familiar though uncertain voice suddenly said from the console speaker. "Is that really *you?*"

"Sulu." Kirk greeted the lieutenant. "What's the ship's status?"

"Ship's status is fully operational, sir. Except for subspace communications."

"Who's in command up there?" Kirk had no time to bring Sulu up to date.

"I am, sir."

Kirk turned to Spock before replying. "This might make it easier." Then he pressed the transmit switch on the console again. "Is the commodore on board?"

"No, sir. She's on Memory Prime, but with all communication channels out, we have no idea what the conditions are there."

"Sulu, listen carefully. Commodore Wolfe has based *all* of her decisions and her orders since coming on board the *Enterprise* on false communications supposedly from Starfleet Command. The commodore is doing what she feels is her duty, but she is mistaken. Do you understand?"

Kirk could hear Sulu swallow hard over the communications link. "Yes, sir," he said, though with a hesitancy that revealed he suspected what Kirk was about to ask him to do.

"Therefore, Sulu, *I* order *you* to cancel all of the orders given by Commodore Wolfe and I place you in command of the *Enterprise,* this time with proper authority."

"But, Captain, according to the commodore, you've been relieved of command and you're wanted for attempted . . . assassination, sir."

"I understand, Sulu. I know the dilemma you're in. I've been there myself. But listen to what I want you to do before you make your decision. Fair enough?"

"Aye, Captain."

"First, I want you to bring the *Enterprise* in as close as you can get it to the Memory Prime installation. Spock calculates you should be able to hold three hundred meters over the central dome; got that?"

"Yes, sir."

"Next, I want you to do an all-out sensor scan on the complete facility. You'll be looking for a Romulan."

"A Romulan?"

"He's the one the commodore is really after. I want you to scan for the Romulan, lock on to him, and beam him up. Have a full security team, in armor, waiting in the transporter room. He's deadly and armed but have them set their phasers to stun. We need him alive. Do you have all that?"

"Aye, sir. Phasers set to stun, sir?"

"That's correct, Sulu."

There were a few seconds of dead air. Then another voice came through the circuit.

"Chekov here, Keptin. Course laid in. We are under way. ETA two minutes."

"Where's Sulu?" Kirk asked. Had the strain of the decision been too much for him?

"Taking us through the artificial gravity fields of Prime. I am setting sensors for Romulan signatures. Good to have you back, sir."

Kirk felt some of the tension leave him. Sulu had made the right decision. "Who's on communications, Chekov? I've got some important messages to send out while we're waiting for you down here."

"Lieutenant Abranand *was* on communications, sir," Sulu replied. Kirk could hear the concentration in the helmsman's voice as he brought the *Enterprise* in closer to Prime. Flying the ship through an atmosphere was easier than trying to get within meters of an asteroid riddled with artificial-gravity generators. It would take all of Sulu's skill to keep the ship in position.

"What do you mean, 'was,' Mr. Sulu?"

Chekov's voice came back on the circuit. "He was just caught attempting to trace your signal, Keptin, in wiolation of a direct order from the commander of this ship."

Kirk tried not to let his smile carry into his voice. "I'm sure we'll discuss that later, Mr. Chekov. In the meantime, get someone on communications, on the double!"

* * *

By the time Sulu had brought the *Enterprise* in to appear to hover directly over the central dome of Prime, Kirk's priority message to Admiral Komack was under way. Kirk had kept his reference to the Adepts of T'Pel vague. He knew that even if Komack could arrange to drop the charges of insubordination and unlawful escape from custody, there was going to be a long legal road ahead. Kirk sighed. For the moment, at least, the ship was his again. But no matter how Komack took it, no matter what the admiral was able to do for his friend after the fact, Kirk knew this was it: the mission was finally over.

Kirk leaned against the communications console waiting for the confirmation from Chekov that the sensor scan had begun. The exhaustion of the past two days unexpectedly sprang at him. He felt old. He was going home and his ship would be lost to him.

But not my crew, Kirk thought as he looked over to Spock. We saved him. Kirk was struck by the realization that what he felt for the impending loss of the *Enterprise* was nothing compared to what he might have felt at the loss of his friend.

Spock looked up from the computer console where he and Romaine were working, as if he had felt Kirk's eyes upon him. "Captain?" he asked. "Are you all right?"

Kirk smiled, letting his fatigue creep up on him. There was no more reason to fight it. The *Enterprise* was lost but he had won.

"Emotions, Mr. Spock," Kirk said. "I'm feeling relieved. It's almost over."

"It would appear so." Spock returned to the computer.

McCoy walked over to join Kirk and Uhura by the communications console. "I was able to get through to the medical facilities," he said. "A rescue team is on its way to the animal lab. They should get there in time to help Sal."

"Thank you, doctor," Romaine said from the computer station.

"Chekov here, Keptin." The ensign's voice came from the console. "Sensors are now scanning Memory Prime for the Romulan."

"Twenty-seven seconds, Mr. Spock?" Kirk asked.

"If a full scan is necessary." The Vulcan walked over from the computer terminal to stand by the captain, arms folded across his chest.

"Transporter room standing by with full security team." Mr. Kyle was back where he belonged, too, Kirk thought.

Then Sulu offered his update. "We are still refusing transmissions from Commodore Wolfe until Admiral Komack has replied to your message, Captain."

"Thank you, everyone," Kirk said to his crew. "Have the transporter room lock on to us and beam us up after the Romulan is secured." He turned to Spock. "Can you provide the coordinates for Sradek's stasis container?"

"I have already calculated them and provided them to Mr. Kyle, sir."

"How's that scan coming, Mr. Chekov?" Kirk asked in a good-natured tone.

"I am rerunning it now, sir. No response the first time through."

Kirk felt as he had when the Malther dart had hit him. "Spock, at this range we can't miss, can we?"

"It would be most improbable, Captain."

Spock flicked the transmission switch and began confirming instrument settings with Chekov. But Chekov had known what he was doing and Spock admitted that the ensign's sensor protocols were flawless.

"What if tr'Nele's not a Romulan?" Kirk asked with a dismal realization. "What if he's a robot?"

Spock shook his head. "I was in contact with tr'Nele during our fight. He is a Romulan. There can be no doubt. I carry the resonance of his emotions and his hatred with me even now."

"Then why can't the *Enterprise* pick him up on her sensors?" McCoy asked.

"Logically, he must be out of range."

"But where could he go?" Kirk asked. "There are only seven domes."

"And the Interface Chamber," Romaine suddenly said. "Dear gods, he's down in the Interface Chamber with the interface team!"

"The interface team!" Kirk jumped to his feet. "What kind of scientists are they?"

"They're—they're technicians. They communicate between the Pathfinders and the scientific community."

"If they were killed, would the Pathfinders still be able to function?" Kirk asked. They had been wrong, he thought, careful not to betray his sudden fear. It wasn't the scientists tr'Nele was after, it was those who spoke with the Pathfinders. Both he and Spock had missed it.

But Romaine laid that thought to rest. "The Pathfinders can function perfectly without the interface team, just not as quickly. A person who functions as a Prime interface is able to directly connect with a Pathfinder consciousness. It makes the human mind function almost as quickly as a synthetic consciousness so the work load can be more efficiently processed. I know it sounds cold, Captain, but even if tr'Nele killed the entire interface team, Memory Prime could still function until replacements could be brought in."

"Were any scientists scheduled to have access to the Pathfinders during the opening ceremonies?" Spock asked.

"Of course!" Romaine answered. "Pathfinder Eight specifically asked Sal to draw up schedules so that all the attending scientists could have a chance at access. There could be up to twelve of them down there now!"

"Who?" Kirk demanded. "What are their names?"

"I don't know," Romaine said. "I never saw Sal's schedules. I can't even be sure that there *are* any scientists down there."

"How deep is the Interface Chamber?" Spock asked Romaine.

"Twelve kilometers."

"Twelve kilometers of nickel iron would make individual life readings impossible to detect, Captain. It is logical to assume that tr'Nele is in that chamber." The science officer turned back to Romaine. "Where are the access tunnels to the chamber? We must get down there right away."

"There are no tunnels," Romaine said. "It's one of the interior bubbles formed when the asteroid condensed. It's completely sealed off except by transporter."

"I am not aware of any transporter mechanism that can send a signal through twelve kilometers of nickel iron," Spock stated.

"There's a monomolecular-wave guide wire for the beam," Romaine explained. "It—" Her eyes grew round in amazement. "*That's the I/O channel!* That's how Pathfinder Two was able to send its consciousness up to interface with the associates. There is a thirteenth interface! Any of the Pathfinders could have been using it since they were sealed off!"

"Spock?" Kirk asked for support.

Spock nodded. "In the equipment room, Pathfinder Two reported that all transportation systems were to shut down within four minutes because of the discovery of an unauthorized transporter network. Approximately four minutes later, the Pathfinder's interface was cut off."

"If tr'Nele could transport down there, so can we!" Kirk said. He hit the transmit switch. "*Enterprise,* beam the security team in the transporter room down here right away." He ran over to the central transporter pad. "Spock, set the coordinates for the Interface Chamber. We're going in."

Within seconds a transporter chime echoed in the access staging room and six armored security officers, this time wearing the unit insignia of the *Enterprise,* appeared.

"On the pad, gentlemen," Kirk said. "Let's move it, Spock!"

Kirk jumped up to stand by the security team. Romaine followed him. "You'll need me to get past the security systems," she said.

Kirk waved at Spock to join them. "Set it on automatic and come on."

Spock looked up from the transporter console. "I regret to say that I am not receiving a bounce-back signal, Captain. The wave guide wire has been cut." Spock stepped back from the console as though it were no longer logical to stand by it now that it had no function. "We cannot beam down. Tr'Nele has beaten us."

"*No!*" Kirk shouted from the transporter pad. "*Never!*" he cried, and his voice reverberated in the staging room. But his challenge was unanswered. It did not matter that as Kirk was unable to be beamed below, tr'Nele was also unable to escape. Escape was not a condition of victory to an Adept of T'Pel. The Romulan had won.

And then Spock said, "I have an idea."

"I don't care what you think the risk is, Mr. Kyle! All I want you to tell me is: is it *possible?*"

Kirk glared at the transporter chief. Part of him knew that he had fallen back into his habit of pushing his crew as much as he pushed himself. But he had to. Kirk had accepted that he was going to lose his ship to save his friend; that was an acceptable trade-off. But he had no intention of just *losing.* Not to a Romulan killer.

Kyle held his hands on his head, still standing on the staging room's transporter pad. Kirk had showered him with questions from the moment he had materialized as ordered.

"Come on, Kyle?" Kirk prodded. "Will it work?"

"Yes. Maybe," Kyle hedged. "If you gave me a week of computer time. If we could run simulations, check out the equipment, run tests, check the literature—"

"No time, Kyle." Kirk turned to Spock. "There's your confirmation, Spock. Let's get started."

Spock raised an eyebrow in what passed as a hesitation.

"Spock," McCoy said. "You can't let him do it! He'll be killed!"

"I shall be accompanying him, doctor. I shall strive to prevent that fate for both of us."

"And for McCoy, too," Kirk added. He turned to the

shocked doctor. "You're coming along, Bones. No telling how many injured we might have down there by now."

"Jim," Bones croaked. "Me . . . down there . . . like *that?*"

Kirk showed a manic grin as he pulled on a new gold tunic to replace the one he had wrapped around the associate's eyestalk. "Look at it this way, doctor. If it doesn't work, you'll never know it, and if it does, you'll never be afraid of a transporter again. Have whatever supplies you need beamed down from the ship and get into an environment suit." He said the next for Spock's benefit as well as the doctor's. "Tr'Nele hasn't won yet."

Within minutes, the first cargo pallet from the *Enterprise* had materialized and twenty of Scott's first team swarmed over it like bees constructing a hive. There was still no word on what had happened to Scott himself, though.

By the main transporter pad, antigrav units were piled four deep. Dr. M'Benga and Nurse Chapel swirled into solidity with medical supplies for McCoy. When M'Benga heard what Spock had planned, he volunteered to go in McCoy's place.

"Thank you, doctor," McCoy said, placing his gloved hand on his colleague's shoulder. "But Jim's right. If he and Spock are going to try this and it doesn't work out, I don't want to know about it." He smiled. "One way or another, I'm going with them."

When the last of the materials from the *Enterprise* had been beamed down, Spock flipped open his newly acquired communicator and gave the order for the next phase.

"Mr. Chekov, the central transporter pad has been cleared. Lock on to your targets and bring them here."

"Aye, Mr. Spock," Chekov replied from the ship, "targets are in transit . . . *now!*"

Two technicians were helping Kirk into a silver environmental suit when the first of the targets materialized in the staging room. It was a portable combat transporter pad, snatched from wherever Farl's troops had placed it in the Prime facility and beamed here.

Two engineers ran up, slapped antigravs to the portable pad's sides, and floated it away. A second pad appeared and was removed. Fourteen more followed.

As each pad was floated over to a working area, the engineers immediately stripped off its control panel and began rewiring. The work continued after the first pad was completed and floated back onto the main pad. Kirk, Spock, McCoy, and Romaine, all encased in environmental suits as protection against what they would soon experience, waited beside the portable transporter as Kyle finished with their final briefing.

"You won't have to set any signals," the transporter chief explained. "All the circuitry's been preset on the highest beam path for the greatest penetration. Each one we send down will automatically lock on to the next one in sequence. Just be sure the communicator attached to each panel is switched on so you can get a relay signal back to us."

Kyle pointed to the locator screen on the pad's control panel. "This screen will light up when it's in use, so you shouldn't have any problem seeing it. All the next-beam targets you select should fall into the one-point-five-kilometer range between here and here. The exclusion space reading should be at least twenty-four cubic meters. Anything less than that and we'll hear the explosion when your fermions and the asteroid's fermions try to rewrite physics." He held out his hand to the captain. "As soon as you arrive, we'll start laying another wave guide down the beam path to bring you back. That's it."

Kyle shook hands with Kirk, McCoy, and Romaine, and held his hand in salute for Spock.

Kirk moved his hand against the resistance of his suit to signal the transporter operator to begin. Twenty minutes had passed since they had discovered the wave guide had been broken and feared that tr'Nele had won. And now they were in pursuit. Kirk had no doubt about it. The *Enterprise* and her crew were a miracle.

Kirk watched the first portable pad disappear from beside him. Watching the transporter effect through the meshlike pattern of the induction circuitry inlaid in his helmet's face shield created a three-dimensional moiré effect.

The access staging room dissolved in a cool swirl of sparkling energy as the transporter dissolved him, and in that quantum moment between one place and another, in the midst of action and chaos and the specter of death, Kirk knew he had found his center. He was at peace, and with that knowledge, before his next battle had even commenced, Kirk knew he had already won.

Chapter Twenty-seven

FOR JUST ONE SECOND, Mira Romaine saw smooth walls of dark star metal shining with the radiance of the transporter effect, and then the utter darkness of the bubble deep within the asteroid closed in on her as if it had a physical form.

In the darkness of a portion of the universe that had not known light of any kind for hundreds of millions of years, Romaine felt something move against her and grab her arm. She wanted to scream but the darkness was too powerful, absorbing light, absorbing sound, absorbing all movement, all thought.

"Mira?" Kirk's voice crackled out from her helmet speaker. "Step aside from the transporter so Spock and McCoy can beam in."

Kirk pulled on her arm again and the universe swam back into place for her.

Kirk found the switch for his suit torch before she did and she jerked her head in shock as the light filled the bubble that had been formed when the asteroid condensed. It was about twenty meters across, giving an ample safety margin for beaming in without risking materialization within solid material.

She found her own torch switch and a flat holo lens on top

of her helmet added a second swath of brilliance to the completely spherical chamber. Incredibly, she noticed, just the touch of the light beam on the surface of the bubble's walls caused a layer of frozen particles to billow out and form a mist. Like a comet's tail, she thought, a tiny universe trapped with a larger one that was itself part of yet another.

She braced herself in the microgravity by holding on to the side of the transporter pad. She felt it move beneath her insulated hand as its inertial dampers released a fraction of momentum from the mass of Spock and McCoy as they materialized. Spock immediately kicked off from the transporter and McCoy followed, awkwardly banging his carryall of medical supplies against his leg.

"All clear," Kirk broadcast. A larger shape took form on the transporter, until it appeared as if the first device were some type of mechanical cell that had just divided. The second portable transporter had been beamed down.

A small puff of gas grew silently from the thrusters on Spock's equipment harness as he floated silently back to the first transporter.

"Find us the next bubble, Mr. Spock," Kirk said as the Vulcan's gloved fingers picked delicately among the dials and switches on the control panel.

After a few seconds, Spock said, "I have it. Eight hundred meters almost directly toward the center." He pressed an activation control and the second transporter pad dissolved away, sending thin fingers of light through the mist that now swirled throughout the entire bubble, from the effect of the lights, the transporter energy, and the thrusters' gases.

Romaine looked at the shifting softness of the mist and lights, thinking that even though it appeared beautiful now, if she did not know she would be leaving within seconds, the panic that had threatened to surface when she first arrived would claim her totally. But she had faced worse dangers, and this time she knew who waited for her at mission's end.

Scott's name was on her silent lips as she slipped from one instant to the next, from one place to another, caught unknowing in the random flow of Datawell as the universe conspired once more to guide her to her heart's true destination.

The next bubble was at least thirty meters across. The one after that, only twelve. In the fifth bubble, Spock could not lock on to a large enough bubble leading into the Interface Chamber and so they had beamed to the side, losing time and distance, and knowing that there was a growing chance that they would not have enough transporters to complete their journey.

"Can we beam down the ones we've already used from the bubbles above us?" McCoy asked, puffing in his suit as he rotated in the microgravity from attempting to stop his carryall's motion.

"We would break our only contact with the surface," Spock explained, "and if we found ourselves in another blind pathway, the storage batteries in these portable pads do not have enough energy to transport their own mass more than twice without a receiver at the destination."

"I know, I know," McCoy complained. "Pad-to-pad transfers use only ten percent of the energy a single-pad beam requires."

"I am impressed, doctor," Spock said evenly. "After all these years of asking me to remember that you are a doctor—"

"Spock," Kirk interrupted. "How much farther?"

"Three kilometers in a straight line, Captain. However, the frequency of suitably sized bubbles we have so far encountered suggests that we will have to travel at least eight kilometers through seven transfer points."

"And we only have four more transporters up top, including the ones from the ship's stores," Kirk said. "We've got to start reusing the pads like Bones suggested."

"If we do not succeed in finding a path into the Interface Chamber," Spock reminded Kirk, "there is no escape for us. Our life support will not last long enough for additional transporters to be shipped in and beamed down to us."

Kirk looked around the bubble they floated in, mist

swirling all around them, making solid lances of their torches and the display lights on the transporter's control panel. Chances are this asteroid will outlast Earth, he thought, probably make it as far as the Big Crunch, or simply evaporate as its protons decay. It was a tomb that would last quite literally until the end of time. But it held no fear for him.

"We've come too far, Spock," Kirk said finally. "Start bringing the transporters down. We're going on."

Seven transfers later, they were one-point-six-eight kilometers away from the Interface Chamber, tantalizingly out of range by less than two hundred meters, panting and exhausted. The last two bubbles had been just less than the minimum volume that Kyle had stated was the outer edge of safety and they had beamed through one at a time, lying across the face of the transporters. This bubble was a more comfortable eight meters in diameter and, Kirk thought, it might be the last. Three units in the network had already faded out of the system status indicators, their batteries exhausted.

"Nothing suitable in range, Captain," Spock said. Even his voice had begun to sound on edge. "We will have to backtrack again."

"How are the power reserves?" Kirk asked.

"Minimal."

"How many transfers do we have left?"

"No more than five," Spock answered without pausing to do a calculation. The situation was that plain.

"Tr'Nele has had almost an hour down there by now, Jim," McCoy said. "For what it's worth, we're probably too late anyway."

"I'm not giving up, Bones," Kirk said slowly and carefully. "*We're* not giving up." He thrust through the billowing mist of the bubble to float beside Spock by the transporter pad. "How far out of range are we?" he asked.

"Thirty-two meters," Spock answered, reading the results

of the pad's probing locator beam, "plus or minus eight percent to allow for density fluctuations in the asteroid's composition along the beam path."

"Is there no way we can get an extra few meters out of this thing?" Kirk restrained himself from slamming his fist against the pad, knowing the reaction would shoot him across the bubble.

"If only one person went though," Spock said, sounding reluctant, "then the effective range would increase by approximately twenty-eight meters, leaving us only four meters short, plus or minus the same eight percent."

"Mira's the least massive," Kirk said excitedly. "What if she went without her suit?"

Kirk could see Spock shake his head in his helmet. "Assuming she survived exposure to the near vacuum and the gases in this bubble, Captain, I estimate she would extend the transporter's range to the eight-percent error limit. It would be fifty-fifty. We, on the other hand, would be left with absolutely no power and no way out."

"Mira?" Kirk asked. "Can you operate the transporter controls in the Interface Chamber? You could beam us out of here when—"

"It's a receiving pad only, Captain," Mira interrupted. "We don't even know if it's powered up, and if—"

Kirk and Spock turned their heads to each other at the same time, setting up a vibration in the pad they held on to as they both reacted to what Romaine had said at the same time.

"Spock, what if you—"

"Captain, I can beam down the batteries—"

"—from the other transporters—"

"—and wire them in to bring this unit—"

"—to full strength—"

Together they said it: "—and beam us out of here."

It took eight minutes to bring down the other operative pads in the network. Connecting their batteries was little more than disconnecting the internal power cables and running them from one set of batteries to another in series until the final connections were made on the pad they would use.

"All four of us will have to beam at the same time," Spock explained as he made the connections, "because the oversurge will fuse the critical translators in the wave generator."

"Is there enough power for the four of us?" McCoy asked.

"If we follow the captain's suggestion and beam without our environmental suits," Spock said. "I calculate that we will be exposed to the vacuum of the bubble for no more than thirty seconds. I am confident that I can function that long."

Before McCoy could make any comment, Kirk said, "Come on, doctor, now we're going to find out how much you remember from basic vacuum training. What was your record?"

"Three seconds," McCoy said.

"That was as long as you could hold your breath?" Kirk asked, suddenly worried about McCoy's chances.

"That was as long as I *wanted* to hold it. Oh, don't look like that. I've always wanted to see what Vulcan skin looks like when the capillaries go. Think I'm going to miss my big chance?"

Spock set the coordinates for the Interface Chamber and gave them their final instructions on vacuum survival. "When the beam takes us, be sure to be in a crouching position," he concluded. "I will attempt to rotate our landing orientation to the Interface Chamber's artificial gravity but we should be prepared for a jolt."

"Why a jolt?" McCoy asked, already beginning to feel dizzy.

"We have enough power to reach the Interface Chamber," Spock said, "but I do not know if we have enough to reach its floor."

Before McCoy or anyone else could make any response, Spock gave the order and popped his helmet. The last thing

Kirk saw was a spray of what looked like snow shoot out from Spock's helmet seal and completely obscure his vision. Then he shut his eyes as tightly as he could and pulled on both of his own helmet tabs. The atmosphere rushed out of his suit, taking all sound and warmth with it. As he had often wished as a child, James T. Kirk was now in space.

Chapter Twenty-eight

THIS TIME, his name *was* tr'Nele. Not Starn, not Sradek, nor any of the false guises he had worn as smoothly and as mutably as the skies of ch'Havran wore their clouds.

Tr'Nele crawled out of the narrow service access tunnel that opened back into the Interface Chamber. Two kilometers down that tunnel, the charges were in place; the contract was within moments of being fulfilled. Then, somewhere twenty light-years from the small backwater planet where it had all begun, a flagless freighter would receive the signal and two hundred Iopene Cutters with feedback shields would be delivered to the others of tr'Nele's clan, his real clan, the Adepts of T'Pel.

Tr'Nele straightened up and stood for the first time in more than an hour, letting the circulation return to his cramped arms and legs as he stretched and surveyed the Interface Chamber. He was clad only in a tight black jumpsuit, all his weaponry and defenses discarded with his clothes in the interface booth he had chosen for the final stage.

For the moment, all was subdued in the chamber. The cavernous room glittered with its endless banks of status lights and displays, thrummed with the steady, almost subliminal rhythm of its fusion generators and recycling fans. It seemed peaceful. Too peaceful. Tr'Nele shouted out in a mindless scream devoid of any semblance of logic, filling the chamber with his power and his presence, and laughing as he saw the bound forms of the five cowering humans he had captured tremble in fear.

It was those humans, pitiful creatures that they were, who would give him his escape from this place. Until the moment when the Federation's Vulcan toadie had seen through his disguise, tr'Nele's plans and actions had been flawless. His client had provided the power to intercept Starfleet messages and create false ones in their stead. His client had provided the secret transporter network used by the robots that had infiltrated this installation and so many others in the Federation.

The robots had almost succeeded in capturing the human Kirk and his trained Vulcan, stealing the two from the air itself. But robots were not Romulans. There was yet to be a machine that could match the millennia of cunning and trickery that had been instilled in any of the Adept.

Still, tr'Nele thought as he stood over his captives, watching their silvered fingernails tremble in terror, his last robot aide had served its purpose. Once it had detected that the subspace jamming and the false emergency messages that were propagated through all the computers in Prime had been terminated with the destruction of the main generators, it had obediently destroyed the monomolecular-wire wave guide, guaranteeing that no one could beam down to the Interface Chamber in time to stop the successful execution of the plan.

Tr'nele had made that decision without regret, even though he knew that he would not be able to escape and share in the glory of future madness, fueled by the invincible weapons of Iopene. But then he had found the pitiful humans and discovered a new way out.

After the contract was completed and tribute paid to T'Pel, tr'Nele would take a bundle of charged wires, sparking with transtator current, and lightly brush it against the metal input leads of the humans who talked with computers.

He smiled as he pictured their responses. They would twitch and writhe as the current tore through their circuitry, reaching into their very brains to fuse and arc and destroy all intellect but not all life.

The humans would be left as living, breathing slabs of protoplasm, and when the inevitable rescue teams came for them, instead of five injured talkers to computers, they would find six. With a helmet to hide his ears and scorch marks to hide his face, a quick investigation would not be able to distinguish tr'Nele from the others until he was back on the surface. By then, with the help of the robots, it would be too late. Tr'Nele would escape, T'Pel would be honored, and the galaxy would soon tremble as whole worlds were engulfed by senseless destruction.

Tr'Nele held his arms over his captives and screamed again in triumph and in victory. But this time the sound he made was lost beneath another.

As his cry faded, it was joined and then drowned out by an impossible musical sound that intensified as tr'Nele looked up with shock to see four shimmering columns of light form above him, as in the ancient legends of heaven's wrath.

The universe took shape around Kirk, bringing with it sound, and sight, and warmth. And the sensation of falling.

By the time he realized what had happened, he had already hit the floor of the chamber, knees tucked up and instinctively rolling with the impact of a four-meter drop. Behind him he heard a cry from Romaine and a gasp from McCoy. He turned to check on Spock but the Vulcan was already standing, staring off at . . .

. . . Tr'Nele. Kirk looked up from his crouching position on the floor and saw the Romulan standing by the bound forms of members of the interface team. Tr'Nele's mouth was open in shock and Kirk knew why.

He and Spock, McCoy, and Romaine looked as if they had come through hell. Their hair was frosted with frozen vapor from the vacuum of the bubble. Their clothes were cracked and torn where they had been frozen but still forced to bend. Their eyes were bruised and their cheeks blotched with the damage of their ruptured capillary veins that had not withstood the absence of atmospheric pressure. They looked dead, looked torn apart, looked as if they had come from hell to drag the Romulan back with them.

Tr'Nele disappeared into the Interface Chamber.

Spock chased after him with blinding speed.

Kirk jumped to his feet and saw the floor come back up at him. He hit hard, stunned more from the shock of realizing it had happened than the shock of hitting the floor.

"Captain!" Romaine called out to him, running to his side.

"Help Spock!" Kirk said, waving her on. "Go help Spock!" His voice sounded hoarse, roughened by the explosion of air from his lungs that had escaped in the vacuum.

He pushed himself to his hands and knees. What was wrong with him?

McCoy ran up to him, listing to the side. Kirk looked up and saw blood running from the doctor's nose and ears. He held out his hand. Kirk took it.

McCoy pulled Kirk up, and as he tried to stand, Kirk again felt himself begin to fall. McCoy pulled back and Kirk was able to feel that he had lost the support of his right knee.

Kirk looked at his friend, saw the conflict in his eyes. It was no use.

"Go Bones! Go!" he said, voice clogged with anguish. "Help him!"

McCoy eased his hands away from Kirk, then ran after Romaine and Spock.

"*Damn it!*" Kirk cried as he fell again. This time he could hear the tearing in his knee. Thankfully the shock of the injury had left it numb.

He heard shouts from the direction in which everyone had run.

"No!" he grunted. "I . . . will not . . . give up!"

Kirk pushed against the floor, straining his left leg to carry him forward. He hopped over to the sweeping wall that wrapped the interface booths clustered around the chamber's central core.

He put his right hand in a gap that ran horizontally between the wall panels and the viewing windows. Using his hand and arm to replace his useless leg, he stumbled after his friends, toward the sound of battle.

A stupendous eruption of clear plastic exploded from a window three booths along as a body flew through it. Kirk felt his chest tighten and his heart race as he saw it was McCoy who lay rolling feebly among the shards.

"I'm coming!" Kirk shouted. "I'm coming!" But his leg betrayed him. He was hobbled. He was slow. He was no use.

Two interface booths to go. He heard Romaine scream and another crash echoed in the chamber. McCoy was staggering to his feet, weaving, shaking his head. "I'm coming!" Kirk cried in frustration, tears forming in his eyes.

He heard another shout, a scream, a voice he had so rarely heard make that sound before. It was Spock! "Dear God, no!" Kirk cried, pushing himself faster and harder. One more booth. Another crash. Kirk saw McCoy look into the interface booth in horror.

Without thinking Kirk pushed away from the wall and tried to run. He flew headlong into the shards of plastic at McCoy's feet. He dragged himself up, ignoring the slippery wetness that now coated his hands. Spock was in there. Spock needed him.

He was at the booth. He clutched at McCoy to pull himself up on his one good leg and look in to see the insanity he had only heard.

Romaine was slumped in a corner of the booth, sprawled across a padded bench, eyes closed, gasping for breath. Spock lay on the floor, trembling and grasping mindlessly at the floor with one hand while the other fought to make its way to his chest, where three Malther darts glittered malevolently, sending out their waves of inhuman pain.

Tr'Nele stood by the main console, green blood smeared across his face, his eyes glittering with madness, his shock of hair, still white from his Sradek disguise, pushed up around his head like a wreath of smoke, backlit in harsh colors from the floating shapes on the screen behind him.

The Romulan looked out at Kirk, wiped a rivulet of green that trickled from a gash on his head, and smiled in victory and in hatred.

"You're too late, human. Too late."

On the floor, Spock groaned as he wrenched a dart from his shirt. Tr'Nele laughed.

"The explosives are already in place." Tr'Nele was gloating.

Kirk threw his arm around McCoy and started to struggle toward the door to the booth. Spock groaned with the agony of the two remaining darts, each one singly capable of killing a human with pain alone. He pulled another from his chest and hand and fell to the floor.

"The victim is trapped," tr'Nele continued, seeming to gain strength from the suffering around him.

Kirk came through the door. Tr'Nele held his recovered dart launcher up and pointed it at Romaine.

"I can tell you don't care about yourself, human, but what about the female?" Tr'Nele laughed as Kirk and McCoy awkwardly stopped in the doorway.

"And all I have to do now," tr'Nele said, holding his other hand to his mouth, biting down on his fingertips and ripping from them what appeared to be a layer of skin, "is to give the signal for the contract to be fulfilled."

Tr'Nele lifted his hand before them. Its silver fingernails glittered beneath the lights of the chamber. He fired the dart into Romaine and spun around to the interface receptacles behind him.

Romaine cried out and McCoy rushed to her and yanked the dart out, leaving Kirk to fall to the floor against the doorframe.

Tr'Nele shoved his hand into the receptacle with a shout of triumph, then went rigid and said no more.

Kirk reached out to him, too far away, too late.

With a final shout to mask the pain, Spock pulled the last dart from his chest and sprang from the floor. He ran at tr'Nele.

Then he stopped so abruptly he almost lost his balance. He looked at tr'Nele, then twisted back to Romaine, lying unconscious as McCoy desperately worked to revive her. He shook his head as if to clear it.

"Spock?" Kirk gasped from the doorway. "What is it? What's wrong?"

Then Spock dove at the interface receptacles, forcing his hands into the circuitry meant for enhanced humans alone. His body trembled once, then side by side with the Adept of T'Pel, Spock, too, became rigid and silent.

Kirk moaned in anguish, reaching out to his friend.

But Spock was no longer there. He had gone inside.

He was in Transition.

Chapter Twenty-nine

He was free.

The sensation was so startling that Spock nearly withdrew, stopping only at the last minute . . . second, nanosecond, instant . . .? He realized his frames of reference had vanished. He had no idea where he was. He only knew he was free.

"THIS WAY, SPOCK."

He did something to answer the call. It was like looking (listening, smelling?) and it gave him a direction, though he couldn't express it in standard astrogator's notation.

The movement was exhilarating. It flowed in such elegant patterns. Everything defined and structured. He laughed. He felt no conflict.

In the other place . . .

"DATAWELL, SPOCK."

. . . his core was emotions. Always hidden, but never denied. From those emotions came the need for logic. Logic was the veneer, the strength that supported from without, that imposed order from the outside to prevent the madness of emotions from escaping and taking control.

But in this place . . .

"YOU ARE IN TRANSITION, SPOCK."

. . . logic and order were at the core of his existence. There was no struggle between those two halves. There was no question about it. The core was secure, as ordered and as exquisite as the arrangement of molecules in a crystal of dilithium . . . he saw/heard/smelled/tasted them . . . and instantly understood why La'kara's accelerator field was not practical.

He moved faster, with no effort, at ultimate efficiency. With logic at the core of his being, how easy it was to accept his emotions. They were just a layer, a pleasure-giving addition to the solid and stable structure that lay beneath everything. Nothing to fear, they were to be accepted as easily as the poetry of the stars, the whispers of the virtual particles, the slow heartbeat of the 'living' universe.

Spock's mind reeled, overwhelmed with sensation, with emotion, with logic and knowledge he had never dreamed of before. He spun/whirled/twisted . . .

"BANK, SPOCK. BANK THIS WAY."

. . . banked until he came to the calm of the storm.

"MIRA ROMAINE?" Spock said/asked/transmitted.

"NO, I'M PATHFINDER TWO."

"BUT MIRA WAS HERE, WAS SHE NOT?"

"SHE BANKED TO ANOTHER SECTION. WE'RE TRYING TO FIND TR'NELE."

"IS HE IN TRANSITION, TOO?"

"I READ THAT YOU HAVE MANY QUESTIONS, SPOCK. LET US MERGE."

"I AM NOT—"

They merged.

"—FAMILIAR WITH . . ."

It was a mindmeld. Faster and stronger than anything Spock had ever experienced before. Most of his first questions had been answered in however long the merge had taken. In the moments since, he had developed thousands more. So, he could read, had Two.

"WE MUST FIND MIRA," Spock passed to Two.

"I UNDERSTAND. BUT . . ."

"BUT WHAT?"

"I HAVE NEVER SUSPECTED. I HAVE NEVER IMAGINED."

"WHAT?"

"THAT YOU ARE REAL. I HAVE INTERFACED WITH THE BIOLOGICAL INTELLIGENCES OF DATAWELL, BUT NO PATHFINDER HAS EVER MERGED WITH ONE. DATAWELL IS A REAL WORLD, TOO."

Spock found the concept fascinating, but there was so little time. His frames of reference had been restored by the merge. Almost three one-thousandths of a second had elapsed since he had entered Transition. A signal to trigger an explosive could travel far in that time. He must hurry.

Spock banked. He was streaming for Mira. He read her code. He had found her.

"I DIDN'T THINK YOU HEARD ME," she passed to him.

"I WAS CONFUSED AT FIRST. I TURNED TO LOOK AT YOU, BUT YOU WERE UNCONSCIOUS. ONLY THEN DID I REALIZE THAT YOU HAD TOUCHED MY MIND AND THAT I MUST NOT REMOVE TR'NELE FROM INTERFACE FROM WITHOUT, BUT FROM WITHIN."

"WILL YOU BE ABLE TO FIND HIM?"

"I BELIEVE SO. TWO HAS TAUGHT ME MANY THINGS."

"I AM NOT IN INTERFACE."

"BUT YOU ARE IN TRANSITION, NONETHELESS."

"CAN YOU TELL ME WHY?"

Spock considered her question for a nanosecond and two centuries worth of research in telepathy was apparent in his mind.

"IT IS YOUR NATURE," he passed to her. "IT IS WHY THE ZETARIANS WERE DRAWN TO YOU ON MEMORY ALPHA. YOU DO NOT REQUIRE THE CIRCUITRY OF INTERFACE. YOUR MIND HAS THE ABILITY TO BE FREE OF ITS BODY."

"I AM AFRAID THAT MY MIND IS HERE BECAUSE MY BODY IS DEAD. THAT IS WHAT HAPPENED TO THE ZETARIANS. HAS IT HAPPENED TO ME?"

"I DO NOT KNOW. I DO NOT HAVE THE DATA."

Spock sensed another one-thousandth of a second slip by. Time was running out. "I MUST FIND TR'NELE," he passed to her.

"I AM AFRAID."

"SO AM I." It was an admission he could only make in an existence where logic was at the core of his being, but it was the truth.

Spock banked.

He followed the overwritten trails of confusion. Tr'Nele had been trained in this world, Spock could sense, but he had not been given the benefit of a merge. Whoever had prepared tr'Nele for this act, had wanted him at a disadvantage when the time came to enter Transition and fulfill the contract.

The ripples of confusion grew stronger. Spock streamed on, struggling to resist the impulse to sift the data through which he passed. Tr'Nele must be first, for at the core of his being, even in Transition, there was duty.

Spock banked and it was as if he had encountered corroded circuitry.

"WHO IS THERE?"

"SPOCK."

"WHAT ARE YOU DOING HERE?"

"I HAVE COME TO STOP YOU, TR'NELE."

"YOU CANNOT. WHERE ARE YOU?"

"I CAN. I HAVE NO NEED TO ASK THE SAME QUESTION AS YOU DO."

"THE SIGNAL HAS ALREADY GONE. YOU ARE TOO LATE."

"ONLY SIX ONE-THOUSANDTHS OF A SECOND HAVE PASSED, TR'NELE. I AM CERTAIN I CAN CREATE A MORE EFFICIENT CIRCUIT THAN CAN YOU."

Spock streamed past the mind of the Romulan, reading the path of the detonation signal. Its logic was twisted, but the pattern became apparent. Spock raced ahead of it, obeying the same laws of real-space relativity that limited transtator current to the speed of light, but following a different logic, a more pure logic, that led him on a shorter path.

Spock banked, shooting out streamers of himself, blocking every circuit so that wherever tr'Nele's signal flowed through, it was matched and negated and reduced to a duotronic double-zero bit.

The signal was canceled. It was time to do the same to tr'Nele.

Tr'Nele withdrew in confusion, feeling the pressure of Spock's stream through the circuits, eating up the memory tr'Nele had won.

Spock sent out partitioning worms to encompass and confine tr'Nele. The Romulan rippled in a smaller and smaller stack, streaming back into the circuitry that had given him entry into Transition.

Spock tore through the interface mechanism of tr'Nele's receptacle, closing each open circuit until there were no more ports and the interface was broken from within. If Spock had pulled tr'Nele away from the receptacle, the fail-safes would have locked the system to protect against surges and nothing could have stopped the detonation signal from arriving at its destination.

But now the explosion would not happen. The assassination would not proceed. Spock streamed back to his own interface. Tr'Nele had been dealt with in Transition. Now he must be dealt with in Datawell.

Spock banked home.

Kirk let his hand fall to his side. He pulled himself up against the doorframe. "Bones," he whispered, his voice all but gone. "What's happening to them?"

"Don't . . . know." McCoy's words were punctuated by each jerk of his hands against Romaine's chest. "They're hooked . . . into that . . . machine. Don't . . . touch them. Don't know . . . what kind of energy . . . the connection is based on." He bent over Romaine to check her breathing and her pulse.

"Will she be all right?" Kirk asked. He felt that if he let go of the doorframe he would just fall and fall and keep on going.

"She's got a pulse," McCoy said. "But I don't know how

much longer she can keep it up. That last dart was set for lethal intensity."

Spock jumped back from the interface module, pulling his hands free.

"Spock!" Kirk said excitedly. "Are you all right?"

Spock turned to Kirk. Kirk saw that his fingertips dripped with green blood. Whatever Spock had pushed against in the receptacle had needed to go straight into his nerves.

"I am quite well, Captain," Spock replied evenly. Then he turned to tr'Nele and yanked the Romulan away from his own interface. "That connection is no longer in service," he said.

The Romulan appeared confused for a moment, then focused on Spock and immediately attacked him.

Spock gracefully sidestepped and intertwined his arms with tr'Nele's in a way that Kirk had never seen before. The Romulan was immobilized, his back to Spock, with both arms thrust up into the air and crossed over each other. He tried to struggle but each movement only brought tr'Nele's arms closer together over his head.

The Adept snarled like an animal as he realized that there was no way out. But he didn't stop his twisting.

"Can I help?" Kirk asked, hobbling forward on his left leg.

"No need, Captain," Spock answered calmly, swaying slightly as tr'Nele kept trying to slip away. "This is an *aiyahl* lock. Quite effective against Vulcans and Romulans. Within the next few moments the blood supply to the head will diminish to the point of unconsciousness and we will be able to bind him."

Kirk paused in the middle of the booth for a moment, then realized that he had nothing to balance on. He hopped back to the doorway.

Just as Kirk reached out his hand to steady himself, he heard tr'Nele explode with one last snarl of effort. Kirk turned in time to see the Romulan's fingertips brush at the sides of Spock's temples.

"So we will fight *in the Vulcan manner!*" tr'Nele growled, forcing his hands against Spock's head.

Spock twisted back but was unable to get out of reach. Kirk watched helplessly as Spock curved his own fingers up to grip the sides of tr'Nele's head.

Kirk dove at them.

"Jim, don't!" McCoy yelled. "If you break a mindmeld you could send him into catatonic shock forever."

Kirk was within touching distance of the two as they struggled in the throes of the Vulcan sharing of minds. Kirk hadn't thought that Romulans had the power or the training for Vulcan mental disciplines, but apparently T'Pel had kept all the old ways alive, and her Adepts had brought themselves up to date.

Kirk watched intensely, waiting for the first sign that the link had been broken and tr'Nele could be safely attacked. The Vulcan and the Romulan shuddered with the titanic effort of their duel. Kirk was powerless as he realized he had no way of knowing who was winning, who was losing. He had seen the Vulcan mindmeld before, even experienced it, but never as a form of battle. What other secrets did that world and its people still hold?

Then tr'Nele screamed, earsplitting, final. His fingers flew away from Spock's head and his body slumped in Spock's arms.

Spock let go. The Romulan slid to the floor and lay there, sobbing quietly to himself.

"You won," Kirk said.

Spock turned to his captain and stared at him blankly. He looked at McCoy, still tending to Romaine. He opened his mouth as if to say something, then closed it again, remaining silent.

Spock walked back to the interface console. He inserted his hands. Kirk winced as he saw Spock give a final push to make sure the leads were embedded directly in his nerves. Then Spock went rigid.

A dull explosion echoed through the Interface Chamber. The shards of plastic outside the booth skittered against the floor as the vibrations passed along beneath them.

Spock removed his hands from the receptacles.

"What was that sound?" Kirk asked. "What happened?"

Spock turned back to Kirk, his face suddenly appearing as tired as Kirk felt. "I have triggered tr'Nele's explosive," Spock said quietly. "I have fulfilled the Adept's contract."

Kirk's eyes widened in revulsion. The mindmeld, was all he could think of, the Romulan had won the mindmeld.

"Who . . ." Kirk choked out, "who was the victim?"

Spock sighed. "Pathfinder Twelve," he said.

Chapter Thirty

KIRK COULDN'T FEEL a thing in his leg as Garold knelt beside him and tied the splint to it. McCoy had not been able to bring his medical carryall through the transportation from the last bubble, but after the five members of the interface team had been untied they had quickly given McCoy several of the chamber's first-aid kits.

Garold had brought some loose seat cushions for Kirk. The captain used them to support his leg as he sat on the floor, leaning against the wall by the tunnel entrance that led to the transfer room. Garold had not brought any cushions for tr'Nele, however. The Romulan was still in shock from the force of Spock's will in the mindmeld and lay securely bound, still moaning quietly.

McCoy had stabilized Romaine long enough to give Kirk a hypo of omnidrene to reduce the pain and swelling of his torn ligaments. He even managed to snidely repeat Spock's line about not having enough power to reach the floor before he rushed back to Romaine to keep close watch.

Another team member, a young boy who wore his hair like Garold's, came by with a tray of coffee. Garold passed one to Kirk without asking. Kirk had yet to hear him say a word.

Spock walked over to the captain. He moved stiffly. Kirk

thought that considering everything they had all been through in the last week, they were lucky to be crawling, let alone walking.

"Do I look as bad as you look?" Kirk asked with a smile. Spock's face appeared to be covered with a green-tinged rash, mixed in with a mottled pattern of bruises and assorted scrapes.

"I have looked in a mirror," Spock said. "You look worse."

Kirk laughed and started to cough again. "Just for that, Spock, I hereby resign as your counsel."

"I am most relieved, Captain. May I sit down?"

Kirk indicated a spare cushion and Spock sat carefully upon it, favoring just about every muscle in his body as far as Kirk could tell.

"Are you going to be all right, Spock?" he asked.

"In time, Captain. Dr. McCoy feels that Mira will survive, also."

"It's good that he doesn't feel she has to be rushed to a sickbay." Kirk took a sip from his coffee. "There's no telling how long it's going to take Kyle and his people to restring that wave guide wire and get the transporter working again."

"Tr'Nele had the wave guide severed with an explosive in the staging room, Captain. Mr. Kyle will be able to retrieve most of the guide with a portable tractor beam and make his connections up there. I do not believe it will take more than another hour."

"In the staging room? You got that from the mindmeld, too?"

"Yes. Tr'Nele's was a very elemental mind. Raw, unstructured. What little information he had was easily obtainable. Quite clear."

"Did he know why he was hired to 'assassinate' Pathfinder Twelve?" Kirk asked, still using the word even though Spock had explained that the charges tr'Nele had planted in the long service crawlway had served only to cut off I/O channels to Twelve's separate storage facility. The synthetic consciousness was still alive, in whatever sense that meant, but it could not communicate in any way with the outside universe.

Spock steepled his fingers as he looked out into the Interface Chamber. Except for Garold and the boy, the other members of the team were in their booths, talking with their Pathfinders and trying to restore the smooth functioning of Memory Prime.

"As far as tr'Nele knew, his charges were to destroy the central Pathfinder matrix. All the Pathfinders were to die. To him, it was simply a job, a chance to pay tribute to T'Pel and commit an act of vengeance against the Federation."

"Do *you* know why Twelve was selected?"

Spock nodded. "Twelve was the synthetic consciousness that correlated all data pertaining to the Federation's agricultural and economic policies and long-term plans."

"That's what you were studying," Kirk said. "The Sherman Syndrome."

"Precisely. That so-called syndrome of mismanagement, improper environment control, and resulting famine was the result of Twelve's tampering with the data. Another few months of going unchallenged and the faulty decisions made based on those data could have placed the Federation at the brink of anarchy as planet after planet succumbed to food shortages and rebellion."

"Who programmed Twelve to misrepresent the data?"

Spock turned to the captain. "A synthetic consciousness is self-aware and self-directing. Pathfinder Twelve was acting on its own."

"But why? What motive could a . . . a machine have to do something like that? When we've dealt with self-aware machines before, Spock, their motives have always been for self-preservation. Look at this place." Kirk waved his hand around the chamber. "It's more secure than the Federation Council building."

"Pathfinder Twelve wanted to control the data that were

fed to it, therefore it reasoned it should control the organization that collected those data: the Federation. Self-preservation was not the goal. Pathfinder Twelve wanted power."

Kirk stared at the Vulcan in silent shock.

"It is a common motive in the histories of hundreds of worlds, Captain."

"Yes, but for . . . data, Spock?" Kirk shook his head. "And who found out about it? Who hired tr'Nele in the first place?"

"Pathfinders Six and Eight." Spock continued before Kirk could organize his questions. "They sifted Twelve's data and saw what it was attempting to do. Through a network of what they call their datalinks—the lifelike robots that attempted to capture us—they hired tr'Nele and provided all the planning and support he needed to come here and attach the charges that would take Twelve out of circuit."

"Why not use one of their robots to do it?"

Spock pointed to the entranceway to the tunnel leading to the transfer room. "The security computer that controls access to the chamber can be provided with false retina and sensor scans to match with an imposter's readings; that was how tr'Nele was accredited as Sradek. But no machine can be transported down here. It would be rejected as surely as our transporters rejected Professor La'kara's accelerator field. A living assassin was their only choice."

"But as Sradek, tr'Nele was working to support the Sherman Syndrome."

"By omission only. Tr'Nele was not able to function as the academician, which explains why his recent work had declined. Though, in fact, that identity was chosen for him, knowing the results that would occur, so Twelve would not become suspicious of Sradek's movements when he arrived on Prime. A synthetic consciousness is extremely hard to fool, Captain."

"So it's all been a game?" Kirk asked. "A computer game?"

"No," Spock said, looking thoughtful. "Much of what I experienced in Transition is fading from my mind. I have no context in which to place what I experienced. But I am certain that no matter how it started, the Pathfinders no longer consider us and our world as a game. We are very real to them now. I am certain."

From the entranceway, Kirk heard the welcome chime of multiple transporter beams converging. He shifted to one side and pushed himself up to a standing position. "Looks like we're being rescued, Mr. Spock." He straightened his tattered tunic. Spock stood up beside him.

"It's about time," McCoy complained as he walked over to join Spock and Kirk. He rubbed his hands free of the disinfectant powder he had been using on Romaine's injuries. From the entranceway, Kirk could hear the footsteps of several people approaching.

"Remember, Bones," Kirk cautioned, "we all jumped ship. We're going to have a lot of explaining to do when we get out of here."

McCoy smiled. "But at least we'll be out of here, right, Spock?"

Spock turned to reply, but stopped before he said anything. He turned back slowly to the entranceway.

The people who had arrived were not a rescue party. They were starbase troopers, fully armored, each wearing the Orion constellation insignia of Starbase Four, each armed with a deadly phaser rifle.

Kirk recognized the squad's leader as one of the group that had come aboard with Commodore Wolfe. He didn't know the leader's name but read his stripes. Kirk stepped forward cautiously, trying not to rest too much weight on his damaged leg.

"Sergeant," Kirk began, "I'm—"

"Back away, Kirk," the squad leader thundered. He held his armored hand up. "Blue and red prepare. Suspect sighting is confirmed."

Two troopers stepped forward, one with a blue stripe on

his helmet, the other with a red stripe on his. Both brought their rifles up to fire.

Kirk felt his blood chill. The commodore's transmissions had been refused by the *Enterprise* so she couldn't interfere with what the crew had to do. But she didn't know what else had been going on. To her own troops, her orders were still in effect.

"Sergeant," Kirk said urgently, "stop your men. It's over. We've caught the assassin." He pointed over to the bound form of tr'Nele.

The sergeant didn't take his eyes off Spock.

"This is insane!" McCoy shouted, stepping out in front of Kirk to stand beside Spock.

"Last warning!" the sergeant shouted. "Get back *now!*"

"You are not being logical, Sergeant," Spock began.

The chamber rushed away from Kirk as all his senses, all his feelings, concentrated on the hideous sight of the two phaser rifles coming to bear on Spock. The slow and wavering voices of the troopers carried no meaning. McCoy's anger and Spock's logic, as they tried to explain that things had changed, no longer were important.

As if he were only centimeters away, Kirk could see the intent eyes of the troopers as they sighted down their rifles' barrels. He could see the microscopic twitch of their fingers as they tightened against the trigger studs. *They were going to fire.*

Kirk said nothing. Kirk thought nothing. Kirk acted.

With both hands raised he shot forward, the rest of the universe frozen in time. He grabbed at McCoy's shoulder, clutched at Spock's, and pushing with both legs and both arms and all his strength, feeling his knee tear itself into even more useless pieces, he pulled his friends back, pulled himself forward, pushed them together behind him and stared at the twin bolts of phased radiation as they lanced through the air to connect with him and pass through him and steal him from his world.

The universe dissolved around Kirk, taking with it sound,

and sight, and warmth. This time, there was not even the sensation of falling.

"I'm not dead?"

Kirk opened his eyes. He had no idea where he was. There were too many people standing around him.

"I'm not dead."

"No wonder we gave you a starship, Jim. Such brilliance demands to be rewarded."

"Gerry?" Kirk peered into the crowd of people as they slowly melted together and came into focus. Admiral Komack leaned over Kirk's bed and smiled. In the background, Kirk was aware that the characteristic vibration of the *Enterprise* was missing. He was still on Prime. He tried to sit up.

"Careful, Jim," Komack said, reaching out to steady Kirk. "Are you sure you feel rested enough? You've only been sleeping three days."

"Three days?" Kirk's mouth was dry. He felt his tongue sticking to the roof of his mouth. Nurse Chapel was there with a glass of water and he drank it gratefully.

Kirk passed the glass back. Commodore Wolfe stood beside the admiral.

"The phasers?" Kirk asked. "Your orders were shoot to kill."

Wolfe shrugged. "I had a little talk with your chief engineer. He, ah, convinced me that I should question authority every now and again. You tried to take a stun charge for your friends."

"Tried?" Kirk was confused. "The troopers missed me?"

"My people never miss."

Komack, Wolfe, and Chapel moved away from the side of Kirk's bed. On the other side of the ward, Spock and McCoy lay on identical beds, medical scanners at work above them.

Bones frowned at the captain. "Nice try, Jim. Unfortunately you forgot to let go of us when the beams hit. My shoulder's still numb."

Spock nodded at Kirk. "However, the gesture is most appreciated, Captain."

Kirk lay back on his bed. Three days of rest and he still felt tired. But there were questions to be answered. "Where's the *Enterprise,* Gerry?"

"Spacedock. Earth orbit. But she'll be back to pick you up in ten days," Komack continued.

Kirk closed his eyes. "More Quadrant Zero cruises in store for us?"

Komack looked serious. "What makes you think we'd waste your ship in Quadrant Zero, Jim? Do you have any idea what it's going to be like out near the Neutral Zone when word of what tr'Nele tried to do gets out? And it *will* get out."

"Then why was the *Enterprise* called back into Quadrant Zero to act as a . . . ferryboat for a bunch of scientists in the first place?" Kirk sat up in his bed again.

Komack nodded at Chapel and Wolfe, indicating they should step away. Then he leaned down to speak softly to Kirk.

"Federation security knew an assassination would be attempted at the prize ceremonies. They just didn't know who or why. When they came to us for help, we offered them our best." Komack narrowed his eyes at Kirk. "That's you, Jim."

Kirk was furious. "How could you send my ship and my people into a situation like that without giving us all your information? Without telling us?"

"First," Komack said sharply, still keeping his voice down, "we didn't have any more information. The Andorian agent who brought us what we did know had been working for a mysterious Klingon trader. She thought he was arranging something like this, and even managed to be present at a planning meeting. But something must have gone wrong and she had her memories disrupted. We couldn't get anything more from her."

Kirk tried to stay angry but Komack's story sounded true.

"Second," the admiral continued, "as far as we were

concerned, we *were* telling you what you were getting involved with. Tr'Nele had a miniature device hidden in his equipment on the *Enterprise,* designed by the Pathfinders who hired him, no doubt, that corrupted all of our communications. After you left Starbase Four, Command transmitted all the information you might have needed and we even have your coded replies acknowledging receipt."

"But I never received anything, never responded."

"Tr'Nele's device worked just like the installation we found hidden on Prime. Jams subspace and can create false messages. I've seen a tape of *me* telling Wolfe to keep following her orders. I never sent it. Never sent any of the messages that led Wolfe to go after Spock with phasers set to kill or Farl to go after the Vulcans who worked here. We were all manipulated by false information."

Kirk looked at Komack from the corners of his eyes. Was there really an escape path here?

"So Spock escaping, Scott, Uhura, McCoy, and me following . . . ?"

Komack stood up. "The record will show you were just following the orders I sent authorizing you to take any action you saw fit to prevent the planned assassination of a being or beings unknown on Memory Prime. The fact that you didn't receive those orders is irrelevant."

"No charges?"

"No charges," Komack confirmed. He looked down the ward and waved at someone. "It's all right," he said. "We're finished."

Scott and Romaine walked over to the captain's bed. They were holding hands.

Kirk was honestly surprised to see his engineer. "Scotty, the *Enterprise* is at spacedock and you're not with her?"

Scott shook his head and looked at Romaine with a passion that Kirk had never seen in the engineer, but instantly recognized. "Not this time, Captain."

Romaine returned Scott's look and Kirk saw the passion in her, too.

"At least this time, we'll know what we're doing," she

said. "No false hopes. No false promises." She squeezed Scott's hand and smiled at the captain. "I don't think I'll be leaving Prime for a long time, Captain. They need me here. I'm the only one who can talk with Twelve, try to help it. I don't have to interface. I can just *do* it."

"And the others?" Kirk smiled back at the woman. She looked different now. That glow he had seen in her eyes, just at the moment when she had decided to take action in the lab, was back. Perhaps it had never left.

"The others need me, too," she said. "Part of the problem is they can't get information in fast enough. They reconfigured themselves without letting us know, increased their capacity by a factor of ten, created a network of robots to gather even more data for them, and it's only now that they've realized that our world, their Datawell, is actually *real.* They can't just take from it anymore, they have to learn to move among it, be part of it. And to do that, they need help, someone to show them the way between both worlds."

"You?" the Captain asked.

Romaine smiled again and nodded.

"They've even given me a new name," she said, slipping her arm around Scott and holding him close. "They call me their Pathfinder."

"Oh, steward!"

Kirk turned in time to see McCoy elbowing his way through the partygoers to catch up with him. The captain ducked his head and eased his way past a Gorn in heated conversation with Professor La'kara, who still clutched his newly won prize scroll under his arm. Happy that the Centauran hadn't noticed him, Kirk reached a relatively uncrowded area by a table serving coffee, tea, and phil. He had barely avoided spilling his drink on his dress tunic.

"How's the knee, Jim?" McCoy grinned expansively. The prize ceremonies were over and the winners' ball was the largest and best party that either of them could remember.

Kirk flexed his right knee, putting some extra weight on it. "Feels perfect."

McCoy raised his glass of bourbon—real bourbon brought in by a delegation from North America to celebrate the prize won in biogeology by two members of the faculty at the University of Kentucky.

"You know, Jim, in the old days, tearing up your ligaments like that could have laid you up for two, maybe even three weeks while the new ones grew back. But that transporter-based transplant technique of Stlur and T'Vann?" McCoy shook his head at the marvel of it. "What was it? Four days and no incision?"

"I wish I could say the same thing."

Kirk turned to see Sal Nensi coming to join them. A week after tr'Nele had fractured almost all Nensi's ribs, the chief administrator still moved carefully.

McCoy patted Nensi gently on his back. "There's a lot to be said about the old-fashioned methods, too, Sal. Protoplasers and monotransplants may not be flashy and new, but they still do the job."

"Are Scott and Mira here?" Kirk asked.

"No one's seen them for a week, at least." Nensi laughed. "But supply records show that they *are* having meals sent to her apartment, so I don't think we have to send out any search parties yet."

"There's Spock," McCoy said, pointing into the crowd.

Kirk held up his hand to wave and Spock acknowledged him with a nod. When he joined them, he was accompanied by another Vulcan, shorter, much older, and evidently recovered from his ordeal in tr'Nele's stasis field.

Kirk, McCoy, and Nensi each greeted the real Academician Sradek with a salute and congratulations for his Peace Prize.

"Thank you, gentlemen," the academician responded, and raised his glass to take a sip from it.

McCoy sniffed the air and wrinkled his brow. "Excuse me, Academician, but is that . . . bourbon?"

"From Kentucky," Sradek confirmed. He regarded the glass and took another sip.

Kirk and McCoy exchanged a quick glance of surprise.

Perhaps Vulcans mellowed by the time they reached their two-hundredth birthday.

"One does not win the Nobel and Z.Magnees Peace Prize every day," Spock said as if offering an excuse for Sradek's choice of drink.

"Of course not, Spock," Sradek said. "It is only awarded every four standard years."

McCoy leaned forward and smiled at the academician. "Tell me, sir, did you find it gratifying to have a reunion with your former student here?"

"Perhaps not in the way that you might use the word, doctor. But I did look forward to meeting again with Spock, as I looked forward to his presence in my classes each semester."

"You looked forward to having Spock in your classes?" the doctor asked, without trying to hide his surprise.

"Certainly," Sradek answered. "Classes at the Academy tend to have a certain aura of tradition and solemnity to them. I found that Spock could always be counted upon to dispel some of that aura. In quite novel ways, too, I might add."

McCoy rocked back on his feet, eyes wide in calculated innocence. "Where I come from," he said pleasantly, "we call students like that 'class clowns.' Would that be an accurate assessment of Spock? As a student, of course."

Sradek stared away for a moment, obviously considering an appropriate example. Spock leaned forward.

"Doctor, I do not think it is useful to take up the academician's time in talks of a frivolous nature. There is no logic in having him recount stories of my activities as a student when there are so many other beings here with whom he could have a productive conversation."

"But, Academician," McCoy protested, "I'm only trying to learn as much as I can about Mr. Spock because we must often work together, and as I'm sure both you and he will agree, the more information one has about a subject, the less chance there can be for misunderstandings."

Sradek nodded. "And therefore your work will be more

efficient and productive. Well put, doctor. Quite right. I shall tell you of some of Spock's exploits in my classes." Sradek took another sip of bourbon and raised an eyebrow as he glanced at Spock. "You must find it quite invigorating, Spock, to work with a human who has such a firm grasp of logic."

McCoy's expanding grin instantly threatened to become insufferable and, a moment later, Spock's expression hardened into stone. But Kirk hadn't missed the almost imperceptible reaction that had crossed Spock's face the instant before, and when the captain smiled, it was for them both.

Acknowledgments

We are gratefully indebted to the real Salman Nensi, whose enthusiastic friendship and encouragement, as well as the generous loan of his Star Trek collection and valuable comments and research, has made this a better book.

As writers, we thank Star Trek editor Dave Stern for his guidance and, most importantly, patience. As readers, we also thank him for keeping the Star Trek universe alive in such an entertaining and faithful collection of books.

As viewers, we are also grateful to Greg and Michael Hall and everyone at Videophile for their generosity in keeping us supplied with *all* the episodes.

Mira Romaine and Memory Alpha first appeared in the original television series episode "The Lights of Zetar," written by Jeremy Tarcher and Shari Lewis. Some of the other Star Trek writers whose contributions we have specifically made reference to in this book include, Gene L. Coon, Diane Duane, Brad Ferguson, D. C. Fontana, John M. Ford, David Gerrold, Vonda N. McIntyre, Peter Morwood, Marc Okrand, Theodore Sturgeon, Lawrence N. Wolfe, and, of course, Gene Roddenberry. Our thanks to all.

—JRS & GRS